The
Dead
QUEENS
Club

The Dead Queens Club

HANNAH CAPIN

ink
yard
press

Recycling programs
for this product may
not exist in your area.

ISBN-13: 978-1-335-54223-6

The Dead Queens Club

This edition published by arrangement with Harlequin Books S.A.

For questions and comments about the quality of this book, please contact us
at CustomerService@Harlequin.com.

® and TM are trademarks of Harlequin Enterprises Limited or its corporate
affiliates. Trademarks indicated with ® are registered in the United States Patent and
Trademark Office, the Canadian Intellectual Property Office and in other countries.

InkyardPress.com

Printed in U.S.A.

To Katharine, Anne, Jane, Anne, Katheryn, Kateryn, and Jane.

And to Cat: you are eternally the Trastámara
and Marck to my Howard girl.

Homecoming

Indiana Teenagers
Demonstrate Poor Study Habits

Henry calls me at 12:01 the night before homecoming. Or technically—and assuming the alarm clock I knock off my nightstand once a day is even in the right time zone—the morning of homecoming.

"Cleveland. I need you. Put some pants on."

I pause the third episode in my *Air Crash Investigation* marathon. I'm supposed to be writing the world's most uninteresting article for *The Lion Ledger*, our school paper, but literal fiery death is better than forcing myself to care about city council elections. "Who says I'm not wearing pants?"

"Come on. I know you're not."

I dangle one hand off the bed, snag a pair of black-and-white cow-print pajama bottoms, and wrestle into them. "I totally am."

"You are *now*."

"Yeah. Pay up. Where are we going?"

"The dump," he says. "The one in York."

"The whole truth."

"And then Walmart. And then school. And then Katie's."

"Okay, Henry, no. I'm just a bystander in your relationships, remember?" I grab a bottle of Mountain Dew from my nightstand and chug the rest of it.

"But you're never a bystander in pranking."

"I'm not helping you torture your innocent girlfriend."

"Right, but what if she's not?"

"Your girlfriend? Then I'd congratulate her."

"Not *innocent*, Cleves." He's laughing. "Come on."

"And yet you're the one conscripting people into pulling off some plot when they're just trying to pantslessly enjoy making themselves afraid of flying."

"Are you watching that plane crash show again?"

I cram my feet into a double-knotted pair of Chucks. "It's compelling."

"It's sick."

"So is torturing your girlfriend."

"It's not torture. It's fair play."

"Dude, she's your fifth girlfriend since January. Maybe you're the problem."

"Not this time, Dr. Phil. Trust me."

"You're a bastard," I tell him, but I'm already opening my window and climbing out. "I'll see you in two minutes."

Summer Camp
Contributes to Life of Petty Crime

I first met Henry the summer before junior year. We were at this camp that's basically school, except with harder classes and more hooking up. Most of the other kids were there on purpose. A lot of them were actually excited about it.

I, on the other hand, just wanted to be home reading crappy thrillers and hanging out with my friends and possibly getting in trouble. Or doing anything other than six weeks of breakneck studying.

The first Saturday of camp, everybody else was pairing off at this '80s party and choreographing how to sneak into each other's rooms. I was in the lounge sending ugly selfies to my friend Sybil back in Cleveland and seriously considering making an Advent chain to count down the days left at Overachiever Camp when I noticed that this guy two seats over was taking ugly selfies at the same impressive pace I was.

So I took a picture of him, obviously, and of course that was the exact second he looked up.

"Hi," he said.

"Um, yeah," I replied, but I went ahead and sent the picture to Sybil anyway, with the caption *"oops busted."* Then I figured we were already at peak awkwardness, so I said, "Great form," and he laughed instead of looking creeped out, which would have been a much more rational reaction.

"Keep a copy for when I'm famous."

He said it like it was this casual but definite thing, the way normal people say *when I brush my teeth tomorrow.* If anybody else at camp said the same thing in the same non-kidding way, I would've added them to my "ugh" list and told them I, too, planned to be famous, as the *Guinness Book of World Records* title holder for owning history's largest collection of toenail clippings. Or something.

But with him, I just figured, you know. Yeah. Accurate. I mean, up until that moment, I hadn't even seen his entire face, because he'd always been in the middle of a swarm of Overachievers when I'd seen him around. He had a full entourage even when he went to grab extra ketchup in the dining hall. I had a few theories about his popularity, one of which involved a form of catnip that attracted academically enthusiastic humans and another that cast Selfie Boy as the favorite son of Harvard's dean of admissions. Which was essentially the same thing.

But now that the entourage was one room over getting their "Dancing Queen" groove on, and I could give Selfie Boy the undivided attention the rest of the universe had been giving him all week, I got it. This sounds borderline culty, but you know how people always say somebody's "magnetic," and you just think of it like another word? Like how "literally" doesn't *literally* mean literally, and "chill" isn't a temperature? Well, as of that instant, I realized what "magnetic" really means. That somebody has this actual invisible force field that draws everybody else in. To the point that I couldn't believe I'd been wasting my time with the kids in my lab group when I could've been doing whatever Selfie Boy was doing, which was undoubtedly much, much better.

Even if he was just grabbing extra ketchup in the dining hall.

Luckily—although perhaps also surprisingly—I have enough social graces that I didn't verbalize this. Instead I went with, "Who's getting the pictures?"

"My girlfriend," Selfie Boy said, holding up his phone. The girl on the screen was crossing her eyes and there was a toy monkey on her head, but she was totally gorgeous in that organic-moisturizer-ad kind of way. Like she did yoga and drank green smoothies and probably meditated, too.

"Damn. Good work."

"I know, she's beautiful, right? And smart. And she kills it on the lacrosse field."

"What's the catch?" I asked, even though everything I knew about natural selection indicated that his girlfriend was probably flawless and likely the result of an international search, several years of think-tank negotiations, and a personal consultation with the Pope. "Heartless mean girl?"

"Try again. She's volunteering in Guatemala this summer."

"Did she also save a busload of nuns from careening off a cliff on her way to the airport?"

He smirked, but it was the proudest, most affectionate smirk I'd ever seen. Like he'd completely won at life by landing such an unsurpassable partner in magnetic-ness. "I wouldn't be surprised."

"So what's her name?"

"Lina. Catalina Trastámara Aragón-Castilla."

"That settles it. I'm stealing her identity and breaking out of here."

He raised his eyebrows. "Why? Is it more work than you thought it was going to be?"

"It's pretty much the same amount of work I thought it was going to be. Unfortunately."

"Oh," he said, but he sounded confused, like *too much work* didn't translate into whatever secret language he and Lina probably spoke. Which might have just been Spanish, but I was taking German, because Ninth-Grade Me went through a deep and inexplicable World War II phase.

"The thing is," I told him, "until two weeks ago, I thought I was going to be spending my summer getting sunburned and going on adventures. Then my parents went all career-counselor on me, and here we are."

"So this is supposed to make you competitive for pre-med?"

I actually started laughing.

"What?"

"Come on. If you had to choose one kid at this camp who's definitely *not* going to be cutting people open for a living…"

I pointed at myself.

"Pre-law?"

"I'd gavel myself to death."

"Political science?"

"Bingo. I'm your future Commander-in-Chief." I went for a presidential pose, but nothing really worked, so I wound up saluting. "But no. They just want to trick me into figuring out a real future day job. Since writing overly opinionated and slightly satirical thrillers isn't the most practical career track anyone's ever thought of."

He took another ugly selfie. "A political career might boost your sales."

"Especially if I come up with a really original scandal. Get Capitol Hill out of the adultery rut. You know, like start an organized crime ring to import exotic animals into the secret tunnels under the West Wing."

I scooted my chair a little closer to his, so we weren't spaced quite as much like one of us had a highly contagious disease. "What about you? I have this terrible suspicion that you're here of your own free will. Even though you kind of look like you got lost on your way to football camp."

"I paid the tuition myself," he said. "And football doesn't start until the week we go home."

"I'm starting to see how you and Catalina Tarantula Amazon-Coachella ended up together. You're a prepackaged power couple."

He flashed a very JFK-looking smile. "We know what we want."

"World domination. Duh." I kicked my shoes off and swung my legs over the arm of the chair. Somehow Selfie

Boy's literally literal magnetic-ness wasn't intimidating at all. It was the exact opposite, actually, like we were long-lost preschool best friends or something. "I guess my main question is why the hell you're talking to me instead of... I don't know. The dean."

"Work hard, play hard," he said. "You're not here for the library time."

"Accurate."

Another campaign-winning grin. "We'll make this summer interesting. Count on it."

And then I realized I didn't know his name, even though we were pretty much jumping ourselves into America's tamest two-kid gang. He must have had the same thought, because he said, "I'm Henry, by the way."

"Annie."

He actually winced. "Annie doesn't work. You're not wearing enough pink."

"I'm allergic," I said, looking down at my outfit. I was interpreting the evening's theme with an off-the-shoulder T-shirt (courtesy of my roommate's nail scissors) and a giant pair of boxers with REAGAN BUSH '84 across the ass.

"Well, where are you from?" he asked.

"Cleveland."

"Cleveland."

He said it like a statement, judgment-free, but I wasn't taking any chances. "We have the Rock and Roll Hall of Fame and a legitimately fancy orchestra. It's the New York City of northern Ohio."

"I'm not knocking Cleveland. I'm saying that's your name."
It was another absolute.

"Cleveland?"

He nodded. "Cleves for short."

"Perfect. I'll put in the paperwork."

While this might not be the expected conclusion to an encounter between a creeper and a human magnet, we had thoroughly boredom-proofed the summer and crafted the foundations of a truly beautiful friendship before our fellow Overachievers had even vacated the dance floor.

I credit my winning combination of shamelessness and boxers-as-outerwear.

Even human magnets can't resist that.

Police Have No Leads in Lancaster Auto Theft

Jumping out the window isn't half as exciting as it sounds when your window is two feet above a porch roof with direct access to Indiana's most climbable tree. It takes cow-print pajama bottoms to make it even slightly interesting.

Potential Future Day Job #327: Stylist for Low-Level Criminals with Branding Problems.

I survive the leap and the climb, then head out to the end of the street and around the gate that's supposed to keep the rabble out of Howard Heights. I'm looking for Henry's old Camaro, but instead, right past the guard booth, there's Katie Howard's Prius, practically glowing in the moonlight. Henry has the windows open, which is good, since I'm not about to open the door and implicate myself in grand theft auto.

"No way. No. Way. I'm not getting in that damn car."

"Come on. It's fine."

"It is NOT fine."

"Shh, Cleves, you're going to wake somebody up."

"And they'll notice you STOLE A CAR?"

"She gave me the keys. Come on. We're on a deadline."

Because I'm dying to know what the plan is—and also because my cow pants are only a third as warm as actual pants—I sigh somewhat theatrically and get in. I do wrap my sleeve over my hand before I open the door, though, because if there's anything I've learned from police procedurals, it's that you can't leave fingerprints, or some cop with a penchant for excessive force will one-liner you straight into prison.

Then I give up on the fingerprint theory, because I can't buckle my seat belt with my hands inside my sleeves. Plus I've been in Katie's car under much less suspicious circumstances, so my fingerprints are already all over it, and if they arrest me, everybody will say, *Yeah, she's ridden with Katie, like, a million times*, and boom, reasonable doubt. No jury could convict that.

We're driving fast out into the country and Henry's not saying anything yet, probably because he wants to wait until we're too far away for me to walk back before he mentions that I was right and he's actually just stealing Katie's car. I turn the radio on, and it's this hideous pop station blasting some guy who sounds like he got kicked in the balls five seconds before they started recording, so I flip to the indie station and Henry goes, "Hey, hey, hey, stop!"

"What?"

"Put that back to her station."

I do the most disgusting gagging noise I can manage.

"Come on. She can't find out we had her car."

I turn the volume up. "I thought she gave you the keys."

"She did. She was wearing my jacket, and I got it back when she was in practice—"

"As in you snuck into the gym and stole it?"

"It's *my* jacket," says Henry. "Not my fault she left her keys in the pocket."

"Pretty sure that doesn't legally constitute her giving them to you."

"It constitutes pissing her uncle off if he figures out she lost them again. I'm doing her a favor. She's at Parker's tonight, and when they stop by Katie's in the morning, the keys will be right inside the front door."

"You're breaking into her house, too?"

"Letter drop," he says, "but I like the way you think."

We hit a pothole, and there's a rustling noise from the back seat. For two seconds, I'm so sure Katie's hiding back there— meaning I'm the real pranking-target—that I practically give myself whiplash spinning around.

It's not Katie. It's a billion water bottles, spray-painted red and white and filled with jingle bells. The cheerleaders sell them before football games so everybody can be even more obnoxious than they'd be otherwise, and the fact that not only students but also full-grown adults willingly pay money for them tells you just how much we care about high school sports here in Lancaster, Indiana.

Henry catches me staring at the spirit bottles. "Hey, can you start going through those? I've already done the ones with the caps off. There's a bag back there for the bells."

"You are NOT serious right now."

"You're already an accomplice."

"Damn you." But I'm laughing, because even though Katie Howard is my best friend in Indiana besides Henry and I love her, she's never going to fit his ridiculous girlfriend standards. And hopefully a prank will get whatever this is out of Henry's system, and then he can either dump her or come to terms with the fact that his ideal girl doesn't exist. Which means that, really, tonight's for the greater good of all of humanity.

I climb into the back and start opening bottles and dumping out bells.

"Isn't it the girl who's supposed to do this?" I ask, sixteen bottles in.

"Do what?"

"Show up in the middle of the night with a five-act revenge plot. Guys are supposed to be the emotionally stable ones."

"I thought you were a feminist."

I shake out another bottle. "I'm just saying. That's the trope."

"I'm emotionally stable."

"Says the guy doing ninety in his girlfriend's car while his wingwoman deconstructs cheerleader accessories."

"We're pranking. It's what we do. And your phone's buzzing, by the way."

I peer over the passenger seat. For a second I'm mildly concerned it might be my mom, who's caught me out of my room a good half-dozen nights so far this fall, but no: This is much worse than a very low-key Mom-lecture. The caller ID says Deadline Police, with a picture of Mussolini filling the entire screen. "Don't answer it," I say.

Of course he does anyway. "Cleveland's phone."

"Hang up!" I grab for it, but Henry ducks out of my way.

"She's in a meeting right now, actually, but I can take a message."

"Hang *up*!"

"No, that's not her, it's—yeah, okay, fine, here you go." He tosses the phone to me.

I kick the back of his seat. "Asshole!"

"Excuse me?" says Mussolini, aka Cat Parr, aka Supreme Leader of *The Lion Ledger*, which you'd assume was actually *The New York Times* instead of a high school newspaper, given how damn seriously Cat takes it.

"Not you, Cat."

"Right." She's not even pissed off, because Cat Parr doesn't get pissed off. She just gets frosty. Like, *Why is everyone so totally incompetent?* "I haven't gotten your op-ed yet."

"You mean the one I turned in this afternoon?"

"I gave you a new topic. An *appropriate* topic."

I mute myself, lean into the front seat, say, "I'm going to kill you, Henry," and then unmute myself. "There's always the option of not censoring everybody to death."

"It's not censorship. It's editorial standards."

"Come on. Eustace and Christina liked my first one."

"Eustace and Christina aren't the editor-in-chief. And neither are you."

"Savage."

"Factual," she shoots back. Without missing a beat, obviously, because she's also vice president of the debate club, and her best friend is the president, and all their conversations are

22

conducted in warp-speed point-counterpoint. "So your re-write will be in my inbox by 6:00 a.m.?"

"Um—"

"Perfect."

She hangs up on me.

I chuck my phone back into the front seat. "Whatever we're getting Katie back for better be good, because I'm going to newspaper jail tomorrow."

He laughs. "We can prank Cat next."

"Let's TP her house with tabloids. The lack of editorial standards will send her over the edge, and she'll be forced out of editor-in-chiefdom, and then I can take over, and we'll have a paper that's actually *interesting*. We'll be heroes."

"I'm down if you're down."

I unscrew another bottle cap. "Seriously, what's up with Katie? You guys were practically shooting a porno at lunch, and now—"

"She's cheating on me."

If he's expecting me to shriek in horror or swoon or some-thing, I'm really under-delivering. But given Katie's tendency to overshare harder than any reality star in the history of the E! network, I'm pretty sure I'd know if she was skulk-ing around on hidden staircases with a dashing stranger. So I just say, "Yeah right."

"She *is*, Cleves."

"I mean, do you have any actual evidence, or is this just helpful bro advice from your helpful bro teammates?"

He turns ever-so-slightly red.

"Ha! I knew it. Dude, they're just being overprotective of

their precious quarterback. And also being really embarrassingly sexist, I'm assuming. What did they even say?"

"Just, you know…she's not girlfriend material. She's hookup material."

"Okay," I say, and yeah, I'm annoyed. "I'm just going to point out how problematic it is to—"

"Did you just say 'problematic' out loud?"

"Did you just reduce the female gender into girlfriend and hookup categories?"

"I love it when you talk social justice," he says, but he's sitting all the way back again.

"Seriously, you can just say you're not a good match. Or you could say, 'Hey, Cleves, I know it's midnight and *Air Crash Investigation* is the greatest show on Earth, but nothing says homecoming like affectionately pranking the queen-to-be,' instead of trying to smokescreen it with some bullshit locker-room talk you don't even believe. I mean, you *don't* believe it, do you?"

He catches my eye in the rearview mirror. He's grinning his stupid human-magnet grin, and damn him, I absolutely would've climbed out my window for this even if it was the night before finals instead of an arbitrarily extra-hyped football game. "Not really. She's—yeah. You win."

"Again," I say. "Must get boring losing all the time."

He shrugs. "Not as long as I'm losing to Indiana's best wingwoman."

Program Attendees Redefine "Progress"

The thing about Overachiever Camp is that it's full of overachievers.

It's not that I don't want to do anything with my life. I totally do. Just not in the Red Bull–abusing, sleep-deprived, academic-champion kind of way. For one thing, I want to have a good time occasionally, instead of spending my teenage years chained to a library table. For another thing, aspiring writers mostly need to be collecting experiences, like road trips and bad decisions and the kinds of memories that turn into good stories. And coming up with ideas for potential future day jobs.

But my family is very, very scholarly. Mom has a PhD in literature and she's written several lengthy tomes on experimental feminist lit, which led to some interesting show-and-telling when I was in kindergarten. Dad has a PhD in psychology and an MD in psychiatry, and *that* led to some interesting analyses of other kids' show-and-telling when I was in kindergarten. And my little sister, Amelie, is definitely going to be one of those freaks who finishes med school at age twenty, at which point I'll be twenty-five and probably still choosing a major.

Although I've tried to turn my adoptee status into a get-out-of-the-Ivory-Tower-free card—you know, "Hey look, genetics! P.S., I quit Academic Decathlon"—the Marck household is all about nurture over nature, assuming you define "nurture" as "horrifying amounts of educational enrichment at every turn."

Plus Amelie ruined that excuse, seeing how she's just as nonbiological as I am.

All of which is to say: Rewind to the end of sophomore year. Specifically, to my sweet-sixteen party at this loft we'd rented with a band that didn't suck. My dad was already at his teaching gig in Germany, but my mom made this huge deal of presenting an envelope and my friends were sure it was going to be a note about how my new car was out front.

Instead, it was an invitation to the Summer Progress Institute of Indiana.

It just sounds menacing, like the House of Special Purpose, or Advanced Interrogation Techniques.

"Is it for writing?" I asked.

"It's for everything," said Mom. "Total intellectual stimulation." Which definitely isn't a weird thing to say at a sweet sixteen.

My parents are actually pretty great. And they're not pushy

in the honor-roll-or-else sense. But they honestly don't get why somebody might not want to spend their summer memorizing formulas. Or formulae. Or determining whether it's *formula* or *formulae*.

So I thanked Mom and got back to enjoying the non-sucking band, and the next day I explained in my calmest, most rational voice that poolside toenail-painting would provide the mental rest I needed to be back on my intellectual A-game by fall, and besides, as a *writer*, what I really needed was *adventures*, like protests and helping somebody bury a body.

But the battle was already lost. I was going to Overachiever Camp, where I would soon realize what an underachiever I was compared to kids who'd won national science fair awards and gotten perfect SAT scores and could play a mean *Moonlight Sonata*, too, which they'd gladly demonstrate on the dorm piano at the crack of dawn.

Then, three days in, Henry came along. And as it turned out, he was as much a fan of reckless exploits as I was. Maybe even more.

An hour after he christened me Cleves, we were up on the roof planning a camp-wide poker black market. He brought a guitar, which I totally wasn't expecting. Eventually we picked out the corner with the best view, and he started messing around on the guitar, and it wasn't your average cringey teenage-boy shit at all.

"What is that? It's good."

"I wrote it," he said. "It's for Lina."

He started playing again, and this time he sang along. At first, it just seemed like it was about winter and storms and holly and ivy—so kind of like a Christmas carol, minus Santa and Jesus—but if you paid attention, it turned into this remarkably non-cheesy love song about how he'd always be loyal to Lina, no matter what.

I'd be lying if I said I didn't have the slightest, faintest trace of a crush on Henry right then. Or that I wasn't the slightest, faintest bit jealous of Catalina Trapeze Armada-Tequila, who'd won the boyfriend lottery in a very serious way.

I mean, Henry was hot. He was tall, with one of those faces that makes you realize what they mean when they talk about bone structure, and he had actual *shoulders*, which never seemed like a particularly significant body part until they were so well done. And he was a million things at once: a smart kid and a jock and a musician and the kind of guy who'd dodge curfew and break out onto the roof three days into Summer Progress Whatever-Whatever.

Plus, the way he was so in love with Lina was kind of nauseatingly beautiful.

But he was taken, and I wasn't about to try to mess with such a devastatingly good couple—not that all the boxers-as-outerwear in the world would've stood a chance against a trilingual humanitarian with kickass lacrosse skills—so we stayed just friends. Yes, really. And at the end of the summer, when I said goodbye to the girls on my hall and promised to text them and knew I never would, I promised Henry I'd text him, too, and I actually did. Before Mom even made it to the highway.

For the record, it so wasn't about my sad little crush or even his human magnet status. It's just that we were completely kindred spirits, and it was a total letdown to be heading back home after the summer we'd pulled off. My Cleveland friends are fantastic, but those adventures were always more like... I don't know. Poorly planned road trips to see possibly shitty bands. Which is a great time, don't get me wrong, but we never really made it out of our comfort zone.

Here's just a sampling of what Henry and I orchestrated during our six weeks of camp:

One: Sneaking into the student union and getting onto that roof, too, which is much cooler than the dorm roof.

Two: Making a fairly hefty amount of cash running the poker black market.

Three: Getting an entire crew of Overachievers to hike across campus to the golf course in the dead of night, armed with fireworks for a bloodthirsty game of roman golf, which Henry swore he and his friends back home played all the time. It consists of shooting roman candles at the opposing team while running for your life.

Four: Dressing up in formalwear and crashing a trustee dinner, which Henry may actually have categorized as "networking" rather than "pretending to be in a spy movie," seeing as he left with business cards and a lead on an internship, while I left with a fake British accent and a new appreciation for the no-carding aspects of old-people events.

Five: Compromising the integrity of the end-of-camp banquet soundtrack, so right after that snobby violin song from every country club scene ever—you know the one—we were all serenaded by Alice Cooper howling "School's Out."

And trust me, that wasn't even half of it.

Anyway, Henry and I made damn good partners in crime, and now that we live in the same town—more on that later—we're pretty much a crack team of midnight marauders.

College recruiters go wild for stuff like that.

Which brings us back to twenty minutes past midnight, off to execute another girlfriend plot and/or continue our shenanigan dominance. And don't even try to tell me you wouldn't also jump out a window in cow pajamas if your other options were (a) study, (b) watch another seven hours of plane crashes, or (c) put together an editorial Cat will actually approve.

For some reason, she had an issue with my latest pitch. Headline: Ten Tips for Surviving Lancaster's Biggest Party. Meaning End of the Road, the annual rager that's happened the day after homecoming since the dawn of time, at least according to every person I've met since setting foot on Hoosier soil. Considering that last spring's after-prom party ended with Henry's second girlfriend blowing up a building, this subject is both timely and topical.

And admittedly a tad on the dark side, since there were in fact two fatalities at said prom explosion. On the other hand, that goes to show that an End of the Road survival guide might be the most practical thing the *Ledger* could ever hope to print.

Anyway, Cat apparently had a traumatic childhood experience involving entertaining journalism, because based on this afternoon's ruling, we can add lowbrow satire to the list of things she won't print. She's never actually *given* us a list, probably because having it all in one place would look too blatantly *Fahrenheit 451*, which is her favorite book, according to our first-day-of-class icebreaker.

I suspect she may side with the book burners.

Since she won't make a list, Eustace Chapman—aka Lancaster High School's very own Perez Hilton—and I have selflessly started making one for her. So far, Cat's given the veto to legit investigative reporting about last spring's prom explosion, a tell-all about every homecoming court candidate, a rate-our-teachers survey, a breakdown of how sexist the dress code is, a highly engaging smear campaign against our rival school's football team, and now a guide to surviving End of the Road.

Basically, if you want to go to print, you have to write about something nobody in our readership gives a flying fuck about. Like religious infighting in countries most Americans can't find on a map, or how to get into colleges that only accept Nobel laureates. Or city council elections.

Spellbinding.

And the thing is, no, I'm not editor-in-chief at Lancaster, but I would've been editor-in-chief at Cleveland Lakes this year if we didn't move, so it's not like I'm some rookie who doesn't understand how to write an article.

Point being, I'd definitely rather be running amok with Henry than euthanizing myself via editorial standards. And anyway, it's not like anyone remembers the nights they stayed in.

Clearly I learned all the right lessons at Overachiever Camp.

Boy, 17, Dumps Recycling Instead of Girl

York is one town over from Lancaster, and it's so small that the main landmark is the high school, even though everybody who goes there lives out on the farms. Other than that, it's just two churches, a bar, a post office, a gas station, a tractor supply, and a dump. And yes, Lancaster does in fact have its very own dump—one that does not require twenty minutes of driving if your starting point is Howard Heights—but the first rule of pranking is that you never do your prep work in a place where your target and/or their spies might intercept you.

We're professionals, damn it.

"Do you think we can recycle the ones that aren't empty?" Henry asks. We're pulled up next to a Dumpster that says *Plastic*. The closest streetlight is yellow-orange and flickering and half a block away.

"WHY ARE YOU WHISPERING?" I answer in my best crowded-cafeteria voice.

"Shh!"

"Is it because we're STEALING A CAR?"

"Cleveland! Shut up!" But he's laughing.

"It's one o'clock in the morning. I think we're good." I flip bottles into the bin while Henry empties a few more.

"Come on. Help me out."

I sit down in the back seat and start dumping out bells again, because he won't leave until we've done this exactly right. A true overachiever, even in pranking. "You have a bright future with Greenpeace," I say. "God, it's cold out here."

"Should've worn something besides the cow pants."

"It was either that or my homecoming gown."

He scoffs. "You in a gown. Right."

"Shut up. I wore a toga to that mythology party at camp."

"The Wonder Woman sheets ruined it."

"Wonder Woman's totally a modern Athena. And it's not like I was going to invest in more authentically ancient Greek sheets just to stand around talking about which AP test is the hardest."

He empties out the last bottle, but doesn't toss it yet. "I can't believe we're never going back there."

"Ancient Greece?" I find a cheerleading sweatshirt on the back seat, but it's way too small because Katie's the size of a seventh grader, so I just hug it to my chest like a blanket.

"I know you hated it. But it was nice to be somewhere nobody knew about my family shit."

Much like most larger-than-life protagonist types, Henry has this sprawling narrative arc of a past, and it's all woven into the history of Lancaster to the point that if I were him, I'd already have a one-way ticket out of here booked for ten minutes after graduation.

But more on that later.

"Come on," I say. "Next fall you're going to be at some genius college, and nobody will give the slightest of damns about your tragic backstory."

Calling it that is pushing it even for me, but he doesn't get pissed off. He just says, "Yeah. You better be right."

"Goals, right?"

He nods. "Right."

As cheesy as it sounds—and last spring was ridiculous, so whatever, it's excusable—Henry and I spent our last night at *Overachiever Camp II: The Second Summer of Scholastic Servitude* drinking room-temperature PBR and coming up with things that we would Absolutely, Definitely, One Hundred Percent For Sure Accomplish during what we swore would be The Best Senior Year To Ever Happen To Anyone.

"Best college ever," I say. "You blood-oathed."

"Yeah, and you blood-oathed to make sure Lancaster noticed you." Henry grins. No more tragic gazing into the distance. Which is good, because I'm here for the adrenaline, not the angst. "You can thank me later."

He throws the last bottle into the bin, and then he's back behind the wheel of a stolen car and I'm back riding shotgun, and we're flying back out into the wide-open darkness of farm fields and straight, narrow roads that are perfect for speeding as much as you want when you're not very concerned about staying on the actual straight-and-narrow.

You know, just a typical Thursday night.

Being the New Kid Doesn't Always Suck:
More at Eleven

It's probably not that surprising that I wasn't quite as opposed to Overachiever Camp the second time around. Drama and all—his junior year was a bit more tumultuous than mine—Henry and I picked up right where we left off. And in the middle of six more weeks of rooftop poker and half-assed studying, my mom called and said, *By the way, we're moving to Indiana.*

She called during my lunch break, and that was already suspicious, so I was expecting the worst. Like, *We're adopting another kid and turning your room into a nursery, so you're going to have to move in with Amelie and her ten thousand textbooks,* which in my defense was only moderately implausible. And I was so busy prepping a speech about how I needed my space for just *one more year* that when she said we were moving, I couldn't even think of any non-baby-related responses.

So I hung up.

Then I skipped my next class and decided to max out my emergency credit card. The only real options were a 7-Eleven, a pizza place, and a musical instrument store. Despite my lack of both talent and training, I briefly contemplated revenge-buying a full set of saxophones, from a tiny, fake-looking one all the way up to a giant monstrosity that looked like those things the lederhosen guys play in Switzerland tourism ads.

In the end, I just went to the pizza place and ate five-sixths of a Hawaiian pizza while texting literally everyone about how unjust the situation was. Then I called Mom back and told her she'd narrowly avoided a catastrophic saxophone shopping spree, and that she could just have the moving guys make an extra stop at Sybil's and drop off my crap there, because I wasn't moving the summer before senior year, and also, this move was definitely a midlife crisis.

Eventually I had to come up for air and Mom said something like, *Well, I'd hardly call it a midlife crisis since it's a tenure-track position, and I'd really like to get away from city life blah blah blah,* and I'd more or less stopped listening to prep my next set of remarks when I heard her say *London College* and I cut her off.

"London?"

"Not the one in England. Indiana, remember?"

"LANCASTER," I yelled fairly ecstatically, which was justified because I'd visited Henry there, not that Mom had been overly worried about the details. Henry actually went to London College for some overachiever-y class, since a mere six AP courses and two varsity sports is a pretty slacker schedule, when you think about it. It was like ten miles from Lancaster, and whatever town it was in wasn't even a real town. Which meant we were moving to Henry's town, and I wouldn't be the proverbial friendless new-kid senior after all.

So the two of us spent the second half of camp plotting twelfth grade instead of just guerrilla-ing a string of misdemeanors. And by our last night in the dorms, there we were on the roof again, with Henry's guitar and the final remains of the beer stash, bloodlessly blood-oathing to have a senior year so fucking spectacular we'd go down in history.

"Best college," said Henry. This was something like our eightieth attempt at nailing down intelligible goals, since we kept getting distracted by the stars and the improv possibilities and estimating exactly how big of a welcome-to-Lancaster party Parker or Brandon or somebody was going to throw for me. "Best parties. Best season—both sports. Best girlfriend."

"Best girlfriend," I sang, and he strummed out a dramatic chord. We were lying on our backs and the guitar was balanced on his chest.

"Best girlfriend," he said again. "For real. For *good*. No more of this bullshit."

I valiantly suppressed my urge to mention how said bullshit had only happened after he made the fatal error of breaking up with the incomparable Catalina Talladega Armageddon-Chinchilla. In my not-especially-humble opinion, both of his replacement attempts had been massively ill-advised. "Fourth time's the charm," I said.

He hit another chord. "Count on it. And you know what, Cleves? If I can just make it all happen, when I come back after college, that town will be mine."

And yes, the first time he'd mentioned this, it did seem totally weird that he wanted to go back home after college instead of conquering New York or Washington or Timbuktu. But Henry's all about family, follow-through, and a healthy dose of personal-narrative-serving symbolism, so his road to the White House has to start in Lancaster.

"Calm down, Napoleon," I said.

He kicked me. "You know what I mean."

"Yeah. I'm just struggling to come up with anything that sounds suitably megalomaniacal for the turn this conversation just took."

"You've got this."

"Okay." I raised a fist to the sky. "I'm going to leave my mark on Lancaster High School."

"Who's the maniac now?"

"Shut up." It was my turn to kick him. "You know what I mean, too. I'm not just going to come in and be that new girl for a year and disappear. I'm going to *do* something."

"Like what?"

"Break a story about how the drama club is laundering car wash money to buy a private island. Get unanimously voted editor-in-chief, Lancaster seniority be damned." I took another drink. "Or maybe I won't even need the paper. Maybe I'll just capitalize on my pranking prowess."

"That could work."

"And also, I'm going to figure out what the hell I'm doing with my life. Or at least what I'm doing after we graduate."

Henry sent some major side-eye in my direction. "Never thought you'd bow to the camp status quo."

"Dude." I threw an empty can at him. "At least it will shut everybody up."

"True."

"And they'll *really* shut up when I go with my 'marry money' scheme and retire to a castle to live off my generous pension by the time I'm twenty-five. Take that, career day."

"You'll figure it out," he said in his I'm-definitely-right-and-it's-definitely-happening voice, which was exactly what I needed to hear. Because even though I could play it off like a champ, that didn't stop the low-key panicking thing that happened every time my deeply bookish twelve-year-old sister or Crown Prince Henry went off on yet another soliloquy about the precise details of what they'd be doing ten years from now, when I couldn't even think of a college major that didn't make me want to barricade myself in my room with a lifetime supply of junk food and a strong WiFi connection.

"And also," I added, before I could kill my own vibe, "have an adventure to end all adventures. The kind I can tell my great-grandchildren about and they'll think I'm losing it, or at least fucking with them, but it will be absolutely word-for-word true."

"It's going to happen."

"Of course it's going to happen!" I shouted into the sky. We usually tried to stick with indoor voices on the roof, to minimize the getting-busted-and-ruining-the-rest-of-summer risk, but it wasn't like they were going to boot us out of camp with ten hours to go. "And bonus points if I can make it all happen at the same time. A trifecta of brilliant ridiculousness."

Henry strummed another three chords. "We're going to have the best senior year ever."

"Hell yeah!" I yelled, even louder this time.

And I didn't even give a shit how cliché and corny and seventeenish it was, because I one hundred percent knew it was going to happen, and I knew Henry knew it, too.

We were going to rock Lancaster so hard, they'd be talking about us for centuries.

Corporations a Factor in Downfall of American Youth

The Lancaster Walmart is on the edge of town across from Howard Heights. It's open all night, but at one thirty in the morning, the parking lot is empty enough that we don't have to worry about anybody witnessing us getting out of a car with three cheerleading bumper stickers and a vanity plate that spells CHR QN.

"So what's the plan?" I ask as Henry steers a cart past the Halloween candy.

"We have to restock the car," he tells me.

"Let's fill it with beheaded Barbie dolls. Threatening, but perky."

"Your mind is an amazing place."

"So is Katie's stolen car." I grab a bag of Twizzlers and throw it into the cart.

"Borrowed," he corrects me. "And we're buying one hundred bottles of water and four cans of spray paint."

"As in, exactly what we just recycled?"

"Exactly what was in the back of Katie's car before she skipped English to do her quarter of the spray-painting in the parking lot."

"Okay, that's just annoying. This is a serious letdown, as far as pranks go."

He angles the cart toward the water aisle. "Nobody else saw the completed project. She left her keys in my jacket, and I took my jacket, and then she rode over to Parker's with Josie."

"Like, totally," I say, because he sounds like a thirteen-year-old at a slumber party.

"She was already late getting the bottles ready. And you know she swore to Parker that she got it done, and then tomorrow, it'll be like she was lying the entire time."

I raise one fairly judgy eyebrow. "That's diabolical."

"She's going to lose it."

"Yeah, because you're literally gaslighting her. What did she even do to you?"

"It's not about what she *did*. It's what everybody's *saying*. That she's a—"

"If you say 'slut,' I'm going to karate chop you in the throat," I say, with the chipperest fake grin post-midnight Walmart has ever seen.

"Damn, Cleves, you could give me some credit every once in a while."

"Well, you *did* say, quote, 'She's not girlfriend material. She's hookup material.' So—"

"*I* didn't say it." He halts in front of the water bottle cases and starts loading the cart while I keep it from rolling away. "*Brandon* said it. And—stop giving me that look! He's looking out for me, okay? He's a good guy."

It isn't totally a lie. Henry's best bro might be on the fast track to winning Most Likely To Keg-Stand Before Noon at whatever frat he pledges next year, but he sort of *is* a douche-face with a heart of gold. I mean, he was so unwaveringly committed to keeping Henry and Lina together that he should've been short-listed for the Nobel Peace Prize.

"Okay," I say. It's a very suspicious *okay*, but it's something. "And what else did Brandon say?"

"That I should be careful not to end up with somebody like—You-Know-Who." He heaves the last case of water into the cart.

Here's the thing: Henry, along with pretty much all of Lancaster, thinks his second girlfriend—You-Know-Who—tried to murder him in the infamous prom explosion last spring. Personally, I don't subscribe to theories that only make sense in a Disney villain context, but whatever.

"Dude. Katie's her cousin, not her clone," I say. "Although I still think it's super squicky to date your dead ex-girlfriend's cousin, by the way. It feels too much like you're pitching your love life to *The Maury Show*."

He starts walking again. "Brandon just thinks I should be with somebody more like—you know. You."

Because I'm still kind of instinctively primed to react when Henry says shit like that—even though I'm also one hundred percent over him—I take a flying leap onto the cart and surf it halfway down the aisle as an extra security measure to make sure he doesn't see whatever renegade *yes I agree* expression he might think he sees on my face.

Yeah, shut up.

He catches up in two steps and says, "Or Jane."

Which completely ruins it.

"Ugh, Jane Seymour," I say, because his third girlfriend— the one who moved away during *Overachiever Camp II: Attack of the Clones*—is the only one Henry still approves of, despite the fact that if you made a Venn diagram of Boring and Basic, the whole overlapping part would just say JANE SEYMOUR in twelve-point Times New Roman. She's a human pumpkin spice latte. Decaf.

"You can 'Ugh, Jane Seymour' all you want, but she had her shit together. And Katie's really damn dramatic sometimes."

Katie lives very passionately—she's always the first one to laugh at shitty jokes, and she legit cries during insurance commercials. But I'm pretty sure her zest for life and parties and being the life of the party is exactly why he liked her in the first place. "Fine," I say. "Then dump her. I'm sure your beloved Jane has a cousin somewhere, too."

He stops in front of the spray paint and grabs two cans of red and two cans of white. "I can't dump her."

"You mean because you actually like her, even though she dares to be more fun than Jane Sey-bore, or because you think she's going to spike your drink with Drano for revenge? Because I promise she's not going to spike your drink with Drano."

He glances at me. "God, I sound ridiculous, don't I?"

"You said it, not me."

"Thanks." He fake-punches me, and I stick my foot out to trip him. He hops it and swings the cart around the end of the aisle. "You know I want to be with Katie. I just—" He cuts himself off.

"You just what? Is this more bullshit from the guys?"

He hesitates for an incriminatingly long moment.

"Okay, what is it? Say it, and I'll shoot it down," I tell him. And yes, maybe I'm disproportionately at the bat for Katie here, but (a) call a girl a slut, and I'll defend her to the death; (b) Katie's such a goddamn sweetheart that she literally bought me a dog two days after we met, although her plan was foiled due to Amelie's inconvenient dog allergy; and (c) female solidarity, kids.

Henry bites his lip.

"Come on. Just tell me. I'm already judging you."

He glances around surreptitiously. "Francis Dereham has her nudes on his phone."

"What the fuck." I boomerang around to the front of the cart and block it. "So, first of all, I don't even want to know how you know—"

"He showed Brandon."

"What the *fuck*. That's fucking *illegal*, for one thing, and fucking *awful*, for another thing. Does she even know? Because if she doesn't—"

"She knows," he says. "She sent them."

"To Francis." I start dragging the cart toward the checkout, because I'm way too pissed off to stand still. "When they were *dating*, right? And I'm assuming there wasn't a memo attached that was like, 'Hey, asshole who doesn't deserve me, please save these after I dump you for someone way better, and also show them to everybody on the team, because that isn't a massive invasion of privacy at all, and—'"

"Cleves!" Henry comes around to my end of the cart and puts his hands on my shoulders. "Chill. I know he's a dick. As soon as End of the Road's over, I'm taking care of it."

"Good. Kick his ass. And then run over his phone."

Apparently that works as a closing statement, because Henry nods like he's mentally penciling in *Kick Francis Dereham's ass, 8:00 a.m. Monday,* and then he pushes the cart the rest of the way to the only checkout lane that's still open and starts loading everything onto the conveyor belt.

But then he goes, "So you think I can trust her?"

"You mean, even though Francis Dickham shares nudes? I thought we'd determined that was a Francis Dickham problem." The checkout guy, who's maybe a year older than us and definitely half-asleep, looks up at *shares nudes,* so I look him in the eye and go, "Not with you, buddy."

"The thing is," Henry says, "Francis told Brandon he and Katie are still talking."

"It's Katie. She's sociable."

"Not talking. *Talking.*"

I stare. "Have you asked *her* about any of it?"

"I can't."

"Oh, yeah?" I lunge for Henry's pocket and grab his phone. He has the most obvious password ever—0008, for his football number—and he never changes it. "Who should I text first? Katie, or Francis? I'm thinking Francis, honestly—"

He grabs the phone back and holds it over his head. I'm not quite shameless enough to jump for it. "I can't ask her. She freaks out when I ask her about other guys."

"Probably because your friends are going around sharing her damn nudes. If you're going to take their side instead of hers, maybe you really *should* dump her."

"I love her," Henry says, out of absolutely fucking nowhere. The cashier stops scanning and stands there gaping at our ever-escalating scene, which is appropriate since we've got at least enough material for a pilot episode here, and possibly an entire season.

"You love her," I repeat.

"I love her."

"Now who's the dramatic one? No offense, but it seems like you two are meant to be together. At least until the midseason hiatus of *The Young and the Ridiculous*."

Scanner Guy finally unfreezes and bags the spray paint, and Henry pays. "That's why this shit is freaking me out, okay? I want this to work, and I'm scared it's all going to fall apart again."

Henry doesn't throw around words like *scared* lightly. The last time I heard him say it, a certain prom explosion had almost blown him off the face of the planet. So honestly, as over-the-top as his random love confession just was, it's pretty clear he means it.

Which stings before the smart part of my brain can remind the ready-for-a-nap part that I'm over him. But then I'm glad, because it kind of explains everything.

"Okay, so listen." I take the receipt from Scanner Guy,

who's been watching us for long enough that he may actually think we're a pop-up improv troupe. Henry loads the cart back up and I say, "We do this prank. And then you go to the game, and you and Katie get coronated—"

"We might not win."

We head out the door. "Who else is even running? Cat and Jonathan? They're boring. They'll never beat you and Katie."

"You're only saying that because Cat's your nemesis."

"She's not my nemesis."

"Mussolini shows up on your screen when she calls you."

I shrug. "She's very skilled at arm-crossing. And dictating."

"Let's do the tabloid thing."

"Can't. Have to write that op-ed. And if this is about sabotaging your homecoming competition, don't bother. Nobody else has a chance."

"Don't jinx it."

"It's hilarious how much you care about a plastic crown."

He takes one hand off the cart to hold up a middle finger.

"Maybe Parker's your perfect girlfriend," I muse. "All that pageant experience of hers has to count for something, if being pseudo-royal is really that critical."

"Hey, I'm not the one who's single."

I dig into the cart for the Twizzlers. "The entire western world is aware of that, buddy."

"What if you went out with—"

"What if I stayed single, since you've got enough relationship drama to cover both of us? Boom. Ten points to Hufflepuff."

He swipes the Twizzler package, which I'm unsuccessfully

mutilating with my economy-sized fingernails, and rips it open in one try. "You need to get back in the game."

"I'm a conscientious objector."

"Best senior year ever, remember?"

"I remember that I'm not the one who made the whole thing about my relationship status. And I also remember that we were actually talking about how maybe the reason FEMA gets called in every time you break up with somebody is because you don't understand the concept of ethical relationships. So as I was saying, you get coronated, and you go to the dance and End of the Road, and then you kick Francis's ass, and at some point you actually *talk* to the girlfriend you love so dearly so you can put this all behind you and move on to more important things, like deciding who gets which seat at which table at your inaugural banquet."

"You make it sound so easy."

"Because it is." We're back at Katie's car. It's cold enough that I can see our breath in the air. "You're dating a junior, not invading Russia in winter."

"You think it will work?"

"You're supposed to be an overachiever. Reach a little."

He sits down in the middle of the pavement, and I sit down next to him, and we stare out at the road. "What the hell did I ever do without you?" he asks.

"You don't want me to answer that."

He wraps one arm around my shoulders and squashes me up against him.

Damn him. And also damn my shoulders for not getting the memo that we're done and he's in love with Katie and if that's what makes both of them happy, then as God is my witness, it's going to make me happy, too.

"We're going to be okay, right?" Henry asks.

"Right," I tell him. "Better than okay. Maybe even good someday."

He laughs. "Now who's the overachiever?"

"Hmm," Says Psychic, Channeling Spirit of Sigmund Freud

Okay, but really, Henry has his shit together. I mean, yes, girls are his kryptonite, but besides that, he's just as infuriatingly high-achieving as you'd figure he'd be, given where I met him. And the whole Tragic Backstory thing—which is a major downer, so let's just get it over with—really does suck.

Once upon a time, Lancaster was practically the only factory town that didn't fall apart when the whole Midwestern manufacturing thing stopped being a thing. And it was Henry's family that kept it going. His dad was running the factory by the time Henry was in kindergarten, and he was so smart about money that he ended up getting elected mayor, too.

Then Henry's mom died.

It was a car accident. They were driving back from Fort Wayne, and a truck in the other lane lost control. Henry and his dad walked away without a scratch. His mom and his brother didn't even make it to the hospital.

Losing your mom has to be pretty much the worst thing that can happen to any kid. And his brother was just enough older that Kid Henry thought he was the actual coolest person ever, as far as I can tell. But that was just the beginning, because after they died, his dad completely changed. He shut everybody out, even Henry. And the factory finally closed.

Apparently it wasn't even really his dad's fault. The end was inevitable, because no matter how thrifty you are, it's not like you can turn the clock back to the golden glory years when Detroit needed an endless supply of Lancaster Manufacturing's car parts.

"But it doesn't matter," Henry said the first time he explained it. It was a few weeks into our first Overachiever Camp, and we were in the library pretending to study. "It happened while he was in charge. It's not his fault that it closed, but it's his fault for not doing anything to fix things since then."

"He's working, though, right?"

Henry flipped pages in his chem book. "He just obsesses over stocks. He doesn't *do* anything. And he won't stop trying to blame everybody—I mean *everybody*, from Congress to my mom's family in York—for why things suck. Things suck. Fine. *Do* something about it."

"Shh," somebody said.

Henry didn't even glance at them. "It's been six years. But every time I say maybe he should start working with everybody who's trying to turn Lancaster around—I mean, he's got money. He could make a difference. But he says I'll never get it, because I had everything handed to me. Like that has anything to do with it."

"So that's why you're…why you want to change things?" I asked.

"I don't want to. I *need* to. Mom and Arthur aren't coming back, and the factory isn't opening back up, and my family's nothing if I don't make it something again. Get in with the people who give a shit about the future." His gaze got so supernova-intense that I was pretty sure I needed to grab a pair of those eclipse-viewing glasses if I wanted to maintain eye contact without permanent retinal scarring.

"And you know what the worst part is?" he said. "My dad thinks it should've been me, not Arthur."

I blinked. "Wait, what? You mean—"

"In the accident."

"No way."

"He *said* it," said Henry. "The night after the funeral. He said it never should've been him."

"Oh, Henry," I said, and honestly all I wanted to do was hug him, but there was a giant library table and an entire rainforest's worth of books between us, and I felt like the ten seconds it would take to circumnavigate everything would've been way too long without a sight line during this intense of a reveal. "I'm sure he didn't mean it should've been you *instead*—"

"He did. My brother was the one who was supposed to grow up and take everything over. He was only sixteen, but you could already tell it was going to happen just the way my dad wanted it. And I was just this nine-year-old kid who liked sports and shit. You don't get it. Arthur was *meant* for this." He nodded at our books and this vaguely menacing metal bust of the crusty ancient guy whose charitable donation had funded our corner of the library. "He was next in line. I was nothing."

Which was so straight-to-the-heart that I reversed my no-moving decision and dodged around the table to sit right next to him. "That's bullshit," I said. "You're so not-nothing, it's objectively unbelievable that anyone could possibly not see your awesomeness quotient even when you were nine, okay? Look at everything you're already doing. Come on."

"He doesn't care," said Henry. "He doesn't see it. It's never going to mean anything to him until I fix Lancaster."

"Fuck," I said, which probably wasn't the ideal response, but honestly, what *is* the ideal response when somebody drops that magnitude of truth-bomb? "That's—"

"Can you please have your therapy session somewhere else?" said the guy at the next table.

Henry's grip tightened on the chemistry book, and I was pretty sure he was about to get up and punch Table Guy. But after a long second, he dropped the book and laughed. "Hey, man, I'm sorry. We're out of here. You good?"

Table Guy's premature brow-furrow-wrinkle situation worked itself out like magic. "You don't have to leave, I mean, sorry I snapped like that—"

"No problem," said Henry the Human Magnet as he dumped our books into his bag and took my hand all in one seamless, casual sweep. "We're done with the library."

At this particular moment in history, he was still Mr. Catalina Tiramisu Arkansas-Casablanca, but he still had me by the hand in the library like some ungodly indie reboot of *Pride and Prejudice*. That nonsense, combined with the extreme emotional realness of the conversation Table Guy had just killed midsentence, explained my uncharacteristic muteness all the way out to the front steps. At which point I finally went, "Dude. *What?*"

There were a bunch of camp kids down by the sidewalk, and they yelled hey to us, or possibly just to Henry. He yelled back, but then he turned back toward me and took my other hand, too. "Now you know," he said. His eyes were so damn clear, I could see his actual soul. "Nobody knows. Only you and Lina."

I just stood there like a fool for a good five seconds. Then I hugged him super hard. He hugged me back just as hard, and he whispered, "Thanks, Cleves."

The hug got slow-mo long enough for a full swooping panoramic shot in our Wes Anderson *Pride and Prejudice*. The whole color palette changed and there were artsy sunflares and everything.

And then it ended, and his Human Magnet self was back, and we were halfway down the stairs as he shouted to the camp kids, "Roman golf tonight! Meet us at the south doors at midnight."

It was weeks before he mentioned Lancaster again, unless he was talking about Lina. *She* was the new Lancaster. Her mom was the mayor now—Isabel Castilla, a literal war hero with the medals to prove it. She and Lina's dad, Fernando

Aragón, had connections all over, and now that Isabel was done overseas, they were focusing their formidable combined talents on stitching Lancaster back together and bringing in new businesses to fill the factory-shaped crater in the economy. So Lina would've been a perfect match even if Henry wasn't completely in love with her. But he was, so it was a win-win, which Henry totally deserved after so much shit.

And so they all lived happily ever after.

Just kidding.

This isn't that kind of story.

Cheer Captain Takes High School Somewhat Too Seriously

"**O**h my God, Katie, you're going to get us both killed!" Hampton Court—possibly the world's most pretentious name for a high school cafeteria—is the eternal home of Lancaster's best theatrics. And the morning after *Mission: Recycling*, it's on.

Parker Rochford is pissed.

"Somebody's messing with me!" Katie has her back to the arc of onlookers, and half of them are not-so-subtly live-blogging everything.

Parker does a hair flip that may have singlehandedly won her the senior cheer captain title. "If you're going to lie, at least give me a *good* lie."

"I'm not lying! I did the spirit bottles yesterday. Just like I told you. Somebody stole my keys and—"

"And got rid of all the bottles you did, and bought a hundred more, and put them in your car, and put your keys through the letter drop?"

Katie looks totally desperate. She and Parker are friends, but Katie's still paying her Lancaster's-New-It-Girl dues. "That's what I keep telling you!"

"That's the worst lie I've ever heard in my life."

"But I'm not lying!"

Parker puts one hand up. "Spirit bottles are *important*, okay? The entire legacy of the Lancaster cheer squad is on the line. Just get them done."

I make a valiant effort not to roll my eyes. I usually would've stepped in before the two of them got quite this intense, but I'm off my game after last night's mission. Fortunately, even though I can't exactly back Katie up here, I have the next best thing: a distraction.

"Merry Christmas," I announce, dropping a giant garbage bag in front of Parker.

"Is this what I think it is?" She dives into the bag and pulls out a cheerleader-sized football jersey. The front says *LIONS, OH MY!* with our mascot crushing a York Cadet under one paw, and when Parker flips the shirt around, it says LANCASTER over Henry's number. "Love you, Cleves. These are perfect."

She tosses the jersey to Katie. Katie pulls it on, and then she spins around and does a cartwheel in the middle of Hampton Court. She lands with a huge smile, and I swear it should be illegal for anybody to be that cute, because Parker isn't even mad anymore.

Parker has her jersey on now, and Josie Bulmer's handing out the rest. I'm not a cheerleader—shocker, I know—but I get a shirt anyway. This is allegedly my reward for using my *Ledger* connections to snag us the last-minute printing job when the batch Josie ordered online fell short of Parker's sky-high demands, although my working theory is that Parker's suiting up her ever-growing army of lady allies. Or possibly just doing her part to even out the cheerleader-to-football-player ratio and get us closer to covering every varsity guy's jersey number. I've got number four for Tom Culpeper, the second-string QB, since Parker's been trying to set us up, despite what I personally view as a glaring lack of chemistry.

The warning bell rings, and Henry and a couple of his friends from the team swing past. Katie runs full-force at him and literally leaps into his arms. He spins her around as she kisses him, and then they're both laughing.

"Hey, Cleves," Henry says when he finally sets Katie down.

I grab the empty T-shirt bag. "You know, I had the strangest dream last night," I tell him. "You showed up at my window and made me come on some Bonnie and Clyde expedition."

"Weird, because I had a dream you came to homecoming in cow pajamas." He grins at me over Katie's head. "By the way, here's that chart you wanted for your article."

He holds up his phone, and my gut reaction is *please God not revenge porn* because (a) that's a deal breaker, and (b) I really, genuinely don't need to see Katie's alleged nudes in any context, let alone in the middle of Hampton Court. But no: It's actually a confirmation page, and it says, *Thank you, Cat! Your subscription to the* NATIONAL ENQUIRER *will begin immediately.* And the next line is Cat Parr's address.

Her street address.

She'll be getting a piping hot batch of editorial standards on her front lawn every week until she leaves for college.

"Holy shit, Henry, that's iconic." I high-five him. "I'd kiss you right now if your girlfriend weren't in my way."

"You're welcome," he says. Katie proxy-kisses him for me.

They head for the foreign language hall, and I'm starting toward calculus, but the second I'm out of the cafeteria Parker pops out of a doorway and latches on to my arm. "Listen," she says, very cloak-and-dagger. "You've got to fix this."

This is a typical Parker encounter. In the five months I've known her, I've accrued something like a thousand scars that match her preferred manicure shape. "Fix what?"

"Katie. Make sure she gets the spirit bottles done. Make sure she and Henry are good. Text me if either one of them starts acting sketchy, okay?"

I raise an eyebrow. "I think that ship might have sailed already."

She doesn't laugh.

So I take it down a notch, because with all the You-Know-Who shit Parker had to deal with last year, I can't blame her for being melodramatic sometimes. "Spirit bottles. Sketch patrol. Done and done."

She looks like I just rescued her cat from an oncoming tornado. "You're an actual lifesaver," she says. "Oh, and also, you need to dance with Tom tomorrow."

"Why is everybody trying to marry me off?" I ask, because seriously? "I'm not dating right now, okay?"

"You better not still be hung up on—"

"Dude. No way." I can literally feel myself blushing, and I'm really not impressed with my face for turning against me in this time of cross-examination.

"Do I need to remind you that you were a walking heart-eyes emoji when he asked you out?"

I will my face back to its non-blushing shade. "That was *forever* ago."

"It was two months ago. And you were still together six weeks ago. That's, like, yesterday."

"Yeah, well, I'm over him."

"Tell that to your face."

"Spontaneous sunburn," I say. Damn her and her precocious levels of social intelligence. "And for the record, that entire two weeks was just my own personal Rumspringa."

She blinks. "You know I don't speak hipster."

"Neither do the Amish."

"Oh my God," she says, but she's trying not to laugh instead of trying not to call the FBI. "I don't know what the hell that has to do with Henry, but—"

"Limited-time-only going wild when you're a teenager. And then you come back to the farm to milk the cows for the rest of your life."

"Milk the *cows*? What the actual—"

"I'm over him," I say. "Absolutely, one hundred percent, swear-on-the-Bible over him."

"Then dance with Tom." She gives me her very best beauty pageant interview smile and ducks back into her statistics class.

So since I'm clearly not getting an explanation for her unsolicited matchmaking enthusiasm, I head back to Hampton

Court and text Katie: let's skip some class. i'm in a spray-painting mood all of a sudden.

Saving lives. One spirit bottle at a time.

New Research
Suggests Attending Class Is Overrated

Okay, so I went out with Henry two months ago. Yeah. I know.

He wasn't always the champion of bad breakups. I mean, he and Lina were together for two *years*. And based on their video chat sessions and the time she visited him our first summer at Overachiever Camp, I was ready to say, *Save me a seat at your wedding. Or don't, because you'll need it for a dignitary, and besides, you guys are self-esteem murder.*

But I couldn't even hate Lina for it, because in addition to being future Secretary of State and also so hot it wasn't fair, she was actually nice. Not Regina George nice, *legit* nice, even though I was the rando who spent too much time with her boyfriend. The weekend she visited, she asked me all about myself and even laughed at my very out-of-control story about Potential Future Day Job #26, Library Table Sleep-Tester.

This conversation happened on the sidelines of a football/ rugby/flat-out-combat match Henry and the guys were play- ing. We got cut off when a kid on Henry's team got kicked in the balls and Henry yelled for Lina to sub in—Lina, instead of any of the guys, even though she's maybe five feet tall.

I said, you know, RIP. And she said, "Imagine me in full armor." And then she ran straight onto the battlefield and scored the winning touchdown.

That is how you girlfriend.

The point is, they were the perfect pair. So you can't totally blame me for thinking maybe he'd revert to his true self once he fully recovered from You-Know-Who. Right?

Anyway, here's the CliffsNotes version: Everything is golden with Lina until You-Know-Who comes in and Henry loses his shit. Then You-Know-Who loses *her* shit, and then Henry rebounds back to the safest of the safe.

(Ugh, Jane Seymour.)

Then my two-week dating mistake, which we're not going to talk about, because according to Parker it never should've happened, and according to Henry it never did, and I still can't figure out why it fell apart in actual record time.

And now it's Katie "CHR QN" Howard, cousin to You- Know-Who and possibly the most fun person I've ever met, but possibly not the best choice for a guy who thinks having a very shitty ex is tantamount to treason.

I mean, I love them both, but I wouldn't necessarily weep if they broke up. For various reasons.

But I don't sabotage people's relationships, even when I'm right in the middle of a very bizarre prank triangle, so I skip calculus and Katie skips French and we meet by her car to speed-spray one hundred more water bottles.

"You're the best," says Katie. "You know I love Parker, but she's going to kill me someday."

So far we've dumped all the water out and peeled all the labels off and added the jingle bells, which was easy enough. The spray-painting phase, however, is feeling straight-up endless.

Katie lines another bottle up. "Do you think Henry's mad at me?"

I attempt a poker face. "He doesn't seem like it."

"That's what I thought, too. But he's so unpredictable. Like, everything was great until two days ago, and then all of a sudden he's acting totally weird, and Macy said Francis said stuff to Brandon, and Josie said Brandon told Henry."

I glance at her, and she's biting her lip like she always does when she's worried. I really just want to say, *Nah, it's nothing*, but this is a girl who has dinner at my house maybe four nights a week, despite Amelie's gratuitous science tangents and my mom's affinity for delivery-based dining. She deserves the truth, even if it's a very unfortunate truth.

So I cave. "Francis showed Brandon some, um, pictures."

She winces and misses the bottle she's spraying. The pavement is starting to look a bit Banksy. "Damn it, Francis sucks," she says, but she's about fifty times less enraged than you'd think she'd be. Like we're just talking about shady subtweets or something.

She shakes her can of spray paint. "I swear I did these yesterday."

"We're practically done."

"That's such a lie." She laughs, but then she gets the worried look again. "But what did Francis *say*? It's just—you know what happened to my cousin."

Sidebar: Katie's cousin—otherwise known as You-Know-Who, officially known as Anna Boleyn—had what you might call a less-than-pleasant breakup with Henry last spring. Long story short: Other Woman becomes Official Girlfriend, becomes Woman Scorned, becomes alleged building-exploder, attempted Henry-killer, and accidental self-immolator.

But that's a tale for a day when I'm not neck-deep in cheerleader labor. The point is, it all happened because Anna cheated on Henry.

Also allegedly, of course.

"Come on," I say. "You didn't cheat. And besides, the prom thing was an accident."

"Everybody says she was a murderer."

"Okay, but do *you* think she did it on purpose?"

Katie looks over her shoulder and lowers her voice. "Of course not. But nobody's even allowed to talk about her anymore. And now it's like Henry thinks I'm going to—"

"Go all Mad Queen on us and burn homecoming to the ground?"

She gives me a big-eyed nod. And let me just say that as much as I doubt You-Know-Who sat down before prom thinking, *Hmm, how shall I kill my boyfriend tonight?*—that still seems about eight million percent more likely than Katie bedazzling a copy of *The Anarchist's Cookbook* and whipping up an explosion.

"Look," I say. I'm crossing into somewhat snitchy territory here, but clearly the Lancaster rumor mill is unstoppable anyway, and besides, I fixed the Henry situation last night. "He knows you're not a secret arsonist. He's just paranoid about cheaters, and—"

"Francis sucks. That's why I dumped him. It's over. So what's the big deal?"

"The big deal is that Henry has girlfriend issues. Monumental girlfriend issues."

She rolls her eyes. "God, it's like he can't stand thinking he's not the only guy I've been with. Like he doesn't have hundreds of exes."

"Thousands."

"Millions." She sets the spray paint down. Her hands are half red and half white. "I'm so jealous of you, you know? Henry never gets mad at you."

"Other than that time he dumped me," I point out.

"Whatever. He still thinks you're the best." She bites her lip again. "I'm trying so hard not to mess everything up. Everybody's so great here, and it's like, so far, so good, but it's so much *work*. And you make it seem so easy." She pauses. "Maybe I should join the newspaper. You guys never have drama."

"We totally do. Trust me."

She pushes her hair out of her face, leaving a giant pink streak behind. "Like what?"

"Cat Parr."

"Homecoming court Cat Parr? She's practically a grownup."

"Yeah, except grownups occasionally trust their writers to make their own decisions."

"What do you mean?"

"Well, for one thing, the very first day of the paper, we were supposed to write about something divisive, right?" I say. "So I wrote about Anna. How everybody basically decided she was a wannabe assassin just because she was kind of too much. I mean, I wasn't her biggest fan, but murder isn't usually the next step after boyfriend-stealing."

"True."

"All I was saying was maybe we should chill out and actually look into it. The cops said it was an accident. Except everybody else said hey, whatever, it's more fun to call the dead homewrecker a murderer."

Katie's not really spray painting anymore. "I think that's a great story."

"Right? And everybody would've read it. But Cat called me into her office—"

"She has an *office*?"

"I mean, it's Mr. Lee's, but she's fully colonized it. So she calls me in, and she goes, 'Do you think this was appropriate?' and I started talking about slander and vigilante justice and how nothing would've played out the same if we were talking about a guy. And Cat literally says, 'You're not editor-in-chief. It's cut. End of discussion.'"

Katie looks moderately alarmed, because I'm sort of yelling, which is maybe a *little* too invested in not being able to heroically change the narrative for some girl I barely even knew.

So I chill. "Anyway, yeah. There's drama. Cat just won't print it."

"Why not?"

"Who knows?" I shrug. "She says it's because last year the paper wasn't professional, blah blah. But we all think she's hiding something."

Katie grins. "You should start your own paper. Like, a secret one that's only things she won't let you print."

"That's actually brilliant. We'll publish all these impossible theories and smoke her out."

"And then we'll do the story about my cousin." She strikes a *Charlie's Angels* pose. "Cleves and Katie, on the case."

"Look out, Lancaster."

She sighs. "Seriously, though, Henry knows we're still good, right?"

"You've got this," I tell her. "We'll beat York, and you guys will win king and queen, and you'll be gorgeous at the dance, and End of the Road will be the End of the Road to end all End of the Roads. The end."

"You're the best," she says, and hugs me.

Fingers crossed that I'm at least half right.

No Charges Pressed in Howard Heights Burglary

I met Katie Howard my very first morning in Lancaster. Henry and I carpooled home from Overachiever Camp, and by the time he dropped me off at my new house in Howard Heights, I was so tired I threw my bags down and passed out with the window open because (a) the air-conditioning vent was stuck, (b) I was used to dorm room hellfire and probably wouldn't have been able to sleep in any sort of reasonable temperature anyway, and (c) what can possibly happen when you live in a gated community in small-town Indiana?

The answer is that you can wake up the next morning with a complete stranger next to you. And yes, that's exactly what happened to me.

So I shrieked and tried to find the pepper spray Mom gave me as a going-to-camp present, but everything was in boxes, so I ended up with a water bottle instead and poured it on my unexpected bunkmate.

"Leave me alone, Francis," the girl mumbled. Then she opened her eyes and saw me standing there in self-defense-class mode, holding the bottle like some sort of useless club. She screamed, which made me shriek again, and I was waiting for Mom to kick down the door, but then I remembered she'd said she was going over to the college early, which was seriously not comforting considering that I was dealing with a breaking-and-entering situation.

Then I started laughing. The whole scene was totally weird, and it was pretty clear this girl wasn't here to steal my diamonds. So I lowered my water bottle and said, "I have no idea what's going on, but hi."

And then she pointed at the doorway and started screaming again, and I spun around with the bottle back up. But it was only Amelie, eating Froot Loops in her regulation mall-goth uniform and looking very unimpressed.

"You probably should've used the door," said Amelie. Then she wandered away and left us in our jumpy scream-aftershock silence.

"Who was *that*?" the girl asked.

"My sister."

She tilted her head to the side. "Are you sure?"

"Well, we think she got switched at birth, but we're holding out on going public in case the hospital agrees to a six-figure payout."

"You...*what*?"

She looked more concerned about that than the whole strangers-in-her-alleged-house thing, which put her several empathy points higher than most burglars. "We're basically the United

Nations," I told her. "They adopted me from China and Amelie from Malawi. My dad's teaching in Germany this year, and my mom's from Florida, but you're sworn to secrecy on that one."

The burglar stared at me for another second, like she wasn't entirely sure she was awake. And then she cracked up, which was definitely a step in the right direction from the screaming.

She propped herself up against my headboard, which still had a layer of bubble wrap around it. "I have the worst headache. Are you sure this isn't my room?"

"I mean, I just moved in, but that *was* my sister."

"Hey!" She looked totally stoked all of a sudden. "You must be Cleveland! Parker said you guys got in last night. Welcome to Lancaster! I'm Katie."

"Wow. You bring *mi casa es su casa* to the next level."

She made a face. "I don't even know how I got here. I had to sneak out because of my uncle, and Francis was like, 'There's this party, you should come,' but you know Francis."

Of course I didn't, so of course I said, "Oh my God, yeah, *Francis*."

"He just wants to get in my pants, but I can't figure out if we're going out. And Parker was like, 'It's going to be gross, don't bother,' you know? But I was bored."

I glanced out my window. The porch roof was right under it, and off to the side, I could see a pretty convenient tree. "Does your house have a tree by the porch, too?"

She nodded. "That's how I sneak out."

"And don't some of these houses kind of look alike?"

"Yeah. There's one, like, a block over from mine that's mostly the same layout, just different colors."

"Pretty sure that's where you are."

"Oh," she said. "*Oh*. Holy shit, I broke into your house. Wow, I'm so sorry." She jumped out of my bed and hugged me.

I gave her an awkward back-pat. "It's okay. Clearly you weren't trying to kill me or anything."

"Never," she said gravely. "But God, I wish I could remember what happened."

There was a leaf in her hair and her makeup was a smudgy mess. Her outfit was cute, but if it had ever involved shoes, they were long gone by this point. "Well, you definitely went to the party," I said.

"Yeah."

"And somebody dropped you off at the wrong house."

She shook her head. "Francis doesn't live in Howard Heights. And I can't put him on the list, or my uncle will find out. So he drops me at the gate and I go around the side so I don't have to talk to the booth guy because—"

"Your uncle would find out."

"Yeah." She pulled the leaf out of her hair. "Do you have any coffee?"

We headed down to the kitchen, which was mostly boxes, but of course the two things my mom had already unpacked were the books—they were piled all over the living room—and the coffeemaker. I started it and we sat down at the table, which was completely covered with London College crap.

"Last night," Katie said. She was biting her lip and staring into space, like she was concentrating on some Overachiever Camp–level equation. "I was drinking. Obviously."

"I couldn't even climb that tree sober."

"You'll learn." She giggled. "It was way easier when I lived with my grandma, out near York. I had guys over and she never knew. My uncle freaked when he figured that out."

"Who's your uncle, anyway? He sounds like an evil overlord."

"Norfolk Howard."

"So definitely an evil overlord."

"Family name." She rolled her eyes. "He and my aunt—like, his sister—they run Howard Estates. He thought I should be in Lancaster instead of out there. That was last spring, after the Tower, and my cousin…"

Katie trailed off and looked at me. Suddenly everything clicked: Her cousin was You-Know-Who. Henry's second girl-friend. The infamous one.

"But it's okay," she said in a rush. "I like it here. It's way more fun than being stuck out in the country, even if I have to climb out my window."

"And back in somebody else's."

She laughed again. "And besides, there are some really hot guys in Lancaster. Forget Francis. I was over him the second I met Tom Culpeper. And Henry, but he's way out of my league. Plus everybody says you guys have a thing."

"Um," I said, and failed spectacularly at trying not to blush.

"Besides, if I never moved here, I wouldn't have met you."

"Yeah. Who knows whose room you would've ended up in then?"

She grinned. "We're Lancaster girls now, Cleves. And you're going to love it here."

"Business Casual Is Always Appropriate," Claims Reincarnated Fascist Dictator

In case you were wondering, I did finish my new and approved op-ed for Editor-in-Chief Mussolini last night. It put me to sleep so many times I lost count, and whatever I sent to Cat may not have made any actual sense, but it was in her inbox by 6:00 a.m.

Nailed it.

This means I can walk into journalism without any type of protective headgear, ready to coast through the last class of the day before we all split for the homecoming parade.

Eustace is already desecrating this morning's *Ledger* at our table with Christina Milano and Hans Holbein. I sit down and grab the op-ed page.

"Looks like you made deadline," says Eustace. Hans—who's really an art kid, but Cat roped him into doing photography for the *Ledger*—finishes drawing an elaborate beard on Henry's homecoming portrait. Eustace adds a quote bubble over Katie's head: *Vote for me and I'll S your D.*

"Looks like you're still a pig." I edit his Katie quote so it says *Vote for me and I'll Shampoo your Dog.* "And of course I made deadline. I'm an editorial standards goddess."

"I still can't figure out what was wrong with your party survival guide," says Christina. "Did you put it on the list?"

Eustace slides our censorship master list across the table. Next to the banned headline roll call, we've vaguely attempted categorizing our offenses. We've tagged my You-Know-Who piece with *too controversial* and Eustace's court exposé with *too gossipy* and everything Christina's ever written with *not depressing enough.*

"There's not even a pattern," I say. "I mean, it's not like End of the Road is serious journalism, but neither are home-coming court portraits."

"Yeah, but Cat's on the court." Hans gives Henry a ridic-ulous feathered hat.

"Cat and her boy-toy of the week," Eustace edits.

"Breaking: Cat's first relationship didn't last forever," says Christina. "Call the AP."

Eustace smirks. "Breaking: Cat and her bestie Erin both upped their boyfriend game this year. And half of what Cat won't print says unflattering things about Lancaster's elite—"

"XOXO, Gossip Girl," I cut in.

He shrugs. "Social climbing only works if you don't talk shit about the asses whose asses you're kissing."

"You should submit that to Girl Genius," says Christina, whose true calling in life is penning the *Ledger*'s advice column. I use *advice* loosely, kind of like Christina uses *genius* loosely. Not that it matters, because Cat cracks down on that column like Vesuvius on Pompeii. This year, Girl Genius only gives advice about college applications.

Eustace digs into his pocket and slaps a couple of dollars and a gas station receipt onto the table. "Cat's climbing. Bet against me."

"Only if you submit your theory in op-ed form if you prove it," says Christina.

"Only if you quote me in Girl Genius."

"You're on." Christina throws a five onto the table.

I add six quarters and a broken hair clip to the pile. "Or maybe she's just a control freak building her portfolio for—"

"Hey, Cat!" says Christina, way too loudly.

I turn around, and of course Cat's right behind me, doing her trademark Mussolini arm-cross.

She's also wearing a blazer. There's nothing inherently wrong with blazers, not that I'd ever voluntarily wear one. But it's the literal day of homecoming, so the teachers don't care if you're wearing your cheerleading skirt, or you have your entire face painted, or—for the newspaper demographic—you're sporting a Eustace Chapman screen-print original with YUCK FORK in typewriter font.

We're all decked out in euphemisms, and she's ready for a job interview.

"Don't let me interrupt," Cat says.

I give her my most winning smile. "We were just saying, you know, looks like you're continuing to build your substitute teacher portfolio, since Mr. Lee's gone AWOL again."

"There's a yearbook situation," she tells us.

"Breaking," says Eustace, because the yearbook is a bottomless pit of dysfunction, and Mr. Lee ends up ditching the paper almost daily just to keep them from imploding. And Cat's always more than happy to step in when he steps out.

"He'll be right back," Cat says. "Cleveland, could I see you in the hall?"

She turns on her heel without waiting for an answer.

"The hall. That's a new one," says Christina.

I stand up. "More room for the firing squad."

Cat's outside, texting at the speed of light, and she makes me stand there for a minute before she looks up and says, "Walk with me," like we're about to exposition-stroll the hell out of some Montague-and-Capulet-level bad blood.

"Certainly, Your Grace."

She blinks.

"I mean, yeah, okay."

Cat starts heading for the science hall. "Your op-ed was really strong."

"I do my best work at 3:00 a.m."

"You do your best work when you're not catering to the lowest common denominator."

"Somebody has to."

She takes a left toward Hampton Court. "Anyone can throw together a few snarky references and a clickbait headline, but I assumed your career aspirations were higher than BuzzFeed."

Small-Town Reporter is definitely topping my Potential

Future Day Jobs list. "Okay, but doesn't it make sense to write things people actually want to read?"

"It makes sense to write things that belong in a newspaper."

"A high school newspaper. For *high schoolers*. Who probably think End of the Road is a little more interesting than politics."

She stops at the edge of the cafeteria. "You wrote about what happened at prom like it was a joke. People *died*, Cleveland."

"Right. Which I tried to write about on my first day, but you blacklisted that, too."

"Prom is off-limits."

"So you're just censoring everything that's controversial?"

"That's not what I said. If you'd read any of my editorials, you'd know I cover controversial topics every week. And I think censorship is abhorrent."

The best thing about talking to Cat Parr is it's a free SAT vocab session. This may also be the worst thing about talking to Cat Parr. "Okay, I get that your religion-and-politics thing is a little more highbrow than whether Henry's ex-girlfriend deserves the murderer label, but—"

She taps her phone a couple of times and then sticks the screen in my face. "You're not the first writer to cash in on Anna Boleyn."

Honestly, it's so weird hearing You-Know-Who's name out loud that it takes me a second to figure out what I'm reading. But it's a back issue of the *Ledger*, from February, at which point Henry and Lina were technically still together, but Anna was unabashedly sirening him away.

The vintage *Ledger* is open to an op-ed from Eustace. Right at the top, there's Anna's yearbook headshot, and the caption says *The Great Whore*.

"Exactly," I say. "That was way before prom, and people were already being completely disgusting to Anna—"

"I'm not finished." Cat scrolls down. The next op-ed has George Boleyn's byline—as in, You-Know-Who's twin brother—and Lina's picture. Caption: *He's over you, sweetie.*

"One more." She pulls up Christina's column. "Read it."

I do my best pompous-documentary-narrator voice. "'Dear Girl Genius, my best friend is hooking up with a hooker—'"

Cat takes the phone back. "That's what the paper looks like when no one draws a line. Bullshit and bullying."

"I mean, if Mr. Lee was okay with it, maybe you should defer to his teacherly wisdom."

She actually hesitates for a tenth of a second, which is possibly my personal record in Parr sparring. She's not the type to throw shade at authority figures, but she's also not the type to lose arguments, even if it means getting dangerously rebellious. "Mr. Lee trusts the editor-in-chief to call the shots," she finally says, which is an expertly executed piece of side-stepping. "That's exactly what I'm doing."

"Right, but couldn't you nix the libel without censoring everything about actual people?"

"It's not censorship. It's ed—"

"Editorial standards, yeah, I know."

"Then I'm sure you also know that my decisions are about responsible journalism." She smiles, and it's a regular smile, like we're just chatting about our mutual affection for midi heels. But the thing about Cat Parr is she's so infuriatingly *mature* that you can never tell whether or not she's being massively passive-aggressive, and if you call her on it, you look like a fantastic mix of a conspiracy nut and a toddler throwing a temper tantrum.

This is just one of the many tools in her argument-winning arsenal.

"I mean, I'm not editor-in-chief," I say, which is as close as I get to playing it cool.

"You're not, but you're a good writer, and if you made a real effort, you could contribute a lot to the paper. And your portfolio." She does a head-tilt when she says the portfolio thing. Totally, *totally* passive-aggressive.

"Right. My portfolio."

Cat starts walking again, so I do, but then she says, "I'm going to the library. Alone."

She gets halfway across Hampton Court before she turns and almost-but-not-quite catches me making an *ugh* face at her back.

"Oh, and Cleveland," says Cat, "you might want to reconsider the company you keep."

Rumors of Lancaster Cheer Squad Hazing True, Sources Say

"'Reconsider the company you keep'? Are you eff-ing serious?"

Parker's sitting on the back of her dad's midlife-crisis convertible, hunting down potential flyaways in Katie's hair with military precision. And yelling over the drumline, which is ten feet away doing the epic drum-off scene from their very own real-life marching band movie.

"That's a direct quote," I tell her. "And I don't know if she meant my newspaper friends or—"

"Us. We're your lunch table," Parker says. "God, like she doesn't wish she sat with us."

Parker Rochford: equal parts brutality and loyalty, topped with Lancaster's shiniest hair.

"Cat Parr?" asks Katie, who's standing Mannequin Challenge–still next to the car.

I nod. "The one and only."

"But she's nice. She put me in the middle when we did the court pictures."

"Okay, Katie, what did I say about trusting everybody?" Parker hops down to the pavement and surveys her work. "Turn."

Katie spins in a circle. "I thought you meant boys."

"Wave," says Parker, and Katie does her best QEII impression. "Don't trust boys. Don't trust girls. Don't trust anybody except Cleves and me."

"And Henry, right?"

"Duh," I say, but Parker goes, "Hell no," at the same time. Katie looks understandably confused.

"Come on." I sit down on the back of the car. "He's Henry."

"Right," says Parker. "And guess who trusted him?" She's got her double-fierce face on—fierce like she's ready to slay on the pageant runway, and also ready to slay her enemies.

"Chill, Rochford, you're freaking Katie out. We can't have our queen looking blotchy, can we?"

Parker laughs. Kind of a nervous laugh, but better than a poison-York's-cheer-captain laugh. "Yeah. You look great, K. Don't touch your hair until after the parade." She sits down next to me, and Katie climbs up and joins us. "So what are we doing about Cat?"

"Um, talking shit and avoiding her? Which is exactly why I'm out here reporting from the field instead of sitting two tables over from her for the rest of journalism." I flip my sunglasses down. "Boom. Goal achieved."

"Okay, but if you're a bitch to my friends, you don't get

away with it." Parker's turning slayer-ish again. "You want to be the newspaper president or whatever it's called, right?"

"Editor-in-chief. And, yeah, but—"

"And she's being a bitch, right?"

"I'd go with a different word, but—"

"She's going down."

"That's kind of overkill, don't you think?" I look over at Katie for backup, but she's totally zoned in on her phone.

"I think I'm making sure she *never* sits with us," says Parker. "Hey, K, you better not be texting who I think you're texting."

Katie swipes to the next page of emojis.

"Katie!" Parker snaps her fingers in front of the screen and Katie jumps. "That better be—"

"It's Henry." She gives us a big, innocent grin. "He says he's going to come tonight."

I side-eye her. "Yeah, I bet."

She laughs. "Shut up! To Parker's party. You're coming, too, right?"

"I don't—"

"She is," says Parker. "And guess who's not invited? Cat Parr."

Katie chews on a fingernail. "Actually, I kind of invited her."

"You what?" Parker slaps her hand away. "Don't mess up that mani."

"I invited her. When we were doing the court pictures. Her and her boyfriend."

"Oh my God. Okay, actually, no." Parker jumps up, heads over to the guy who seems to be in charge of the Battle of the Bands, and stands there until he stops drumming. She says something I can't hear, but apparently it's persuasive, because two seconds later the drumline is hiking toward the football field and Parker's back in our section of the parade lineup. "Now that I can effing hear—*no*. Tonight's supposed to be exclusive."

"I'll cordially decline," I tell her. "Cat can fill the newspaper quota."

"No. You'll be there." Parker's grin is ninety percent glee and ten percent Crest Whitestrips. She literally photosynthesizes drama. "You'll keep Henry chill, and we'll show Cat you're one of us and she's not."

"Am I, though?" I ask, because even UFO crash survivors could pinpoint me as the outlier in our trio. Or our entire lunch table, for that matter.

My Lancaster popularity remains a mystery.

"Stop it," says Parker. "You're everyone's favorite. You're coming tonight, and we're icing Cat out. And let me tell you something, Cleves." She looks me straight in the eye with her notorious Rochford dagger-stare aggressively in place. "By Christmas, you're going to be running that paper."

Peanut Gallery Offers Insights into Intramural Inveiglement

By kickoff, aka seven, aka finally, everything is looking significantly less apocalyptic than expected, although this may be due to the triple-espresso abomination the barista concocted when I zombied my way into the coffee shop after the parade. Parker and Katie are in cheer-land, I don't have any deadlines, the JV squad's selling the spirit bottles for way more than anybody should spend on spray-painted trash, and the only thing Henry's worried about is winning the game.

And another plastic crown, of course.

I'm in the bleachers with the newspaper crew, since Parker and her Exclusives are busy cheering and intercepting. And yes, Cat's with us, because it's not the newspaper crew without the editor-in-chief. But the blazer is off, and so far she hasn't bleeped anything.

For real, I don't actually hate Cat Parr. She can be a tad

bit insufferable sometimes, but I don't want her to break her ankle walking out to get her sash at halftime, and I don't want Parker writing threats in lipstick on her locker until she caves and forfeits her editor-in-chiefdom. Not that she strikes me as the caving type.

The real question is why all my Lancaster friends are so invested in *Dateline*-level mental warfare. This never happened in Cleveland.

"Henry and Katie are such a lock for king and queen, it's not even worth counting the votes," says Eustace. "No offense, Cat."

Two seats over, Cat laughs. "None taken. I'd put my money on them, too."

I nod. "Henry could bring a blow-up doll as his date and they'd still win."

"Sorry, did you say 'could'?" Eustace raises an eyebrow in the direction of the track, where Katie's at the top of a pyramid doing some especially enthusiastic smiling.

"Eustace, *no*," Cat and I say at the same time.

"Damn, wrong crowd."

Katie launches into a gravity-defying flip-thing. "You don't even know her," I say. "Just because she's pretty doesn't mean she's stupid."

"If she's cheating on Henry, she *is* stupid," says Eustace.

I kick him. "Breaking: She's not."

"Wanna bet?"

"Yeah." I hand him my ticket stub. "Consider this an IOU. She's not cheating."

He shrugs. "She might be."

"And I might win homecoming queen as the darkest dark horse in the history of horses."

"You came close," Cat says. Because of course she's everybody's designated fact-checker, and of course she's the only one who's not on board with helping Henry and me pretend we never went out.

But I don't debate Cat in recreational settings. "Thankfully, he closed that chapter."

Eustace laughs. "When's he closing this one?"

Then Cat has to head down to the field to line up for the court announcements, and the rest of us wait exactly until she's out of earshot to shift the topic to—

"Okay, spill, Cleves," says Christina. "What happened in the hallway?"

"The usual. Blah blah editorial standards, blah blah I'm the boss, blah blah prom explosions are off-limits."

Eustace zeroes in on me. "She said that about prom?"

"Among other things. Like—"

"Not finished. What else about prom?"

"Chill," I tell him. "Nothing. Just that your op-ed war with George is why nobody's allowed to write anything entertaining."

Christina claps him on the shoulder. "Good work."

"Prom," Eustace says again.

"Yeah. Prom." I watch Cat get in line behind Katie. "Which we've already covered."

"Maybe it's not about social climbing," he says. The scoreboard clock runs down to zero, and the homecoming court heads for the fifty-yard line. "Maybe it's about prom."

Cat's boyfriend is the only guy on the court who doesn't play football. He's more the tennis-and-trust-fund type, and his suit looks beautifully ridiculous next to all the shoulder pads.

"Cat Parr and Jonathan Latimer are a match made in sport coat heaven," I say. "Touching. But what does prom have to do with anything?"

"Cat was Team Lina." Eustace proclaims this like it's some game-changing revelation.

"Everybody was Team Lina," says the entire newspaper crew.

"Everybody except George."

I do a grand, sweeping gesture at the track, where Parker's hanging back by the fence instead of hitting the field with the queen wannabes. "George is kind of dead."

"Yeah, and Ms. Parr doesn't miss him."

Hans slow-claps. "You solved it, Eustace. Cat's the one who blew up the Tower. She's afraid Cleveland's going to blow that story wide open."

"No pun intended," the rest of us chorus.

"Fine. You don't have to believe it. But I'm sticking with my theory. Cat hates Cleves because Cleves writes essays about how we should canonize Anna."

The Student Council kids are giving out loser sashes. Katie doesn't even look nervous. "Dare me to do another Anna op-ed to test that hypothesis?" I ask.

"You're on." Eustace holds out his hand, and we shake on it.

"Brilliant," I say. "But I can tell you there are exactly zero links between Cat and Anna."

He grins. "Prove it."

Breaking: Ledger Reporter Isn't Actually Rabid Anna Fan

I guess I need to back up and explain what's going on with this Shakespeare-worthy feud. And also explain that no, I'm not particularly Team Anna.

At least I wasn't at first.

Rewind back to junior year, aka the midseason hiatus between Overachiever Camp and *Overachiever Camp II: Henry and Cleves and the Chamber of Secrets*. All year, Henry and I video-chatted once or twice a week, and half the time Lina was with him. But after Thanksgiving, she stopped showing up. I didn't notice at first, like how you don't notice when a song stops playing on the radio and then boom, you realize it's been ages since you were screaming the lyrics and embarrassing your best friend or your sister or the Wendy's drive-thru lady. Besides, it was her senior year—Lina, not the Wendy's lady—and she was always future-Secretary-of-State levels of busy anyway, so I didn't really think about it until I happened to ask about her in January.

Henry didn't say anything. He looked slightly ill.

"Hello? What happened to Saint Lina?"

Then I heard somebody laughing, and it definitely wasn't Lina.

"What's going on?"

"God, just tell her already," said not-Lina, and then my view did a very artistic swoop and I could hear Henry freaking out.

The screen came back into focus, but the only thing I could see was a girl's face—everything behind her was a blur. "Hey, Cleveland, didn't Henry tell you he's going to dump Saint Lina?"

She was scary-charismatic in a way that made you worry she might brainwash you into, like, robbing a bank and splitting the money, but you'd wake up the next morning missing your kidneys. If Henry was a teenage James Bond, Lina was the uber-classy ally you wanted him to end up with. And Anna was the KGB operative who tricked you into forgetting which country you worked for.

Yeah, I got all that from ten seconds of spinning before Henry yelled, "I'M SERIOUS!" and the screen went black.

He called back an hour later, and he looked so flustered that I kind of wondered if the bank-heist, kidney-theft phase of *The Spy Who Stabbed Me* had happened during that one missing hour.

"Dude, Henry, what the hell was that?"

"Yeah. I know. I don't know. It's—oh my God, I'm going to dump Lina."

I stared. In the sitcom of my life, this was definitely a Break-The-Fourth-Wall-For-A-Very-Long-Moment moment. "Okay. No."

"I'm going to dump Lina." He buried his face in his hands and made a profanity sound without using any actual words.

"No, you're not."

He uncovered his face. "I've never met anyone like Anna. She makes those kids at camp look like idiots. She makes *me* look like an idiot."

"She definitely makes you *sound* like an idiot."

"I'm serious. She practically runs her mom's company."

"I'm assuming that by 'company,' you mean some online shop where they sell crocheted toilet-seat covers that say, you know, 'God Bless America'—"

"Howard Estates. It's a corporation. Remember how I told you Isabel was getting people to build Lancaster back up?" Isabel, as in Lina's mom. As in (a) an adult, (b) the mayor, and (c) a war hero. None of which barred Henry from first-name-only status, apparently. "Well, it's happening."

And then he waxed poetic about how the Howards had bought a crapload of farmland on the northeast side of town and thrown all the family money into turning it into a gated community with fake lakes.

"There's a *spa*. In the middle of a *cornfield*," said Henry, like it was one of the seven wonders of the modern world.

"Exactly what the Founding Fathers fought and died for."

He totally ignored my witty repartee. "And it's not just the new development. They're fixing up the whole downtown, too. Lancaster's in the *Wall Street Journal*. Look it up."

So I did, and it was, and they quoted Anna's mom like six times. And Anna once, buzzwording about how she had to hightail it back from studying in France to help her family "make the Rust Belt shine again."

You can't make this shit up.

"So she's in college?" I asked Henry.

"She's our age. She's been here since August."

I decided right then and there that print journalism was dead. "She's sixteen and they're *quoting* her?"

"She's going places, Cleves. She's going to own this country by the time we're thirty."

"So you're dumping a future president to get your foot in the door with a future billionairess?"

"Give me a damn break. Nothing with Lina is working."

"Seriously?" I kind of wanted to get Dad in on a conference call, so he could confirm that Henry was in fact brainwashed, and we could electroshock him back to normal, which is exactly how contemporary psychiatry works. And then we could get back to how I'd literally gotten called to the principal's office over my latest editorial, which was what we'd been trying to talk about before Anna commandeered everything.

But apparently girlfriend drama takes precedence over my steroid-dealing baseball coach exposé.

"We're done," Henry said. "Lina's just—she's gotten so serious. She never wants to go out. And she's… I mean, you know how Catholic she is—"

"Oh my God, you're sleeping with Anna?"

"Cleveland! Stop it! For your information—even though

it isn't any of your damn business—she won't until we're official."

I was getting actual vertigo from the soap opera–level theatrics. "I don't know what kind of hallucinogens you're on, but for *your* information, you're being a dick, and Lina's perfect for you."

"God, Cleveland, no, she's not! You know she wants to be an ambassador."

I blinked. "So?"

"So we can't leave! Lancaster's not fixed yet."

"It's a town. It's not, like, your family legacy."

"But it is. That's the point. And my dad gave up on it." His jaw tightened. "And you remember what I told you about my brother."

I *really* wasn't sure what Anna the Conveniently Uncatholic had to do with the whole wrong-brother thing. Or Lancaster. "Dude, this isn't about what's going on in your town. It's about what's going on in your pants."

"Stop."

"I'm just keeping it real."

"So am I. Lina and I are over."

I stared at him. "Then dump her. Man up."

"She's—it's complicated, okay? I have my internship in Isabel's office, and—"

"Henry. Your girlfriend is not a *political alliance*."

"Exactly. Alliances don't blackmail."

I snorted. "She said, 'Hey, if you dump me, my mom's going to nope out on your internship'?"

"She said staying together is in our best interest. And that we've been together too long to throw it away over—" He cut himself off.

"Over some wannabe femme fatale who jets in from France and bribes you with theoretical sex and the *Wall Street Journal*? Yeah, I'm with Lina on that one."

"Don't talk about Anna like that."

"Well, don't treat Lina like that. You *love* her, remember?"

He wouldn't even look me in the eye.

"Come on! You literally wrote a song about how you'd never cheat on her."

He was pissed and confused and totally off his game. "You don't *get* it, Cleves."

"Yeah. Because I know you, and I know Lina, and—"

"You don't know Anna."

Then he hung up.

So no, I didn't exactly subscribe to the Anna Boleyn news-feed, because (a) she was way too look-at-me for my taste, and (b) what the hell, and (c) I'll always place my allegiance with lady ambassadors who can kick ass on the rugby field. And Henry kept not-dumping Lina for so long that I started wondering if he was actually afraid of what the angry hordes would do if he did. Or afraid of Lina's ass-kicking skills. Or afraid of Isabel's machine gun collection.

My phone started autocompleting *Stop being a dick and dump her.*

Finally, aka the last week of February, Anna video-called me from Henry's phone and announced—yes, announced, and all that was missing was some trumpets with banners hanging off of them—that they were Officially Going Out.

Of course I asked if this meant Henry had, in fact, stopped being a dick and dumped Lina.

"Finally," said Anna. "It feels like it's been seven years, doesn't it?"

"Seven years of treating her like shit when she's never been anything but humble and loyal and—"

"Wake up," she snapped. "She isn't humble. She's proud and stubborn and a stage-five clinger."

"Nice."

"I know you hate me. But don't pretend I don't love him, because I do. Probably too much." She said it so straight-up that I believed her, even though I definitely didn't trust her. "George thinks I'm going to get hurt, and he's always right."

"Yeah," I said, "but Lina loved him, too."

She blinked, and her lower lip twitched, but then she shook her head. "She's the saint and I'm the whore. I get it." And just like that, she was back to her look-at-me self. "But they're over. *Ainsi sera, groigne qui groigne.*"

"If you want your insults to mean anything, you're going to have to hire a translator."

"Complain all you want," she said. "This is the way it's going to be."

All of which is to say we didn't exactly skip off down the yellow brick road together. But that was before things ramped up from annoying to legit stop-the-presses. Unless you're Cat Parr, that is, and you think exploding buildings are more of a look-the-other-way deal.

Seriously, as soon as homecoming is over, I'm rewriting that article and setting the story straight, because maybe I'm not Team Anna, but I'm also not Team Anna-Was-A-Murderer.

Come on. It's high school.

Sometimes Lancaster really needs a reality check.

Do Homecoming Kings Have Any Actual Responsibilities? Correspondent Goes Deep Undercover to Investigate

Henry and Katie win king and queen. Shocker. They get their crowns and sashes and everybody cheers and the band plays "Hail to the Chief," for some reason, and for a moment, all is right in Camelot. Even Eustace says, "Well, they look good together anyway."

He's right. They might not be the most made-for-each-other couple ever, but Katie's got the sparkly cheerleader thing going on, and Henry is Henry, and right now they're looking delightfully drama-free.

"Ten bucks says they're over by Thanksgiving," says Christina.

I give her a thumbs-down. "Way to kill the mood."

"Ten bucks says Katie's still sleeping with Francis," says Eustace.

"Ten bucks says Francis is over in every world except the one in his dreams," I tell him.

Christina nods. "Besides, I heard she was with Tom now."

Everybody swivels around to see if she's kidding.

"Tom Culpeper? Bullshit." I'm leaning into Christina's row and shouting over the halftime show and the excessively extra fans behind me. They're having an ear-damage competition with a few of the spirit bottles I'd be happy to never see again. "Parker's trying to set me up with him."

"Maybe Parker's covering for Katie," says Hans.

"Maybe Parker's a raging bitch," says Eustace.

I smack him. "Seriously, Useless?"

"Guys. Come on. Shut up and listen to this." Christina has her phone out and her gloves off. "'Dear Girl Genius, my friend is cheating on her boyfriend. He's getting suspicious—'"

Hans laughs. "Wonder why."

"'—but she doesn't want to break up with him because he's so popular, and he really hates cheaters. I don't want her getting hurt, but he deserves to know. Should I tell?'" Christina gives us the smuggest look possible.

"Fake," says Eustace.

I squint at Christina. "People actually send you questions?"

"I get plenty, thank you very much."

"Plenty of fakes," Eustace tells me. "Last year she got one that went, 'Dear Girl Genius, I tried to murder my boyfriend because he found out I'm a total cheater, but I fucked it up and now I'm dead. What should I do?'"

Cat's back from the field, and she sits down with us again

in her non-queen sash. "That's a perfect example of why we need editorial standards."

Eustace stares at her like she's the human equivalent of stepping on a Lego. "It's a perfect example of why every submission Christina gets is bullshit. Or she just makes them up."

"I only make them up because none of the real ones are printable!"

Cat reads the message over her shoulder. "That's somebody trying to start something."

"Whatever," says Christina. "I think it's real."

"Then who sent it?"

"I asked around. Josie Bulmer freaked out, and Macy Lascelles said I should talk to Tom. So there you go."

"It's not real," I say. "Anybody who knows as much as they're claiming to know also knows the entire world could figure out who it's about. And—"

"Breaking: Cleveland admits she sent the message," Eustace interrupts.

"And," I repeat, because by God, I will get through this thought no matter how many attempts it takes. It's my cross to bear as the only person in the world who doesn't automatically assume a person has ten secret lovers just because she has one nude-sharing dick of an ex. "If Katie's cheating, which would be astronomically reckless—"

"Breaking: Cleveland cheated on Henry."

"It's fake," Cat says again. "They make the suspects clear, but the story's generic. It reads like the writer wants to break them up."

Eustace clears his throat way too dramatically. "Breaking:

Cat sends fake Girl Genius email, destroys the holy union of Henry and Katie, and secures coveted position as Girlfriend Number Five."

Cat and I say it in unison: "Six."

Designated Driver Tells All, and No One Else Can Remember Enough to Know If It's True

Tom Culpeper is exquisitely drunk.

Correction. Every single person in Parker Rochford's tricked-out basement is exquisitely drunk. Other than yours truly, who drew the Designated Driver straw. And also the sit-next-to-Tom straw, which is possibly the bigger letdown, since I can't even begin to contemplate why Parker's shipping us so hard.

"Cleves," Tom's saying. "Cleves Cleveland. Is that your real name?"

I knock back the rest of my pop. "Yes."

"Damn, that's a good name. Your parents must be badass."

We're sitting at one end of a giant leather couch. The rest of the couch is a sea of football guys playing an NFL video game, because apparently they didn't get enough tackling action on the actual field an hour ago. "LEFT LEFT LEFT! Damn it," Henry's best friend, Brandon, shouts at some kid with a controller, and half the guys *oooh*.

"And you're, you know, a reporter, right?" Tom asks.

"I'm the Nellie Bly of Lancaster High School."

"Right on." He nods several more times than necessary. "Hey, you should write about—"

"Culpeper, I need you." Parker swoops between the couch and the TV, and the footballing footballers bless us with a truly imaginative collection of expletives. "Shut up, losers, it's my basement," says Parker. "We need more ice, Tom. Can you run over to Katie's garage and grab some? And Cleves, take Katie's car and get that boy out of my house." She points at the least-drunk non-DD in the room.

"Is he...did he just puke or something?"

"He's JV," she says scathingly. "Pick up Henry, too, okay? Love you."

I sneak a glance at Tom, who's also sneaking a glance at me. He's got the exact same Rochford-induced resignation face I'm wearing right now, because the thing is, when Miss Indiana's Outstanding Teen starts tapping into that Ruthless Popular Girl archetype she loves so much, the easiest course of action is just to go with her decrees.

In other words, we both keep our lips firmly zipped.

Parker stands there waiting until we drag our asses off the couch and hack our way out of the basement with the JV interloper five paces behind us. It turns out Katie's car isn't just unlocked—the windows are open, and the keys are on the dashboard. The garage door is open, too, which I'm sure her uncle will be super jazzed about when he gets home.

One drunk-bus run later, I'm pulling up in front of Henry's house in the car we stole twenty-four hours ago. He comes down the steps carrying his football bag and his guitar case, and he throws the guitar in the back before he climbs into the passenger seat. Then he turns on the radio and switches Katie's pop station to the hard rock station, which he listens to for exactly two seconds before he tells it to go fuck itself. And *then* he flips to the classi-cal station and literally goes *hell yeah* to some soundtracky thing.

"Hell yeah is right," I say. "But I think you overpacked."

"We're taking the scenic route." He unzips his duffel bag and pulls out an ice pack and a can of spray paint.

I hit the brakes. "Hard no. I'm getting flashbacks."

"No more spirit bottles." He slaps the ice pack onto his leg. "We're hitting the away stands."

Here's another piece of Lancaster lore: Behind the stadium, there's this ten-foot-high concrete wall that faces the road into the student parking lot. And since approximately forever, up-standing LHS students have been decorating it. The school paints over dicks and death threats, but otherwise we have free rein.

I start us up again. "What's our message?"

"Whatever you want it to be, Voltaire."

Five minutes later, we pull onto the cross-country trail that cuts through the woods by the stadium. I glance over at Henry, and he's looking at me, too, with this indescribably up-to-no-good expression.

I raise an eyebrow. "What?"

"Just thinking about the last time we were out in the woods at night," he says. "You know, when—"

"I'm not making out with you. You have a girlfriend, remember?"

He laughs. "You miss me."

"Hard to miss you very much when we're co-running an unauthorized valet service."

"You love it."

"So do you." I open the door. "Are we doing this or what?"

"You know it."

He grabs the duffel bag, and we head for the fence. Which isn't nearly as Everesty as my window tree, so I handle it with grace and aplomb, and Henry pretty much leaps it. Then we're facing off against the back of the away stands, armed with an entire sack of paint plus a flashlight as big as a headlight, because this is Henry we're talking about. Half the wall's been painted over in white with LANCASTER LEGENDS written in creepily perfect letters—but I wouldn't expect any less from a cheer squad homecoming rite under Captain Rochford's command. Everything else is beautiful, beautiful chaos.

Henry takes the first sweep. Gold, obviously. I grab the biohazard orange and start in on what I've been training for since my first day at LHS.

Editorial standards. Duh.

First victim: *KATIE H = SLUT.* The Cleves edit: *KATIE H = HOTTER THAN YOU.*

"I heard you walked out on Mussolini," Henry says from his half of the wall.

"Yeah, but did you hear Parker's plotting a showdown when Cat shows up tonight?"

"Wouldn't be a Rochford event without somebody on the chopping block."

Way up in the corner, a TEAM LINA tag is hanging on for dear life. Across the LINA part, there's a spiky yellow H+A from the Anna Boleyn era.

"You should watch out for her," says Henry.

"Wait, who?"

He laughs. "Rochford. Don't want to end up guilty by association when her George shit comes back to haunt her."

"Dude, really? He's dead." I add an exclamation point to a YORK SUCKS tag. "And they were pretty true-love-forever, right?"

"She was using him."

"Come on. She's some mutant hybrid of a stalker superfan and those Spartan wives that murder anybody who dishonors their absentee shirtless yelling husbands."

"Do you get all your history references from movies, or just most of them?"

"Quality movies," I say. "Films. But you know it messed her up when George died. She's all...intense now. You know what I mean?"

"I know *she's* mean."

I legit don't get the Henry-Parker rivalry. Which wasn't even a thing until prom, despite the fact that mutually surviving a deadly explosion is the type of thing that usually brings people closer together. "Whatever," I say. "Let's skip the party."

"And miss hazing your nemesis?"

"Still not my nemesis."

"Still Mussolini in your phone." Henry steps back from the wall. He's added a subtitle to LANCASTER LEGENDS: *We rule this town.*

"Very democratic message," I tell him. "Seriously, I appreciate the anti-Cat campaign support, but it's not that big of a deal. And it's not like I can actually oust her anyway."

"Why not?"

"She got editor-in-chief fair and square. I'd be less of a noble revolutionary and more of a partisan power-grabber. That's really not my style."

"God, I love you." He laughs and grabs my non-painting hand and pulls me closer to the wall so the flashlight shadow-puppets us onto the graffiti. "If you ever change your mind, I'll help with the partisan power-grab."

I sigh. It's highly tempting, and if anybody could pull it off, it would be Henry the Human Magnet. But Cat's actually damn good at her job, even if she does run things a little more toward the dictator end of the spectrum than I'd personally go with. "It's just the paper."

"It's what you *do*." He's got his When-I'm-Famous face on. "You're good at it. You have things to say. Fight for it."

He's still holding my hand. Sidebar: He needs to stop doing this shit, because I need to remember I'm over him.

"I'm a pacifist," I say. "A very lonely pacifist."

"Goals," he says.

"I'm making a mark. Several." I spray biohazard orange into the air, and it rains down like the chemical weapons I'm apparently supposed to be using on Cat. "See?"

He weaves our fingers together. Totally normal ex-who-has-a-new-girlfriend behavior. "I see editor-in-chief material."

"Only if I institute a bloody coup."

"I see the coolest girl Lancaster's ever had."

"Careful. Parker guards that title as hard as you guard your plastic crown collection."

"I see a girl who could change everything if she wanted to." He's so close I can practically feel the breeze when he blinks. "And she wants to."

The words hang there for a second like the literal definition of double entendre.

And then the stadium lights come blazing on. I yank my hand back and javelin the paint into oblivion and sprint for the fence. "And I see a guy who has a girlfriend!" I yell over my shoulder, except Henry's already passing me and world-championing his way over the chain link. I make it to the top, and then my hoodie sleeve snags and I'm stuck thrashing around with Henry laughing his ass off from the ground.

"Just because I have a girlfriend doesn't mean you're not my favorite," he calls.

"Then get up here and rescue me!"

"Fight for it."

"Henry!" I thrash a few more times. "This is *not* a teachable moment."

He pulls his phone out. "It's photogenic, though."

I give him the middle finger with my free hand. "Photogenic that."

"You want to be editor-in-chief. Admit it."

"Pretty sure I already did. Several hundred times."

"Then prove it."

I thrash so hard I almost backflip to a tragic demise. Then I come to my senses and strip like a reasonable person.

I jump down hoodie-less and punch Henry in the chest. "No fighting necessary. Think outside the box, king-boy."

He tags my entire shirt with a giant *X* before I can duck and cover.

Schoolboard Rules That All Parties Must Include a Fight

We hit the Rochford basement in matching gold-X shirts, since Henry's chivalry might not include rescuing damsels in distress, but it does include letting them return the duel shot. Which is a brand of equality I'm willing to stand behind.

Everybody notices, even though the virtual football tournament has escalated to full-fledged leaping and the music is so loud it occupies physical space and the Jacuzzi in the back room is overflowing. It's so clichéfully high school rager, I have to pinch myself to make sure I didn't swan-dive off the fence and end up in some teen movie alternate reality.

But then again, this is Lancaster. So even post-pinching, I'm walking through the aforementioned mayhem to the cheers of dozens of drunk Exclusives, and they're parting like the Red Sea for us, because that's how it goes when you're with

Henry. Honestly, I'm not sure why nobody's rolled out an actual red carpet.

"Where's Katie?" Henry shouts at the twenty people in the hot tub when we finally high-five our way through the French doors and into the other room.

Parker yells something.

"What?"

She stands up. Her bikini is Lancaster colors, with the lion logo on her left boob. "She went home to change. But listen, Cleves, Cat's coming. Like, now."

I'm so not feeling a manufactured fight. "Damn it. I forgot my battle ax."

"It's fine," she says, like I actually have a battle ax chilling in my room, which kind of makes me wonder what she has chilling in hers. "The paint's perfect."

"It's…what?"

"It's totally in her face that she's not on your level." Parker climbs out of the tub, grabs a towel, flings it over her shoulder, and spins. "Am I good?" she asks. She's got this huge scar crossing down her back, all the way from her right shoulder blade almost to her left hip. Honestly, she could rock it, but she's more about the pageant aesthetic.

"Flawless," I tell her.

She leads the way back to the entertainment room. "You need lipstick."

"She's fine," says Henry, who's got one arm around me in human-shield stance. "When's Katie coming back?"

"In like two sec—oh my God." Parker zeroes in on the stairs.

It's Cat Parr and Erin Willoughby. Walking in as uneventfully as possible.

The music cuts off, and everybody *ooohs*, but Parker just stands there full-on brandishing the remote like it's Excalibur.

"Come *on*, Rochford," somebody yells.

"I don't want to hear it." Parker does a shut-it gesture with her free hand, and then she focuses back on Cat. "Can I help you?"

Erin rolls her eyes and starts in on a comeback. But Cat whispers something to her, and Erin rolls her eyes again before crossing the no-man's land to sit with Brandon.

"This party's invitation-only," says Parker.

"Girl fight," some guy calls. Somebody else adds a solid angry-cat sound effect.

Actual-Cat stands her ground.

"You're not on the list," says Parker.

Cat gives her frostiest smile. "Who made that call?"

But Parker's loving it. "You did. Maybe you should reconsider the company you keep. Or the company you're *trying* to keep."

Next to me, Henry snort-laughs. I'm still not feeling this entire encounter as much as I'm probably supposed to be, because Censorer-in-Chief or not, it's not like Cat *did* anything. A private lecture session doesn't exactly warrant this full-on public humiliation.

Parker has a slight tendency to go overboard with—well, everything, basically.

"Dude," I whisper to Henry, "Maybe we should—"

"You really don't know what you're talking about, Parker,"

Cat says before I can triage some kind of damage control. She's looking at me. "There's a reason some stories are dead."

Suddenly Parker's very much *not* loving it. "What did you just say?"

The room goes so quiet, I can actually hear somebody texting everything to whatever non-Exclusive isn't catching it live.

"Rumors can kill," says Cat. Which is so clearly a dead-George reference that I officially retract that part when I said, you know, *It's not like Cat actually did anything.*

Parker's gone from drama-for-entertainment to drama-for-real. "Don't you effing dare."

"And there are things you don't want in print, aren't there?" Cat smiles again. If I didn't kind of want to slap her for the dead-George thing, I'd be applauding, because she's zero-fucks fearless and it's weirdly inspirational. "For example, where's Katie?"

My eyes go straight to the football couch, and when I spot Francis, I practically do a victory dance. Then I feel like grade-A shit for checking.

Henry's hand tightens on my shoulder. "Watch it," he tells Cat.

She looks him in the eye. "I'll see myself out," she says. She gives him this little nod, like she's low-key *bowing*, and starts back up the stairs.

Parker snaps back to life. "Get out of my house," she shrieks. "Get the hell out, and don't come back, or you'll get exactly what you deserve for saying one word about George and—"

Henry grabs Parker's arm. The towel's sliding off her shoulder, but she doesn't even notice. "Rochford, get yourself together," says Henry. "And find Katie."

"Vicious," some girl sings from the Jacuzzi. One of the football guys is whispering to Francis, who's doing this dicktastic grin, and I genuinely wish I knew how to juggle or something just so I could break the Antarctica-level ice we've got going thanks to Cat the Brat.

Potential Future Day Job #69: Court Jester.

"Okay, so—" I start to say, but then there's a burst of laughter from upstairs, and Katie emerges in her sash and her crown and a silver cape and a pink bikini and platforms, and holy shit, I have never in my life been so pumped to see such a patently absurd outfit.

Literally every boy whistles. And most of the girls, too.

"Hell yeah, Lancaster!" Katie shouts. She catapults herself into Henry's arms and boom, insta-makeout.

Brandon grabs Henry's guitar and starts bashing out the world's worst rendition of everybody's favorite Henry-the-rooftop-songwriter original, and two seconds later, we've gone from fight club to karaoke night. "'We're ride or die, live fast, live high—'"

Before we can make it to the second line, a very familiar vise grip drags me into a corner.

"She can't say that." Parker's at whisper volume, but dog-whistle pitch. "She knew I was just messing with her, and she still has the nerve to talk about—" She inhales half the air in the basement. "She *can't*."

"'We run the night, drink-love-dance-fight—'" the football glee club shouts.

I try to back up, but I'm against the wall, which is an excellent metaphor for Lancaster's inescapable thrill ride. "She went way overboard, but—"

"She's done," says Parker. "You're going to find out what she's really trying to do, okay? Because that was on purpose. We're going to bury her."

Then she spins around and links elbows with some random girl and goes, "We *have* to talk about Erin's outfit, because it's the worst crime against fashion since Jane Seymour wore that headband to prom," with her toothiest pageant smile.

Wow.

"'We're all the best, fuck all the rest,'" the team chants. And suddenly I'm laughing, because that Henry-the-rooftop-songwriter original they're singing? It's called "The Company." As in *reconsider the company you keep.*

Sorry-not-sorry, but I'm not reconsidering being part of this unfathomably dramatic, thoroughly ridiculous company of headline-worthy Exclusives.

Best senior year ever, right?

Cat Parr is going down.

End of the Road

Slumber Parties:
Not Just for Sexy Pillow Fights Anymore

The morning after this season's most-viewed episode of *Keeping Up with the Lancastrians*, I'm the first one awake. And yes, this is a personal record.

I roll over and practically crush Parker, whose face is half-covered with a literal silk eye mask. So I roll over the other way and end up halfway under Katie's bed, drowning in nine layers of blankets and sheets and pointless bed-skirt crap. It takes me way too long to extract myself and my phone.

When I finally manage to *check* my phone, I have three billion texts. The first one is from Eustace: Did you and Bitchford really fight Ms. Parr?

Aftermath. Ugh.

I text him back—to the death. can i borrow a shovel?—and then make the executive decision not to answer the infinite other people who want to know who started it and who said what and how many collective teeth were knocked out at what's clearly an already very fictionalized version of last night's fight. Which, in the harsh light of day, I'm wishing I'd stopped, because now Cat's probably ready to kick me off the paper for letting Parker go clique-master on her in front of the entire football team. And Parker's probably ready to kick me out of the Exclusives for being an employee of the editor-in-chief who felt the need to bring dead boyfriends into a petty drunk-girl party fight.

I toss my phone across the room, and then immediately regret it, because every square inch of floor space is covered with cheerleaders and cheerleader belongings. It disappears into the sea of bags lined up along the wall.

RIP, phone.

So I sigh and dig around in Katie's nightstand for something to write on, ending up with a notepad I strongly suspect has never been used, because the monogram looks so Cat-level professional that it would definitely bum Katie out.

Title: VERY SERIOUS REVENGE PLOTTING.

I cross that out two seconds later and write *Parker can do the actual revenging.*

Second draft: EDITOR-IN-CHIEF PROGRESSES FROM CENSORSHIP TO THROWING PEOPLE'S DEAD BOY-FRIENDS IN THEIR FACES; CORRESPONDENT CON-NECTS EVERYTHING, WINS PULITZER.

This is a headline I can work with.

After five minutes of scribbling, I have some disorganized rants about all the things I've been banned from writing, *re-*

consider the company you keep, Eustace's upwardly mobile dating theory, *rumors can kill,* and like five notes about prom.

So I get to the point and jot down *What really happened at prom?*

I'm really not sold on Henry's Anna-was-a-murderess ideology, but I'm not even close to enough of a jerk to quiz Parker about the night her boyfriend died. And I can't exactly ask Anna for her side of the story.

The thing is, as much as Eustace obviously binged way too many conspiracy documentaries before he decided Cat was the one who blew up the Tower, the everything's-connected-to-prom concept is sounding less and less out there, the more I think about it. Cat's editorial standards definitely never have room for Anna, so what the hell was she *doing* last night? I mean, bringing up Dead George and the cheating girlfriend parallel when Parker was just flexing her popularity muscles—that's basically bringing a gun to a knife fight.

Or, you know, bringing heavy explosives to prom.

Which I guess means I need to pause the tangential theorizing and go back through everything I *do* know about prom. And the unkillable drama of Anna Boleyn.

Pulitzer-worthy. Trust me.

Overly Ambitious Girlfriend Both Better and worse Than Anticipated

Okay, so I'm going to start out by admitting that I'm a terrible person, because the main reason I kept up the anti-Anna sentiments after Henry quit being That Two-Timing Asshole was that he practically stopped talking to me once he and Anna were official. Apparently he was too busy for anything besides rampant hometown revitalization and Pope-free sexcapades.

Yeah. Shitty, shitty me, because Lina's the one who had the *right* to throw a fit, and as far as I could tell, she was continuing to win at life. Nothing drives the shame home like seeing the ex post glorious Notre Dame campus shots with a countdown to her first day and *blah blah varsity lacrosse, blah blah international studies*, complete with sixty million likes each, when you're just the weird camp friend and you're feeling totally abandoned.

All of which is to say that when Henry called and asked me to come to Lancaster in May for a Howard Estates thing, I said yes, even though it sounded phenomenally unfun.

And that's how I ended up being passed off like shady human cargo in a Toledo parking lot at 4:00 a.m. on a Saturday. That, plus my mom assuming that anyone from Overachiever Camp wouldn't traffic me into the Hunger Games or harvest my bone marrow or whatever parking lot strangers are supposed to do.

We made it to Lancaster right before sunrise. Downtown was Stepford-tier charming, with wrought-iron street lamps and brick sidewalks and old buildings redone with all the details exactly right.

"It's like the town you're supposed to grow up in," I said. "Good for the establishing shots in your biopic."

Henry hit the gas a little too enthusiastically. "I can trust you, right?"

I held one hand up in a vague approximation of swearing myself into office. "Cross my heart and hope to die."

He hit the gas again, and we zipped past a couple of blocks of perfect houses. Then he took us through another intersection and slowed back down.

"Welcome to the other Lancaster," said Henry.

It was like whatever filter they'd slapped onto the rest of the town had missed a street. The houses were kind of the same—mostly big, mostly Victorian, mostly too much lawn space—but instead of the maintenance overdose from one block back, it was like nobody had bothered fixing anything for a decade. Like whoever lived there had given up.

"Every town has a shitty street," I said, even though I kind of felt like I wasn't supposed to say anything.

Henry kept driving until he rounded a corner, and then he pulled up in front of a chain-link fence.

It was the factory. In the half dark, it looked creepy as hell. Strips of loose shingles were flapping against the roof, and big black letters spelled out *LANCASTER MANUFACTURING* on the front of the main building, with *A subsidiary of Plantagenet Industries* underneath.

Under that there was a line in red spray paint: *NOT ANYMORE.*

The pause dragged out. Finally I said, "They should do something about that graffiti."

"Paint over it, and they'll just put more up. At least this one doesn't have my last name in it."

The streetlights blinked off.

"Fifteen hundred and three," said Henry.

"What?"

He was still looking at the graffiti. "Fifteen hundred and three people lost their jobs when the factory closed. You know what that does to a town?"

I kept my mouth shut. Miraculously.

He put the car back into Drive and pulled up to the gate to turn us around. We slid back past the empty buildings and the boarded-up houses, and Henry said, "This is what the whole town would look like if Isabel never talked the Howards into building in Lancaster."

We crossed the intersection again. And just like that, we were back in the land of matching porch furniture.

Henry turned onto Broadway and pointed at a banner in a storefront window: *Another classic reimagined by Howard Estates.* "That building's already full. It's businesses. Real jobs. People moving in. Money coming in." He looked at me. "Do you get it now?"

I really wanted to hug him. Instead I just nodded.

Then we drove up and out past the fake new downtown to an unbelievably pretentious pair of signs—Indiana limestone with *HOWARD HEIGHTS* in gold. There was a gate across the street and an actual guard booth in the median.

"I'm on the list for the Rochfords," Henry said to the actual guard in the actual guard booth about the apparent actual list for people daring to enter Howard Heights.

"Morning, Henry," said the guard, and a second later the gate swung open.

So that was when I met Parker Rochford, my volunteer hostess. Junior cheer captain—"I'm senior captain-elect," she told me—and pageant winner and Pi Beta Phi legacy. Her dad was Chief Financial Something for Howard Estates. "And I'm dating George. You know, George Boleyn," she said, like he was a celebrity.

You have to respect a girl who can make you feel dumb for not knowing some random high school boy. Especially when she can do so while holding a blow-dryer in one hand and a straightener in the other, carrying out a ridiculously complex hair ritual without setting off any smoke detectors.

"Honestly, my main focus here is how obedient your hair is. It's like those dogs on ESPN. The ones that do obstacle courses. But it's *hair*."

"Anna *will* make you feel like shit if you're not runway-ready. She won't even say anything. She'll just, like—" Parker gave me a zealous side-eye. "And then she'll do—" This time there was a half-smirk. "You know? And then you'll be right back in sixth grade when you had braces and she was the glitter eyeshadow queen."

"Glitter eyeshadow? That's the appeal?"

She laughed. "She totally leveled up when she was in France."

"I've heard. Just ask Henry."

No comment.

"So, about the Lina thing…"

"Mmm," said Parker around a hair clip.

"'Mmm,' as in, 'Yeah, I'm just tolerating Anna because I'm dating her brother'?"

She stuck the clip into her hair. "I'm so not taking sides."

"You're practically Lina's lady-in-waiting, though, right? I mean—" I pointed at the wall by the vanity, which featured ten thousand cheerleading and pageant and lake house pictures, and right in the middle, there was a super-BFF-y shot of Henry and Lina and Parker and George at homecoming, complete with king and queen and court sashes.

"That was a long time ago."

"True. That's a really high-quality daguerreotype you and Cicero got with King Tut and Guinevere."

She was trying not to laugh. "Okay, but George and I have been together since forever, and Anna and George are really *twin*-twins, and she's getting so much shit right now—"

"So you're playing nice, but you're really on Lina's side?"

126

Parker gave me a pointed look in the mirror. "They're both amazing girls, okay?"

"One of them teaches orphans to read. The other one steals people's boyfriends."

"That's really reductive, don't you think?"

And there I was, called out by a girl most people would write off as plastic on sight. "Damn. Point taken. But—"

"She's really smart. And she's almost as funny as George."

"But she—"

"Shh." Parker mimed a lip-zip with the straightener. "She'll be here any—"

"Park!" her brother yelled from downstairs. "The hobag's here!"

"Don't call her that!" we shouted back in actual unison.

You'd figure that in a town where social climbing is everybody's top priority, Parker wouldn't be my biggest fan, given her mastery of hair arts and her excruciatingly on-trend ensemble next to my road-trip outfit, which featured combat boots that were only semi-ironic. But there we were, cracking up together over our mutual intolerance for fourteen-year-old misogynists.

And then the door opened, and we shut it straight down, because there she was, in the flesh, wearing indoor sunglasses and an oppressively yellow dress and shoes any self-respecting zero-tolerance-policy school would categorize as weaponry.

Anna Boleyn.

"What the hell are you looking at?" she said. Then she laughed, and Parker laughed, too, even though nothing was funny.

"Just...it's a little early for this much saturation."

Anna laughed again, and she put a lot of shoulder into it—like she was making sure we knew she wasn't just beautiful, she was the *most* beautiful. She wasn't just fun, she was the *most* fun. She wasn't just happy, she was the *most* happy. Or the happiest. Or both, probably.

"It's never too early to make a statement." She pulled off the sunglasses and shook her hair out. The light caught on her necklace: a gold *B*. Not dainty little script like you'd expect, but a bold block letter. Hester Prynne in rapper bling.

"Was it Churchill who said that, or the Dalai Lama?"

Anna did the exact side-eye smirk combination Parker had predicted. "It's a Boleyn original."

This was accompanied by an actual wink.

Then she burst out laughing and grabbed my hand. "Seriously, I'm so excited to meet you. Henry never shuts up about you." She was staring right into my eyes, probably in an attempt to hypnotize me. "Hey. Come on. I don't bite."

It was way harder than it should've been to keep myself from smiling back and thinking, *Maybe she's okay after all.* Which I'm sure somebody thought about that guy who cyanided his entire town to prep for that comet. Point being, don't let hypnotic eyes make your decisions.

Then Anna glided off to some pre-event thing, while Parker and I got breakfast and showed up just in time for the clubhouse groundbreaking, which was mostly people posing with shovels. At the end, Anna attacked Henry with a hug so aggressive it would've qualified as battery if she'd done it to a stranger.

"God, I feel like celebrating," she said, and proceeded to eat his face.

I left them to it and went over to join Parker and George, aka Lancaster's Next Top Everything, given that he'd ridden in on a mint-green Vespa wearing boat shoes, pastel shorts, and an Oxford monogrammed in the exact same font as Anna's necklace. They had the back gate of a Howard Estates SUV open and they were sitting in the shade scoping out the scene from a safe distance. Parker scooted over to make room for me.

"She's enthusiastic about property management," I said as Anna vogued for the cameras.

"She's enthusiastic about the expansion of her empire," said George.

Parker laughed and kissed him—a very venue-appropriate kiss, by the way. "Like you don't do the exact same thing behind the scenes."

"Don't spill my secrets." He watched Anna. "I don't give a shit what anybody says about her. She's herself. And she's damn good at it."

Anna was pointing at a bunch of nothing next to the ceremonial dirt pile, so invested it was like she could already see the clubhouse. "Pardon my lack of imagination," I said, "but I really don't get being that excited about a building."

"It's not just the building," said George. "Lina's gone."

Apparently I sucked at internet stalking. "What do you mean, gone?"

"Adios. She took her finals early and left for Guatemala yesterday."

"It's not like she's been having a good time here lately," Parker added. "Anna's totally been icing her out."

"But everybody else still loves Lina, right?"

"Obviously. But Henry and Anna are so, like, *public*, and Anna got Lina on the Howard Heights blacklist, so last week she was coming in for this lacrosse party, and the guard was like, 'Sorry, management says you're not allowed in.'"

"It wasn't Anna's fault. That's bullshit," said George.

Then Anna came sweeping over with Henry, and it was all Howard Estates this, shareholders that, and, in ten seconds, George's eyes glazed over and Parker started surreptitiously texting and I pushed up my aviators and said, "Okay, so maybe you guys should go chill with the VIPs, and we'll meet you later?"

"Later" ended up meaning "midnight," so we lowly peasants found other ways to amuse ourselves. By that point, we were fairly exhausted from a day of rampant consumerism and full-throttle gossip, and it was a perfect night—clear skies and just the right temperature for making stupid decisions— so we ended up at the park. George and Parker and me and Tom Culpeper, whom I'm pretty sure Parker recruited just so I wouldn't feel quite so third-wheely.

The Lancaster City Park is about a million years old, and every piece of equipment violates the Playground Safety Code of America or whatever PTA moms write to their congressmen about. It's got high swing sets and a domed jungle gym and three wooden seesaws and a merry-go-round that screams bloody murder when you spin it. But the best part is the slides. There are two of them: one built into the hill down from the main part of the park, and one freestanding in the lower part by the basketball court.

These aren't your little sister's playground slides. They're twenty feet high, rickety as hell, and *steep*.

Anyway, we sprawled out on the jungle gym under the giant old trees and got busy getting buzzed on a six-pack of shitty beer Tom brought and some liqueur George swiped from his parents' stash.

"Hell no. Get that shit away from me. I'm an American, damn it," Tom said when I passed the liqueur his way.

I took another sip. "It's decent once you get past feeling like you're drinking your grandma's perfume."

"Sorry my palate is too refined for you," George said in a singsongy wine snob parody.

Parker stared at the sky. "God, tonight's perfect, isn't it? I don't even remember the last night there wasn't any drama."

Of course that was the instant the world's most blinding headlights cut through the trees and five seconds later there was Henry in his khakis and Anna in her banana dress, standing next to the bikes we'd come on, since that had seemed like a more appropriate mode of transportation to accompany park drinking than, you know, a swanky sports car.

And yes, Parker the Perpetually Pageant-Ready on a bicycle was very much a scene suitable for a *Stars: They're just like us!* page in *Us Weekly*.

"Aren't you four straight out of a Norman Rockwell tableau," said Anna in George's wine-snob voice.

"How was the cabinet meeting?" George said in the exact same voice, and next to me Parker dissolved into helpless giggles.

"Your trust fund's going to thank me someday."

Then Tom, who I guess thought the pretentiousness level was un-American, chugged the rest of his beer and announced with the absolute self-assurance found only in North Korean dictators and drunk high school boys, "Bet you ten bucks I can bike down the slide."

"Bet you fifty Henry can, too, and he'll look twice as good doing it," said Anna.

"Don't," Parker started to say, but Anna cut her off.

"God, Rochford, live a little."

Henry and Tom were already crashing over to the hill with Anna right behind them, so Parker and George and I hauled ourselves off the jungle gym and, in my case, did a quick review of ninth-grade health class CPR skills, which mostly served to establish that I didn't remember any CPR skills from ninth-grade health class. By the time we got to the edge, Henry was doing a site assessment, and Tom yelled, "LIONS!" and took off.

Then he hit the side and did a flip over the handlebars and rolled the rest of the way down the hill.

At the bottom, he jumped back up and yelled, "Who's prom king now, Henry?"

Anna grabbed the bike away from Henry and said, "Are you planning to take seven months on this decision, too?" She jumped onto the bike, banana dress and all, and plunged down the slide.

"Take a damn risk," she shouted. So Henry snatched Parker's bike and followed Anna down.

There was one bike left. George looked at Parker and me

and said, "I mean, peer pressure, right?" and went over the edge with Parker shrieking next to me.

Tom was already back at the top for round two, so Parker and I found a bench with a prime view of the tiltyards. She was covering her eyes every time somebody took another header down the slide, but I couldn't look away, either because I'm such a good friend or because I'm a horrible friend.

Parker peeked out just as George kicked off again. "Oh my God oh my God oh my God," she shrieked for twice as long as he was actually biking. Then she peeked out again and said, "Jesus, he's going to kill himself."

"More like Anna's going to get him killed."

"He would've done it anyway." She snuck another glance. Tom was about to go again, but Anna was grabbing his shirt and making some huffy scene. He threw out a couple of f-bombs and took off.

"Yeah, run away," Anna shouted. Then she marched over to our bench and sat down next to Parker.

She held up a TEAM LINA pin. "You know how sick I am of this shit?"

"Probably not as sick as Lina is of yours," I said.

"He's not her property, you know. He chose *me*." Anna glared at me for a second, but then she laughed. "Come to Hampton Court some morning when Henry's not there, and you'll see. They hate me ten times as much as you do."

"They don't hate you," said Parker.

Anna pinned the TEAM LINA button over her heart. "Right. That's why you couldn't find even one guy who doesn't wear one of these. Eustace Chapman owes me royalties."

I watched Henry crash-land at the bottom of the slide. "Yeah, and you owe Lina an apology."

Parker kicked me, but Anna just laughed again. "That works really well when she looks me in the face and smiles like they never broke up. She won't even let me say it."

"Maybe because, I don't know, she's somewhat *gracious*—"

"You don't even know her."

Which was closer to true than I wanted it to be. But it's not like I needed ten years of documented sisterhood to be Team Lina, especially when Anna was trying to play off her Henry-stealing as Lina's fault. "Maybe she—"

"Maybe she knows her lacrosse girls take care of everything. She doesn't have to get her hands dirty. She just has to play the martyr, and everybody falls all over themselves to talk shit about me, like it's my fault she won't move on."

I snorted. "Maybe you could be nice for once and they'd like you, too."

"You think I haven't tried that? I'm nice, okay? I'm a nice person. They liked me in middle school. They liked me in Paris. They'd like me now, if they gave me a chance, but they won't. So fuck them. I'm done." She picked up the bottle of liqueur and drank.

"They don't hate you," Parker said again. "They—"

Anna flung an arm around Parker's shoulders. "Rochford, you're one loyal little bitch, and I love you. But they do. Everybody except you and George." She glanced down at the guys, and then over at me. "It sucks. I'm lonely. I miss being able to trust people."

She didn't put on any of her theatrics this time. She just said it straight to my face, and yeah, okay, I was starting to feel pretty shitty.

But then she jumped up and said, "I've got Henry, and she's gone. It's going to get better, right? She's *gone*." And then she cracked up, like it was the funniest thing ever that she'd chased Lina out of the country.

She shook her hair over her shoulder and went for the bike again. Parker did her oh-my-God refrain until Anna made it down the slide, and then she said, "She's right. Henry wouldn't have left Lina if he was still happy with her."

"Wow. That was way harsh, Tai."

"Who?"

"I just mean, you know, way to blame the girl when her boyfriend cheats."

She made a sound that was half giggle and half slide-terror. "You're kind of blaming Anna, though. Just like everybody else."

"Wow," I said again, and then I sat back and watched the Darwinism Olympics for a second while I reevaluated my life choices. Between Anna turning out to be an actual human and Parker turning out to be a one-girl callout squad, I was kind of ready to dial up Guatemala to ask Lina how many Hail Marys it would take to keep my feminist card from getting revoked. "I mean...yeah. Henry's the one who cheated."

Parker gave me a very stern look. "They didn't cheat, okay? Anna—*oh my God*."

She sounded significantly more traumatized this time, and

sure enough, when I looked back at the Hill of Questionable Decisions, it was empty. Because Henry was on the other slide—the freestanding one. Not even a questionable decision, just a blatantly moronic one, because that slide didn't come with a built-in gutter guard.

"DON'T," Parker and I yelled.

But Henry wasn't looking at us. He was looking at Anna, and she was standing at the bottom of the slide with this ultra-intense smile, staring at Henry like if he didn't ride down the slide, he might as well not come down at all. Like he had to choose: her, or everybody else. And he was staring right back like she'd gone one step too far, but he couldn't stop her.

They held their electrified staring contest for another second, and then Henry set the bike down, swung onto it, and pushed off, while Anna laughed with actual delight.

And then—because what the hell were we expecting—he bumped over the edge and dropped straight to the ground.

So our night ended with a trip to the emergency room. Except only Anna ended up going with Henry—and her dad, who was pissed at us, but even more pissed at Henry's dad, which may have had something to do with the fact that Henry's dad didn't answer the phone for any of us.

Parker didn't stop freaking out for a good two hours, until Anna texted to say Henry was finally awake. There was a pretty nasty gash on his leg and he had a concussion, but he was going to be okay, and he could still play football next fall.

Probably.

Why we needed that last part is beyond me, but I've never been quoted in *The Wall Street Journal*, so what do I know?

Anyway, I had to figure out a new ride back to Cleveland, so Parker and George volunteered. On the way out, we stopped at the hospital to say hey to Henry. But as it turned out, he was asleep, and Anna was asleep next to his bed in the most uncomfortable-looking chair I'd ever seen.

"What do we do?" Parker whispered.

George shrugged. "We could rearrange all the furniture."

"Or put them on the roof," I said.

"Excuse me," said somebody behind us. We turned and saw a nurse with her hair pulled back so tight, it was giving her a face-lift. "Henry needs his rest. You can leave your names with the volunteer at the visitors' desk."

Then she stepped to the side and stared straight ahead, like those guards with the tall hats who don't laugh even if you poke them in the eye, and we all stood there waiting for the queen to enter until I finally figured out she was just waiting for us to leave. So we did, and we found the desk at the end of the hall—we'd walked right by it on our way in.

"It's so nice of you to be here for Henry," said the desk girl as George wrote *Ben Dover* and *Hugh Jass* in the guest log.

"My turn, babe." Parker grabbed the pen.

"I'll tell him you guys were here." The desk girl was still talking, which seemed a little excessive until Parker said, "Thanks. See you Monday?"

"Yeah," said the girl, and I finally glanced at her. It was pretty understandable how she'd blended in with the scenery the first time around—she was wearing the exact same color scheme as the wall. Beige and white. She practically screamed "unobtrusive."

Or whispered it, I guess.

She looked down at the log, which now included George's aliases, Parker's extraordinarily cheerleadery signature, and my all-caps CLEVES, because brevity is the soul of wit. And possibly the soul of communicating with post-concussives. "Oh, so you're Cleveland," said Desk Girl.

That was weird, because as far as I was aware, I wasn't a celebrity. "Depends on who's asking," I told her.

She smiled a little tightly, although it might've just been her ponytail, which was even more face-paralyzing than the nurse's. Hospital dress code, maybe.

"Nice to meet you," she said. "I'm Jane Seymour."

Courtly Intrigues: Coming Soon to a High School Near You

"**C**leves. Oh my God."

Parker is the actual goddess of the drama-whisper. Normal humans yelling at the top of their lungs can't compete with her Maximum Impact Whisper-Scream.

"Last night literally happened." She has her eye mask pushed halfway up and she's staring at her phone like it's dripping blood.

"And I was assuming you didn't do regrets."

"I don't. But your newspaper boss better." She glances at my notes before I can strategically block the giant prom question from her view. "You know what I can't figure out? Why Cat switched sides."

I'm still feeling residually guilty for letting Cat walk into Parker's slam-fest in the first place, but my nosiness takes priority. I mean, I'm on a story. I'm doing it in honor of my editor-in-chief. "What do you mean?"

"George really liked her."

"Yeah, right. He's her poster child for repealing the First Amendment."

"He was super close with her and Erin before everything happened with Anna. They were, like, the debate A-team from Hell. And he—" She cuts herself off and clenches her jaw for a long second. "I'm just saying, she never hated him. So why would she be so shitty?"

I shrug. "Eustace thinks she's social-climbing. And hating Anna is a pretty popular pastime, right?"

"Cleves." Parker pulls her mask the rest of the way off. "She didn't do it."

"I'm not saying she did. I'm just saying that if Cat's trying to ladder-climb, maybe she thinks shit-talking the Boleyns is a no-brainer."

She jaw-clenches some more. Then she says, "You're ready to take over, right?"

"The world? Definitely."

"The newspaper."

"I'm kind of more about Katie's idea. You know, starting my own."

Parker finally laughs. "Do it. I'm serious." She reaches for her suitcase-sized makeup bag. "Hey, what did Henry say about Katie last night?"

"Nothing."

"Not even after Cat tried to start shit?"

I glance at the bed. Katie's still sound asleep, even though we're not even trying to whisper anymore. "Francis was sitting right there. So A for effort, but C-minus for execution. And anyway, you know she's not cheating."

Instead of the obvious *Yeah, duh, of course she's not*, she goes with, "Francis! Yeah, okay," and starts laughing again, for no reason, but I'm not judging. "Listen, you're still on Henry duty tonight, okay? If he says anything—like, anything at all—you have to let me know."

"Dude, it's fine. He doesn't give a shit what Cat said."

"You never know."

"You're—"

"Don't you dare say I'm paranoid. You know what happened at prom."

I look back at my notes. So far, my Anna backtrack has yielded exactly one insight: *Hating Anna = official sport of LHS*. Case closed, basically. "It was an accident."

"Right," she says. "But that thing Cat said yesterday—you know, 'rumors can kill'? That wasn't an accident." She looks at Katie and then back at me. "It was a threat."

"That Escalated Quickly," Says Absolutely Everyone

Okay, so yes, Parker can be slightly overdramatic from time to time. But I barely even blame her, when you put it in the context of what happened at prom. Because maybe Part One of the Anna saga sounds like your average high school dumbassery, but Part Two is so next-level, somebody should secure the copyright and write an actual opera about it.

Assuming they don't have to report to a power-tripping editor-in-chief, of course.

The Monday after his magnificent bike-slide face-plant, Henry called me in the middle of my pre-calc class. And then he proceeded to call eleven more times until I finally faked sick and went to the newspaper office to wait for the thirteenth call, which took thirty seconds to come in.

"Welcome back, Sleeping Beauty."

"Cleveland," he said with the gripping urgency usually reserved for a lead-up to something like *We've lost him* or *They're not even going to slap together a series finale, it's just over.* "Anna's cheating on me."

He sounded totally ghastly, and he was in the hospital with a scrambled brain. But if he was expecting eternal fidelity from a girl who'd hypnotized him into slide-diving and polygamy, that was some very wishful thinking.

"Are you sure?" I said, probably not as skeptically as I should've.

"Cleves!" He was sounding more desperate by the second. "She was gone when I woke up. Jane said she left with a guy."

"Who's Jane?"

"Jane Seymour."

"Is that supposed to be somebody I know?"

"You met her. The volunteer desk girl."

"Oh, right," I said. All I could piece together was a hospital-colored blouse and a voice that sounded remarkably like the GPS lady.

"Jane said it was some senior. And Anna *hugged* him."

"Stop the presses."

"I'm serious!"

"She was probably upset because her boyfriend fell off a slide and landed on his HEAD. People hug people in hospitals. It's kind of a thing." For the record, defending Anna did feel a little counterintuitive. But Henry really needed a voice of reason.

"Everybody's been telling me to look out for her."

"Well, yeah, because she made it her life's work to get you away from—"

"It's not about Lina! It's about Anna." He wasn't even attempting to chill. "I can't trust her. I trust Jane more than I trust Anna, and I barely knew her before yesterday."

"I think that's the concussion talking, buddy."

"I have to call Parker. She talks to George, and George talks to Anna. They're so close it's stupid."

"Or maybe you could—"

He hung up.

"—give yourself like five minutes to calm down," I said to nobody, which was pretty much who I'd been talking to the whole time.

So basically, in one anecdote from the most forgettable hospital volunteer ever, Anna went from the Savior Of Lancaster to the Wicked Witch Of The Midwest in Henry's mind. And Henry went from Most Fun To Hang Out With Under Any Circumstances to Most Likely To Believe The Moon Landing Was Faked And It Was Anna Boleyn Who Was Responsible.

Yeah. One hundred and eighty degrees of WTF.

He had a new theory every day for a week. Literally. As in five different guys he decided she was sleeping with, which seemed more than a bit unlikely. But the only alleged paramour he decided probably didn't deserve torture-based questioning was the only one who actually fell into the realm of believable—some sophomore who was YOLO-reckless enough to write actual poems about her.

I'm not making any of this up. I swear to God.

Anyway, Henry's next stop on the express train to tinfoil-hat land was a radio silence so complete I had to text Parker for proof of life. She texted back: Can't talk. It's bad.

Which was super reassuring.

So based on a few more Parker texts and some online recon, I was on high alert even all the way from Ohio by the time Lancaster's prom night rolled around. Henry and Anna were still together for tax purposes, and Anna was planning some after-party at "the Tower," aka the new Howard Heights clubhouse, aka still just scaffolding and No Trespassing signs.

Plus some metaphorical red flags, of course.

Back in Cleveland, it was your typical Marck family weekend, featuring several bloodthirsty rounds of *Clue*. I was Colonel Mustard, obviously, and I was building a pretty solid case against Amelie's Mrs. Peacock until my phone started blowing up. One text. And then three. And then six hundred.

"Maybe you should check that," said Mom. "I'd hate to hear that somebody bled to death while you were solving a recreational murder."

I moved five squares closer to the billiard room. "It's just prom drama."

"Well, it would be especially tragic if they bled to death at prom."

"Okay. Fine. I'm checking," I said.

Henry was definitely over his radio-silence phase. Every single message was from him. *Blah blah Anna's cheating, blah blah she's up to something, blah blah I don't know how I'd be dealing with all this if it weren't for Jane.*

I briefly considered flushing my phone down the toilet and/or using it to call in a police raid on their prom hotel, but instead I typed ugh jane seymour and threw my phone onto the couch.

Then Henry upped the ante and started calling, and after several more minutes of nonstop buzzing, Mom said, "For the love of God, answer that or I'm regifting your phone to Amelie, effective immediately."

So I went out onto the porch and Henry called again two seconds later. I answered with, "You're interrupting an evening of domestic bliss in the New York City of northern Ohio, so this better be—"

But it wasn't Henry. It was Anna, and she was screaming, "Where's my necklace?"

"Dude. You have the wrong phone *and* the wrong number."

"Don't play stupid. I've been onto you this whole time. You and Jane—"

"I'm hanging up."

"No!" she shrieked, and I moved the phone six inches away from my ear. "Please. You can't. He's—" She took a gasping breath. "Don't go."

Either I'm a glutton for torture-by-proxy, or I'm too damn nice, because I didn't hang up. She sounded so freaked out that I couldn't. "Hey. I'm here," I said. "Are you okay?"

She started laughing. "I'm about to win prom queen, but everybody hates me. Henry's going to dump me, and I didn't even do anything. He's making it all up because he wants to get rid of me and everybody knows and nobody cares."

I was pretty much knocked flat by the Anna Boleyn emotional roller coaster. "Um, so—"

"God, what am I saying? You're on his side, aren't you?"

"I—"

"Of course you are. Everybody's on his side. Team Lina forever. *Ainsi* fucking *sera*." She laughed again, except it turned shaky, like she was about to cry. "Whatever. I get it. But just tell me where my necklace is."

The mood whiplash was strong enough to decapitate somebody. "What necklace?"

"You know what necklace! The Boleyn *B*. He took it. It's gone."

I was pretty sure she was at prom right that second, surrounded by hundreds of witnesses. "Are you sure you didn't—"

"Forget it." She wasn't laugh-crying anymore. She was pissed off and imperious and definitely not the kind of girl who'd beg her almost-ex's long-distance friend to listen to her self-esteem issues. "God, he's going to pay."

And then she hung up.

A minute later, Parker sent me an obscenely blurry ten-second video: Anna shouting at Jane Seymour, then lunging forward and ripping Jane's necklace off. But five minutes after that, George sent a snap of Henry and Anna getting crowned. Caption: *Drama always wins.*

Then I guess they all got busy partying, because they shut up for so long I fell asleep before the last text of the night came through.

May 19. 3:00 AM.
Anna: Ainsi sera

Two minutes later, the Tower exploded.

And that's how they wrote Anna and George off the cast of *The Young and the Ridiculous*, which on an actual soap opera would be a jumping-the-shark moment somebody would cut in post-production or at the very least rewrite as an it-was-all-a-dream episode half a season later.

But it was real life.

I told you Lancaster parties need survival guides.

"I Love the Smell of Drama in the Morning," Claims Combatant

"**C**leves! Hey! Are you up?"

Katie's hanging halfway off her bed, looking immeasurably more excited than anybody should be ten seconds after they wake up.

"Shush, we're sleeping," somebody mumbles from across the room.

Katie claps one hand over her mouth and pats the space next to her with the other. I climb up, and she pulls a blanket around both of us and checks out my notes. "What's that?"

"Our secret newspaper. Duh."

"Prom?"

"Yeah." I glance over at the bathroom door. The shower's running, but I'm still kind of expecting Parker to be standing there, waiting for me to talk shit about Dead George. "Hey, so how did *you* hear about the Tower?"

"My uncle called my grandma's house at like five in the

morning, and my grandma slept through it, so finally I answered just to make the phone stop ringing." She bites her lip. "He just went, 'George and Anna are dead,' like he was talking about the freaking weather."

"Nice."

"I know, right? So I'm crying, and he goes, 'Pull yourself together, Katheryn, it's going to be a long week.'"

"Are you sure he's not a really lifelike robot?"

"Robots don't give curfews," she says. "But anyway, that wasn't even the worst part. I mean, you know what they found."

And I do, because Henry told me, and because I checked the *Lancaster Tribune* to make sure he hadn't actually concocted the entire cheating-Anna story arc as some magnum opus prank to poach me away from Team Lina. "All the big fireworks under the scaffolding," I say. According to the cops, somebody must've dropped a roman candle before it burned out, and that set off the stockpile. Which was Bicentennial-in-the-Town-Square-level fireworks, by the way.

Presto: Exploding Tower.

"And...you know." Katie pulls the blanket all the way up to her chin. "Anna's necklace."

Yeah, that was the other thing the cops found: Anna's missing necklace. *Under* the mountain of fireworks. Which is why everybody decided it was Anna's fault, even though the police technically ruled it an accident. Even though the most revenge-obsessed of vengeful girlfriends still don't *blow up buildings* because their boyfriends think they're cheating. Especially buildings their families *own*.

I mean, at least blow up Henry's house instead. Or Jane Seymour's.

"You know Anna didn't do it," I say.

She peeks over the edge of the bed to see if anybody else is awake. "I'm not even allowed to say it. My uncle thinks she did it."

"Norfolk Howard thinks his own niece was a suicide bomber?"

"I don't know. Basically. Yeah. Because of the necklace."

Lancaster family dynamics continue to surpass my wildest definitions of dysfunctional. "Dude. That's majorly shitty of him."

She nods really fast, like her evil overlord uncle is going to barge in and catch her making actual sense.

"Seriously, even if you believe she put the fireworks there, doesn't it seem like she probably had a way different plan? I mean, to prove she wasn't cheating?"

Katie literally shivers at the word *cheating*, and I feel a tiny bit guilty for dragging her through the Howard–Boleyn highlight reel of doom. On the other hand, I'm the future editor-in-chief of whatever we're calling our underground paper. So hard-hitting interviews are kind of my thing now.

"Plus she texted Jane and me that quote," I remind her. "That sounds like she was prepping for some big dramatic stunt to win him back, and then...celebratory fireworks, I guess? But not *killing* everybody."

"Holy hell," Macy Lascelles mumbles from the floor. "Do you guys ever shut up?"

"Excuse you. That's your queen you're talking about," I say. "And FYI, this is important research."

Macy sits up. "You want to know what happened last

spring? Anna slutted it up all over Lancaster five seconds after she broke up the two most popular people in school. And then she couldn't handle the consequences."

"Sexist slurs and factual accuracy aside, she kind of did handle it," I say. "Unless you think being flammable is a negative character trait." Everybody's wide awake now, which makes me slightly suspicious that they've all been fake-sleep eavesdropping for the last ten minutes.

Macy scoffs. "I'm just saying Katie might want to learn from Anna's mistakes instead of sleeping with half the football team."

"Wow. Good morning to you, too," I say.

"My cousin goes to York." Macy's looking super, super pleased with herself. "He says Katie was really...*popular* last year."

Katie grabs my hand under the covers. "Mace. Don't."

"He says you've been really popular since middle school," Macy adds.

"Dude, we get it," I say. "Katie's a full-on traitor for sleeping with somebody besides Henry once upon a time. Can't we just calm down and paint our toenails or something?"

But Macy's still smirking at Katie. "End of the Road's always a good time, isn't it? Even when you're in eighth grade, I guess."

Katie's grip gets blood-pressure-cuff tight.

"Shush," Josie Bulmer tells Macy. "Just because we know her dirty secrets doesn't mean we have to talk about them."

"Exactly. Way to be a passably decent human being," I say.

"Whatever, Cleveland." Macy rolls her eyes. "Just because you won't admit Katie and her bitch cousin are skanky little—"

"Somebody's jealous." Parker steps back into the bedroom in a robe and shower hair. Despite the attire, she's still pulling off an enormously successful withering glare.

Macy stiffens. "What would I be jealous of? Not interested in cheating, thanks."

"I could say something about your nose." Parker pauses, and everybody pretends they're not inspecting Macy's very slightly crooked nose.

Which I use as my chance to go, "Right, and maybe we could keep this on topic instead of insulting people's faces—"

Parker holds up one index finger and says, "But I won't."

"Anna wasn't even pretty," Macy protests.

"Or I could say something about your boyfriend, but—" Parker pauses again. "Oh, wait. You don't have one."

Everybody *oohs*, of course.

And then Macy says, "Well, neither do you."

The room goes so dead silent, I can practically hear Parker's hair drying under the heat of her fury.

But she's totally ready with a comeback. "Yeah, except you're not going to bring that up. Because if you got cut from the squad, you'd really be nobody. Right, Mace?"

Louder *oohs* this time. Katie lets go of my hand and giggles.

"Anyway." Parker pageant-smiles for the whole room. Macy's over and done with, apparently. "It's eleven. Get up and get beautiful, because tonight's going to be the best night of your lives."

Girls at Corner Table Definitely Not Plotting to Overthrow Government

When you hang out with Lancaster's varsity cheerleading squad under the Rochford administration, there are certain realities you have to accept. Such as how any sleepover can turn into footage for *The Real (Future) Housewives of Greater Fort Wayne*. Or how there's an actual itinerary for homecoming dance prep even though nobody cares about the dance itself.

What they actually care about is End of the Road. It's just outside town, in a section of woods you can't get to unless you drive all the way down this maintenance road on the Lancaster side of the bridge and walk across the drainage pipe over the river.

A horror movie setup, basically. And the biggest party of the year.

Anyway, we're almost late to our hair appointment because Parker takes a year doing her hair. To go to a hair appointment. Pierre's is right outside Howard Heights in the fake downtown area, between the spa and a bakery that mainly sells overpriced croissants. Katie and I are done first, so we escape over to Le Overpriced Croissant because Pierre and his minions are starting to get highly frenzied by Parker's diva-ish demands.

"Congratulations, Katie! Best queen ever," sings the register girl as she rings up one five-dollar pastry for us.

Then Parker blasts through the door sporting the most intricate hair-sculpture I've ever seen. Ten points to Pierre for grace under fire. "Okay," Parker says, all business. "We need to plan."

She pulls us over to a corner table, slices the croissant into thirds, picks up her portion, and starts peeling the outer crust off. "So. End of the Road. It's going to be huge."

Katie laughs. "It's always huge."

"You have to be perfect, okay?"

I eat my third in two bites. "She's always perfect. Smile, Katie."

And she does: perfect pearly whites, bright eyes, and curls Pierre pulled off in ten minutes with a reverent, "Your hair is so very *malleable*."

"See?" I say.

Parker peels back another layer. "I see a girl Henry fell for. He needs to see a girl he wants to stay with."

"We're okay now, I promise!" says Katie. "We won. He's happy again."

"Like the old Henry?" Parker asks. "The way he was before the Tower?"

Katie hasn't touched her croissant third. "I didn't know him then."

"He was different," Parker says. "And he started acting like that again six weeks ago. Like he remembered life could be fun."

I cross my eyes. "Because Henry's fifty years old, and Katie's a midlife crisis?"

"He does seem like he's fifty sometimes, doesn't he?" Katie says with a giggle.

"Better fifty than Francis."

"Shh!" they both hiss.

"Don't talk about Francis." Parker picks off another strip of pastry with feverish concentration.

I do a conspicuous visual sweep of Le Overpriced Croissant. Besides the three of us in the corner, there's a duo of yoga moms and two perfectly coiffed older ladies. Rule me out, and the café would be three generations of the exact same table. "Nobody here gives a damn about Katie's exes."

"Henry does," Parker says. "He holds his girlfriends to a standard—"

"—so high not even an Olympic pole vaulter could clear it? Yeah, I know. But he's happy now."

"Unless somebody's telling him Katie's cheating."

I really thought we'd settled this line of inquiry. "Okay, but she's not."

Parker glances at Katie. "People talk when they're jealous. Cat Parr and Macy Lascelles would both effing love to see Katie go down if it got them closer to the top."

I steal a piece of Katie's croissant third. "Can't we just rock-paper-scissors for the best spots in Hampton Court? Normal high schools don't actually operate like the Reign of Terror."

"It was different last year," says Parker. "Before Henry dumped Lina."

"Classic." I start counting on my fingers. "Beloved leader dethroned. Power struggle ensues. Freedom of the press dies a swift death. With nowhere to turn for an honest account of the world around them, the people devolve into unchecked rumormongering—"

"What the hell is rumormongering?"

"—until deep in the heart of the dystopian wasteland, three girls unite. They come from different families, but they share one goal: to liberate their homeland. And thus, the resistance is born. It all begins with those revolutionaries and their underground paper. The..."

Parker and Katie stare at me like I've just hurled my last marble over a cliff.

"Come on, you guys, I need a snappy title!"

"Pretty sure you've got this," Parker says.

"The Lion Ledger?" says Katie.

I shake my head. "That's the school paper."

"The Lancaster Tribune?"

"That's the Lancaster paper. Damn it, resistancing is harder than I thought it was going to be. We're going to need another croissant."

Parker finally eats one dismembered pastry shred. "Let's postpone the resistance until Monday, because tonight's going to be enough work just making sure everything goes the way it's supposed to."

"Tonight's just a party." Katie grins and pulls us into half a group hug.

"So was the Tower," says Parker.

"Well, *that* got really dark really fast," I say.

Parker blinks. "God, no. I didn't mean it like that. It's just—George, you know? And Anna. They should be here. Right now, with us."

"They *are*," says Katie, which is the kind of inspirational woo-woo I'd normally laugh at, but Katie's so damn earnest I can't. "And as your queen, I proclaim that today, we're only allowed to have fun. No being sad. No fights. Even if everybody else is being the worst. We're the underground resistance for having a good time."

I crack up, and even Parker smiles. "That's the best mission statement I've ever heard," I tell Katie.

"Obviously," she says. "Because we're the best secret club ever. We're the *queens* club. And we've got this."

Scientists Determine That Time Slows Down During School Dances

We roll up to the homecoming dance an hour and a half late, except we're not late because we're with Henry and Katie, and the party doesn't start 'til they walk in.

On the surface, it's the most generic high school dance setup possible. Streamers and balloons and those lights that make patterns on the walls, like it's a '90s movie where the guy is a chain-smoking bad boy or possibly a jock who can't reveal his secret love for quiz bowl, and the girl is kind of plain until she takes off her glasses and discovers she's conventionally pretty.

"I can't believe they're having it here," says Macy Lascelles behind me.

Parker holds up one hand. "Don't even go there, Macy."

"I'm just saying what everybody's thinking."

Because the non-generic underbelly is that we're having

the dance at the Lancaster Country Club. You know, the one that blew up on prom night.

But still. "Come on," I scoff. "You know at least eighty percent of the guys here aren't thinking about the venue. They're thinking about how many more minutes they're socially obligated to *spend* at the venue before they can get their half of the bargain in the back of a car."

"Or in the woods," Katie says, because End of the Road is hookup central. Nothing says romance like dead leaves and wayward spiders.

"Exactly."

Macy rolls her eyes and slinks off, and the rest of us get down to what you do at a dance: wait for it to be over. We're just in time for the court presentation, which means everybody has to clear the floor for the most awkward slow dance ever, where we all stare at the four homecoming court couples and, in Parker's case, pull out a flask without even the slightest attempt at subterfuge.

"Dude, there's a teacher literally one table over," I say.

"I miss my boyfriend, okay?" She takes a sip and spins the lid back onto the flask—which, by the way, looks straight out of *The Great Gatsby*. "Before the Anna thing, everybody loved him, even though he was arrogant as hell."

She slips the flask back into her purse half a second before the teacher at the next table looks over at us. "But then he was dead—*dead*, Cleves, I mean, seriously!—and nobody would even say, *Wow, it sucks that George died. It sucks for Parker that George died.* It was like, since everybody decided it was Anna's fault, they had to blame George, too."

The slow dance is still going. It's the longest dance in human history.

"I caught one of my girls—Beth Somerset, her sister was with Brandon when you visited—saying, like, 'You know Anna and George were creepy-close, he was probably in on it, too,' and I kicked her off the squad right there. I swear to God, I almost smacked her."

"You should've done it," I say. "Not some wimpy slap, either. Belted her in the eye."

Parker finally cracks a smile. "Where the hell were you five months ago?"

"Cleveland."

She gazes out over the dance floor, and it freaks me out how together she looks. Like, she's drinking from a Gatsby flask and talking about her dead boyfriend and how she wants to smack people, and that all evokes a particular picture, right? Sloppy and loud and flapping her hands around with at least one strap of her dress falling down.

Instead she looks perfect, and her voice is totally normal. If you weren't sitting right here listening to her say, *I want to smack Beth Somerset*, you'd have no idea that she wanted to smack Beth Somerset.

The song finally ends, and Henry comes over with Katie. "Holy shit," he says. "My leg is *killing* me." He smacks himself on the thigh, right where he got his bike-inflicted stab wound during the slide-dive. He probably shouldn't be saving the day on the football field quite as often as he does, but come on. This is Henry we're talking about. He's not going to let a mere hospitalization-worthy bike-stabbing interfere with his quarterbacking.

"Sit with me," Parker says.

Henry shoots her a somewhat suspicious look.

She pulls the flask out again. "I have vodka."

"Ooh, gimme." Katie grabs for it.

"Katie, we're practically at school!" Henry hisses, but he sits down next to Parker after all.

"Practically," Katie says with a wink, and something about it reminds me of Anna, even though they don't look anything alike.

And I can tell Parker sees it, too, although maybe she's seeing the other Boleyn twin, because she grabs the flask right back again for another drink.

"Come on, let's dance!" Katie shouts over the music, which is in throwback mode with a timeless pop-punk masterpiece I'm pretty sure came out before we were even born.

Henry shakes his head. "I'm going to make sure Rochford doesn't turn into a drunk mess."

Parker does her talk-to-the-hand thing. It's especially impactful given her level of fanciness: You might've had a girl in a cheerleading uniform give you the hand in the face, but a girl in a bespoke homecoming dress? Transcendental.

"I don't turn into a mess," she says. "You should know that by now."

"Come on, this is my *song*!" Katie's grabbing Henry's hand.

He winces. "You saw that hit yesterday. I'm done dancing."

"Fine. I'll find somebody else."

I swear she's actually looking at Francis, who's shoulder-slapping Tom three tables over, so I grab her arm and say, "You owe me at least fifty dances after all that spray-painting I did yesterday. Let's go."

I kick my shoes off, and we run out onto the dance floor, crashing into Christina Milano and the rest of the newspaper girls.

"I'm so ready for tonight," Katie shouts. She grabs my hand and I spin her around, like she's a poodle skirt girl and I'm her extremely uncoordinated powder-blue-tux guy. "I can't believe you've never been to End of the Road!"

"It's kind of a long commute from Ohio."

"You'll be fine. I'll make sure you have the best time." She giggles. "I really did start going in eighth grade."

"Dude, your grandmother *was* cool with everything."

"Fake sleepover. Duh."

I try a spin this time. The barefoot thing doesn't work in my favor, and since my astonishingly subpar dancing skills can use all the favors they can get, I look decidedly less than ready for *Swan Lake.* "How does an eighth-grader from York get an invite to Lancaster's biggest party?"

"My guitar teacher asked me."

"Aww."

She makes a face.

"Not aww?"

"Definitely not aww. Guitar is so not my thing. Not that he ever taught me much about how to play the guitar, if you know what I mean."

I'm doing a mental inventory of guitar guys. If Katie was

in eighth grade, Guitar Guy was probably a freshman, so he's a senior now. My age. "Do I know him?"

"Doubt it. He was a senior."

"Like, a child prodigy guitar-Mozart senior who was fifteen?"

"No, he sucked. And he was almost nineteen, I think."

I stop dancing and stare at her. "He was almost nineteen, and you were thirteen, and he asked you to a party guys call 'the devirginizer'?"

She's still dancing, but she doesn't look quite as in love with the universe as she did a minute ago. "I knew what End of the Road was about."

"Katie! You were in *middle school.*"

"What are you saying? I'm a slut?" Her smile wavers.

"Of course I'm not saying you're a slut," I say way too loudly, but I'm not about to tone it down. Not about this. "I'm saying he's gross. Nineteen hitting on thirteen isn't romantic. It's pervy. And illegal."

She blinks three times, fast. "I didn't say no or anything."

The music is still sing-yelling, and the newspaper girls are still bouncing around next to us, and the whole thing is so not the setting for a conversation this level of awful. "It doesn't matter if you said it or not."

"I kind of liked him. He was nice."

"He wasn't nice if he was trying to lure some kid into the woods!"

And of course that's when the song ends, so I wind up screaming "INTO THE WOODS!" into relative silence. A good slice of the dance floor—including Cat, who pretty much counts as a chaperone—turns to stare.

"Theater!" I say, with one of those dramatic hand gestures the theater kids are always doing. "Got to love it."

Some drama girl yells, "Hell yeah!" and everybody else either laughs or goes back to ignoring me. Then the next song starts, the same whiny crap that was playing when Henry stole Katie's car. So I pull Katie into slow-dance formation, which is much better suited to my remedial dancing skills.

"Listen, that guy was a creep. And if you ever want to do anything about him, I've got your back, okay?"

She's dancing the girl part, arms around my shoulders, and she turns it into a hug. "You sound just like Anna."

Which is the last thing I expected her to say, with the possible exception of *let's go home and study.* "Anna Boleyn?"

"Yeah. She was always like, 'We're going to ruin him, we're going to'—I don't even know. She had all these revenge plans, and she kept yelling at me when I said it was probably just, you know, okay, because I kissed him back and stuff."

I skip over the Anna thing. "It wasn't okay. He was *nineteen.* And you were skeeved out, right?"

"I don't know. Kind of. I mean, yeah, a little bit." There's still a tiny piece of her smile left. She's doing her damnedest to hold on to it. "I guess I was. But I didn't say no."

"Well, yeah, but you didn't say yes, either, did you?"

She doesn't answer, but her arms get tighter around my shoulders.

"Does anybody else know?"

She shrugs into my chin. "Not at Lancaster. And hopefully everyone at York keeps their mouths shut."

"Hopefully?"

"I had kind of a reputation. Like Macy was saying."

Possibly the shittiest part of this entirely shitty thing is that she's right. Even I've heard the Katie-was-a-slut-at-York rumors, and anyone who's exchanged two sentences with me knows that saying that type of thing to my face is going to earn them a *War and Peace*–length lecture. "Katie," I say. "That's not fair. It wasn't your *fault*."

"I'm different now. I'm with Henry. So it's okay."

"Dude." I tilt my head so I can see her better. "You need to tell somebody."

"Like at confession?"

"Like somebody who knows how to deal with this kind of thing. Like the cops, or a therapist, or something."

"I'm okay. It's whatever."

"It's not whatever!"

"I told Anna, and I told you, and you were both perfect." Her smile almost doesn't look like it's being held in place by sheer willpower anymore. "Just keep this a secret. Please?"

"Only if you promise me you're really okay."

"I promise. It's over. Look at me, I'm homecoming queen! I won."

We're still slow-dancing far enough away from everybody that nobody can listen in. "Okay. But if you ever change your mind, we'll make him pay."

She pulls me into a hug again. "You're the best. You're, like, the only person at this whole school who wouldn't just call me a slut and go tell Henry."

"Listen, Katie—" And I'm about to tell her that anybody who thinks it's their business to police her life choices doesn't deserve the effort it would take to tell them to go fuck themselves, but the song cuts off and all of a sudden we're being bludgeoned in the eardrums with a rap track that spent all summer being "this summer's anthem" and is now apparently "this football season's anthem," too.

"This is my JAM!" Katie shouts. She squeezes the hug tighter for just a second, and then she's dropping it right there while half the football guys catcall.

Katie Howard knows how to work it on the dance floor.

And she knows exactly how to make it look like she's fine, even when she's not.

"Come on, Cleves!" Katie calls with a combination body roll–hair flip that's probably illegal in Utah. Some guy who's worked his way up behind her has his hands on her hips, but she's just watching me and laughing as I do my best attempt at a barefoot moonwalk, and then I'm dancing like she is, and so's Christina and everybody, and ten seconds later even Parker's running out to join us.

It's all because of Katie.

Henry got it right when he fell for her.

Lancaster Youth
Carry on Time-Honored Traditions

If the Lancaster County sheriff's office actually had any interest in cracking down on underage drinking and general teenage shenanigans, they could just follow the caravan from the clubhouse back downtown, across the railroad tracks, and out to the last turn off the main road before it crosses the bridge over the Wabash River.

"What exactly are they maintaining all the way out here?" I ask Parker as she inches down the gravel road behind a truck full of Lancaster guys.

"What?" Her eyes zip back and forth between the truck and the headlights in her reverse mirror. "If these assholes ding my car, I'm pressing charges."

"It's a maintenance road. But it just goes out to the drainpipe, right? Why does an old pipe over the river need my taxpayer dollars?"

"Because without it, there'd be no homecoming party," she says.

"Unless you want to hike a mile around to the other side," Josie adds from the back seat.

"Not in this outfit," says Macy. Out of the four of us, I'm the only one who wimped out and changed into jeans instead of staying in my homecoming dress.

A guy in the truck in front of us lobs an empty can just clear of the car, and Parker pounds the horn. "Some of us are trying to *avoid* depreciation, thanks!"

"Need me to drive?" I ask.

"Nobody's touching this steering wheel." It's exactly what she said fifteen minutes ago during the carpool choreography. When I mentioned the flask, she walked a straight line across the parking lot while reciting the alphabet backward, then did a back handspring without even flashing anybody. "And anyway," she says, "we're here."

Macy and Josie are already out. In the glow of everybody's headlights, I can see the road widening into a makeshift parking lot. I've been here once before, with Henry, for the only reason anybody ever comes out on nights that aren't homecoming: to hook up.

Yeah, classy, I know, but whatever. It's a rite of passage, okay?

So Parker pulls in, and we body-block her Fiat so nobody can get too close. "Okay. We're golden," she finally says after every vehicle in Lancaster has found a spot no less than fifty feet away. We follow a troupe of band kids past the cars and down a dirt path.

"You sure you want to ford the river in your ballroom attire?" I say.

"You sure you want to look like a peasant all night?" she shoots back.

"Looking like a peasant feels pretty pleasant."

She laughs and links elbows with me. "God, Cleves, you're in for a great night."

And then there it is: the old drainpipe across the Wabash. "Yeah. I just have to do that Indiana Jones trial scene first."

The pipe isn't *that* narrow, and it isn't *that* far above the water. Theoretically. But when it's pitch-black—the sky is solid clouds tonight—the whole situation looks damn precarious.

"It was nice knowing you, Rochford."

"You, too, Cleveland."

Then she's on the drainpipe, lighting the way with her phone, and I'm right behind her. "Okay, I really don't get how you're doing this in heels."

"I'm Miss Indiana's Outstanding Teen," she says, stepping over a section of metal that's rusted to the point of basically being a hole. "I could walk in heels by the time I was three."

"And people say pageants don't give you any transferable skills."

"They so do. Poise, self-confidence, discipline, philanthropy…"

While she's listing the merits of the Miss America Organization, I'm just focusing on staying right in the center of the path. And it's not too bad, since I'm wearing tennis shoes, and it's too dark to see much—

Then I get cocky and look down, and we're thirty feet up.

"Hello, are you coming?" Parker's looking at me over her shoulder. Totally unruffled.

Maybe there's something to pageanting after all.

"I'm there. Let's do this."

I catch up, and we make it across, praise Jesus, and bash through the woods for a couple more minutes. By now, we can hear people yelling and laughing, and there's firelight flickering through the trees. And suddenly there we are, in some combination of a caveman encampment and Hampton Court. There's a line of bonfires—we're at the first one, but I can see a few more stretching out deeper into the woods— and half the school is here.

"You go on. I've got to scheme this," Parker says, pointing at her phone.

I head for the fires. The first one isn't anybody I know— freshmen and York kids. But the second one is all Lancaster juniors and seniors.

"Cleves! Get over here!"

It's Katie, sitting on a blanket with Henry next to a pile of purses and a giant tree. I sit, and there's a beer in my hands a second later, and I'm not even sure where it came from.

"Spontaneous beer generation. Impressive."

"That's End of the Road." Henry pulls Katie in for a kiss.

"Katie!" Parker yells from the other side of the fire. "Emergency!"

Katie jumps up and flits past a couple making out so close to the flames, their hair is probably singed. Parker says something, and Katie nods. The firelight's gleaming off her dress, and she looks like a teenage Tinkerbell. "We're going to the car," she calls. "I'll be right back."

"Have fun," I shout, and then they're disappearing back toward the first fire.

Henry leans back against the tree. "Cleves," he says, "I can't even tell you how much better this year is because you moved here."

"I live to please."

"Can't believe next year we'll be gone."

"We could stay. Keep coming to high school parties until we're fifty. You'd never have to miss a single second of turning Lancaster into the next Dubai."

"Dubai's definitely what I'm going for."

I point past Francis and a few of the other football guys, who are currently—and very loudly—attempting to shotgun their beers. "Right over there, you could have a three-hundred-story hotel."

"And over there," Henry adds, pointing past the human rotisserie couple, "an underground mall. Nothing under two thousand dollars."

"There better be a food court with gross state fair food."

"We can put the whole state fair under there."

"Subterranean Ferris wheel," I say. "The walls will be shark aquariums."

He wraps one arm around my shoulders. "I'm going to miss you, you know that?"

"Yeah, and I'm going to miss your sappy drunk side."

Then the guys call him over, because apparently they've come up with the world's best drinking game, which seems

THE DEAD QUEENS CLUB

to have some major flaws in both planning and execution, but hey. One blanket over, the newspaper crew's breaking out s'more supplies, so I work my way in.

"Right," Eustace is saying. "Time to bet on tonight's best story."

"God, remember last year?" says Christina.

"Who doesn't?" Eustace angles a marshmallow into the flames.

"Those of us who were in Cleveland," I say.

"George—" Christina glances around, like she's making sure nobody else is going to hear her say the forbidden last name. "George Boleyn rode his damn Vespa across the drainpipe."

"Are you shitting me?"

"He did," Cat says, which confirms it better than a ten-page annotated bibliography. "Anna talked him into it."

Christina grabs the marshmallows. "I miss George."

"Sucks for Parker." I keep an eye on Cat when I say it. Potential Future Day Job #007: Supersleuth.

"Sucks for everybody who has to *deal* with Parker," Eustace edits.

"I'm sorry, what?" Cat asks.

I actually laugh. Which isn't very sleuthy of me, but whatever. "Pretty sure you were the one shit-talking Dead George to Parker's face last night."

"I wasn't insulting George," says Cat, because apparently *shit-talking* doesn't meet her editorial standards. "I was making a point about unsubstantiated gossip."

"And I'm making a point about how you didn't exactly take the high road. Pick a side."

Cat gives me a long look. Then she smiles, which is definitely the most punch-worthy thing she could do right now. "Whatever you say, Cleveland." She stands up and heads over to where Erin Willoughby and Brandon Suffolk are sitting.

"Now look what you've done." Eustace shifts his flaming marshmallow spear to the other hand and high-fives me.

"You're welcome," I tell him. "Let the unsubstantiated gossip begin."

"Best story," Eustace repeats.

"Breakup," says Christina.

"Is this a Girl Genius tip?"

"A good journalist never reveals her sources."

"Fake," says Eustace. "Unless you count Cat and Jonathan. They barely talked at the dance. Ten bucks says she's got a new target in mind."

I reach for the chocolate. "She killed her Lancaster prospects with that fight yesterday."

"Yeah, okay, this is old news," Christina says. "Cat's going to dump Jonathan. She's talking to a London College guy. It's TJ Seymour. Jane's brother."

We stare.

"Fake," says Eustace.

"Where the hell do you get your intel?" I ask.

She laughs and lip-zips. "Moving on. There's a queen who's poised to fall."

"So your column is a psychic hotline now, is that it?"

"Say what you want. But if we're betting on tonight's best

headline, I'm putting my money on a breakup. And it's going to be the biggest one we've seen since—"

She doesn't finish the sentence. She doesn't have to.

United States Congress Bans Texting

Fifteen theories later, Henry calls me over. "Hey, have you seen Katie?"

I squint through the fire at the guys. They're doing one of the cheerleading cheers, and Francis is getting really into the pom-pomming. "Not since she and Parker left."

"That was forever ago."

"It was probably a hair emergency. You know Parker."

"Yeah, I know her." He says it like he's definitely not talking about hair emergencics. Like maybe she and Katie are out there, you know, sacrificing goats or something.

"Sappy drunk has progressed to paranoid drunk?"

"It's End of the Road. Anything can happen." He pulls his phone out and thumbs a text.

We sit there without saying anything for a minute, leaning against the big tree.

"She should be back already." Henry's voice is tighter now.

"Come on. They're probably just talking to somebody."

"She's not texting back." He calls her and waits.

On the other side of the fire, the guys have moved on to the fight song. Or at least I think it's the fight song, because they started out with *We're loyal to Lancaster High*, but since then it's been mostly unintelligible.

"Want me to try Parker?" I ask.

He calls Katie again.

"How far could they have gotten anyway?" I'm hoping he won't answer, because I have an irrational suspicion that this patch of woods stretches all the way to Canada, and it would be a major downer if I'm right.

"—a victory for Lancaster High!" the football quartet bellows, and everybody cheers.

Everybody except for Macy, who's suddenly right in front of us holding Katie's turquoise clutch like it's the Lost Ark. I couldn't tell you the name of the pop princess who's singing through Macy's petty-thieving hands, but I *could* tell you it's the ringtone Katie's had for a month, because the last thousand times I've heard it, I've politely begged her to please, for the love of God, switch it to something exponentially less likely to get stuck in my head all day.

"Maybe you should check Katie's phone," Macy says.

I raise an eyebrow. "Maybe you shouldn't steal people's purses."

Henry grabs the clutch and pulls out the phone, which is finally finishing that damn song. A second later, the screen lights up with a text. We both look, like the nosy assholes we are, but it's just Parker.

"She was *with* her," Henry says, and right then Parker pops out of the dark halfway between us and the football quartet. Macy takes a few steps back, which is probably her first good decision all day.

"Rochford!" Henry yells, but she's already on her way over. "Where's Katie?"

She shoots me a glance, and I feel like I'm supposed to understand it, but I'm as clueless as Henry. "She's, um—we ran into Josie."

"Awkward," I say, because when Josie took off with her linebacker of choice ten minutes ago, I'm pretty sure they weren't looking for company.

Henry swipes Katie's screen open, and there's Parker's text: I'm back, H is with C.

Then he's jumping up, and I am, too, because I'm not about to miss this.

"Rochford, where's Katie." He's not even asking.

"I told you, she's with—"

"Then what the hell is this about?" He shoves Katie's phone in her face. Parker looks how a deer in the headlights would if it had homecoming hair.

"Where's. Katie."

Parker's radiating freakout vibes. "Just give me the phone."

"No." Henry swipes another conversation open. The name at the top says *Culpepyyy* with a turtle emoji, of all things, but I don't get any time to analyze its significance because suddenly we're dealing with Henry's seriously intimidating jealous-boyfriend wrath.

"Rochford. What the hell is this." The way he's leaving off

the question marks is freaking me out. Like he already knows the answer, but he needs her to say it out loud.

We can all read the screen anyway.

Katie, at 2:35 this afternoon: Culpepy

Katie: Culpepyyy hey

Tom: hey

Katie: When can I see you??

Katie: Are you ok? Josie said you got beat up at practice

Tom: thats football lol

Katie: When can I see you

Katie: I just want to see you i miss you

Tom: u saw me last night lol

Henry's grip is so tight, it looks like he's going to crush the phone. And yes, he's mad, but he also looks legitimately scared, which is infinitely more concerning. Almost as concerning as this very concerning text conversation. "Last night," says Henry. "What does she mean, last night?"

"Just—the game, you know, my party—"

"Shut up, Rochford!" He keeps scrolling.

Katie, at 4:58: Culpepy

Katie: It's killing me that I can't be with you

Katie: Right now

Katie: And always

Tom: tonight

Katie: !!!

Katie: I can't wait you don't even know!

And then she sent a bunch of pink hearts and turtle emojis, the latter of which are starting to condition me into a cold sweat. I mean, I'm not accepting this as absolute proof that Katie's cheating, but it's looking Very Not Good for literally everyone involved.

"It's not what it looks like—" Parker starts to say.

Henry just points at the screen.

Katie, 10:37: Culpepy are you here yet?

Tom: idk if this is a good time K

Katie: You promised!!

Katie: I need to see you idc

Katie: Parker's coming, she'll cover for me

Tom: u sure?

Katie: Culpepy seriously!! Need you

Katie, 11:08: Parker's here I'm coming where are you

Tom: northwest of fire

Katie: ???

Tom: past the guys

Katie: On my way!!

Heart. Turtle.
Thirty minutes ago.
I'm pretty sure I'm going to puke.
Henry throws the phone against the big tree, and the screen shatters. Parker reaches for it, but Henry grabs her and pulls her back up. "What the hell were you thinking, Rochford?"
I finally remember how to talk. "Maybe it's not what it looks like. Maybe we can just wait for Katie to get back, and—"
"You mean Katie and Culpepy?"
"They're just talking." Parker's face is totally white. "She's—"
"I don't want to hear it, Rochford. And I don't want to hear where she was last night, either." He takes a step away from us and hits himself hard in the leg, but it's not like at the

dance when he was trying to break the pain up. He's making it worse. And I guess it works, because he yelps and grinds his foot down.

"Henry—" Parker tries again, but he gets right up in her face.

"I think you should stop talking," he says. "Because every time something happens, you're standing right there when it all goes to shit."

"What's that supposed to mean?" she gets out, but the way she's gone six shades whiter, it's pretty obvious she already knows.

"I mean when you stand too close to the fire, you're bound to get burned," says Henry. And then he takes off into the darkness, and it's just me and Parker Ghostface Rochford and Katie's shattered phone, which is serving as a lovely metaphor for my shattered expectations of End of the Road somehow not turning into all of my friends hating each other.

"Cleves—" says Parker, but then she just sort of trails off, like she can't come up with a suitably good explanation for (a) those texts, (b) her new snow-inspired complexion, or (c) whatever web of trickery I've stumbled into—which, no matter what the actual story is, can't be great.

And then I'm having one of those TV detective sudden-flashback-pieces-clicking-together moments. It's both unrequested and unwelcome, but once I think it, I can't unthink it, so I go, "Wait. Last night when you had Tom go over to Katie's house when I was picking up Henry—"

"*Cleves,*" she says again, and her extra-whiteness has now progressed to Shrek-green. "Don't ask. Please just don't ask."

The football singers start up a rendition of "Back Home

182

Again in Indiana," which is a not-that-fantastic song under the best of circumstances, and an objectively crap song when sung by drunk football players, and truly nightmarish when it's accompanying this nuclear meltdown of a wilderness kegger. I'm trying not to be mad at anybody, but instead I'm mad at everybody, including myself. *Especially* myself, for not seeing whatever I didn't see, and not stopping whatever I didn't stop, and also apparently accidentally lying to Henry, and god *damn*, she can't be cheating.

It's a prank. That's what I'm going with.

"Okay," I say. I'm channeling Cat Parr, because at least Cat doesn't end up in the middle of school dance–centered alleged cheating scandals for two seasons running. "I'm finding Henry. And if by some chance this is the prank to end all pranks, this would be a really fabulous time to mention that."

She just says, in a very un-Parker-like death whisper, "Fix it? Please?"

Which isn't an impossibly tall order at all, but I head for the woods anyway.

"I'm here," Henry says right after I scream his name at full earsplitting volume. He's literally ten feet away, which is the first good thing to happen in the past few minutes. If there's one thing that isn't on my End of the Road bucket list, it's getting lost in the woods and dying of starvation while trying to find my best friend to console him over the fact that my other best friend might possibly be cheating on him.

I bushwhack my way over and sit down next to him. I have exactly zero ideas about what to do right now.

"Cleves," he says. His voice is totally devastated and it almost kills me flat. He rubs the back of his hand across his eyes, and he's crying, and that *actually* murders me. "It's true. She's cheating. Fuck."

"Maybe… I mean, maybe she's not."

He laughs the most tragic laugh ever. "Seriously, Cleves?"

"I mean…maybe there's an explanation?"

"She doesn't care. She doesn't give a shit."

"Yes, she does," I say, which is the first thing I've said that I actually believe. "No matter what's happening with Tom—"

"Tom Culpeper. Jesus." He laughs again, and then he takes a breath that's all ragged and shaky. I scoot closer and wrap one arm around him. "Of all the guys on the team, she had to pick Tom. I throw with him every damn day, you know that? I trusted him. I trusted *her*."

We sit there not-talking for a painfully long moment.

Then Henry sighs and stands up, pulling me with him. "He's over," he says.

"You mean—"

"Tom. He's done. He's out of here." He's sounding more pissed off with every syllable, and I sort of want to de-escalate this before it turns into a brawl, but on the other hand, I don't exactly blame him.

Also, attempting to stop a fight between two drunk guys at End of the Road feels like a very poor decision, in terms of self-preservation.

But I still go, "Well, maybe if you talk to Katie—"

"It doesn't matter." He shakes his head. "That's over, too. For good."

Correspondent Miraculously Does Not Get Lost in Woods but Everything Else Continues to Be Shitty Anyway

In the two seconds it takes for me to catch up with Henry and reemerge at the bonfire, he's already got Francis Dereham by the shoulder. To Henry's credit, he's keeping it together pretty well, all things considered. To the newspaper crew's credit, there are at least three people filming already, and nobody's even thrown a punch yet.

"Francis," says Henry in the most this-means-business voice imaginable, "you better come clean right now."

Pregaming for Tom, I guess.

"Henry, chill," Brandon says, getting halfway up from where he's sitting with Erin.

Henry's shoving Francis the way guys do when they're trying to assert their manliness. Like, *bump*, look at this! I'm, *bump*, the king of the woods! "You slept with Katie."

"Breaking," somebody mutters from the newspaper blanket. I'm pretty sure it's Eustace.

"What, you're too good for my sloppy seconds?" Francis has a big grin on his face, like he can't tell how much Henry isn't kidding.

"Did you even break up?"

Francis shrugs. "Have to be going out in the first place to break up."

"She was going out with you. Everybody says she was."

"She was going *somewhere* on me—"

Henry punches him in the mouth.

"Fight!" one of the football guys bellows.

Francis swings, but Henry ducks. Francis stumbles, almost nosediving into the flames, and Henry takes a step back, like he isn't even worth fighting.

That's when Tom steps out of the woods, slowing to a dead stop as he takes in the punching match by the bonfire. Henry strides forward and claps Tom's arm. He's smiling, but it's deadly.

"Hey, Henry," Tom says. He's outstandingly oblivious.

Parker pops up out of nowhere and digs her manicure into my arm. "You've got to find Katie."

"Me?"

"I'm so dead right now," she says. "He'll lose it if he finds me with her."

"Culpepy." Henry's smile is too tight. The light gleams off his teeth.

"Go." Parker's voice turns even more desperate.

"Where is she?" I whisper.

"You having a good End of the Road?" Henry asks Tom, a little too loud. Francis spits blood into the fire.

Parker nods past them. "Hurry."

"Retract the claws," I say, and she finally realizes her nails are fusing my sweatshirt to my skin. She lets go. She's still got the pageant poise going, but I can tell she's hardcore panicking underneath it. "It's okay. I'm on it."

I edge out of the clearing, and the good thing is nobody's watching me at all. The bad thing, of course, is that it's because Henry is ten seconds from knocking Tom's head off.

"Hey, Tom, I was wondering if you could tell me where Katie is."

He flounders. "Who?"

"Katie Howard. Wearing a tiara? Going out with me?"

"Uh, maybe Parker—"

"Don't give me that shit, Tom!" For a second I think he's actually going to start crying, but instead he shoves Tom so hard he almost falls. "Where the hell is Katie?"

I run.

Let me just state for the record that I am devoutly unathletic. I'm a charter member of the school of Don't Run Unless You're Being Chased. But if I survive the night, I'm amending our constitution to allow for running when you're attempting to do some unqualified mediating of a very endangered relationship at a party where too many things are already burning.

Away from the fires, it's stupidly dark, and of course I left my phone back at the punching arena, so I'm mostly just trying not to slam into any trees. I couldn't even tell you whether I'm still heading in the direction Parker pointed.

Should've stayed in Girl Scouts, but God, I hated the arts and crafts.

So now that I'm alone in the dark and the slasher-victim aesthetic has reached alarming levels, I finally stop and do a three-sixty to check for—I don't know, zombies? Then I give up whatever token attempt at covertness I was theoretically going for and shout, "Katie!"

No answer.

I take a few more steps. "Katie!"

"Cleves?"

I crash a little closer to her voice. "Where are you?"

"Over here."

I see a glint of light off the sequins on her dress and I swerve toward it, and of course now that I have an audience, this is when I trip over a giant root. I crawl the last few feet, and then I'm next to Katie, who's leaning against a tree drinking a wine cooler.

"Hey," she says, reaching over to give me a hug. She's still wearing her crown.

I'm not sure if it's because (a) Katie is too damn adorable for her own good, thus making it impossible to be mad at her under any circumstances; (b) I have no moral compass at all when it comes to standing up to people I love, even if it's also *for* people I love; (c) I have the best moral compass ever and am a staunch disciple of Innocent Until Proven Guilty; or (d) I'm in some type of drama-induced shock and am compartmentalizing this situation until we're out of the woods, both literally and figuratively, and I have the psychological bandwidth to handle it. Regardless, I can't even talk myself into yelling at her.

Instead I just say, "Dude, we have a situation."

"What do you mean?"

"Henry saw your phone. The texts with Tom."

She goes stiff. "Shit."

"Yeah. Serious shit."

"Where is he?"

"Well, he punched Francis in the face, and then Tom walked into it."

"Shit," she says again, and she starts to stand up.

I grab her hand. "I seriously don't recommend entering that demolition zone."

"I have to talk to him."

"Not right now."

Even in the dark I can tell that all the color's drained out of her face. "I have to."

I scoot around so we're knee-to-knee with the bottle between us. "He's really upset. And he's drunk. He's not going to listen."

She stares up at the branches. "No. I can't—this can't—" Her voice is going breathy, like she's not getting enough air.

I take her other hand, too, and hold on while she sits there blinking and blinking, like she's not allowed to cry. "You've got to give him until tomorrow. It's a mess back there. It's like if everybody in Lord of the Flies was a drunk football player."

She finally looks down from the trees. "Is that the one with the elves?"

And then we're both laughing way too hard and knocking our foreheads together. Her tiara and curls and my hoodie and ponytail. Then she's crying instead of laughing. Grabbing on to my shoulders and shaking like a freaking leaf.

Hi, I'm Cleves Cleveland, and I specialize in being cried on in forests.

"You've got to help me," she says. "He trusts you."

I nod, even though he won't anymore whenever he finishes his boxing match and finds me out here aiding and abetting a girlfriend with an overdue expiration date. "We're waiting until tomorrow, okay?"

Her makeup is smeared a little—dusty gold eyeshadow mixing into the tear tracks down her cheeks—and her tiara is crooked. "Okay," she says. "But I can explain about Tom. Or I guess I should start with Francis—"

"Who cares? He's your ex. You can have as many exes as you want. Henry sure does."

"He's not even my ex. Not really. We were just, you know, that started when I was at York. And he—"

She closes her eyes. She looks so young somehow, like she's just a kid instead of the homecoming queen who dropped it on the dance floor with all the boys whistling.

"Francis won't leave me alone. He knew me back then, and he's holding it over my head, and he has those damn pictures. And Tom—it's not like it looks. I swear."

She drinks and passes me the wine cooler. "You know, when I first moved here, I had the biggest crush on Tom. I went to this party with Francis, but he got really wasted and passed out and I had to get home somehow. So I was walking down the driveway, and Tom came running after me, and he was like, 'You can't walk home, you're drunk, look at your outfit, you're asking for something to happen, let me drive you.'"

"God, if I never hear anybody say 'asking for it' again, it'll be too soon," I say, taking a sip from the bottle like it's a very sad drinking game.

"He was being nice."

"You see a drunk girl trying to walk home, you don't get brownie points for not throwing her in the trunk."

She honestly looks like she doesn't get what I'm saying. I'm starting to feel really glad Henry punched Francis, and not just because of those damn pictures.

"Dude, it doesn't matter what you're wearing or if you're drunk. I mean, good for Tom, but that's, like, the lowest bar for qualifying as an intelligent life-form."

She giggles again, right on the edge of hysteria, and then she takes the bottle from me and drains it. "Tell that to my uncle. Come home with me right now and say that whole speech and flip him off."

"I'm there. Let's go."

She tosses the bottle over her shoulder, and it clangs against something in the dark. "But for real, Tom's nice. He helped me get in his car and he gave me a Gatorade and we're driving back and then I saw a turtle in the road, and this is over by the park so there's kind of a lot of traffic and I started freaking out and he was like, what the hell? And I thought he was going to make fun of me. But he stopped and we got out and I couldn't walk that well, so he picks up the turtle. It wasn't, like, a little box turtle, either. It was a great big snapper."

"You're leaving me in the dust on the turtle nomenclature."

"The ones that look like dinosaurs. It was hissing and trying to bite him, but he grabbed it and carried it to the pond and then we got back in the car and he drove me to the gate and walked to the house with me to make sure I got up the tree okay."

I'm honestly so done with Lancaster boys. "And they say chivalry's dead."

"It was really sweet, I swear. None of the other guys I've been with would've done that."

"You need to meet some less shitty guys."

She shrugs. "It's whatever. It's fine. Anyway, I kind of liked him, but then, you know, we went back to school. And then Henry liked me. No offense."

The "no offense" part is because that was technically when Henry and I were dating. For an illustrious fifteen days. Except that was already unraveling by the time he noticed Katie.

"But you liked him, too, right?" I ask.

"Who doesn't?"

Touché.

"He's hot," she says. "He's popular. He's got that, like, knight-in-shining-armor thing."

"He's a human magnet."

"Totally." She shrugs again. "So yeah. But I still liked Tom."

"Because of the snapping turtle rescue?"

"He's not, like, homecoming king, but I don't know. Tom's sweet. So I liked them both, but Henry asked me out first. And my uncle told me to say yes."

"Wait, what? Norfolk Howard sat down to dish on which boy was more dateable?"

We're both laughing. Way too hard. "He was——" Katie can barely speak. "He was like, 'Henry's right for your *future*, Katheryn. You need to think about your place in this family, and'——I don't even know. Basically, like, Henry has a good reputation, and you don't. Fix it."

"Damn."

"Yeah."

"Pushing your niece's ex on another niece is kind of creepy and weird, when you think about it."

"My uncle's kind of creepy and weird, when you think about it."

Then we're both cracking up again. "Okay, but after Anna, that's dark."

"We don't talk about her," Katie says, one index finger in the air. She's not laughing anymore—she's doing her high-speed blinking thing. "Nothing good, I mean."

There's a flicker of lightning, and we both look up.

"The thing is," she says, "about Tom. We——"

"Don't."

"What?"

I want to know. I mean, I'm a newspaper kid. Much Too Nosy is the first line of my job description. But I also really *don't* want to know, because the whole world cares entirely too much about who Katie has or hasn't slept with. Like it's the only thing that matters about her when actually it's no-body's damn business.

"Don't tell me," I say. "I mean, tell me if you want to. But don't tell me because you think I need to know. I don't give a flying fuck whether or not you slept with him."

"Really?"

"Really. We're done talking about guys, okay? Let's pass the damn Bechdel test."

"The what?"

"Let's talk about something better than this shit. Tell me something good."

She hesitates.

"Like, if you could have a superpower, what would it be?"

"Flying," she says.

"Yeah, I guess that would be pretty convenient for cheer-leading."

"Parker would love me. We'd win everything." She's slowed down to a normal human blinking speed instead of the hummingbird-wing thing.

"I'd pick teleporting. Be anywhere, anytime. Like right now, we could zap out of here without having to cross that drainpipe."

"Zap to the Bahamas."

"Zap to college."

She tilts her head to one side. "Wow, I'm going to miss you next year."

"You've only had me around for two months."

"Yeah, but they've been *good* months," she says. "Are you going far away for college?"

There's another bolt of lightning, a little closer. "Want to know a secret?"

"Obviously."

"I have no fucking idea where I want to go. Or what I want to study."

"Oh. Wow."

Somehow there's something comforting about exploring my future-related angst. It's so refreshingly hypothetical compared to this very non-hypothetical clusterfuck of a homecoming party, that I'd gladly discuss all the majors I don't want to major in for the next seven hours if it meant not seeing any more punching.

"Yeah," I say. "Exactly."

"Not, like, newspaper stuff?"

I fake-gag. "I'll leave that to Ms. Parr. I'm not a newsroom personality, trust me."

"I bet you'll end up somewhere super cool. Doing super cool things."

"Or unemployed in my mom's basement. One or the other," I say. "What about you?"

She shivers and wraps something around her shoulders. Tom's sweatshirt. "I want to go someplace where I can be on the dance team. Or cheer, if I'm good enough. Parker thinks I am."

"Especially once you can fly."

"Yeah." She pulls the sweatshirt tighter. "I don't really know what I want to, you know, be when I grow up? That sounds dumb."

"Well, I want to write thrillers. That sounds dumb, too."

"It sounds amazing. I'll buy all your books."

Katie Howard is the actual best. "I'll come see you at a game, even though I hate football."

"Don't say that! That's practically—what's that word?

Where they burn you at the stake because you're the wrong religion."

"Heresy?"

"That one." She nods. "I want to go to a big school. I want to take all different classes. It's so cool, you know? We can do whatever we want. When we're, like, thirty, we could be anything."

"Zap to thirty. Where are you?"

"Paris," she says. "No, I take it back. I'd miss Anna too much." She's looking up at the sky. "I don't know where, but I want to travel and meet people and see the world. And I want to help people. Like old people, or people in jail. Or maybe work at an animal shelter."

"The Howard House for Displaced Snapping Turtles."

"You can write my commercials."

"They'll be really thrilling."

"Perfect."

Maybe it's the impending shitstorm, but I can't even say anything snarky about what Katie wants to do. I mean, think about her sitting in prison teaching teardrop-tattoo guys how to write a résumé. It's the nicest life ambition I can think of.

"Okay," Katie says, sitting up straighter. "Let's promise. In ten years, we'll both come back for homecoming. No matter what."

"Zap to Lancaster High School."

"Even if we never talk anymore."

I nod. "Even if a militant Amish dictatorship bans cars and we have to trek back to Indiana via buggy-hitchhiking."

"Even if we have to walk. We'll come back for homecoming. Sit at the fifty and watch football, so nobody burns us for heresy."

"A crime second only to treason, which is reserved for those who hate basketball." I'm feeling weirdly sentimental about the concept of high school, given how the actuality of high school is absolutely not proving itself all that nostalgia-worthy this week.

"And we'll remember tonight, and we'll see what we did. And I bet it'll be pretty great."

"Because we're pretty great."

It's raining now, tapping off the leaves that haven't fallen yet. "Let's go," Katie says.

"You sure you're ready?"

She isn't fighting back tears anymore. "Yeah. And I'm going to talk to Henry."

"Please note that you're doing this against legal counsel." We start picking our way back through the woods, and I'm crossing my fingers that Katie's sense of direction is stronger than mine, because I couldn't tell you whether we're headed for the bonfire or Botswana.

"I have to." She lifts her chin. Very proud. Very Howardy.

"You'll talk to Henry. I'll get Parker. And we'll zap out of here and back to—'"

Then the rain starts for real, freezing cold and coming down in sheets. Katie shrieks and pulls Tom's sweatshirt over her hair, and we run.

Ready or not, here we come.

Nothing Goes Wrong and Everyone Makes It Home by Curfew

Two minutes of storm-sprinting later, we're back to the disappointing and unfortunate reality of End of the Road. The rain's hissing off the fire and a couple of drunk girls are spinning in the downpour. The newspaper crew is hiding under the blanket, which they've turned into a tent, and the football guys are drinking like they don't even notice the rain. Which is possible, given the staggering number of beer cans everywhere.

"Oh my God, Tom!" Katie shrieks, and she leaps over the Great Wall of Beer Cans to where Tom's slumping against a tree. His head's bleeding and his left eye is swollen shut. "Are you okay?"

"Never better," he rasps out.

The other football guys shoot sidelong glances Katie's way. They're on Henry's side. You can tell.

It's still pouring, but Katie's kneeling down next to Tom, draping his sweatshirt over him. It's a lovely moment, but it's raining so hard we're all about two minutes from getting washed away, plus I'm really not excited about what's going to happen if Henry walks in on this.

"Katie!" Parker pokes her head out of the newspaper tent. She's got somebody's jacket over her hair. "Get out of here!"

"I can't—" Katie looks up at me, wide-eyed, like she can't figure out what she's supposed to do, and I know exactly which of these roads diverging I would travel by. But it doesn't matter, because that's when Henry's voice cuts through the rain and the music somebody's phone is playing and the laugh track from one bonfire over.

"Katie."

Just that one word.

Her whole body tenses up. Then she snaps upright, and her crown slips off and hits the ground. "Henry!" she bursts out. "I—"

"Don't," he says.

"Henry, I can explain, I promise, I can—"

"Don't," he says again. He stares at her through the driving rain, like Tom isn't slouched against the tree and I'm not standing there panicking and some wondrously drunk couple isn't making out next to the fire ignoring this entire scene.

He's barely bleeding. He won the fight.

But he looks like he just lost everything.

"Henry—"

He shakes his head once, quick and curt, and then he turns

and disappears into the woods. He's not even walking. He's running away from this damn disaster.

"Henry!" Katie shouts after him. "Henry! Please!"

"Whore," somebody coughs from the football huddle.

Katie spins to look at them, but nobody meets her eye. Everybody's looking and not looking at the same time, like she's some anthropology exhibit instead of the girl they voted homecoming queen.

Her reign is over.

"Katie, come on, let's—" I start to say.

"Henry! Wait, Henry!" she shrieks again, and then she takes off after him, stumbling in her heels.

The rain falls so hard, it feels like hail. "Does anybody have a flashlight?" I call.

One of the football guys mutters something about how Katie's probably going to get lost down somebody's pants on her way to find Henry, and somebody from the newspaper tent says, "Breaking: Katie's a slut."

Parker slides out of the tent. "You can all go to Hell. Have fun in social Siberia for the rest of your lives, because I can make it happen."

"Not if Henry hates you for setting him up with another cheater." It's Eustace, as usual.

"Grow up, Eustace." Cat crawls halfway out and hands Parker a flashlight.

"Thank you," Parker says to Cat. "And fuck the rest of you."

She takes off after Katie, and then I'm running through the woods again. And let me tell you, even in heels and a dress with a jacket around her hair, Parker is *fast*.

"Where are we going?" I call as we cut past the first bonfire.

"The river." Parker's not even out of breath. "Henry's going to get out of here, and Katie's going to try to stop him." She runs even faster.

I try to say something back, like, *Well, we're about to break the sound barrier, so we'll definitely catch them if I don't die first,* but I can't budget the oxygen. The rain's letting up, at least, but the leaves are slick and I'm spending more effort staying upright than moving forward. Parker's not even slipping.

In my next life, I swear I'm doing pageants.

"Do you hear that?" Parker yells.

"What?" She's ten yards ahead of me and doesn't seem to be on the verge of puking up two beers and half a wine cooler, like some people.

"That's Katie." She speeds up *again,* and I stop for a split second to get my hair out of my face. Then I hear it, too—Katie, shrieking something. Henry shouts back, and their voices blend together like the most disturbing opera ever. We've got to be almost to the river, but I can't see a damn thing because Parker and the flashlight are too far ahead of me.

Katie's voice gets desperate. "You can't, you don't understand, Henry, listen to me, listen to me!" Then there's a clattering and clanging.

Then a scream that shuts my pulse down from a million to zero.

The scream cuts off.

Then Henry's the one screaming. Parker bolts again, and we both dash out of the woods. Straight ahead of us, the ground drops away to nothing, and it's just the drainpipe across the river, slick with rain, and Henry's crouched half-way across, yelling at the water.

Katie's nowhere.

"Oh my God, Henry, what did you do?" Parker leaps for the drainpipe, but her Barbie shoes slide straight off the metal. She shrieks, and I grab her arm before she can slip off the edge.

"You can't go out there, Parker, you'll fall!"

"But Katie—" She's wide-eyed and blanched.

"I'll go. Get your phone and call the cops. And don't let anybody else out here. It's way too dangerous."

"But Katie—"

"I'm going."

Then I'm running out onto the stupid drainpipe I never wanted to cross in the first place, and I swear my heart has dropped all the way into my feet. The metal's so slippery I can't believe I'm not falling, even in tennis shoes.

I finally get to Henry, and he's still crouching there in the middle of the river, his whole body shaking. "Oh my God, Cleves," he says, grabbing my hand and pulling us down to sit on the drainpipe. "She fell. She's—she—she was freaking out, and she was wearing those damn shoes, and—I couldn't get to her—"

I wrap my arms around his shoulders, thinking about the dumb drunk newspaper topic from an hour ago: *Time to bet on tonight's best story.*

"We have to do something," Henry's saying. "We have to— What if—"

"Parker's calling the cops."

He shakes his head and pulls away from me, struggling to his feet. "She can't—we have to—"

"We can't get down there, Henry. We shouldn't even be up here. Let's get across to the parking lot, okay?"

He nods. He looks like an actual ghost. Like you could poke him in the arm and your hand would go all the way through.

We head for the other side. We don't look down.

I've never been quite so thrilled to have solid ground under my feet. Or to see a bunch of terrible parking jobs with Lancaster-colored paint running down their windows in the rain.

Henry goes over to his car and half sits on the trunk. There's spray paint dripping all the way down to the fender, red and white smudging together.

"She's gone," he whispers.

I lean against the trunk next to him. He's right. I know he's right, no matter how much I don't want him to be, but there's no damn way I'm about to go down without a fight—even if I'm fighting against actual reality. "You don't know that."

"She's gone. Why the hell did she have to run out there?"

"She just wanted to tell you what happened. She—"

"I know what happened. She was cheating. She never loved me at all."

"Yes, she did. She *does*."

There's panic in his eyes. "I'm trying so hard, and it's all so fucked up, and now she's gone and—"

He buries his head in his hands. He's crying again, for real this time, and nothing I can say is going to make any of it better.

But I try anyway, because being hopelessly encouraging is the only thing left to do. "They're going to find her," I tell him. "It's going to be okay."

"I believed in her." He looks back up. "I *loved* her. I'm so fucking stupid."

"I'm not going to argue that last point," I say, and he tries to laugh, but it comes out sounding more like he's getting strangled.

The thing is, as much as I want to slap him for acting like it even matters what Katie did, I really just want to fix everything for him. He lost his mom and his brother and pretty much his dad, too, and then he almost got blown up. And now everything's falling apart again.

"She's gone. I hate this. I hate myself," Henry whispers into the dark.

"We don't know anything yet."

"It's so far, Cleves." He's breathing too fast. "She's dead. I swear to God, she's dead."

"Don't say that!"

"It's true." He drops to his knees next to the car.

"Henry, no, she's not." It feels more like a lie every time I say it.

"Everyone's going to say it was me."

"No, they're not. That thing is a death trap."

"They will." He looks up. "Because of Anna."

Somehow I want to laugh, which thankfully I manage not to do, because it would be wildly inappropriate and it's probably a whistling-in-the-graveyard shock reaction anyway. It's just— I don't know. Conspiracy theories, even about fatal explosions, are a blinding bright spot compared to freezing rain and Katie being dead. But I snap out of it in roughly two seconds, because—you know. Freezing rain and Katie being *dead*.

"Everybody knows the Tower wasn't your fault," I say.

"But they won't say it was her fault. Not the paper, and not the cops."

I sit down next to him. "Okay, but everybody's on your side. And tonight was an accident. And Katie's going to be okay."

He looks right into my eyes and says the dumbest thing possible. "I wish Jane never moved."

"Ugh, Jane Seymour."

He can't even smile. "If she didn't move, we'd still be together. None of this shit would've happened. Katie never would've died."

I don't say anything. He doesn't say anything else, either. But he takes my hand, and a little jolt of electricity binds us together, and it feels like it matters.

Like there's way more to us than fifteen days of awkward dating can explain.

So we sit in the mud and try not to think about the only thing there is to think about: Schrödinger's ex, completely fine and completely not fine at the exact same time.

I'm not sure how long we wait, but suddenly there are voices and flashlights, everybody else from the party, finally back from the bridge since nobody's about to cross the drainpipe anymore. Parker's the first one into the clearing. She's soaking wet and carrying her shoes, and there's a gash right over her collarbone.

I stand up. Then I hear a burst of static and I realize that, mixed in with Parker and Brandon and Eustace and everybody, there are two cops with their radios yammering in little blips.

Parker's makeup isn't just running because of the rain.

She sprints the rest of the way to where I'm standing, like

she doesn't even feel the gravel under her feet. There's mud halfway to her knees.

In my head I'm repeating *ugh Jane Seymour ugh Jane Seymour ugh Jane Seymour* because it's the stupidest thing I can think of. I have to think about something that doesn't matter, because I know exactly what Parker's about to say.

Katie's dead.

Number Six

Bad Times at Lancaster High

The cops found Katie a hundred yards downstream. She didn't drown, thank God, because everybody's a death expert all of a sudden, and they all say drowning's one of the worst ways to go. Which is fantastic information to have on hand.

It was quick. The river's shallow. She broke her neck. The cops say she didn't feel anything.

Pretty sure nobody believes them.

November sucks so much it's not worth talking about. I'm not going to act like it's about me, because I only knew Katie for a couple of months. She was my best friend in Lancaster except Henry, but it's not like we went way back. It's not fair to act like it's my personal tragedy.

But it really, really sucks.

Tom and Francis quit the team. Francis quits everything— he drops out of school and books a flight to Alaska to get a job on a fishing boat or a pipeline or something where you might make bank, but you'll probably die in some heinous winching incident that's essentially modern-day drawing and quartering. He doesn't say goodbye to anybody. Tom moves in with his brother, outside town, so he can go to York instead of Lancaster. He only says goodbye to Parker.

After that night in the woods, Parker never looks bad again. She looks better than ever, which I didn't even think was possible. And she and Katie have *actually* been friends forever, or at least since their middle school summers at the Howard-Boleyn lake house. But apparently excessive outfit-planning is the key to overcoming deathpression.

Or maybe she's just transferring the negative shit straight to the squad, because her captaining has gotten so abusive that everybody's calling her Tyrannosaurus Rochford. I run into her after practice one afternoon while I'm waiting for Henry, and the coach is yelling at her.

"Parker, I know you're upset, but you can't take it out on the girls."

"What the hell are you saying? That it's my fault?"

"No! You—are you even sleeping? Are you okay?"

"I'm fine!" She's fifty percent Miss America and fifty percent provoked pit bull. "I'm *winning*."

Then she storms off with literal daggers shooting out of her eyes.

So Parker has the approximate warmth of one of those cryogenically preserved billionaires, and Henry's always in a mood these days. And Katie's...you know.

Dead.

I spend a truly impressive amount of time alone.

Then, the Wednesday after Thanksgiving break—the worst Thanksgiving in Marck family history, because Dad couldn't come home and Mom was trying to outrun some journal article avalanche and Amelie decided she was vegan and boycotted everything turkey-related—I stop in the bathroom on my way to German class and hear this exact sentence:

"She'd still be alive if she didn't cheat."

I freeze right there in the doorway.

"Everybody says it wasn't the first time, either."

"It definitely wasn't *her* first time."

The two girls at the sinks—whom I've never talked to before, but I'm pretty sure they're juniors—crack up like that's the most original joke in comedy history.

"I heard she was the school slut at York." The first girl's leaning toward the mirror, layering up on mascara.

"Well, she was the school slut at Lancaster, too. In like two months." The second girl's texting. "That's a record."

"I can't believe she thought Henry wasn't going to find out."

"Seriously. How stupid can you be?"

I can't handle this. I slam into the bathroom, eyes blazing. "How stupid can *you* be if you think somebody deserves to die because they cheated? *Allegedly* cheated."

Mascara and Texter look at me. Mascara still has her makeup wand in front of her face. "I'm just saying it wouldn't have happened if she wasn't screwing three different guys. She wouldn't have been running after Henry, and she wouldn't have fallen."

Texter shrugs. "Karma's a bitch."

I'm so indescribably pissed that I can't even hear right. There's this high-pitched buzzing in my head, which I'm assuming is some evolutionary feature that's supposed to block out what they're saying so I don't rage-combust. I'm scrolling through my insult inventory, but nothing's even close to insulting enough.

So I glare at them for an awkwardly long moment, and then I turn around and walk out. I get two steps into the hallway before I turn around again and barge back into the bathroom. Mascara and Texter are exactly where I left them.

"You," I say as damningly as I can, "are a disgrace to the entire female gender."

They just sort of stare.

"That's all. The end. You suck."

I storm out again, and I keep on storming straight to class. Then I park my ass in my seat and hide my phone in my textbook and start typing the world's most vitriolic op-ed. About Katie. About Anna. About how much everybody sucks for their slut-shaming and their victim-blaming. About girls who can't say no and boys who share pictures nobody was supposed to see. About *whore* and *bitch* and *tease*.

I wrap it up ten minutes before the bell and don't even bother proofreading. I just scroll to the top and add my headline: ASKING FOR IT.

And then I send it straight to Cat.

Best Day Ever Continues to Improve

Of course Cat vetoes my article. It takes her exactly eight minutes to make this fantastic decision, and she emails me a very thoughtful response:

Not appropriate. —KP

And yes, her first initial is *K*, and she spells her nickname with a *C*. Contemplating this for the trillionth time is far more enraging than it should be.

I literally cannot deal with Ms. Parr today.

So I text her: what the hell.

No reply.

I text her again: WHAT THE HELL

Still nothing. So much for the power of caps lock.

Third try: THAT STORY NEEDS TO GO TO PRINT

The bell rings. It takes me a second to figure out what that even means, because I'm so zoned in on my own personal fury road that I didn't hear a single word all class. Which is fine, because I doubt I'm going to be using my shitty high school German during Potential Future Day Job #1984: Starting a Masked Brigade That Identifies, Captures, Tars, and Feathers High School Newspaper Editors Who Censor Everything That Actually Matters.

I stand up and text Cat one more time: WHY THE HELL DO YOU SPELL IT WITH A C

I mean, I'd be a negligent journalist if I didn't ask the probing questions.

Fortunately-slash-unfortunately, she can't avoid my warpath forever, because we've got newspaper after school—aka right now. Aka, it's going down.

So I resume my storming. I don't even stop in Hampton Court. I just head straight for the journalism room and fling the door open—

And there's Henry kissing Cat Parr.

No.

Clearly I'm hallucinating. Somebody's pumping drugs into the air vents. That's the only logical explanation for this splendidly vile scene.

Except they don't disappear or turn into purple kangaroos or whatever hallucinations are supposed to do. They just finish kissing, and then Henry says, "See you later, Cat. Hey, Cleves," and walks out like everything's normal.

Literally nothing is normal.

So now it's just me looking at Cat across a table of layout prints, and the phrase *catfight* does in fact cross my mind as I'm weighing whether or not it would desecrate Katie's memory to deck Ms. Parr right in the middle of the classroom.

"Hey," says Cat.

Fighting her would probably be a bad idea, because my unparalleled rage levels might result in me tearing her limb from limb, and I'm really not about Potential Future Day Job #24601: Life Without Parole.

"Did you talk to Hans about the cast portraits?" Cat asks. She's infuriatingly nonchalant.

I don't move. "Um. Yeah."

"Great. Could you start the outline?"

Okay, so just to be clear, (a) she still has kiss-spit on her mouth from making out with a dead girl's boyfriend four seconds after the funeral, which might not beat Jane Seymour's record but it's still Not Okay; (b) the last thing she did before said makeout was snub my texts; (c) she's STILL snubbing my texts; (d) she just shot down the most necessary article any *Ledger* writer has ever written; and (e) her name is spelled with a *K* but she spells her damn nickname with a *C*.

And (f), she's ignoring this laundry list of felonies like maybe I'll go gentle into that good night.

Breaking: No fucking way.

I look her in the eye and say, "You need to leave Henry alone."

"Excuse me?"

"I said, 'You need to leave Henry alone.'"

She blinks. "I don't think that's your business."

"He's my best friend. Somebody's got to look out for him, because he's still not over Katie." I say her name as meaningfully as I can.

"Katie's accident was terrible," Cat says. "But it's Henry's choice when he wants to start dating again."

"Wait, you're an actual couple?"

"Yes."

Somehow that makes it infinitely worse. "Are you KID-DING me?"

She gets out her laptop. "This is the last time we're having this conversation, because you're way out of your jurisdiction. But no, I'm not kidding—yes, I'm dating Henry—and no, I don't need his ex's input in how I manage my relationships."

The most fitting response I can think of is *Oh, no, she didn't.* "I'm not saying it as his ex. I'm saying it as his friend."

"But you did date, right?"

"For like five minutes!"

"A month, if I remember correctly," she says.

"It was two weeks, but I really appreciate your investment in my personal life."

"Likewise."

Damn her debate-club ways. "It was a mistake. Henry and I both agreed to pretend it never happened."

"That's not how relationships work."

"Come on! My relationship with Henry is BEING HIS BEST FRIEND."

"And my relationship with him is as his girlfriend, and as somebody with some distance," says Cat. "Somebody who's willing to help him through this without dredging up the past."

It's like she actually wants me to flip out. "Okay, what?"

"You won't let go of the Anna story."

People are coming into the classroom now, but I don't even care. "It's a *story*. I'm a *writer*."

"And now you're writing about Katie, too."

"Yeah, I am." I check in with the mini crowd behind me to make sure somebody's witnessing this. Eustace is front and center. "Because she's *dead*, and people are running around calling her a slut. That's not okay. We need to talk about it."

"We need to respect her family. It's not an appropriate topic."

"Okay, but silence is siding with the oppressor, right? We—"

"Cleveland." Cat squinches her eyebrows together like I'm giving her a migraine. "You need to separate your journalism from your social life. And you need to find a crusade that doesn't revolve around girls your ex used to date."

"You know it's not about that."

"Then what is it about? Because this conversation started with you attacking me for going out with Henry."

There's an audible gasp from the kids behind me, because of course they didn't have the privilege of walking in on the magic makeout moment, meaning Cat just broke her very own front-page headline.

"It's about defending the things that matter," I say. "We're the ones writing the paper."

She smiles. Yes, really. "And I'm the one running it. We're not dragging Katie's name through the mud, and that's final."

"It's not—"

"Cleveland," she says again. "This conversation is closed. I'm the editor-in-chief, and I'm with Henry. I suggest you get used to it."

She opens her laptop like, *checkmate*, and fine, okay, I should

217

definitely just let it go like the civilized semi-adult I'm supposed to be.

Or not.

"Godspeed," I say, smiling right back at her. "Just don't forget you're number six."

Hell Hath No Fury Like a Writer Scorned

I'd like to take this opportunity to personally thank Editor-in-Chief Cat "KP" Parr for being thoroughly extra enough to jolt me out of my post-Katie sadness quagmire.

Thank you, Cat. You're the worst.

Here's how it plays out: Mr. Lee comes out of his office and heads off to Kyrgyzstan or wherever, meaning Cat sets up shop in the office, meaning everybody else loses their goddamn minds.

"Social climbing. Social *climbing*," Eustace yells. "Pay up."

"I'm the one who called the breakup," says Christina.

"Yeah, but you said she'd end up with TJ Seymour. You can pay up, too."

I kick my feet onto the table, pull out my phone, and get to work. Not on anything for the *Ledger*, obviously, because the *Ledger* can kiss my inappropriate ass.

I'm starting a new paper. Just like Katie said I should five minutes before she died.

I pull up Tumblr and make a new account. A month ago I couldn't think of a name, but today I don't even hesitate.

The Dead Queens Club.

Yeah. Try forgetting that.

I snag *deadqueens* for my URL, because apparently God sees my torment and is cutting me some slack for once. And then I say, "Hey, Hans, do you still have everybody's court portraits? Last year's, too?"

He looks up from sorting Eustace's betting spoils. Half the pile is collector's-item TEAM LINA pins. "Yeah."

"Can you send me Katie's? And Anna's?"

"Anna...Boleyn?"

People are listening. Which is absolutely excellent, because I'm three formatting choices away from living my Overachiever Camp dreams. "Affirmative," I say. "Anna Boleyn. And Katie Howard."

"Interesting," says Eustace. "Ten bucks says whatever Cleveland's doing, Cat's going to yell at her about it before Christmas."

Christina shakes her head. "Sweet summer child. Cat's going to yell at her by Friday."

"Sent," Hans says.

One questionable editing job later, I've made myself a shitty banner with both of my dead queens grinning under their tiaras. And an ask box. And a submissions page, because this paper is for the people and by the people, in case you were wondering. And a tagline: *Always relevant. Rarely appropriate. Never censored.*

My ASKING FOR IT essay is ready to go before Cat even checks on us.

I hit *post*, and I get this rush that's equal parts nerd and revolutionary.

"Hey, Eustace." I grab a Sharpie off the table and scrounge up a dollar bill and write my *Dead Queens Club* URL across the back. "One dollar says we've escaped editorial standards forever."

Transatlantic Lecturing Proves Ineffective

Resistance organizers definitely don't wait around to hear what everybody says about their resistances. So I ditch the journalism room two seconds after I drop my pre-platinum debut.

I put on my obnoxiously large headphones and take my soundtrack in a much more old-school direction than usual, because all I want to hear is angry guitars and girls shouting. Then I walk seven hundred miles home and my hands freeze into blocks of ice, since I cut the fingers off my gloves in order to be able to type at cold outdoor events, which in retrospect was an incredibly unwise decision.

Or maybe it was an incredibly unwise decision for my parents to send me to Overachiever Camp instead of getting me a car, like any normal parents would do if they cared about my independence and also my hand-health instead of my intellectual stimulation. Thus rendering this situation their fault and not mine, so there.

It's dark when I get to Howard Heights. I don't even look at the guard, but either he recognizes me or he hears Joan Jett yelling all the way through my headphones, because he opens the gate anyway. I walk right down the center of the street feeling more badass and less shitty than I've felt in a very long time.

Somewhere out there, somebody's reading my very first *Dead Queens Club* post.

Secondhand redemption. Hell yeah.

I really want to kick the door in, cop-style, but I demonstrate my immense maturity by flinging it open instead and throwing my backpack across the floor, which is so slick that Katie and Amelie and I spent a full afternoon sock-skating on it before the furniture arrived and ruined our Olympic dreams. So my bag slides all the way to the other side of the foyer and hits an end table. The vase on it starts to fall, and I do a full-body dive to catch it before it hits the ground.

This is definitely my superhero transformation montage.

I get to my feet and put the vase back, and then Amelie's in front of me saying something.

I pull my hood back. "What?"

She yanks my headphones off and sighs like I'm history's greatest trial and tribulation. "Stop yelling. Mom wants to talk to you in the living room." Recently, Amelie's gone even gothier, so much so that all she's missing for the full deck is a couple of flying buttresses. Her current lipstick color is probably called either *Souls of the Undead* or *You Will Regret This Phase When Pictures Of It Show Up In Your Wedding Reception Slideshow*.

"Thank you, Princess of Darkness," I say.

"You're welcome, Princess of Chaos."

I head for the living room, which is more of a library even though there's an actual library on the second floor, because our family is disguising a hoarding problem by channeling it into the socially acceptable realm of book acquisition. Mom's in the beat-up fuzzy recliner better known as the Professor Chair, and it's non-reclined for the first time in history. Next to her, on a stack of books on the coffee table, there's a tablet propped up, and there's my dad in his apartment in Duisburg.

I pause at the top of the three stairs down to the living room. "Is this an intervention? Because this really feels like an intervention."

"Sit down, sweetie," Mom says.

"Thanks for the warning!" I yell over my shoulder at Amelie.

"Ignorance is bliss!" she yells back.

I hop the stairs and pull up a chair and say, "Isn't it, like, 3:00 a.m. in Germany?"

"Midnight. Ish," the digital Dad answers.

"For the record," I announce, "I'm not pregnant, suicidal, or participating in gang activity."

"We just—" Mom starts.

"For the record," I repeat. Nothing they say is going to faze me right now, so they can bring it on.

"We know you're upset about your friend," Dad says.

"Katie," I correct him.

"We know you're upset about Katie. And grief is a complex process."

"Was it the dissertation that uncovered that incredible insight, or the med school all-nighters?"

"Come on, let's try to have an adult conversation here," Mom says, and of course that's the second Dad's face freezes and the tablet makes some ominous blooping noises.

"Damn it." Mom flips the keyboard out and starts typing, and they IM for a minute while I visualize Henry and Cat kissing, just to keep my anger fresh.

God, I can't wait until *The Dead Queens Club* goes viral.

"Okay," says Mom, setting the tablet back on the table. "He says they're doing electrical work out on the street, and the WiFi's been fritzing out all evening."

"That's a very linguistically appropriate technology problem for the Fatherland."

"It doesn't mean we're not having this conversation."

"I don't even know what this conversation is."

She sighs, but there's a smirk in there somewhere. The serious-parental-confrontation gene never even got close to her section of the pool. "I know you're not over Katie, and that's fine. That's healthy. But you still need to think about next year at some point."

"Next year," I say grandly, trying to buy some time to decide what to tell her, but I draw a blank. So I just nod.

"Have you thought about any schools yet?"

"Obviously. I'm not going to join the circus."

"Good, because I've never even seen you land a cartwheel."

"That doesn't mean I wouldn't be a fantastic lion tamer."

"Right." She starts to recline the Professor Chair, but changes her mind and just tucks her feet up instead. She's wearing wool socks that are begging to be reunited with a pair of Birkenstocks. "But really, do you have a list?"

"Um," I say. "Harvard. Roll Tide."

She actually laughs at that, but then she points a finger at me, like, *I'm onto you.* "Not the same school. And you'd hate them both."

"I think I'd make a spectacular Skull and Bones pledge."

"As much as I'd love to see you become their first female initiate, that's Yale. God, I've failed you as an academic elitist. Anything else you'd like to pull out of your ass?"

"I'm waiting until *Playboy* comes out with their top ten schools for alcohol poisoning." I wait a beat. "Roll Tide."

"Listen, I know you don't like talking about it, and I don't care where you end up, as long as you're happy. But you're way more likely to be happy if you think about it now instead of waiting until June for whatever schools are still doing rolling admissions." And then she catches what she said and adds, "Roll Tide."

"Somewhere I can major in air crash investigation with a minor in lion taming."

Mom sighs. "You're smart. You know that. And you work hard when it's something you like. That's why we sent you to the summer program. We wanted you to explore your options."

I flop back in my chair, which is more painful than it sounds, given that it's a straight-backed mahogany monstrosity. "Ugh, Jane Seymour."

"Who?"

"Nobody. Never mind. I'm just fully occupied making sure Henry doesn't get mauled by another rogue girlfriend."

"Maybe you should back off a little."

"I can't. He needs a full-time bodyguard."

"Noble. God sent you to Lancaster to manage a teenage boy's love life?"

She's hardcore judging me, but whatever. She's never experienced Lancaster at trench-level. "God sent me—well, to keep him sane. And at least somewhat chill. And to get him the hell out of high school, so he can fast-forward to the part where he leads the masses into a new golden age."

"Too bad you're more invested in his future than yours."

"Ouch."

"I'm serious. I'm glad you're a good friend, but you've got to think about yourself here, too, and what you want to be doing in ten years."

I am emphatically Not About this conversation. "I don't even know what I want to be doing next weekend."

"Researching colleges," she says triumphantly. "Roll Tide."

"When I find a school that offers lion taming, you can't tell me I can't go there."

"I won't, because I'll be too busy saying I told you so."

"Noted." I stand up. "Is this intervention over?"

"Do you feel intervened upon?"

"Unbearably so."

She gets up, too, onto her plaintively Birkenstockless feet, and gives me a kiss on the forehead. "Just look out for yourself, okay? You're barely going to remember Henry in a few years. And I mean that as unpatronizingly as possible, I promise."

Local Basement Surprisingly Classy when Footballer~Free

It takes me two minutes of college searching—which I only attempt because it beats homework on Maslow's Hierarchy of Awful—before I break out in figurative hives. In those two minutes, I've searched "lion taming for the absolute beginner," "do you have to take math to be an air crash investigator," and "fiction programs that don't suck." That last item lands me on some interview where famous writers talk about how they studied underwater basket-weaving or pre-law or basically anything *other* than fiction.

College research is a boundlessly confusing bummer.

So I check *The Dead Queens Club* instead, and high-five myself for having a non-zero follower count and four submissions. I post one—Contributor: Girl Genius—and queue the rest, plus another of my many rejected op-eds.

I still feel future-bombed. But now I'm pissed again, too.

Which totally justifies grabbing a couple of books and yelling, "Mom! I'm going to Parker's to study."

"Roll Tide," she yells back.

I cut through our neighbor's lawn to the next street over. Mrs. Rochford, who was Miss Indiana like twenty years ago and is now the football team's unanimous MILF, answers the door. "Parker's in the gym," she says. "Tell her to keep an eye on the phrase endings."

When I open the door to the Jacuzzi room, the AC's blasting, and I kid you not, Parker Rochford is running on the treadmill while belting out something very dramatic. The sound system's playing a sweeping orchestra track.

"Keep an eye on the phrase endings!" I shout. Parker gives me a quick nod and practically knocks me over with a piercing high note.

She wraps it up in thirty seconds and slows down from rabid-wolves-are-on-my-heels pace to rabid-wolves-are-in-the-vicinity pace. "How were the phrase endings?"

"I wouldn't know what a phrase ending was if I tripped over one on the treadmill. Which is never going to happen, because the day you catch me on a treadmill is the day the world ends," I tell her. "But dude, you should be in chorus." My one and only encounter with the Lancaster High School chorus was at Katie's memorial assembly. They were so bad, Parker and I started cry-laughing and were politely asked to get a grip or leave.

She kills the music. "God, no."

"You're better than all of them put together."

"But then I'd have to be in *chorus*," she says, like she'd rather saw off her arm.

"And their lack of treadmills is a deal-breaker?"

"This," she tells me, doing a vague wave that seems to refer to her disturbingly perfect body, "is training. When you're nervous, your pulse speeds up. You can fake it with cardio."

"That sounds like literal torture."

"No pain, no gain."

"Remind me never to hire you as a life coach." I sit down on the edge of the Jacuzzi. "Speaking of which, my mom just did a college intervention."

"Where are you applying?"

"I could tell you, but then I'd have to kill you."

"Don't. We just ordered my new evening gown." Parker slows down a little more. "I applied to Indiana and Michigan and Illinois. Winter's totally booked, since I'm going to have cheerleading tryouts and voice auditions on top of my pageant schedule."

"I didn't even know you sang."

"Only at pageants. I have, like, talent-specific stage fright. For now." She stops the treadmill, finally, and starts a stretching routine that makes my muscles cry just watching her.

"So do you want to hear something hideous?" I ask.

"Obviously." She pulls one leg back in that archetypal cheerleader pose—you know, foot behind the ponytail, hands on the tennis shoe.

"Henry's got a new girlfriend."

She drops her foot. "No. Hell no."

"Told you it was hideous."

She pulls her other foot up. "Just a second. Symmetry." When she comes back down, she says, "Okay, who? And if you say he dug up some obscure Howard third cousin, I'm going to take this goddamn hairband out of my hair and asphyxiate myself."

"You're safe."

"It better not be one of my girls."

"Not unless Cat Parr is one of your girls."

"Oh my God. That bitch. I can't." She hops off the treadmill and grabs a towel. Her scar looks especially angry today, like it can't have been very long since she got it. But I'm absolutely not the type of person to go asking people rude questions about their bodies, so its origin story is going to remain a mystery.

Parker sits down on a yoga mat. "Cat effing Parr. I totally didn't see that coming."

"Right? She's not nearly Howardy enough to be his type." She squeezes her eyes shut.

"You okay?"

"I. Miss. Her. So. Much." She leaves a space after each word. "Why does everybody have to die? It's so stupid." But then she opens her eyes, and she's Miss Indiana's Outstanding Teen again. "What even *is* his type? Genius lacrosse queen. Ambitious business bitch. Boring hospital chick. Indie best friend. Sweetheart party girl." She counts off on her right hand and then brings her left up to finish: "And now the party-crashing newspaper boss."

"Can't even profile him."

HANNAH CAPIN

She wrinkles her nose. "I still can't believe you made the lineup."

I'm not sure whether that's an insult or a compliment. Honestly, it feels like both. "Hans helped me catfish him. By the time Henry realized it was me, it was too late to back out."

Breaking: Parker almost laughs. For basically the first time since End of the Road, not counting our memorial hysterics. "Stop it. You're pretty."

"I'm not going to sleep with you just because you said that."

"I'm so serious." She's pulling her shoes off. "You wouldn't be sitting with us if you weren't."

"Having superficial friends is the only way to make sure I'm still presentable."

"Having sarcastic friends is the only way to make sure I'm still superficial." She takes her hair down and combs one hand through it. "But I meant I can't believe you fell for him."

"Rookie mistake."

"Really, though? Cat Parr?"

"Cat Parr," I say. "I mean, even if you ignore that part where she practically started a brawl at your party, she's just—"

"Stuck-up and bitchy?"

"Funny, that's what people say about you."

She almost-laughs again. "Jealousy."

"Obviously."

"Whatever. She needs to watch her back." Parker stands up. "Hey, I've got to shower. But do you want to stay and work on the English homework after?"

I hold up my copy of this week's masterpiece. As of today,

we're supposed to be done reading *Othello*. I haven't even started.

"God. Nothing I'd rather do than read about murdered wives," she says.

"Spoiler alert. Damn, Rochford."

"You can thank me when you pass the quiz. And by the way, Desdemona was innocent. Put that on *Dead Queens*."

"You saw it?"

"I linked the entire squad," says Parker. "Desdemona. Post it."

"Are you making cheeky Shakespeare references?" I pull out my phone and type Parker's post. And byline it *Miss Indiana's Outstanding Tyrannosaurus*, because contributors can't be choosers. "God, what's happening to the world? What's happening to *you*?"

She flips the towel over her shoulder. "I could tell you, but then I'd have to kill you."

Sordid Past Haunts
Teenage Revolutionary

I guess at some point I have to suck it up and recap my brief term as Lancaster High School's first lady. Especially now that Cat's getting so much mileage out of it.

It started at *Overachiever Camp II: Electric Boogaloo*. Lina was dumped and Anna was Towered and Jane had passed over to a better place—aka Chicagoland—which was devastating only because Henry wouldn't shut up about the boring end of his boring five-week relationship with a girl so boring that looking at her picture for eight seconds cures clinical insomnia.

But he was mostly done with the Jane-mourning by the time I found out I was moving to Lancaster. So anyway, we were the only ones left on the roof after one of our poker nights, and he was playing guitar and I was watching some college kids play in the fountain across the street.

Then he stopped his chord-strumming and said out of absolutely nowhere, "Cromwell says we should go out."

My first instinct was to tell him that whoever the hell Cromwell was, he was a goddamn genius. Instead I took several deep breaths and said as casually as possible, "Who's Cromwell?"

"One of the Thomases."

Half the guys on the football team were named Thomas, so they all went by their last names or, you know, their first pet's name plus the street they grew up on. "Interesting," I said, and immediately wanted to kick myself in the face.

"Yeah," said Henry. He was totally hiding a smirk. Either this was the lead-up to a prank, or he agreed with Cromwell. "Because I talk about you so much. Everybody liked you when you visited. He thinks I need to get over Jane."

I was somewhat unenthused about being the rebound from the most boring girl in Indiana history, but Henry really *did* need to stop whining about her. So I said, "Amen to that."

He wrapped one arm around my shoulders. He was always doing shit like that, and I could never tell whether he was broing around or flirting with me. "What do you think?"

"You better write me songs."

"Already did. 'The Company,' remember?"

"You're a true romantic. How's that one go? 'I like to drink. I like to dance. I'll bike down a slide if I get a chance'?"

He picked the guitar up again and started playing. "'We party hard. We all play sports. Cleveland wears Ronald Reagan shorts.'"

I jumped up. "'Anna was awful. Jane was a bore. Time for girlfriend number four.'"

He stood up, too, without missing a note. "'Prom was the worst. I can't get a date. You're the girl I'll never hate.'"

He was standing so close, the guitar barely fit between us, and we were both laughing.

So I kissed him. It was actually perfect.

"Cromwell is a goddamn genius," he said.

Which totally sealed it.

We didn't make it official for another month, because I had to move and he had football death-hazing. But he asked me out for real the night before school started, and the next day I walked into Hampton Court on King Henry's arm.

And we all lived happily ever after, right?

Still not that kind of story.

I mean, I was happy. Embarrassingly happy, because we were friends, and I had my stupid crush, and he liked me, too. So on day two we went to the end of the maintenance road, because that's what you do in Lancaster. It was moderately creepy, since teenage-couple-making-out-in-the-woods is the opening of every slasher ever, but once we got a few minutes in, I definitely wasn't worrying about that anymore.

At least until Henry stopped kissing me and said, "Did you hear that?"

"Very funny."

"I'm serious." He untangled himself and peered into the dark. "I'm going to check it out."

"Do you *want* to be an urban legend?"

He pulled his shirt back on. "I'll be right back."

Which is every slasher character's final line. But he was already out, so I plastered my face against the window and waited for the chain-saw noises to start. I counted down from one hundred, and he still wasn't back, so I finally decided to text Parker. At least she could tell the FBI where to look for our bodies.

Then the other door banged open, and before I could even turn around, somebody was grabbing my arm and shoving their mouth onto my face. I screamed and went in for the palm-to-nose death punch, except I didn't have an angle, so I ended up punching the unsub in the eye and rebounding back into my own face.

"Cleves! Chill!"

It was Henry.

"What the hell?" I twisted around to face him and smacked my head against the window in the process.

Henry was rubbing his eye. "Okay, that didn't go how it was supposed to go."

"How the hell was it supposed to go? You know how many true crime shows I watch!"

"I thought you'd know it was me."

"I thought you were the damn Zodiac Killer! If you pulled that shit on Lina, she would've smashed your face in with a lacrosse stick."

He sat back against the door. "Lina liked it."

"Lina liked being attacked out of nowhere when there was supposedly something making weird noises in the woods?"

He blinked like he'd never noticed how batshit his make-out strategy sounded. "It was...exciting?"

"Sneaking onto the roof is exciting. Attacking your girl-friend when she's alone and creeped out is a good way to get maced."

He looked the slightest bit sheepish, and really, it was about damn time. "Sorry."

We both sat there listening to the crickets. After a minute, Henry brushed my hand and I almost screamed again.

"Sorry," he repeated. "I just thought we could pick back up where we left off."

"Dude. The mood is officially dead."

But by the time we got back to Howard Heights, we were both laughing so hard we were almost crying.

"I can't believe you punched me," said Henry.

"I can't believe you attacked me."

"I can't believe you didn't know it was me."

"I was expecting you to be classy."

He pulled into my driveway. Before I could reach for the door, he jumped out and ran around to my side of the car and opened it for me with this ridiculous bow. When I stepped out, he kissed me and said, "Good night, sweetheart," in falsetto.

He was still laughing when I got to my front door.

So it was all good until the next morning, when Parker yanked me aside as soon as I walked into Hampton Court. "What happened last night?" she whisper-shrieked.

"Um," I replied brilliantly. "It's quite the story."

She pulled me closer. "You went to the river, right?"

"Yeah."

"And what happened?"

She was a little overly invested. "Well, he kissed me, and then he said 'Good night, sweetheart.' Very swoony."

"That's all?"

Then Katie came up and started pulling us back over to the guys and everybody, which I was pretty sure was going to spare me from answering, but then Parker said over her shoulder, "So you're still—"

"Thrilled to be having this conversation, yes, totally!" I shouted, and ran straight to Henry.

Except that conversation turned out to be the beginning of the end.

For no reason. Obviously.

Parker kept grilling me, and I kept being as flippant as possible, and we had our football season opener, and Cat Parr was demonstrating how demanding she was going to be. So Henry and I barely saw each other except in Hampton Court.

And I felt like somehow, I'd fucked everything up. Like something was off, even though I couldn't figure out what it was.

But it didn't matter, because the morning after the first game, Parker texted me: He likes Katie.

I stared at the screen. Katie was actually in my room right then, because she'd gone a little overboard at the post-game party and some guy had been getting skeevy with her, and since Henry was busy yelling at Cromwell over a bad play, I'd peaced out and brought her home.

Parker texted me again: He thinks it's going to F up your friendship if you stay together.

So I wrote back: nice of him to tell me to my face??

Parker: If he says anything you need to go with it

Me: i can handle it

Parker: Remember Lina?

I sat there feeling shittier and shittier, partly because of Lina, and partly because what the hell? And then I said: fine. whatever he wants.

Because clearly the dating thing wasn't going to happen, and at least maybe this way we could still be friends.

So we broke up in an exceptionally amicable manner, and Henry took it out on Cromwell instead of me. It was stupid and frustrating and highly unrequited, but whatever, it could have been worse.

I mean, no, I wasn't actually over him. But I survived.

Unlike some people.

True Life: My Internet Persona
Is Cooler Than Me

By Thursday, as in one day after the kiss heard 'round the world, everybody in the galaxy knows Henry and Cat are an item. They walk in together. They sit at lunch together. And they make out in the doorway of the journalism room before our regular class block instead of just the after-school session.

While this last bit takes place, a sizable audience sits at the classroom tables and doesn't pretend to look away. I'm pretty much expecting applause when Henry finally detaches himself.

"Damn, Cat, moving on up," says Eustace when she walks by our table to get to her seat.

She has the decency to blush, which is surprising.

"Settle down," Mr. Lee says. "We're having a slight emergency in the yearbook arena—"

"Breaking," three of us cut in.

"Understood. But I've got to run to the vendor, and I'm leaving Ms. Parr in charge—"

Somebody does an obligatory wolf whistle.

Eustace grins. "Watch out. Henry's got a thing for guys who have a thing for his girlfriends."

Everybody *oohs*.

"Breaking," I say. "Useless Chapman reaches new levels of tastelessness; scientists determine he is genetically identical to the smallpox virus."

"Breaking: Cleves is just jealous that Henry wants a piece of the editor-in-chief instead of running back to her."

I'm very, very over Eustace at the moment. "Breaking: Cleves punches Useless; 'thank you,' sources say."

"Breaking: I'm leaving, and when I get back you comedians better have tomorrow's stories submitted." This last contribution is Mr. Lee, who's literally backing out the door.

We all stare at Cat.

"You know what to do," she says. "I'm available if you need input." Then she disappears into the office, which should really just have MS. PARR etched into the door at this point.

"So," Eustace says when the din gets loud enough that our table can have a semi-private conversation, "Cat's climbing. We know that. But why did Henry ask *her* out?"

"Blackmail," I tell him.

"Is that going on *Dead Queens*?"

"As soon as it's fact-checked."

Hans flips a page on his list. "It's weird, though. She's nothing like Katie."

"And she doesn't have sex-eyes like Anna," says Eustace.

"Or a once-in-a-generation triple threat of fashion exper-
tise, extreme hotness, and glamorous Ohio appeal," I add.

"Time out," says Christina. "You're overthinking it. Henry
can't keep it in his pants. It's that simple. He was going to ask
me out when Jane moved."

I side-eye her. "I'm going to need a source on that."

"Parker Rochford. She had that going-away party for Jane—"

"Rochford chased Jane out on purpose," says Eustace.

I give up on my *Ledger* op-ed and log into *Dead Queens*.
"Parker got Jane's dad a job in Illinois? That's a stretch, but okay."

"Jane was going to stay with one of her horseback-riding Girl
Scout buddies for senior year," he says. "But then all of a sudden,
she and Parker are best friends and bam, Jane's moving after all."

"Anyway," says Christina, "Parker dragged me into a corner
and said Henry was going to ask me out. She was flipping her
shit about how I had to say no, even though there was already
no way I'd say anything else. I mean, this was basically a month
after the Tower, and sorry, but I'm not fireproof enough for that."

Eustace literally ruffles her hair like he's her proud papa and
she just hit her first home run. Or said her first words, but only
if they were *I pledge allegiance to Team Lina and the gossip and
the glory forever, Amen.* "And that was *before* End of the Road."

"Careful," I say. "Murder insinuations are just as bad when
you throw them at Henry instead of Anna."

"Yeah, and they're just as fun, too."

"It's not about murder." Christina picks up a marker and writes
DONE across a copy of last week's *Ledger.* "Just tempting fate."

"Spoken like a true girl genius," I tell her. "Want to do as-
trology for *Dead Queens*?"

"Right, but there you go," she says. "You're calling it *The Dead Queens Club*. That's not really a club I want to join."

Eustace smacks one hand against the table. "Exactly. If I were Cat, I'd make damn sure I didn't cheat."

A new ask pops up in my inbox: if anna didn't blow up the tower who did?? parker???

I type the point: you missed it, then look back at Eustace. "Let's all cross our fingers that five hundred years from now, your glittering social commentary is the only remaining record of our generation."

"I don't see you complaining when I submit my glittering social commentary to your glittering social media site."

I swipe to my front page and point at the tagline. "Never censored. And besides, people like what you write. It's very Page Six."

"The whole thing is Page Six," says Christina. "People are talking. I don't know how much of that you're catching in your head-table bubble, but—"

"Holy Very Special Episode, Batman. Cliques are in the eye of the beholder."

"—*but*," Christina repeats, "everybody's reading *Dead Queens*."

"Good. That's the point."

"Somebody painted your URL on the away stands last night."

"Seriously?"

She holds up her phone. And there it is, in stencil-perfect black letters, right under Henry's *We rule this town*.

Which gives me the type of high I generally associate with skydiving, cocaine, and born-again jogging addicts. "Hell yeah. I've got a marketing department."

"Right, but some people are pissed."

"Good."

"My entire college fund says you're going to reevaluate when the principal sues you for cyberbullying," Eustace says.

"Or he'll just anon me to ask who smokes in the bathroom."

"Forget Dr. Farnese," says Christina. "There's no way Cat hasn't heard about *Dead Queens*. She's going to call you out eventually."

"Bring it on." I glance at the office. Objectively Cat's just sitting there typing, but at this point she could be feeding a homeless baby and I'd still be able to come up with a reason to rant about it. In my preferred interpretation, she's currently either swiping left on every single article anybody submits or picking out china patterns in preparation for the day she completes the ultimate social climbing coup and marries the president right after the first lady is fortuitously assassinated.

"Look," I tell Eustace, "as long as you're betting, go ahead and place all your money on me for the final Cat-Cleves match."

He laughs. "I'm going to spend most of it on front-row tickets."

"In that case, you can wire fifty grand into my offshore account. And in the meantime, I'm going to be getting the insider information we all want."

Hans looks up from Christina's old *Ledger*. It's now fully illustrated. "Which is…?"

I do my best game-show-host hand motion toward Ms. Parr's executive suite. "The reason my best friend is dating my nemesis."

Correspondent Baffles Literally Everyone with Her Shockingly Poor Decision-Making Skills

I walk home again, because in the eloquent words of Christina Milano, I am DONE. Done with Cat Parr, which I shouldn't even have to mention. Done with the *Ledger*, which I didn't even attempt to work on during class or the debate club scrimmage I was supposed to be covering after school—yes, there really is such a thing, and yes, it's just as electrifying as it sounds. Done with school itself, which is a stellar waste of everyone's time, other than as a means of producing new *Dead Queens* material.

Anyway, I walk home again, except I don't go home. That stupid Tower ask is bugging me, because even though the question itself is obviously bullshit, I'm still not any closer to solving *Anna Boleyn and the Mystery of the Exploding Scaf-*

fold. Or to accomplishing the recon I promised my three top contributors.

So I head past the park and across the railroad tracks, straight into the old downtown. I'm in Howard-Boleyn territory. Dead center.

No pun intended.

With all the Christmas lights up, the nostalgia-meets-new vibe is working just like it's supposed to. But the longer I wander, the more creeped out I get, because I'm seeing Anna everywhere. Big compass letters on the corner of Broadway and Main in the same font as her necklace. A bright yellow dress in a window display. A French flag outside the bakery.

It's a little trippy, given how (a) she's violently dead and (b) everybody decided she was a murderer and ran her parents out of town, which Norfolk Howard may or may not have seen as his luckiest dead-niece side effect ever.

I'm also damn cold, so I hang a left at the end of Main Street and hike up a set of wrought-iron steps built into Lancaster's one and only hill. Technically it might not even count as a hill, since it's really just the land remembering it's supposed to slope back up to the level it was before it dipped down for the Wabash River, but you know. It's northern Indiana. If it slopes, it's a hill, okay? We deserve it.

Shut up, Colorado. Nobody asked you.

The iron steps shortcut you up to another row of big old Victorian houses, and the house right at the top is the biggest and oldest and Victorianest on the block. Maybe in all of Lancaster, not counting Lina's house, which is several midsize countries out of everyone else's league.

This doesn't make Henry's house any less imposing, particularly in the dark when you're mildly to moderately suffocating after ascending the iron steps.

But I suck in some oxygen, straighten my metaphorical cuff links, and head up the driveway. There's a big formal front entrance—complete with stupid amounts of red and white roses, although at this time of year they're more like a garden of thorns—but I always use the kitchen door, since it feels less like I'm going to stumble into a *Wuthering Heights* reenactment.

Henry answers right away, because his room has this hidden back stairway that comes straight down into the kitchen. "Hey," he says. "Nobody's home."

He takes the stairs crooked, because he's got a bag of ice taped around the old bike-slide injury. There's a freakishly organized set of books laid out on his desk and the radio's on. He sits down in his desk chair, and I flop across the bed.

"So," he says. *"The Dead Queens Club."*

"So," I answer. "Cat Parr."

"Don't start."

"Fine. I'll just sit here." I stare him down somewhat vindictively.

Finally he kicks his foot up so it's propped up on the bed. "You need to leave her alone."

"She's my boss. I couldn't if I tried."

"Not that you're trying."

"So," I say again, "you talked to Jane lately?"

"Who?"

"Ha!" I sit up just enough to do a one-handed air-punch

like I'm the final freeze frame in every sports movie ever. "So much for true love."

"That's not fair. She's out of the picture."

"She moved to Chicago's Wonderbreadiest suburb. It's not like she's—"

"Don't say it."

"—on a trek across Antarctica."

He starts peeling off the plastic wrap that's holding the ice to his leg. "So?"

"Just… I didn't even know you liked Cat. And I thought she was talking to some guy at the college."

"TJ?"

Because naming Cat's former future love interest is what matters in this conversation, as opposed to actually answering my deep and important questions. "Sure," I say.

"He's studying abroad this semester. Belgium."

"How convenient for you."

Henry drops the ice. "Can you give me a break for once in my life?"

"I already did that when I agreed to go quietly, remember?"

He snorts. "Generous. You were so broken up about that breakup."

Which stings, because I actually kind of was. I just didn't broadcast it, because I'm the queen of decorum and self-control. "We could've had it all," I half sing. It's a terrible idea, since I never rehearse on a treadmill.

"Anyway, I do like her," he says, like he's talking about an ice cream flavor.

"Calm down. Your torrid passion is making me un-comfortable."

"What the hell has 'torrid passion' ever gotten me?"

He has a point. Madly-in-love Henry dumped Lina for Sex-Eyes Boleyn and dumped me for a girl who, guilty or not, probably wasn't the best choice for someone with chronic cheaterphobia. "Something to write in your application es-says?"

"Thank God for that. God, and my right to remain silent, so I can have a normal college life."

There's a stack of catalogs on his nightstand. The top one says PENN in big sporty letters, and the one under it is for Dartmouth. "Theoretically, it might be easier to have a nor-mal college life at a normal college."

He flips a page in one of the books on his desk. "Yeah, but you know me."

And of course I do: He's the guy who won the overachiever award at Overachiever Camp. So I just nod. The radio guy cuts in to say something in that velvety posh classical DJ voice about something being *fantastique*, which strikes me as a very Sex-Eyes Boleyn move.

"So. Cat Parr." This time Henry says it.

I roll over onto my stomach so I'm looking at him. "Cat Parr."

"What do you know about her?"

"Less than you do, hopefully. You're the one fused to her face every time I turn around."

"You're on the paper."

"Yeah, and Cat's all business. You want intel, ask Erin. Or, you know, ask Cat, since she's your girlfriend." I'm working pretty hard not to sound like a jealous bitter harpy, which is a challenge since I kind of feel like a jealous bitter harpy, if we're being honest. This is not only embarrassing, but also Not a Good Look. "What do you need to know, anyway?"

He puts his book down. "I don't know. I never really noticed her before, but lately she and Erin have been around a lot when I'm hanging out with Brandon, and the things she says—she's not afraid to say what she thinks."

"That wasn't a question. And it wasn't an answer, either. Not your best work."

He laughs. "You saw the way she handled Rochford at homecoming. I—she's intriguing."

"Gag me."

"Two minutes ago, you were getting me for not writing a sonnet. Now you're getting me for using adjectives."

"You're looking at the shit-stirrer-in-chief of Lancaster's latest publication sensation. If you think you're off the hit list just because we're car-theft colleagues, you're sadly mistaken."

"Wouldn't expect any less," he says. "Just watch out whose posts you let through. Some opinions don't need to go on blast."

"Sorry, I think you're confusing me with your girlfriend." I bat my eyelashes at him as obnoxiously as possible. "'Intriguing'? Seriously?"

"She's impressive. She had a letter to the editor printed in the *Indianapolis Star*, did you know that?"

"Must've been a slow news week."

Henry smirks. "You're jealous."

I throw the Penn book at his head, but he catches it and smooths the cover down.

"Jealous."

"Not jealous."

He sets the Penn book on his desk. "Jealous."

I grab the Dartmouth catalog and throw that one, too.

"Keep throwing things. You're still going to be jealous as hell that Cat has a byline."

I stick my tongue out. "Fine. I'm the smallest, tiniest, most infinitesimal amount of jealous—"

"Knew it."

"—but she's still just the blazer-happy editor-in-chief who aspires to a society more like the one in *Fahrenheit 451*. She's only intriguing because you have an uncontrollable—"

"Intellectual curiosity, which she shares?"

"So that's what they're calling it these days."

"You're so over the line." But he's laughing.

"Just wait until your wedding. I'll be the best man, whether by official appointment or because I got Brandon drunk and stole his tux and left him naked and alone in a port-a-potty—"

"There will be no port-a-potties at my wedding."

"—and I'll give the best best-man toast a best man has ever toasted, and by the end of it the only thing your, um, 'intellectual curiosity' is going to care about is how the hell you let this get away." I do a feast-your-eyes gesture, which works especially well since I'm sprawling on my stomach in a sweatshirt.

"Who says I let you get away?" he shoots back. "It seems more like I kept you around."

I roll back over and reach for the rest of the college books, but Henry's on his feet and knocking them out of the way before I can weaponize them. He flops down next to me, and I hit him. "Thanks for nothing."

"Anytime."

"I just hope Cat's good enough for you."

"You know I only date exceptional women."

"Present company excluded."

We laugh again, and the music swells. "Thanks, Cleves," he says, but suddenly he means it. He's not just being dumb about our two-week dating mistake and his rampant womanizing and our mutual commitment to pranking excellence.

"You're welcome."

"Really. You just—sometimes I wonder—"

He cuts himself off, and after a pause I turn to look at him. He's looking at me, too. So of course now I'm staring straight into his eyes, and it's like I'm right back at Overachiever Camp, one of those nights we talked for hours about everything. Nights when I could forget he had history's most perfect girlfriend waiting for him in Guatemala. When we were laughing for no reason, and I was getting distracted by how ridiculously blue his eyes were and how his face just *worked* so much better than anybody else's, and it was all the dumbest cliché but God, as much as I was sick of overachieving, when I was with him, I didn't ever want to go back to Cleveland.

"We could've had it all," I say again, not singing this time, and I can't tell if I'm being serious. I'm just hoping Henry will figure it out for me.

"Maybe we still can," he says.

I forget why I came over here in the first place. I forget everything that happened since August. I forget to breathe.

He leans in just a little bit, and we're already so close that that's all it takes. And then he's kissing me, and I'm kissing him back, and for a second all I can think is *why the hell did we break up*, and then I'm not thinking at all. My hoodie is off and so is his shirt, and he slides even closer and I almost fall off the bed. I shriek, and he laughs and grabs my shoulders so I won't fall. We're kissing again, and really it's way beyond kissing at this point. I start to pull my tank top off, and it catches in my hair, but Henry gets it free and then he's on top of me and I really can't understand why the hell we're still wearing pants. And I guess Henry agrees, because his lips are on my neck but his hands are unbuttoning my jeans and this is really happening—

And then the music goes *Psycho*-shrill, and it's like somebody dumped an ice bucket down my nonexistent shirt.

Holy shit, what am I doing?!

Henry has a girlfriend, and Katie's barely dead, and here I am literally unzipping his jeans because I'm the worst goddamn friend in the universe.

I jerk myself back, which mostly means smashing my head into the pillow, and I say, "No, Henry, stop," and he looks at me like I'm totally out of my mind, and my entire body agrees with him. I actually lean back up to kiss him again, but then the music does another angry twitch, and all I can think about is Katie shrieking *Henry, I can explain, I promise!* and dashing after him in that damn Tinkerbell dress.

"We can't," I gasp out, and finally my body stops staging a mutiny. I brace against the mattress and push myself back up so I'm halfway sitting.

Henry sits back, too, and says, "Why not?"

"Katie."

His eyes go dark, but still he says, "She's gone."

"Cat."

"You hate her."

"Oh my God, Henry." I try to hike my jeans back up. "This is *not* a revenge booty call."

He blinks, and then he says, "Holy fuck," and that's literally all it takes before I'm laughing so hard I can barely breathe. And so is he. We're straight-up losing it.

Then somebody yells, "Henry!" and one microsecond later, the door bangs open.

It's Henry's dad.

I die right then and there. The end.

Except no, I don't, because I'm still hearing everything. Which begins with Henry's dad going, "Jesus Christ, Henry, again?" like this is more of an everyday annoyance than a cataclysmic humiliation.

"Dad, what the hell, can't you knock?" Henry finally climbs all the way off of me and zips his pants, which you'd think would be an improvement, but it's actually the opposite since now I'm one hundred percent exposed while wearing just a bra that's only marginally functioning as a bra and jeans that still aren't pulled up past my fluorescent orange under- wear. And my Chucks. Hurrah.

"Not much of a point when you're this deep into things." His dad hasn't even looked at me.

"By the way, Dad," Henry says, "this is Annie Marck."

I swear he's never said my actual name before. And of course I've never met his dad, either, because he's practically a recluse, and let me tell you, this is not the meet-the-parents scene I had in mind.

Henry's dad shrugs. "No shortage of easy girls at that high school, is there?"

And then he finally looks at me. He looks me right in the eye, in fact, and true story: If I were wearing one of those medical alert heart monitors, the spike in my pulse would be bringing every ambulance in the county straight over.

"Excuse me?" I say, and yes, I'm pissed off. I sit up taller and cross my fingers that neither boob is popping out of my bra in the process.

He doesn't answer.

"You don't know a damn thing about me. And I bet you wouldn't ever call your son easy, even if you found him in here with a different girl every week."

Then I stand up and swipe a shirt off the floor and barge straight out the door and down the stairs, still in the unbuttoned jeans and crooked bra ensemble.

I may be the shittiest friend ever, but I am a goddamn fashion icon.

Lancaster Homeowners Lament Presence of Unchaperoned Teenage Pedestrians

I grab my jacket and my backpack off the kitchen table, and I'm all the way past several rooms of judgmental antique furniture and charging across the front porch when some man on the sidewalk with a poodle glances over and literally drops the leash.

Which makes the poodle look up, too.

So Poodlemaster and Poodle are both standing there with their mouths hanging open, and I yell, "WHAT?" Poodlemaster turns Crayola red and kicks into full-out speedwalking toward the end of the street.

"NICE TALKING TO YOU, TOO!" I shout. Something falls out of my armload of crap, and I snag it off the step.

Henry's shirt.

Oh. Right. I'm semi-topless. Semi-topless and verbally assaulting random passersby from the ex-mayor's front porch.

This does not appear to be my week.

I pull on the shirt, which is way too big and says LAN-CASTER BASKETBALL in gigantic letters, but it's also my only option since I'm definitely not going back inside to collect the correct clothing. Then I put on my jacket and my backpack and start running, because that seems like the kind of dramatic escape I should attempt if I want any shot at fending off the impending guilt.

It only takes me half a block to trip over a sidewalk tile. I fall all the way down. And then I stay right there on the concrete and marvel at my own astounding stupidity.

I just tried to sleep with Henry.

Ten seconds after Katie died.

When I've spent the past two days being truly insufferable about how he has a new girlfriend.

And *he has a new girlfriend.*

Go hard or go home.

If I don't yell about this ASAP, my brain is going to implode. So I call Parker, but she doesn't answer, because this is International Bad-Luck-For-Cleves Day. I text her: answer your phone!! Then I get up and head for home, which is eighty light-years away.

She texts back a minute later: Running, what happened?

Me: i kind of hooked up with henry

Parker: NOT FUNNY

Me: not kidding

Parker: WHAT THE HELL

So I call her again, but she still doesn't answer, because apparently she's actually running away from a pack of pissed-off bears, since that's the only valid reason I can think of for not answering right after this particular truth bomb.

Me: answer your phone!!!!

Parker: Please stop talking

Me: i feel like shit

Me: because of Katie

Me: because of cat

Me: WHAT IS WRONG WITH ME

Parker: Stop talking!!

Me: dude i know i messed up but you're being kind of awful tbh

Parker: NOT EVERYTHING IS ABOUT YOU

Me: wow, ok

I call her one more time. She declines it so fast it doesn't even ring.

Me: SERIOUSLY??

Parker: Don't talk about this EVER AGAIN

I'm about to throw my phone into the street and throw myself into a dumpster. I mean, yes, I'm a shitty person, and this entire sequence of events goes against my life philosophy of "try not to be a total dick." But that's the *point*. That's exactly what I was telling Parker when she decided to be a dick right back.

I turn right at the corner. It's freezing, and this damn walk is starting to feel like one of those penance sentences from the middle ages, or maybe just TV interpretations of the middle ages. Either way, I should count my blessings that I'm not naked or on fire. If this were the TV middle ages, things could definitely be worse.

This is not a very comforting internal monologue.

I'm at the park now, and of course it makes me think about Katie's turtle rescue, and of course that puts me over the edge, and if I could remember how I punched myself in the face that time I thought Henry was going to kill me, I would do so again right now with great enthusiasm.

But since I can't, I sit down on the sidewalk and get my phone back out. I pull up *Dead Queens* and start typing with the frozen remains of my thumbs: WALK OF SHAMELESS.

Slightly tricky topic, since I'm not excited about outing myself for out-Anna-ing Anna in the seducing-other-people's-boyfriends department. But then again, this isn't about that, because let's be real: I'm not the one in the relationship.

Live from the field, I type. *A certain correspondent who shall remain nameless just ran screaming from a botched hookup. Said correspondent is now traversing the streets of Lancaster in full Walk of Shame regalia.*

For the record, your faithful correspondent doesn't ascribe to the Walk of Shame concept. Hookups aren't a sin, and solo hikes home in somebody else's shirt aren't degrading. They're actually kind of empowering. Pairing up with your makeout buddy of choice is a good time. But sticking around for brunch? Not necessarily. When you've got places to go and deadlines to miss, booking it out the door exactly when you want to is a very healthy choice. Sorry not sorry.

I squint at my screen. This is the touchy part, since I have to make the jump without declassifying that one nagging detail of tonight's *Iliad*-level epic.

But here's the rub: Your shameless correspondent was about to seal the proverbial deal when the ghost of a certain dead queen haunted the hell out of me. Slamming doors, creepy music, the whole nine. Which was exactly when I hit the brakes and hightailed it out of there, because call me lame, but it felt totally wrong to be rolling right along with hookups and banter and Business As Usual when Katie's never going to get to do any of this again.

So that was my shame-factor right up until now. Shame on me, and everybody else who's just carrying on like normal. Hooking up and going to practice and whining about who gets her seat in Hampton Court.

It's not fair. She's supposed to be cheering for Lancaster for another year and a half, and helping turtles cross the road in perpetuity. She would've married an NFL quadrillionaire someday. She would've had two annoyingly perfect kids and sent care packages to death-row inmates and made everybody's lives suck less.

Instead she's dead, and it's like we already forgot about her.

My fingers are so cold, I can barely feel my screen, but I keep going. I don't even care if I get twelfth-degree frostbite and lose my fingertips. Plus then I won't have fingerprints, which will be helpful in any future crimes I commit.

We can't do that. She deserves better. She deserves to be remembered, and not just for her shitty death scene.

Here's the thing—and work with me, because I'm winging this, and I'm also so cold I can see some type of afterlife figure in the distance, and I can't even cross my fingers that it's Saint Peter and not whoever got the gig as Hell's bouncer, because my fingers are officially at icicle status.

Maybe hookups and cheerleading and basketball games are exactly what we're supposed to be doing. Not like forget-her-and-move-on, but more like seize-the-fucking-day. If you're reading this, you know Katie was the life of every damn party. She didn't let the past hold her back. She didn't let the future freak her out. She just LIVED.

When I sat down here on the sidewalk, I felt like shit for living like nothing was wrong when Katie's still figuring out how to rematerialize in Hampton Court. And I was going to write such a downer of a post that it might have even qualified for certain papers with slightly higher editorial standards. I was going to yell at us for having the goddamn audacity to act like normal high schoolers.

Fuck that. It's time to live. No more teen angst bullshit.

Tomorrow might be my day to join The Dead Queens Club.

Today I'm going to be shameless.

I hit *post* with great theatrical flair, and right at that exact second, a car honks two inches away. My resulting jump of terror launches me off my frozen ass and into orbit.

"Cleveland?" There's a car pulled up to the curb, and Erin Willoughby's leaning out the shotgun window. "Are you okay?"

I stand up, except my feet aren't totally with me on that decision, and I almost fall over in the process. "I, um. My ride bailed on me."

"Get in!"

"This is character building," I say, and then I shiver so hard I almost knock a tooth out. "I'm having a defining moment."

"You live in Howard Heights, right? That's barely out of the way."

Good enough for me. Although at this particular intersection of hypothermia and Zero Regrets, I'd probably jump into the back of a van to help Ted Bundy move a couch.

I slide into the back seat. "Thanks."

"Hey, no problem," says Erin.

Then the driver turns around and I can personally confirm to you that God is real, and not in the deist clockmaker sort of way. In the Zeus-actively-fucking-with-the-mortals sort of way. And also I'm an idiot, because besides Brandon, who else would Erin be riding around with?

"Glad to help," the driver says.

It's Cat Parr.

Alien Abduction Likely Cause of Students' Disappearance

I fake sick on Friday.

Although I'm not even sure it counts as faking, because the second my alarm goes off, I remember every single detail of yesterday and almost puke. I don't even have to pull out my acting skills to convince Mom I'm better off staying home. Which is good, because I have no acting skills.

Shameless or not, I can't face Henry. Or Parker. Or Cat, especially after yesterday's Telltale Heart carpool. I was *wearing Henry's shirt*. And I swear I thought Cat was going to (a) look away from the road long enough to inspect the back seat, even though she's an infuriatingly safe driver; (b) activate her night vision; (c) activate her X-ray vision; and (d) intuitively know that the reason I was wearing a Lancaster Basketball shirt under my jacket was because I'd been inconveniently shirtless during a mad rush out of Henry's bedroom.

Rational, I know.

So I fake sick. And I turn my phone off. And then I deep-clean my room, because compared to Henry, I live in literal squalor. And then I attempt *Othello*, but the first word is "Tush!" with the exclamation point and everything, which is far too much for my modern sensibilities, so I elect not to proceed.

Instead I embark on a marathon of that unsolved disappearances show, and at some point this strenuous effort knocks me out, I guess, because suddenly I'm jolting awake and somebody outside is honking nonstop.

This is generally considered a no-no in the highly curated world of Howard Heights.

After a minute the honking stops, and after another minute Mom knocks on my door and says, "Not to alarm you, but they're storming the Bastille."

"Who?"

She opens the door a couple of inches. "The very perfect one."

When I get outside, Parker's idling with her window open. The second I hit the pavement, she yells, "Cleveland! Where the hell have you been?"

I swing around to the passenger side and get in. "Sick."

"Bullshit." She shuts her window and hits the gas. "Why was your phone off?"

I turn it back on, and it blows up with six thousand missed calls and an equal number of texts that all say some variation of *Answer your phone!!!*

"My, how the tables have turned."

She doesn't laugh. She just guns it at the corner and hits the brakes five seconds later to wait for the gate to open.

"Is this a kidnapping?"

She doesn't answer. It feels like three in the morning, but according to the dashboard clock, it's nine o'clock at night.

"Look, I'm sorry about yesterday," I tell her.

"Don't talk about that," she says. Then she turns left at the clubhouse and takes off like we're trying to outrun a tornado.

"If it makes you feel better, I feel like shit and—"

"It would make me feel better if you'd stop talking about it!" She drives her foot into the accelerator. We catch up to the car ahead of us in two seconds, and it's a double yellow line, but Parker passes anyway.

"I said I'm sorry."

"Shut up!"

So I do for a minute, while we pass the dark fields so fast everything blurs into nothing. And then I say, "For the record, this is a really unenjoyable kidnapping experience. Zero stars. Would not be kidnapped here again."

She slams on the brakes and takes a ninety-degree turn off the road, and at first I think we're actually just driving into the middle of someone's trampled post-harvest corn, but it turns out there's a dirt lane leading off into the field.

"Um, not to be rude, Rochford, but what the hell are you—"

Before I can finish, she hits the brakes again, turns the car off, jumps out, and spins around in a full three-sixty. There's nothing to see except the occasional pickup truck flying by on the road half a mile behind us and a few farmhouse lights scattered out across the fields.

It crosses my mind that perhaps Parker is on something. Or about to murder me.

She slides back into the driver's seat and says, "Give me your phone."

"What?"

"This is your only chance."

I hold my phone out. She grabs it and turns it off. She turns hers off, too, and then she reaches out the door and puts both phones on the roof.

"What the hell, Parker?"

She slams the door and turns the car back on and turns the radio all the way up.

"WHAT THE HELL, PARKER?" I scream over the noise. It's not even music. It's a mattress commercial, and the entire population of Australia can hear it.

"Okay," she says. "This is the only time I'm going to say this, and if you ever say anything about it, I'll end you. That means no *Dead Queens*, too."

"I get it. Can we turn the radio down?"

She takes the volume down exactly one notch.

"I'm suing you when I need hearing aids at graduation."

She does her trademark one-hand-up stop-talking thing. "So last spring. Prom night. There was this after-party."

"Wait, this is about the Tower?"

"Will you let me tell this effing story? You're the one who brings it up every five minutes, okay? If you interrupt me one more time, we're done."

I nod in case "okay" counts as an interruption.

"You know what everything was like before Henry had that bike crash. You know how obsessed he was with Anna.'"

She turns the volume back to max. "But the day he came back to school, they had the worst fight. He was yelling that she was cheating, and she was yelling right back, and everybody loved it. Because everybody thought she was a whore for making him dump Lina."

So she's here to Other Woman–shame me. "I'm not trying to break them up. I—"

She shoots me a look so heated, my eyebrows singe. "Yeah, and thank you for agreeing that Anna was a whore."

"I didn't say that! I'm just saying Lina—"

"Can you shut up about Lina? You didn't even know her!"

I'm pretty sure my head is literally spinning, old-school cartoon style. This is the most confusing kidnapping-slash-ambush in the history of kidnapping-slash-ambushes. "I thought you liked her!"

"Of course I liked her. Everybody liked her. She was everything you could want from the most popular girl in school, okay? Not that anybody will let me forget that. It's not my fault I don't spend my summers saving the world."

The radio is finally through the commercials, but now we're on a remix with bass so heavy my teeth are vibrating. "Dude. I don't know where you're going with this, but—"

"Stop *talking*," Parker practically snarls. "The point is, that week sucked. And Henry wouldn't stop interrogating me. His friends were all ganging up on Anna, and that effing hospital girl was in the middle of it."

"Wait, who?"

"Jane Seymour."

I almost lose it, even though I know this is Extremely Serious. But the harder I try not to laugh, the harder it is not to laugh, and four seconds later, I'm fully choking on my own suppressed inappropriateness.

"Okay, what the hell is funny right now?"

I choke for another few seconds and then I go, "Um. Nothing."

Parker looks at me like I'm the actual worst person on the face of the earth. *"As I was saying,"* she huffs, "I was just trying to not piss anybody off. But Anna kept talking shit. It was all stupid, like, 'Henry cried when Lina left,' or 'Henry sucks in bed.' And of course I wasn't telling Henry, but I told George, because I had to tell somebody, okay? And George can't keep his mouth shut, either, and the next thing you know Henry grabs me out of French class and he's grilling me like it's life or death."

She stops for a breath. It's too bad my phone is on the roof, because I'd kind of like to send a surreptitious mass text with our latitude-longitude coordinates.

"So," I finally say. "That's exactly what Henry told me six months ago. Except that your version is pro-Anna."

She does her eye-dagger thing.

"I'm not saying I think she wanted to kill him. Chill."

More eye-daggers.

So I circle back to the facts, which is the cubbiest of reporter tricks, but whatever. "Henry thought she was cheating. She said she wasn't. The Tower blew up. I know the story."

269

"No, you don't." She gets out of the car again and stands there staring at a bunch of dead cornstalks and breathing super deliberately. I could make a run for it, but we all know how well I measure up to Miss Indiana's Outstanding Teen Cardio Expert.

Parker gets back in and turns the heat on full blast. "That was the first week," she says. "By the second week, Anna was the one on the brink. Freaking out about Jane and screaming at Henry for being such a hypocrite. When Anna's pissed, it's like, get out of the way."

Her dead-girl present-tense is creeping me out. "You're kind of setting her up to be the villain," I say. "Just FYI."

Parker flinches. "Stop it. If you were on her bad side, you were screwed. But if she liked you, she was the best."

"Yeah, and that's why the first thing you ever did was tell me about her disdain-face."

"Because when she came back from France she made us all feel like stupid hicks, okay? She came to the homecoming game in all black. Like she was too effing Parisian to wear Lancaster colors. Like we were so lame for caring about football."

Frankly, when I'm kidnapped against my will, I prefer not to get blamed for the social dynamics of an institution I didn't even go to during the year in question. "I mean," I say, "not everybody lives and dies for high school athletics."

"Oh my God." She glances at the radio like she might be about to turn it down, but then she looks back at me. "I'm just saying, she made me feel like shit sometimes, and yeah, I care what people think. We can't all be everybody's favorite quirky girl."

"I'm not—"

"Look at you! What are you even wearing? Are those rockets on your pants?"

Wardrobe-based verbal assault is also something that seems like it could happen by text, or at lunch, or really anywhere other than top-secret cornfield conventions. "They're pajamas. From the boys' section."

"Yeah, well, if I put on some effing rocket pants, I'd be out of the game in ten seconds. Being popular is work, okay? So when somebody comes in and makes you feel like your version of cool is never going to be as cool as theirs, it sucks. But that doesn't mean we weren't friends. She trusted me. And she was trying to get rid of Jane—"

"Like, cement shoes and sleeping with the fishes?"

Parker blinks. "I literally have no idea what you're talking about."

"'Get rid of her' sounds like murder."

"You *know* that's not what I meant," she says. "Not *kill* her. Make her look bad. We started a rumor about how Jane was hitting on Henry at the hospital, and how she was only volunteering so she could get the hot doctors to give her references for nursing school—"

"Sounds legit."

"—and when none of the hot doctors noticed her—which hello, why would they?—she went for the most popular guy in school."

"That does make her seem a little schemey."

"She *is* a little schemey." Parker shrugs. "But Henry figured out it was us. He cornered me in the hall again, and I
thought I was going to be, like, excommunicated, but he was
really chill. Like, laughing it off. And then he started talking about the party."

"You mean Anna's party?"

"Okay, see, this is why you need to stop listening to your
dickhead of a best friend."

The radio slams into an unbearably stupid love song. I want
to throw the radio, the singer, and the object of his affection
into the field and run over them. "I didn't say—"

"The party wasn't her idea. Like, we'd talked about roman
golf at the Tower, but that was before the bike crash. And it
didn't make sense anymore, because it was totally obvious he
and Anna were over."

She stops and takes a drink from a bottle of Coke Zero,
which is somehow the most bizarre thing she's done all night.
Very mid-speech politician.

"Anyway," she says, "one second he's like 'I know she's
cheating,' and the next second he's like, 'You have to get Anna
to throw that party.'"

I'm pretty sure Parker's trying to convince me that Anna's
not a backfiring attempted murderess, but her approach leaves a
lot to be desired. I mean, I entered into this kidnapping thinking prom was just a case of win-him-back gone stupendously
wrong, but the more Parker hypes up the feud, the more I can
almost see Anna going full Tarantino.

Not in the murdering Henry sense. More the blow-up-the-
Tower-to-teach-him-not-to-trifle-with-her sense.

"So I told Anna, and she loved it, because she was still obsessed with him. But I felt like she was walking into a trap, so I was like, 'It was Henry's idea, maybe he's going to dump you in front of everybody or something,' you know? But she was like, whatever."

Parker's checking every damn box in the establish-Anna-as-the-prime-suspect column. We've got motive. We've got the misguided friend unwittingly encouraging the crime. And of course we've already got the proof that she's the one who set up the stockpile.

This looks Very Bad.

And as much as I love a killer story, I do *not* love the idea that some girl I shared a bottle of liqueur with—and may have given an accidental pump-up speech to right before trigger time—went full domestic terrorist.

Over a boy.

"Anyway," Parker's saying, "the next time Henry talked to me, he wouldn't shut up about that band kid who wrote the poems. Mark Smeaton. And finally I was like, fine, yeah, she flirts with him, but that's just Anna."

She shoots me a pointed look. "He punched a locker so hard he left a dent in it."

"Well, yeah. He hates cheaters."

"She didn't *cheat*, okay? But he calms right back down and then he's back to talking about the stupid after-party. And he gets all nostalgic, like he really thought he was going to get the past back. Hello. No."

She shivers, even though the heat's still blasting. "You know what happened next."

I really hope she's not saying what it sounds like she's saying. "The fireworks?"

She nods.

Damn it.

This is really not the headline I was hoping to throw onto *Dead Queens*. Which may need to be retitled *Dead Queens, one of whom killed her brother while intentionally blowing up a building in an attempt to maim her boyfriend.*

And also, no wonder Parker's flipping out. She thinks she's an accomplice to her boyfriend's public execution.

"Dude, it's not like you were supposed to know Anna was going to do it," I say.

"It wasn't her fault!" Parker shrieks.

"It... What?"

"She didn't kill anybody!"

Apparently the two of us speak very different dialects of Midwestern English, because in my language, Parker definitely just framed Anna. "She put the fireworks under the Tower, and she knew Henry was going to dump her, and she knew you guys were playing roman golf. I mean, I don't think she meant to kill people, but she meant to blow up the Tower. You just *said* that."

"She didn't do it!" Parker starts counting on her fingers. "Henry wanted to have the after-party. Henry thought it should be at the Tower. Henry started talking about roman golf. Henry set the entire thing up, don't you get it?"

I absolutely don't. Because (a) it's fucking ridiculous, (b) she literally just set up an open-and-shut case, and (c) is she actually trying to frame Henry for MURDER when everything points straight at Anna?

Which brings us back to *it's fucking ridiculous.*

"Parker. Anna did it. You just pretty much convinced me, and I've written a million op-eds about how she didn't."

"Are you even listening?" The fact that she has to scream this over the radio doesn't faze her. "How was it her if he's the one who set it up?"

"He set up a party. She set up an explosion."

"She didn't do it!"

"You told the cops she did!"

She glances out her window like she legit expects somebody to be out there listening in. "I told them what I had to tell them."

"That Anna did it?"

"That I agreed with Henry's story."

"Which was that Anna did it."

"Oh my God, I lied, okay? I had to." Parker closes her eyes for a second. "It was awful. It was so awful, Cleves. They're climbing up the Tower—Henry didn't go that high, but Anna and George were all the way at the top. And then the fireworks went off, and Henry jumped, and then one side of the scaffolding caved in and—"

She's crying now. "George—I just started screaming, okay? I was sitting on the back of the car, and Anna and George were making fun of me because I wouldn't go up. And then when it happened, I went running in like I was going to save him. And something fell and knocked me down, and it felt like my whole back was on fire and I don't know what happened, but I guess Henry got me out, and then he told me he was so sorry about what Anna did."

"He *saved* you."

"Bullshit," she says. "I was freaking out, like, what do you mean, and he said she must've set up the fireworks, and I kept saying no. She was a bitch sometimes, but she was a good person. And Henry kept saying, 'You're confused. You're in shock.'"

"I mean, you probably were."

"That doesn't change the facts, okay? So I kept telling him no, I knew what happened. And then he put his hand on my back right where I got burned and he said, 'Parker, it was Anna's fault,' and it hurt so bad I started to black out. And then the fire department got there."

I sit back and stare at the mangled cornstalks. Which are a really excellent visual representation of my brain right now, by the way.

"It wasn't Anna's fault," she says. Like she's begging me to believe her.

I turn toward her again. "But it wasn't an accident."

She shakes her head.

"You can't think Henry did it."

She looks right at me with her hand hovering next to her cheek, shaking so bad it looks like she's about to poke her eye out with her acrylics. "Please, Cleves, just trust me."

"He didn't do it."

"He *threatened* me."

"Wait, what? How did he—"

"Okay, I know you're in love with him or whatever, but

what else do you think he meant when he put his hand on my third-degree burn and blamed Anna when we both knew it was his fault?"

When you put it that way, it does sound pretty incriminating. On the other hand, everything she was saying two minutes ago made it sound like Anna was a closet pyromaniac. Which just goes to say that the entire Anna Boleyn story can be whatever the storyteller wants it to be, for better or for worse.

"Parker, I really don't think he meant it like—"

"You don't have to blame anybody if you're innocent!"

I hit the power button on the radio and the silence slaps us in the face.

"Listen," I say. "There's got to be a logical explanation."

"Yeah. Henry lost it, and two people ended up dead, and five months later, he came back for round two."

We've now advanced from unbelievable to unbelievably unbelievable. "You're not saying Katie—"

"You seriously think it's a coincidence?"

My ears are still ringing. "End of the Road was an accident. You almost fell, too."

"But you caught me. Henry didn't catch Katie."

"Maybe he was ten feet away."

"Or maybe he pushed her." She reaches for the radio again but I grab her hand. "I'm turning it back on!" she shrieks. "You never know who's listening, okay? He's watching me. And you're done if you get back with him."

And suddenly it makes sense—well, that's being way too generous, because her actual theory doesn't make any sense at all. But last night's freakout and tonight's borderline nervous breakdown do fit together, if you play fast and loose with reality.

She's trying to save me from a guy who, in Tyrannosaurus Rochford's twisted parallel universe, is a ladykiller in a very literal sense.

Batshit, but heroic.

I unbuckle my seat belt, which is still on because personally I think I'm more likely to die in a car crash than get ex-murdered, and lean over to hug Parker.

Her nails stab me through my sweatshirt. "I knew," she says. "About Katie and Tom. I didn't—"

"Stop. It's not your fault."

The nail-stabbing intensifies. "Don't get back with him."

"I won't. But also, let's get to the bottom of this," I say directly into her hair.

"What?"

I sit back. "I mean, maybe we can go all Sherlock Holmes and figure out what happened. Like I was trying to do before End of the Road and Cat and the general Lancaster disaster."

"I *know* what happened."

"Yeah, and I respectfully disagree on the details. But either way, let's prove it."

She reaches across me to get a tissue out of the glovebox. Then she grabs her purse and fixes her face, and thirty seconds later, she looks better than I did in my damn homecoming makeup.

"I'm in," she says.

"Can you drive?"

"Oh my God. My car. My driver's seat. My driving."

I'm tempted to high-five her just for that garden-variety Exclusives jab, because praise Jesus: Parker is back. "Then get us out of this cornfield," I tell her as I climb out and rescue our phones from the roof.

"Hell yeah," she says. "Where are we going?"

I slam the door. "To talk to Lina Aragón."

College or Exile?
Reports Remain Unclear

W e're in South Bend by midnight, and when we finally pass a big UNIVERSITY OF NOTRE DAME sign, Parker laughs. An actual laugh, unlike everything else she's managed so far, including when I called my mom and gave her history's least believable cover story, which started with a cheerleading competition and ended with something about lion taming.

"What's so funny?"

She shakes her head. "Anna. After she went to France, she started pronouncing Notre Dame the French way, like, 'No-treh Dahm.' George would, like, go out of the way to get her to say it." She slows down to let a herd of coeds jaywalk in front of us. "Where am I going?"

I glance at my phone. "Assuming your lacrosse informant

gave you the right address and the map is right and I'm reading it right, that's her dorm." I point across a quad.

Parker pulls into a visitor spot and we get out and cut across
the grass. "Lina Aragón," she says. "God, they probably already named the library after her."

We stop in front of Lina's building, and Parker looks at me.
"What are we going to say?"

A couple of girls crash out of the dorm into the cold, and I
grab the door before it can lock behind them. Breaking and
entering made easy. "You know," I say, but I can't think of
any bullshit, so I just shrug. "Yeah."

"Great plan." She nods toward the stairs. "Lina's on the
third floor."

We hang out in the lounge fake-texting until somebody
comes down the stairs, and then we do the same grab-the-
door-before-it-shuts thing. When we get to Lina's floor, somebody's propped the door open with a flip-flop, and a few yards
later we're in front of a door with name tags for Catalina and
Kim. And also an extremely over-the-top calligraphy sign that
says *Catalina Trastámara Aragón-Castilla*, which looks less like
it belongs in a college dorm and more like it belongs outside
the office of a benevolent but terrifyingly badass queen. And
also like ten sports-y bumper stickers, various Lina-fan Post-it
notes, an actual mini crown hanging from the doorknob, and a
whiteboard with several hundred Lina-kicks-ass type messages.

I'm assuming we're in the right place.

We stand there looking at the door until a girl from the
next room comes out and gives us a weird look on her way to

the water fountain. Down the hall, somebody's yelling about football in a very passionate tone.

"Now what?" Parker asks me.

"I'm brainstorming."

We stand there until the girl comes past again with an armload of filled-up bottles, like she's prepping for the End Times, and she says, "Are you guys lost?"

"Um," I answer.

"We're looking for Lina," Parker says with a flash of ultra-white teeth.

"Oh." She reaches for the door. "Hey, Li—"

"Shh!" Parker grabs her hand before she can knock. "It's a surprise."

Doomsday Prep looks at us like we're the weird ones. "Whatever," she says, and disappears into her room.

So I knock instead.

The door opens, and there's Lina, looking more intimidatingly regal than ever, if that's even possible. It would feel one hundred percent on-brand if all the doors on the hall came flying open and a full band started playing the National Anthem. I have to actively resist the urge to curtsy.

In other words, just what I was expecting, given whose room this is.

Except Lancaster Lina hugged me the first time we met, despite the fact that the star-power differential of that moment was approximately equal to when Beyoncé takes a selfie with anyone other than Beyoncé. Notre Dame Lina isn't even going for a handshake.

The pause drags out, and finally I say, "Surprise!"

"What are you doing here?" Lina asks. Which, granted, Beyoncé would probably have a similar reaction if we showed up on her doorstep at midnight without even texting. But still.

"We're investigating," I announce, because at this point it couldn't get any weirder.

Except it could, because Lina looks at me like I'm several suits short of a full deck. "We?"

I turn around, and Parker's flat against the wall. "What the hell?" I hiss, and then I remember the whole Catholic school thing and say, "I mean heck." Parker gives me dagger-eyes again and smooths her hair down before she joins me at the door.

Lina goes straight from not-feeling-this to really-not-feeling-this.

"Parker, what the hell?" she says, which clears up the H-word issue.

"Hi, Lina," says Parker. Brightly, but also somewhat nauseously.

Lina just stares. It's a very threatening stare, and this is coming from someone who's had months of acclimating to Parker's eye-daggers.

"So," I say with what I hope is a diplomatic smile, "can we come in?"

Lina keeps staring at Parker, who seriously should have given me a heads-up. I mean, I knew things weren't awesome between them, but I didn't know I was going to have to play mediator as well as investigator, neither of which I'm at all qualified to do.

Finally she steps back and opens the door the rest of the way.

Her room is reverse-hoarder neat. Besides two laptops and two stacks of books—one on each desk—the only sign that humans actually live here are a lacrosse team picture, a world map, and a crucifix. Which is especially disappointing, since based on the door-décor alone, I was expecting a shelf full of trophies and a monogrammed throne.

Apparently the only design style Lina and Invisible Kim could agree on was Bleak Chic.

Parker sits right down at one desk and says, "Katie Howard is dead."

So much for small talk.

"I know," Lina says, and she sits down on her bed. This might sound like an unremarkable thing to do, but the way she does it, it isn't. Even in leggings and a lacrosse T-shirt, she has this chart-topping poise factor that makes everything she does feel important. And also deliberate, like all of this is a chess game and she's definitely going to win.

"Henry killed her."

Lina literally doesn't react. Not even an eyelash flicker.

"Hello!" says Parker. "Did you hear me?"

"Yes."

Parker tosses her hair. "So what are you going to say about it?"

Still nothing.

"I can't believe this." Parker tips her chair back and looks up at the ceiling. "You *have* to get a lamp. This fluorescent thing is gross."

I should probably be brainstorming, but I'm just watching Lina watch Parker, and I swear Lina's an entirely different per-

son from the girl I remember. A year ago, she was the definition of warm and welcoming, ass-kicking tendencies and
all. Now she's icing us out so hard, even an unholy alliance
between Cat and Parker couldn't compete.

And if her door-décor means anything, it's pretty clear she's
still the well-beloved queen as far as the rest of the population is concerned. So this is definitely personal.

"Are you mad at us?" I blurt out.

She finally stops staring at Parker. "No."

"Then what the hell is going on?" I ask, because that's the
type of unbiased, productive question six years of journalism
classes have taught me to ask.

"Nothing."

"Come on, Aragón, we can all see *that's* a lie," says Parker.

"Maybe you'd like to explain it," Lina fires back.

"How am I supposed to know why you're hiding in a tragic
dorm room on a Friday night being a bitch to the people who
drove eighty-five miles to see you?"

"I have practice in the morning and finals next week, and
now I'm reliving the worst part of high school, and you expect me to be happy about it?"

Parker executes the most impressive eye-roll I've ever seen.
"You got dumped. My boyfriend *died*."

Lina picks up a rosary from the table by her bed. It reads
like another power move, because nothing says Queen Lina
quite like a subtle reminder that she totally has God on her
team. "I won't pretend to understand what that's been like.
But last year wasn't just a breakup for me."

"Because your ex turned out to be a murderer? Congratulations. That's why my boyfriend is *dead*."

"Because Henry put me through hell. And I actually loved him."

"Congratulations," Parker says again. "I loved George."

Lina gives Parker another long look. Then she stands up and walks over to the mini fridge. When she opens it, all that's inside is a jar of pomegranate seeds and a couple of ice packs.

The more I experience Lina's personal dungeon, the more I'm getting pumped up for college. Prison camp furniture and transformative coldness? Sign me up.

After a long moment of communing with the refrigerator, Lina shuts it again and goes back to the bed. She still hasn't put the rosary down.

"So are you always this much of a bitch now, or just on weekends?" Parker asks.

Lina ignores her. "I didn't just lose a relationship. I lost someone I'd loved for two years. I trusted him. We shared everything. And then he ruined all of it. He was cruel, and so was she."

"Come on. Everybody hated Anna."

"That didn't change anything. You know how humiliating it was? To have Henry flaunt her in my face like that?"

"You could've dumped him yourself," says Parker.

Lina glares again. "I thought he'd move on. He always did before."

"Wait, what?" I ask, with great journalistic gravitas.

Parker smirks. "Guess Henry forgot to tell you Anna wasn't

his first side piece. There was Liz Blount, and then Mary Boleyn, and—"

"Please tell me that last name is a coincidence."

"Anna's sister."

I'm still standing next to the door, which is great, because if I were by the window instead, I'd probably jump out. "Nice try. If there's another Boleyn kid, how come I've never met her? Check and mate."

Lina looks profoundly unamused by my sparkling wit. Parker, however, looks straight-up gleeful. "Mary's two years older."

"Bullshit."

"She's at IU now."

"Bullshit."

"Oh my God. You've seen her picture." Parker gets her phone out and starts scrolling lightning-fast, then waves the screen at me two seconds later. "Lake Max. Mary and Anna and George and me."

I don't look. "When did it even happen?"

"Five seconds after Henry got back from your first summer thing."

I aggressively don't want this to be true, because those were the days of uncheesy guitar love songs and Henry Plus Lina Equals Power Couple Forever, and if that was the backdrop for serial cheating, I'm about to get a lot more cynical about the whole concept of relationships. So I just say, "Bullshit." Yes, again.

"Truth," says Parker.

"Bullshit. Bullshit. Bull—"

"Cleveland." Lina cuts me off. "Stop. It happened."

This is ten times more concerning than Parker's murder theory. "He cheated before Anna? For real?"

Parker nods. "Totally. Lina was for the image. Those other girls were for the action."

"Holy shit," I say. "Could you maybe not be quite so ragingly mean about—"

"It wasn't like that," says Lina, because of course she doesn't need backup. "He loved me."

I literally can't believe any of this. "He cheated, and you just let it go? Like those senators' wives who stand there during press meetings in pearls and on Xanax?"

"Exactly," Parker says.

I sit right down on the industrial carpet. "What the fuck. You're Lina Aragón. You're a goddamn queen. You bathe in the blood of your enemies. You don't stand there and take it."

Lina sets her jaw. "I happen to believe that forgiveness is a real and valid thing, and I wasn't going to throw everything away because some girl with no standards was willing to give it up for a guy in a committed relationship."

Parker glances at me like *are you really going to let her say that*, which yeah, normally, no, but this is one time when I'm not going to sidetrack myself into a *Dead Queens* post. "Right, but *he* wasn't committed to *you*. That's the point I'm trying to make here."

Lina turns just enough that I get the full force of the Imperial Stare. "I don't expect you to understand."

Somehow it's the most stinging thing anyone's ever said to me. Ever. As in, I need to unload the ice packs from the mini fridge and put them on my face and also my soul. Instead I just blink it off for a long, bruised moment, and then I channel all my press-corps impartiality and get back to the sad, sordid facts. "So if you were just letting him get away with it, why did he escalate to actual dumping when Anna came along?"

Lina doesn't flinch. "She was manipulative and dis-respectful. And he fell for her lies."

"Hey, that's not fair," Parker says. "She really liked him."

"He was taken," says Lina. "He loved me. I slept with him, okay?"

After a beat I say, "And…?"

Lina crushes her hand around the rosary. "I wasn't going to sleep with anybody until I was married. I don't care if you think that makes me a prude. It's something I believe in. And Henry understood."

"Obviously," Parker mutters.

"Parker! Jesus!" I burst out, because seriously? And then I remember there's an actual mini-Jesus on the wall, so I try to save face and cross myself, but I'm ninety-nine percent sure I'm doing it backward, which given my luck this evening probably means something horribly offensive.

Thankfully Lina ignores my one-girl shitshow. "But then I finally did, because I'm an idiot, and everything was getting so bad," she says, and for the first time all night, her full-armor glare cracks open and she looks totally, completely broken. It's blink-and-you'll-miss-it fast, but it's there. "I thought maybe, if— I thought maybe he'd just let the whole thing go, all right?"

Somehow seeing Lina showing weakness is exponentially

worse than seeing Henry cry, which was my previous barometer for shit being Very Bad. "Dude," I say, which might not be the best salutation when you're pep-talking an exiled queen, but whatever. I'm trying. "It doesn't change who you are. You could sleep with, like, hundreds of people, and it wouldn't—"

"Cleveland." She's sitting up so straight it feels like she should be holding a scepter instead of a rosary. "It's not about your values. It's about mine." She holds her ground, like she's making sure we get it.

And we do. Clearly. Because she just flat-out decreed it.

"I can't believe he cheated," I say, like the absolute moron I may in fact be.

"You knew about Anna."

"I thought that was completely out-of-character. He seemed so into you."

"He *was*." Lina's still in scepter-wielding mode. Or possibly sword-wielding. In her case, it's too close to call.

Parker side-eyes me. "He's into a lot of people."

"Shut *up*," I say, because the last thing I need is for Lina to know about yesterday. And also, tragically, because my go-to rationalizing technique every time I've thought about yesterday is that I'm the exception. I don't have Anna's powers of hypnosis, but there's something special about the Henry and Cleves duo, and something something something and therefore it's not really normal cheating at all. The end.

I'm strongly interested in not exploring the alternatives. I'm very strongly interested in not exploring the alternatives in front of Lina and Wall-Jesus.

"*Anyway,*" says Parker, "Henry killed Anna."

And just like that, Lina's back to non-reacting.

"Come on. We're trying to figure this out."

She shrugs. "It sounds like you already did."

"So? Do you agree with me?"

Lina finally sets the rosary down. "I think it was an accident."

"Nobody thinks it was an accident."

"I think whoever set up the fireworks was trying to scare the right people and end the right relationships. Not kill anyone."

"Come *on,*" Parker huffs. "Was it Anna or Henry?"

Lina hesitates, like she's deciding if she can trust us. "I think," she says carefully, "Anna Boleyn wasn't capable of something like that."

"Exactly!" Parker's practically jumping out of her chair. "She was a good person. She wasn't a *killer.*"

This is one of those times when all I can do is assume everybody's sidestepped into a murder mystery dinner-party-theater thing without warning me, because none of this makes any sense, no matter how much of a cheating cheater a certain someone might be. "Right, but Henry's not a killer, either. And even if we ignore the fact that he's fundamentally not a trench-coat train wreck who axes people, he still doesn't have a motive."

"You mean like killing Anna so she can't get revenge?" asks Parker.

"Um. No."

"Teaching Anna a lesson for supposedly cheating on him?"

"Parker. This isn't a soap opera. It's high school."

She rolls her eyes and goes, "Is there a difference?"

Which is why I love her, but still. "Seriously, let's look at it like a prank gone wrong. It's the only idea that doesn't sound like you just took the high dive into the deep end of an empty pool."

"What about scaring Anna into letting go?" Lina says.

"If he wanted to scare her off, why didn't he do that with you, too?"

"Because we were real, and he knew it. Anna was a mistake."

"Seriously, Aragón?" says Parker. "You're not *that* much better than everybody else. He was just afraid of your mom." She glances back at me right as I'm opening my mouth to attempt another blasphemous can't-we-all-just-get-along interjection. "You know it's true, so don't start. And it wasn't a prank, okay?"

I shrug. "Prove it."

"*You* prove it. You're the one who thinks it was a prank. Trick him into telling you."

"It wasn't even him."

She stares me down. "Well, we can't exactly ask Anna, can we?"

"So I just go, 'Hey, Henry, remember that time you blew up the Tower? Those were the days, am I right?'"

"Whatever," she says. "I don't see you coming up with any better ideas."

Then Lina laughs. Which is so miraculous that Wall-Jesus does jazz hands to mark the occasion.

And Lina says, "Let's call Jane."

Illinois Sues Indiana Over Seymour Expatriation

I wake up thinking I've had the weirdest dream ever, but then I roll over and start to fall off the itchiest couch known to man, and while I'm clinging on for dear life, I look over and Parker's on the floor doing pushups.

Not a dream.

She flips onto her back and starts firing off crunches. "Lina just left for practice. I'm going on a run in a minute. Want to come?"

Here's what I know: Parker and I spent the night in the lounge on Lina's hall, and we're calling Jane after lunch. Also, my hair is so knotted, it might not be worth salvaging.

Oh, and Parker and Lina think Henry killed Anna. Which seems a hundred times less compatible with reality now than it did at one in the morning.

I roll back over. "I gave up cardio for Lent."

So she goes on her run, and I wander around fake-researching Notre Dame just in case I ever decide to smash gender roles via Future Day Job #316: Lady Pope. There are a number of perks, such as how you can break into a dorm fairly easily, but in the end I vote no, because I'm not all that sold on organized religion. And also, everybody's so Gryffindor it freaks Hufflepuff-me out.

Parker and I get to the dining hall fashionably late, and Lina's already sitting with the team. Correction: They're sitting with *her*. Because even though she's only a freshman, it looks like she's holding court.

Which is weirdly comforting on a weekend as twilight-zone as this one.

Lina waves us over. "Guys, this is Cleveland and Parker," she says, and the way she says it apparently tells the team we're worth their time, even though one of us is in rocket pajamas. They start making room for us, but Lina tells them not to worry about it and herds us over to a table in the corner.

Parker kicks me, and I can tell she sees it, too—Lina's still Lina, if you can ignore how deeply unfriendly she was last night in her sad draconian dorm room.

So yeah, it was definitely just us. This is equal parts insulting, understandable, and a damn relief.

"Okay," Lina says when it's just the three of us. "We're calling at one thirty, and I'll handle the introduction. No wild accusations."

"Do you ever talk to Jane?" Parker asks.

Lina shakes her head. "Do you?"

"Not since she left."

Which isn't all that promising, but oh well. Once we finish our preview of college dorm fine dining, we head up to Lina's room to call my favorite piece of hospital furniture.

"Don't talk about murder unless she does," Lina tells Parker as she pulls Jane's number up and sets the phone on her desk.

"Whatever. It's not like she didn't know."

"She's way too milquetoast to mess with a killer," I say. "Hypothetically. And she wasn't ambitious like Anna."

They look at me. "Jane is ambitious," Lina says, one finger hovering over the call icon.

"Like volunteer-at-the-hospital-to-get-a-reference ambitious?"

"Like gold-digger ambitious," says Parker.

I snort. "Henry isn't rich."

"He isn't poor," Lina says. "They lost the factory, but his dad's a genius with investing."

"Besides, she was gold-digging, like, socially," Parker adds.

This conversation is already ten miles into the Upside Down, and we haven't even gotten Jane on the line yet. "So she's a *metaphorical* gold digger."

"Sure. What are we waiting for?" Parker reaches for the phone, but Lina gets to it first.

"I'm taking it off speaker if you go rogue," she says.

And then it's ringing, and we're staring like something really interesting is about to happen. Which is unlikely, given who we're calling.

"Hello?"

Parker grabs my arm.

"Jane. It's Lina Aragón."

"I know," Jane says. Her voice is guarded. Probably because she can smell the what-the-fuckery lurking behind this casual greeting even from one state over.

"She's hiding something!" Parker hisses.

"Hello?" Now Jane sounds straight-up suspicious.

"Jane." Lina shoots a warning glare Parker's way. "I'm here with Parker Rochford and—you know Henry's friend Cleveland, right?"

"They're more than friends, if Henry's relationship status was accurate in September."

"You're two girlfriends behind, Seymour," says Parker.

Then Lina gives Jane a deeply abridged version of last night's theory, which still sounds absurd, but Jane doesn't say a single thing during or after.

I'm not saying Jane's an alien who doesn't quite understand the way people are supposed to respond to shockingly tabloid-tastic stories, but I'm not saying she isn't, either.

"Hello?" Parker's two seconds from hopping back in the car and booking it across the border to Illinois to give Jane the full eye-dagger treatment. "Say something, Seymour."

"I think it happened like everybody says it did," Jane says.

"Anna wasn't capable of something like that," Lina tells her.

"I'm surprised to hear you say that," says Jane, and I almost miss it because she's still using her default blandness, but it's actually a pretty pointy little remark.

And Lina gets the message. "That's why you should be taking this seriously."

"I understand." Jane's speaking so carefully, it's like she's playing some massively complicated version of *Taboo* where half the English language is off the table.

"So help us," says Lina.

Silence.

"Come on," Parker says. "You know something,"

"I'm really not part of your world anymore."

"Okay, but this is about last May."

"You were a little more involved in that than I was, weren't you?" Jane asks.

Parker's getting Tyrannosaurus-y. "What are you trying to say?"

"Well, you were the one who told Henry about Anna, weren't you?"

Jane's really good at this, especially for an alien.

And Parker's really pissed. "That wasn't me! Why the hell would I hurt Anna?"

"The rumor-spreading seems like a pattern, doesn't it?"

"You can drop the innocent act," Parker snaps. "We all know you're even more of a snake than Anna. You just don't have the balls she did."

Lina reaches for the phone, but Parker grabs her hand.

"Look," I say while they do some intricate fight choreography, because somebody has to be the voice of reason, and nobody else is looking particularly qualified at the moment. "If you think it's Anna, you think it's Anna. Just—"

"You know it's not," Parker cuts in. "Do you really want to be guilty by association when Cat Parr bites it? We're trying to keep her *alive*. You're lucky you—"

Lina clamps one hand over Parker's mouth.

"I understand the survival instinct. But you're being over-dramatic," Jane says. Behind Lina's hand, Parker makes a totally disgusted expression.

"And I can't help you," Jane finishes.

"You can't, or you won't?" Lina asks.

Jane gives us another full year of illuminating silence before she finally goes, "I think it was an accident."

And then the screen says *Call Ended*, and Parker pushes Lina's hand out of the way. "So that's what I get for throwing her that going-away party. Selfish bitch."

"Self-preserving," Lina corrects her. "And you and Anna did start those rumors about Jane."

"God, okay, stop," Parker says. "I fucked up, okay? But I'm *sorry*, and at least I'm trying to fix it, and Jane won't even help." She flicks her hair out of her face and scowls.

And I say the only thing we can all agree on right now: "Ugh, Jane Seymour."

Shit Hits Fan

Just for the record, my general philosophy on everything from whether Anna blew up the Tower on purpose to whether Henry might actually like me versus just seeing the hookup opportunity and, you know, *carpe pantalonem*, is this: Choose the most survivable tactic, and go for it.

So that's what I'm doing on Monday, two days after the Jane Seymour conference call. Which in this case means avoiding Henry in all nongroup situations and refusing to think about Parker and Lina's theory. It's all going spectacularly, thank you very much.

But when I walk into journalism one strategic minute late, because it's a three-for-one—avoid Henry, avoid Cat, and avoid seeing Henry make out with Cat—Cat looks at me and says, "We need to talk."

Shit.

Not only is Cat about to verbally decimate me for at-

tempting to sleep with her boyfriend right after I unsuccessfully attempted to verbally decimate her for going out with
him in the first place, but she's going to do it in front of the
entire class, including Mr. Lee, who's in his office with the
door open.

Public humiliation. Lovely.

"About…what?" I finally manage, which may not sound
like the wittiest response, but given how loudly my instincts
are screaming *run right now because she'll follow the rules and ask
for a hall pass and you'll be out of here and on a flight to a country with no extradition before she can catch you*, it's damn Shake-
spearean.

"I think you know," she tells me, and I hope nobody's
fooled by her pleasant tone, because she's definitely about to
destroy me.

"Breaking: girls go wild," Eustace says. Everybody's watching, with an even split between the ones pretending to be en-
grossed in something else and the ones flat-out staring. That's
how obvious it is that there's about to be blood.

And of course Cat notices, too. She taps on the door frame
of Mr. Lee's office and says we have to run over to the auditorium for the drama club story, and just like that, we're out
in the hall and Eustace has the floor. He's narrating our up-
coming brawl before we're even out of earshot.

"Opening night is Thursday. It's Eustace's beat, but the
play's the biggest thing on his calendar, and he'll probably
try to pull something like he did last year."

So that's how she's going to play this? Okay, fine. "Which
was…?"

"Skip the play, bullshit two paragraphs, and give the rest of the space to George for a parody. I'd like it to be covered well this year."

"High school drama. My favorite."

"I trust your reporting." Her tone is still neutral, and she's leading us toward the auditorium at an all-business clip. It's like those political shows where everybody's always running from one press conference to another, and if you stop walking, the terrorists win.

"My journalism won't disappoint you," I say.

She pivots and opens a random classroom door, except clearly it's not random because it's empty, which she seems to have either known in advance or detected with her heightened editor-in-chief senses.

I follow her in. It's a history classroom, so at least there aren't any Bunsen burners ready to be appropriated for torturing out confessions. Just desks and books and walls so postered-up you can barely see the paint. Plus an actual suit of armor, which I strategically sit next to, because it never hurts to have some defensive options.

Cat sits down across from me. She's in front of a wall dedicated to *Queens Who Changed History*, with Nefertiti over her right shoulder and Cleopatra over her left. A trifecta of deliberately killer eyeliner and well-informed stares.

"Cleveland," she says, "I trust your journalism, but I'd like to be able to trust *you*, too."

I'd be lying if I said I didn't have a cold-sweat situation happening.

"We both know what's going on here."

Maybe if I give her something tiny, she'll be okay with running some verbal circles around me and leaving me to contemplate my poor choices in front of another set of dead queens. "I don't know what Henry told you, but nothing happened," I say.

Now she just looks irritated. And slightly confused, which I can work with.

"I mean, he was studying, and we were talking about, you know, college."

She blinks.

"Penn," I tell her. "They have a great program in lion—" And then I realize I'm about to say *lion taming*, because it's as close as I've come to choosing a major. "Linguistics."

Cat holds up her phone, and there's my *Dead Queens* header. "Oh. That."

She raises her eyebrows.

"I mean…wow. Damn. You caught me."

"This really isn't appropriate."

"So, first of all," I say, "as a friend, it's my duty to tell you that maybe you should check out a thesaurus, because I'm sure there's something else out there you could use the next time you want to go with 'appropriate.' And second of all, the Bill of Rights. Look it up."

"The First Amendment doesn't cover threats."

"Yeah, and there aren't any threats on *Dead Queens*."

She scrolls down without breaking eye contact.

The top post says CAT PARR SHOULD WATCH HER BACK.

"Dude. I didn't write that."

She waits.

"I'm serious!"

"It's your blog, isn't it?"

"I mean, yeah, but I didn't write *that*."

She keeps on waiting.

"Okay, look." I grab my phone and pull up *Dead Queens* myself, since as of lunch, which was barely even an hour ago, there wasn't even a Cat-threat submission. Not that I would've queued it, anyway, because I do have *some* editorial standards.

Except I'm signed out of the account, and when I enter my password—it's my birthday, so yeah, go ahead and judge me, but that means there's no way I'm typoing, okay?—it tells me I'm wrong. So I try four more times, and I keep being wrong, and two feet away, Cat's annoyance is evolving into a literal thundercloud over her head.

"Care to explain?" she asks.

"I…think I got hacked."

"Really."

I smack my phone down on the desk. "Look. I'm locked out."

"Interesting timing."

This is a very morally confusing situation. I mean, on one hand, I'm pissed that she's framing me for a threat I didn't post. On the other hand, I'm apparently in the clear about the objectively much-more-offensive offense of trying to sleep with her boyfriend. "Come on," I say. "What would I even be telling you to watch your back about?"

She just looks at me.

"Oh my God, Cat, I'm not trying to break you guys up."

"See, that's where I'm not sure I trust you. You were pretty territorial last week."

"I was mad, okay? It was about Katie. And there's nothing I can do about it now."

"Except try to break us up."

"I'm over it."

"And that's why you're suddenly so into the Ivy League?"

I walked right into that one. "I would've just told you to your face if I thought you should break up. I already *did*."

She keeps her eyes on me. "I hope you're telling the truth, because I'd hate for this to interfere with the paper. You know I respect you as a writer."

I can't decide whether that's supposed to be a backhanded compliment or if it's just Cat being Ms. Parr. So I get up and leave. One of the queens on the wall—the Columbus-sailed-the-ocean-blue one, I think—has those Mona Lisa eyes that follow you, so she and Cat both watch me beeline for the door.

"Cleveland," Cat says right as I'm reaching for the handle, and I freeze because this was probably her strategy all along, and this is the part when she springs her I-know-what-you-did-last-Thursday speech.

"Yeah?"

"Hypothetically, if you deleted that post right now, I'd let this go."

I turn around. "I got hacked. I'm locked out."

"And hypothetically, if you're going to leave it up, I'd appreciate if you pushed it down the page before the end of the day."

"I'm *locked out*."

She smiles.

I almost wish I'd let Henry complete the cheat. Almost.

"We don't have to be enemies," she says.

"Is that hypothetical, too?"

She does a long blink. Full-on Ms. Parr. "I don't want a guy to come between us."

"I'm sure he wouldn't mind."

Anybody else would laugh or roll their eyes or whatever, but Cat just says, "I would."

She's doing this on purpose—getting me to keep talking. But I'll play. "Why did you say yes?"

"To Henry?"

"Obviously," I say. "And don't tell me it's not my business."

She pauses. "Off the record?"

"Yeah."

"I like him," says Cat.

"Good thing that's off the record. God, and I could've gotten so many hits on *Dead Queens* with that headline."

"He's smart," she says. "We can really have a conversation."

I wait.

"We have a lot in common."

I keep on waiting. Because yes, I actually do want to know, and there's no way she just *likes* him. He's not even her type. She likes quiet preppy nerd-boys she probably meets at the tailor, not hot jocks half the population of Lancaster has a crush on.

"Why did *you* say yes?" she asks.

This is why I don't debate Cat Parr. "It doesn't matter."

"Off the record."

"Politics. Securing our families' fortunes."

"Seriously, Cleveland."

If I tell her, it's going to be totally obvious that I'm not over him. And that's the most embarrassing thing ever, because why the hell *do* I still like him when Parker thinks he's a murderer and Lina thinks he's cruel and everybody knows he's kind of an ass where girls are concerned, and God, I should seriously have more self-respect than this. I *do* have more self-respect than this. Besides, if she knows I still like him, she'll be even more suspicious.

Which is fair.

So I give her the exact same punch-worthy smile she gave me a minute ago, and I say, "Ask your boyfriend."

Suspect Apprehends Self

I leave Cat alone with the armor suit.

Here's the thing: (a) I really am locked out of *Dead Queens*, so I can't delete the post; (b) deleting it wouldn't do much anyway, since it's already been reblogged; (c) Eustace just texted me Too far for Ms. Parr?, which means the entire newspaper has seen it by now; and (d) clearly the Phantom Hacker is looking for a reaction, so it's probably smarter to give them one before they graffiti the message behind the away stands.

So I go to my own damn ask box and type you need to stop. she gets it. Then I decide to take a page from the Malicious Compliance handbook by going straight to the auditorium for some top-notch school play reporting instead of going back to the journalism room, aka Enemy Territory.

I can't believe Cat thinks I'm lame enough to defile *Dead Queens* with a pointless vaguepost. Maybe I'm a little ethically challenged lately, but I can think of at least ten better ways to break them up.

One: Find, in the eloquent words of Parker Rochford, "some obscure Howard third cousin" to dangle in Henry's face. Problem solved.

Two: If you're posting threats, go with something better, like, *Cat Parr should watch her back, because Henry probably has syphilis by now.*

Three: Or *Cat Parr should watch her back, because Anna and Katie didn't*, which is fifty shades of gross, but hey, all's fair in love and libel.

Four: Tell Cat that Henry's cheating. Hypothetically.

Five: Even better, tell Henry that *Cat's* cheating. Although this might be overkill.

Six: Tell Mr. Lee that Cat's love life is endangering her editor-in-chief availability, and let him do the rest.

Seven: Or post *WHY ARE YOU GOING OUT WITH HENRY ANYWAY, CAT?* and leave THAT up until she gives in and confesses the bottomless depths of her popularity-grubbing, or whatever it is that's motivating her weirdly fragmented behavioral patterns.

Eight: Just sleep with him.

Nine: Or maybe refuse to sleep with him, since that worked so well for Anna.

Ten: Wait a few weeks, and he'll be done with her, too.

And that's just off the top of my head. In conclusion, of course I didn't post that crap. It's probably Eustace doing his part to feed the drama flame. In which case I'll just hire Anna's ghost and/or Henry to explode him ASAP, because locking me out of *Dead Queens* is a very shitty thing to do to a fellow journalist.

I set up camp at the very back of the auditorium. From what I can tell, they're still getting ready, unless what's going on now—which involves a lot of yelling and a lot of people sitting in the front few rows ignoring said yelling—is in fact performance art.

"It's going to be a shitshow, am I right?"

I turn around, and there's Eustace, carrying everything he owns plus a bag of vending-machine cookies. Because he's utterly inescapable, and also Cat is sublimely gifted at punishing me.

"Probably," I say. "But I'm onto you."

He sits next to me in the last row. "You mean you didn't post the Cat thing?"

"Of course not."

"Ha. Called it. Christina owes me five bucks."

"Of course you called it." I get my phone out and try logging in again, just for the pure senseless hell of it. "You're the one who hacked me."

He tears open the cookie bag. "Flattering, but wrong."

Which is too bad, because now I'm back to square zero.

"It's weird, right?" he says. "Nobody else even hates her."

"I don't hate her." I reach over and grab a cookie. "And I can't be the only one who doesn't think she's some gleaming marble pillar of humanity."

"Pretty much. Just you and Parker."

"Are you kidding me? She grabbed Henry five seconds after Katie died."

He shrugs. "Why do you care, unless you really *are* trying to get back with him?"

I would very much like to be excluded from this narrative. "Who told you that?"

"I never reveal my sources."

"Because they're fake."

He grins. "Word on the street is you begged Henry to take you back."

"Hell no!"

"Word on the street is you were on the iron steps Thursday night. Visiting a certain ex."

The drama teacher screams something at a kid who appears to just be standing there. I deeply relate to both parties. "Who told you *that*?"

He does an exaggerated lip-zip. "And then you hitched a ride back to Howard Heights with Ms. Parr."

"So Cat's starting all this gossip?"

"Yeah, no."

"Erin?"

"Unlikely."

I'm running out of options here. "The Howard Heights guard?"

"Doesn't matter. I'm right. And I'm right about the steps, too, aren't I?"

I glance around in a shout-out to Parker's paranoia. "If you say that one more time, I'm going to unleash the fury of a thousand cheerleaders on you."

He bites into another cookie. "So you *do* want him back."

"No."

"Then tell me why you went to his house on Thursday."

"Homework."

"Holy shit." He stops chewing. "You're hooking up with him, aren't you?"

"NO!" I yell, and all the theater kids turn to stare.

"Shit," says Eustace. "No wonder you're trying to break them up."

"I'm not trying to break them up," I whisper-hiss, because the last thing I need is the entire drama department spreading this rumor around. I'm not about to be That Girl Who Can't Get Over Her Ex Even Though They Only Went Out For Two Weeks, Who Also Is a Stalker. "And I'm going to kill you. I'm actually going to kill you with my own hands if you ever say, or *write*, a single word about this."

"Damn." He's shaking his head. "So that's why you hate Cat all of a sudden."

"I don't hate her! And it's not sudden. You were whining about her censorship habit way before I was."

"That was professional," says Useless Eustace. "This is personal."

"She's the one who made it personal! She's being totally shitty to Katie, going out with Henry this soon."

"As opposed to just sleeping with him?"

"I'm not SLEEPING with him!"

The drama kids turn around again. One of them is a total Amelie doppelganger, and she does a giggle-smirk thing my sister would definitely do in this situation. It's weirdly unnerving.

"I'm just saying, you care a lot about Ms. Parr's love life for someone who supposedly doesn't have a thing for Henry. Don't you think?"

I channel my best Parker Rochford eye-daggers straight at his unbelievably meddling face. "I think," I practically growl, "*Ms. Parr* is taking quite the burden on herself."

"You'd know, wouldn't you?"

"You better watch what you're saying."

"Kind of like Cat Parr should watch her back?"

I'm about to kick him in the balls. And leave him lying there, where the drama kids will circle him like vultures and slowly peck his eyes out. Or just sing annoying theater songs at him until he succumbs to his ordeal.

But before this can unfold, the back door opens and there she is: Miss Indiana's Outstanding Teen.

I have never in my life been so pumped to see Parker Rochford.

"Get out of here, Eustace," she says, hands on her hips, the absolute epitome of everything a cheer captain should be.

He glances back and forth between me and Parker, looking wonderfully dumbfounded. "When did you even text her? I was watching you the whole time."

I roll with it, because it's about time fate or the universe or Wall-Jesus cuts me a break. "Angry cheerleaders. As promised."

"Fine. I'm leaving." He gets up, and I fight the overpowering urge to follow through on my ball-kicking dreams. "But just so you know, I've got an ironclad alliance with the lacrosse girls."

"Reconsider," Parker says, standing next to our row of seats like she's the bouncer waiting to throw him out. "Because I'm friends with Aragón again."

He gives us both the side-eye. "Calling your bluff."

"We stayed with her at Notre Dame and everything."

"*Really* calling your bluff."

Parker pulls her phone out and brandishes a picture in Eustace's face. It's a selfie-creepshot hybrid—Parker's grinning on one side of the screen while Lina inspects the fridge behind her. Very stealth.

He takes a half step back, which is unreasonably gratifying. "Should I be terrified or thrilled?"

"Terrified," I answer.

"Thrilled," Parker says at the same time. "And keep your mouth shut, or you're going to regret it."

He looks both confused and impressed. "Fine. I won't tell."

"Swear."

"Uh, I swear."

"Or Lina will hate you forever."

"I get it." He puts both hands up, like, *I surrender.* Then he backs out of the auditorium and Parker shifts her glare over to me.

"Come on. We have to go set up for practice." She heads out the door and across the hall to the auxiliary gym.

I'm right behind her. "How'd you find me?"

"Cat told me where you were."

"Because you guys are so tight these days?"

"I was looking for you in the newspaper room. And anyway, we're friends."

"Last week you were about to put a hit out on her."

"No, I wasn't." Parker unlocks a closet and we both start hauling out putrid blue mats.

"Dude," I say, because she might be living in a semi-fictional world of her own creation, but I prefer to inhabit reality. "Quit the gaslighting already. I was *there*."

"We're friends *now*, okay?"

"Right." I manhandle a stack of mats onto the court. "Don't you have JV minions to do this for you?"

"They can't blow off last block. And if we're set up when the bell rings, that's ten more minutes of practice."

I let the mats slap down onto the floor. "They don't call you Tyrannosaurus Rochford for nothing."

"Whatever." Parker starts unfolding the mats, and I head back to the closet. Maybe I should major in whatever would land me Potential Future Day Job #XLVIII: NFL Cheer Squad Manager. I could probably get a scholarship, since I suspect that major is mostly composed of stalkers. Or aspiring professional cheerleaders who weren't quite good enough and are planning to take a baseball bat to somebody's knees five minutes before the show.

I grab the next stack of mats, but before I turn around, the closet door slams shut and somebody has a vise grip on my arm. It's Parker—her acupuncture pattern is pretty familiar by this point—but I shriek anyway.

"You can't tell anybody it was me, okay?"

I detach her nails from my arm. She might need a new dinosaur name—whichever one had razor-sharp talons and sliced its prey to death. "In the conservatory with the lead pipe?"

"What the hell are you talking about?"

"What the hell are *you* talking about?"

She crosses her arms. The lighting situation in here is sub-par: one fluorescent panel in the ceiling, and it keeps flick-ering. "Don't give me away."

And then the lightbulb in my head goes on, beautifully synchronized with the actual light overhead buzzing to the brightest it's been so far. "You hacked *Dead Queens*?"

She looks at me like, *duh*. "Like you pointed out an hour ago. And all I did was guess your password."

At least I'm not the only one on the self-incrimination train today. "I didn't know who it was when I sent that ask. I was just pissed because Cat practically waterboarded me over it, and I thought it was about—"

"Don't say it."

This might actually be good advice, but still. "You should really consider seeing somebody about the paranoia thing."

"Yeah, well, you should really consider seeing somebody about the sleeping-with-the-enemy thing."

"He's not the *enemy*, Parker."

"Fine. The suspect."

"And nobody's doing any *sleeping*."

She finally cracks a smile—it's wry, but it's there. "That's exactly what I'm saying." Then she's back to business. "Cat thinks it's you?"

"Apparently I'm the only person alive who doesn't think she's flawless."

Parker makes a face, but then she says, "I asked her to go shopping this weekend."

"You're the architect of your own destruction."

"I'm protecting her." Parker pulls the door open. She checks the gym for possible spies, and then she grabs another set of mats. "Get the other end. It's easier."

I grab it and follow her out. "You hate her."

"No, I don't."

"The last time I saw you together, she was shit-talking George and you were evicting her from your basement."

"That was *forever* ago," she says. "Besides, after Saturday, we're going to be totally bonded. Drop it here." That last bit is in her drill sergeant voice. We drop the mats and start unfolding them.

"And then you'll be like, 'By the way, I posted that threat'?"

She crouches down, nudges the mats into place, and pops back up. "The plan was that she'd mention it and ask me what I thought. And then I could tell her Katie told me Henry was totally sketchy."

I raise one eyebrow.

"Or something."

I maintain the eyebrow-raise.

"Okay, I haven't worked that part out yet."

The longer I fraternize with the classically popular crew, the less I understand them. "Have you ever tried not getting into everybody's business?"

"You're the newspaper girl." She jogs back to the closet and grabs a set of speakers.

"And I still know when to keep my head down."

"This is important, okay? Cat's screwed if she doesn't watch her back."

"Yeah, and you're screwed if you don't watch yours."

Parker stops in her tracks. Because holy shit, I just made

a watch-your-back comment to a girl with a scar down her back from trying to save her boyfriend from a building explosion. I've officially won every sensitivity award ever created.

"Shit," I say. "I'm sorry. I didn't mean it like that."

"I know." She sets the speakers down. "But listen, Cleves. After End of the Road, I stopped giving a shit what happened to me."

"It wasn't your fault."

"It kind of was."

"Parker. It was NOT."

"Whatever." She snaps back into Tyrannosaurus mode. "I'm not letting anything happen to her. Not this time."

Parker starts for the door, and I follow her like the good future manager I am. "Noted," I say. "But you have to give me my account back. She got your message."

She hesitates for a second, then nods.

"Give me the new password. I'm taking the post down."

"Okay."

"And then we're going to talk to Cat."

Reporter Seeks Political Hunger Strike to Join Following Lunch-Related Injuries

Of course Parker has cheerleading and I have newspaper, so we schedule the Cat-frontation for Thursday, before the basketball game. And at first, I'm thinking, you know, great, that will give Parker some time to chill about this whole deal.

Except Parker's definition of "chill" is letting fifty people get wasted in her *Cribs*-worthy basement, and/or kidnapping people from their actual driveways. So of course when I walk into Hampton Court for lunch on Tuesday, she's camped out right across from Cat's new seat.

I squeeze in on Henry's non-Cat side, aka exactly where I've been sitting every damn day since September, and give Parker a *what the hell* look.

"Hey, Cleveland," Cat says, like yesterday never happened.

Parker texts me: Shut up.

I write back: a normal person would actually call the cops if they thought somebody was a MURDERER which henry definitely ISN'T so can we stop pretending to be bffs with my nemesis??

Two more football guys push their way past everybody. "Yo, Henry, move your fat ass. This table's too crowded," one of them says, and Henry laughs.

Cat smiles at the guys and goes, "Let's try this," and slides onto Henry's lap. I hit the question mark on my screen several times very emphatically, so what I actually send to Parker is a series of upside-down Spanish question marks, but that's fine, because my WTF levels can't be fully articulated within the confines of English.

The guys shove the Henry/Cat duet a little closer to me, which is a true delight. And then everyone has a seat, thanks to Ms. Parr's innovative PDA.

Parker texts me a few exclamation points, but then she pageant-smiles and says, "Love the necklace, Cat."

Cat narrows her eyes, even though she's clearly doing her damnedest to play the lovestruck girlfriend, no matter how many Parker-traps she has to weather along the way. "Thanks," she says. Then she finally seems to pick up on the undisguised stink-eye I'm giving her, and she takes her acting up to Oscar-bid levels. "I'm in for Saturday, by the way."

"Perfect. Cleves and I can pick you up at ten."

It's unfortunate that real life doesn't come with a soundtrack, because I could really use a needle-scratch right now. "Um," I say. "What?"

"Saturday? Fort Wayne? I told you."

I pull a Tyrannosaurus Rochford and smile at her—at everybody, really, in a grand gesture that consists of baring my teeth and waving my face back and forth—and say, "Right! I'm so there," as unsarcastically as I can manage.

Parker kicks me, because I guess I don't sound as euphoric as I'm supposed to be about spending all day with my enemy-in-chief.

"Seriously, Rochford?"

She amps her smile up a level and kicks me again.

"Ow!"

"You know, maybe we can do a sleepover after Fort Wayne," Parker says to Cat.

Disclaimer: This goes against my general MO of Go With It, but Cat's practically giving Henry a lap dance and Parker seems to have taken up full citizenship in her murder-centric alternate universe. So I get up, planning to walk around to her side of the table, but that's going to kill the momentum. Instead I climb onto the bench and step up onto the table, and the guys do the *oooh* thing as I jump down on the other side and haul Parker out of her seat.

"Oh my God, Cleves, what are —"

"Emergency," I say, giving everybody a rock-on sign with the hand that isn't dragging Parker out of Hampton Court, and the guys transition the *oooh*ing into cheering while I yank her around the corner.

"Cleves. What the *hell*."

"If you think I'm spending twenty-four consecutive hours with a girl who—"

"We're getting her on our side." Parker squirms out of my grip.

I grab her arm again and pull her a few more feet away from Hampton Court. "If I have to listen to your conspiracy theories, you can listen to mine." And I'm about to say, you know, *Henry did the cover-up at Area 51*, but then Eustace walks by at slow-mo gossip-harvesting pace, so I take a left back into Lancrapster. "Tell me why Cat's dating Henry."

"Because he's popular."

"Go home, Chapman," I yell at Eustace, and then I zero back in on Parker. "Bullshit."

"She's social climbing. We knew that way back at homecoming."

"We *said* that way back at homecoming. But she practically pariahed herself at your party. You don't do that if your life goal is sitting at the mythical Exclusives table."

Parker pulls her arm free again. "Who cares?"

"It doesn't make sense."

"Who *cares*?"

"Listen, Cat's all about her illustrious future. She basically told me not to hang out with you guys, remember? She liked a college guy. Then all of a sudden, she's third-wheeling with Erin and Brandon until Henry notices her, and then *boom*, she's giving him mouth-to-mouth in the middle of journalism."

Parker wrinkles her nose. "Ew."

"You're not the one who had to see it," I say. "But combine that with how she shit-talked George at your party and how she shuts down every op-ed I write about Anna, and..."

"What?"

And here I was hoping Parker's overactive imagination

would slam all the puzzle pieces into place. "I don't know. But that's a lot of weird shit."

"Not as weird as killing two girlfriends in six months."

She says this while casually checking her reflection in the window behind me and smoothing down her hair.

This school. Holy shit.

So I say, "Tone it down, Agatha Christie. I'm just saying I think Cat's up to something besides winning a popularity contest."

"Are you finished?" Parker asks. "Because I'd like to get back to the half of my lunch you didn't step on."

"Well, yeah. I mean, we've left Henry unattended for a full two minutes. He's probably smothering Cat with a cafeteria tray right this very second."

Parker gives me an exceptionally foul glare.

"Right, but before you go, consider this: Jane Seymour did it."

"Cleves."

"Kill Anna," I say. "Date Henry. Flee the state before the FBI notices you aren't actually an inanimate object."

"Cleves."

"Or consider *this*: Cat did it. She's on an undercover mission to destroy the Lancaster social hierarchy. She paid Anna off to break up Henry and Lina, and then Anna knew too much, so she had to go. And now she's infiltrating the Exclusives from the inside. Holy shit, *she's* probably smothering *Henry* with a cafeteria tray right this second."

"Cleves!"

"OR," I say, because honestly, I'm starting to see the ap-

322

peal of wildly irrational murder accusations. It's entertaining. Too bad there isn't a way to spin *that* into a potential future day job. "Consider this: Lina Aragón. Destroy the ex. Destroy his new girlfriend. Destroy the newspaper kid who cashed in on your breakup. Destroy the backstabber who ditched you for the Boleyns—"

"I'm not an effing backstabber!"

"And while you're at it, frame Anna for the whole thing." I pause. "Wow, that's actually pretty solid. Are we sure she was in Guatemala that week?"

"CLEVES."

"You know what, scratch that. She hired Eustace as a contract killer."

Parker actually walks away. Which is good, because I'm running out of ideas other than, you know, it actually *was* Anna, but in a non-murdery sort of way, since that's the only story that doesn't feel like we plagiarized it directly from a telenovela. And Parker's definitely not open to that version of events.

I'm not all that stoked about voluntarily subjecting myself to our lunch table again, so I pull up *Dead Queens* to do some quality procrastinating.

Except something's wrong. My entire dash is just *so-and-so reblogged your text post* times infinity, which never happens, because *Dead Queens* is definitely more of a lurk-and-screenshot type of blog. An anon-ask-and-chill type of blog.

"Parker!" I yell, even though she's already back in Hampton Court. "If you hacked me again, I'm sabotaging Saturday!"

But then I click through on one reblog that includes a

brand-new wall of text, and okay, never mind. It's not a glitch. It's like nine hundred people legit reblogging my very first post. The ASKING FOR IT one. And it's not Lancaster people—it's random internet strangers leaving tags and comments like *@deadqueens PREACH* and *finally someone said it*.

This is not a drill.

Dead Queens is going prime-time.

Editor-in-Chief Is Life of Party, Says No One

"**O**h my God, Cleves, you could have at least dressed for the occasion," says Parker.

"I'm sorry, what? I look awesome." We're outside the journalism room, about to stage the Cat-frontation. I'm in an old-school *Jurassic Park* T-shirt with a zip-up hoodie, and I'd argue that I'm far more dressed for the occasion than Parker, who's in heels and a skirt even though it's thirty degrees outside.

"This is Cat Parr."

"Right, and she wears blazers. To school. As a student."

"*Designer* blazers."

"So you're saying she doesn't just dress like a teacher, but she also spends ridiculous amounts of money to dress like a teacher?"

Parker sighs. "I don't even know why I'm trying to have this conversation with a girl who owns rocket pants." She pulls a mirror out of her purse and does a quick face check. "Do we have a plan?"

"Do we ever?"

So we go in. As expected, Cat's typing aggressively away in Mr. Lee's office with a Starbucks cup on the desk and a pair of purple heels on the floor by her chair.

"*How* did you get your hands on those?" Parker's staring at the shoes.

Cat swivels her chair toward the door. She's in black pants and a blazer—because of course she is—and she's sitting cross-legged with her feet up on the seat. Her pedicure matches the shoes. "My mom was in New York last week."

"They're perfect," says Parker. She looks around for somewhere to sit, which, good luck, because Mr. Lee hasn't cleaned his office since the Carter administration. Finally she goes back out to the classroom and grabs a chair. I pick up a stack of yearbooks and dump them onto the floor to sit in one of those folding chairs people bring to parades. The seat has York's logo on it, but that's an investigation for another day.

"So," says Cat. "What's going on?"

This feels uncannily like being sent to the principal's office. Except we sent ourselves.

But Parker's beaming her sparkling-white teeth at Cat like a weapon. "Well, this is awkward. But I was the one who made that post. You know, about—"

Cat nods.

Parker looks over her shoulder and out the office window, and then she twists the blinds shut. A cloud of dust puffs out, because nobody's touched them in ten generations. "Is anything recording? Is your webcam on?"

Cat pretends Parker doesn't sound insane. "No."

"Good." Parker lowers her voice. "I had to warn you."

"About what?"

"You're in danger," she says, like she just rode fifty miles on horseback over the misty moor—wearing a black cape, probably—to deliver this melodramatically vague message.

"In danger," Cat repeats.

"It's Henry. He—" Parker stops for another furtive glance around the room. "Anna. And Katie. It wasn't—"

"Just a minute," Cat cuts in.

"But—"

"I know what you're going to say."

"Henry's an effing mur—"

"Don't say it."

"You need to be careful," Parker says. "You weren't at the Tower. You don't know."

Cat doesn't look like she thinks Parker's living in some very dark fantasy realm. She just looks like we're having one of our Monday meetings and she's standing at the whiteboard with a marker, crossing out ideas that aren't worth printing. "This isn't an appropriate conversation."

Parker hesitates, and then she starts laughing a little too hard. "Oh my God, you're right."

Okay, clearly I don't believe her Henry theory, but Parker believes it so much she yelled at me in a cornfield for an hour. So why the hell is she faking it for Cat?

Cat's laughing, too, like murder accusations and immediate retractions are everyday fare. "No, it's fine. You've been under a lot of pressure lately."

I mean, congratulations to them on their blossoming friendship, but that drugs-in-the-air-vents hypothesis is looking more plausible every hour.

"We're still on for Saturday, right?" Parker asks.

Damn it.

"Absolutely," says Cat, who's gotten so damn comfortable in her Henry's Lovestruck Girlfriend persona that I'm starting to suspect she's been body-snatched. "By the way, good luck at the game tonight."

"Thanks! Are you coming?"

"Of course. Can't miss Henry's senior-year debut on the basketball court." Cat slips her feet into the shoes I'm not fashion-qualified enough to be impressed by and steps over to open the door. "I'll see you there, okay?"

I get up with Parker, but before I make it out, Cat says, "Cleveland, hold on. I need a second opinion on a couple of articles."

"I'll catch up with you later," says Parker. And just like that she peaces out, which I guess is her personal way of thanking me for yesterday's lunchtime vignette.

Awesome.

Cat shuts the door again, and this time she locks it. Then she just stares me down.

Double awesome.

"Why are you here?" Cat asks.

"Like, existentially? Great question."

Slow blink.

"Emotional support, obviously. I'm an award-winning friend."

"Do you agree with Parker?"

If this conversation goes on much longer, my face is going to get stuck in a permanent WTF expression. "Do I think Henry's a murderer? Seriously?"

She sits back down and drums her fingernails across the desk. "I'm wondering why you talked her into having this conversation in the first place."

"It was all her, okay? I'm not trying to break you and Henry up. Move on."

She raises her eyebrows. "I didn't say anything about that, but—"

"You're totally leading the witness. Entrapment. Objection sustained."

"People are talking about you and Henry. You should know that."

Once upon a time, I lived in a town where everybody did not know everybody else's business. No, I can't believe it, either. "And here I thought gossip was below your editorial standards," I say.

She waits.

"Nobody's even talking. Because nothing's *happening*."

"Cleves," says Cat, "you know how rarely Eustace keeps his mouth shut."

"I'm leaving," I tell her, and try for a dramatic door-fling, but of course it's locked, so instead it's a dramatic doorknob-shake followed by some undignified fumbling.

"Why did you come here with Parker?"

I turn back around. "In case you haven't noticed, she's one Kool-Aid shot away from joining a cult. I'm on high-stakes babysitting duty."

Cat lets me figure out how to unlock the door before she says, "And I'm sure it's been interesting reporting back to Henry, hasn't it?"

"I don't know what the hell you're talking about, okay?" I answer, which probably sounds way too defensive, but seriously, it's like those cop shows where they get confessions by making shit up and letting the bad guys incriminate themselves. And (a) I *don't* know what she's talking about, (b) Henry and I haven't even talked since our intellectual curiosity episode, and (c) I'm not a *bad guy*.

So for good measure, I add, "I'm an innocent bystander. And I'm onto you, KP." I'm flat-out bluffing, but it's worth a shot.

Then I try door-flinging, Take Two, which is pretty damn successful, if I do say so myself.

And then I leave her there with her corporate coffee and her overhyped shoes and head off to kill three hours and possibly Eustace Chapman.

Marine Police under Investigation in Negligence Suit

Except as it turns out, I can't kill Eustace, on account of how I don't have scaffolding, fireworks, or an angry girlfriend to pin the whole thing on. And also because when I get to the auditorium to wait for the play to start, Eustace isn't alone. He's with some lighting guys, and when I crash in, he goes, "Great, we needed a fourth," and then I'm suddenly in the middle of a game of euchre. Which is a game no one outside of Indiana gives a damn about, but everyone in Indiana loves more than their own children, unless their children are especially good at basketball.

So since we have witnesses, I have to be a charming mustache-twirler and wait until eventually I put down a jack after the lighting kid to my right puts down a queen. Then I say, "Can't beat your queen, but here's her faithful inferior, reporting for duty," and stare at Eustace ominously while the other lighting kid trumps in with a two of spades.

Eustace overtrumps with the queen of spades and says, "Sorry. Looks like there's a new queen in command."

Which is a solid comeback. "Okay," I say, "but seriously, it's not like Cat's going to promote you just because you fed her some gossip."

He smirks.

"You asshole. You're literally just trying to generate drama for your own entertainment, aren't you?"

One of the theater guys deals the next hand, and Eustace shrugs. "You're the one running *Dead Queens*."

"My blog is both transparent and democratic, thank you very much."

"We'll see if it stays that way now that you're getting your fifteen minutes," he says with the kind of wicked grin that can only be accomplished with months of dedicated practice time.

But I don't get around to a rebuttal because that's when Henry starts texting from the basketball bus, and in the euchre game of life, Henry will literally always trump Useless Chapman.

Henry: We need to talk

Me: word choice? or was that intentionally threatening

And then, like a tenth of a second later, Parker texts me, too: Btw don't tell H anything!!

Me: about what?

Parker: NOT FUNNY

Parker: Delete these messages

Parker: Delete ALL messages from me

> So much for laughing it off.
> Then Henry's back: What are you doing?

Me: reporting. wearing a dinosaur shirt but this isn't the best time for sexting, sorry

Henry: Not funny

> Tough crowd.
> So I get boring, because he's in Serious Game Mode: I can hang out later if you want.
> I survive the play by spending the entire time on *Dead Queens* while Eustace puts together a review so ridiculously scathing, it would make Dead George proud. That's what Cat gets for putting me on editorial standards watchdog duty for a guy she's using as a spy.
> She's pretty savvy, but we're pretty obstinate.
> Anyway, by the time we're walking out, the bus is pulling back in from the game, and Henry meets me at his car looking like he literally just conquered the world.
> "Cleves!" he yells, and then he picks me up and spins me around like I'm some dainty Katie Howard type.
> Keep in mind that this is our first face-to-face interaction

since our attempted hookup. Or at least our first interaction that didn't also involve Cat Parr doing her best vampire impersonation on his neck. Before he literally swept me off my feet, I was planning on going for a cordial, platonic, and professional high-five.

This does feel like the better choice, though. At least to the anti-establishment contrarian in me.

He sets me back down and I almost lose my balance. "Good game?"

"We destroyed them." He gets into the car.

I get in, too. Now that we're talking again, I can't even remember why I was so sure things were going to be awkward between us. I mean, as long as we're not meeting his dad for dinner, I'd say we're solid. "Where are we going?" I ask him.

"Wherever," he says, and then he cranks up the radio and turns the heat on full blast and opens the windows. It's like a loud blizzard in Hell, and I love it. As we drive out to nowhere, I can almost forget the last month even happened.

I'm definitely a fan.

Eventually we're out of the fields and onto a road lined on one side with big houses spaced claustrophobia-close. Henry pulls into a driveway and shuts off the radio, and that's when I realize how freakishly quiet this overcrowded mini-mansion commune is. And *dark*.

Nobody's here.

"So…did the rapture happen while we were driving? And this used to be a colony of devout rich guys?"

Henry laughs and gets out. "Welcome to Culver," he says. He heads up the driveway toward one of the empty houses.

It's three stories high and looks slightly precarious, given how skinny the lot is.

"Is this the town with Lake...Madagascar?"

"Maxinkuckee." Henry's on the porch now. He runs his hand under a windowsill and goes, "Ha!" and holds up a key. Then he bounds back down the steps and over to the garage— bounds, even though he's got an ice pack sealed onto his leg with two hundred square yards of Saran wrap—and unlocks the side door. Something inside starts beeping, but Henry ducks into the dark and after a second, the beeping stops.

"Let the record show that I had no hand in this home invasion."

But of course he ignores my reservations, grabs my hand, and pulls me inside. He flips the lights to reveal a garage that has more interior design than your average living room. There's *art* on the walls and even the shelving is color-coordinated. The space could fit three cars, but instead there's just a Jet Ski on a trailer, which in context looks kind of like a sculpture on a pedestal.

"It's not a home invasion if it's your own place," Henry says.

"I'm dying to hear the mental gymnastics you did to categorize this as your house."

"Technically it's the Howards'," he tells me.

"Sounds like a fairly significant technicality."

He hits a button on the wall and one of the doors starts to roll up. "My dad's grandfather owned this property. He gave it to Norfolk's grandfather."

"In that case, I totally stand by whatever we're doing."

"What we're doing," he says, "is cashing in a debt."

"You're a terrible influence."

"You love it." He crosses the garage to check out the Jet Ski.

"So this is the lake house Parker's always talking about?" I ask. Which seems like a better approach than bringing up any dead Howards or Boleyns.

"God, everything's bragging material for her."

Whenever Henry talks about her, he gets annoyed. Which is retroactively understandable, since she's running around telling every living girl he's ever dated that he's a killer, but that's a new development. And he doesn't even know about it. "What's up with you guys hating each other, anyway?"

"Rochford and me?" He starts unwrapping the ice pack on his leg. "Can't trust her."

"Yeah, but why?"

"She's self-serving as hell. She'll throw you under the bus when she's done with you."

"Okay, but if that's true, wouldn't she have done it when we broke up?"

He drops the bag of ice and goes around to the front of the trailer—the part you'd hook up to a truck. "You sell yourself so short."

"Right. That's why you dumped me."

"Don't be like that. You know it was mutual."

Mutually stupid. "Whatever. But there's no strategic reason for Parker to stay friends with me."

"People like you. You're different."

"Because I'm not like other girls?" I accompany this with an obnoxious foot pop and eyelash flutter. It's too bad I don't

have a flower crown or something to help me fully capitalize on this dumb trope.

"Come on. You do it on purpose."

I give him the double middle finger.

"Anyway, she's probably using you for something. I just
don't know what it is."

"Nice."

"That's what I'm saying. She's not nice." He picks up the
front of the Jet Ski trailer and starts wheeling it out into the
driveway. "Give me a hand with this?"

"I don't even want to know what we're doing," I say, but
I start pushing the trailer anyway. We're probably going to
take it back to Lancaster and leave it on Cat's lawn. "But back
on topic: I don't have anything Parker *wants*. Unless she's in
it for my encyclopedic knowledge of Netflix documentaries
or my off-brand aviator collection."

We have the trailer all the way out of the garage now, and
Henry swings it onto the grass. "It's not going to be obvious.
You won't even notice."

"Your confidence in my observational skills is incredibly
inspiring," I retort.

"Did you know she was helping Katie and Tom hook up?"

"Of course not," I say way too fast, because I'd definitely
rather have him knock my powers of deduction than group
me into the helping-his-girlfriend-cheat category.

"So you probably wouldn't notice if she set you up for
whatever she's plotting."

"She's not plotting. Don't be dumb. You're the one who
plots."

"Takes one to know one," he says grimly. "She's getting friendly with Cat lately, isn't she?"

I stop pushing the trailer. "Wow, Henry. You really know how to make a girl paranoid."

"I don't want her using you."

"She's not. She trusts me."

"Right." We pass the end of the house, and Henry aims for the lake.

"Seriously, the shit she's told me lately—" I stop, because let's be real: Parker's murderer story really doesn't deserve any publicity.

"What did she say? That I'm going to dump Cat?"

"It doesn't matter. It's stupid."

He powers through the last few yards to the water. "Cleves. What did she say?"

"Not worth repeating."

"Come on. Tell me." He comes around to my side of the Jet Ski and takes my hands, and we stay like that, looking into each other's eyes, and I swear it's like he's reading my mind.

"Just prom stuff. You know. The fire wasn't Anna's fault, blah blah."

He laughs. "Classic. Did she mention she was the one who told me Anna was cheating?"

"Yeah, right. That was Jane Seymour."

"It was all Rochford."

"But I thought you told me—"

"Listen," he says. "She was obsessed with George. And she was jealous of how close Anna and George were, so of course

338

she spilled Anna's secrets. She's all about payback bullshit." He shrugs. "But then Anna lost it, and then the Tower happened."

I'm beginning to question my prom investigation, because every new version of the story sucks worse than the previous one. It's way less fun than originally anticipated. "You mean—"

He nods. "If Parker didn't tell, Anna wouldn't have done the Tower. If Anna didn't do the Tower, George wouldn't have died."

His words hit me like an exploding scaffold. I don't know what's true and what's not. I don't know if anybody really knows—nobody who lived through it, anyway. But I do know Parker would swear by any possible excuse if she thought there was even a one-in-a-million chance that her clinical addiction to gossip is the spark that lit the fireworks.

She can't believe she killed George. It might actually, literally, kill her, too.

"Fuck," I say, sitting down on one of the trailer wheels.

He pulls me back to my feet. "I won't let her screw with you, okay?"

"I mean, thanks, but I'm more thinking she's just…losing it."

"She's not."

"Hypothetically?" I say. Maybe Henry's type is girls who overuse hypotheticals.

"You've seen her mess with people. She's a pro. You know that."

"I mean, yeah, but—" And I'm trying exceptionally hard to pretend Henry's wrong, but I'm thinking about Parker and

Lina bestie-ing it up before Anna bulldozed her way to the center of Parker's precious Exclusives table, and how everybody says Parker was Jane Seymour's number one fan before Anna was even cold, and how Jane's just another ex-friend these days.

And how Parker barely has time for me anymore now that Katie's gone and Cat's the new queen bee.

"But we're *friends*," I say, and then I'm literally crying right here in the middle of the Howards' yard. Which is even more embarrassing than it sounds, trust me.

Henry pulls me in against his chest.

"God, I miss Katie," I mumble into his jacket.

He hugs me tighter, snot and tears and all. "I miss her, too."

We stay like that for a minute, and then I'm the one who kills it, because suddenly I'm laughing instead of crying.

"What?" Henry says.

I shake my head. "It's so dumb. We're so dumb. We're worse than the kids whose parents force them onto talk shows to scare everybody else into parenting their kids better."

He starts laughing, too. "And we were supposed to be growing up."

"We're regressing. I'm a side piece, and Parker thinks you're a murderer, and—"

"She said that?"

"I told you she's unhinged. And Cat's just over in the journalism room trying to be useful in all the things she does, and we're all so useless, and she's like, 'Where the hell is my corner office in the *New York Times* building?'"

We're laughing so hard we're almost back to crying. They

can definitely hear us all the way across Lake Maximillion-aire, and somebody's probably going to call the Marine Police or the National Guard or whatever. But I don't care, because the only thing I need right now is to forget about Ms. Parr and Judas Rochford and Anna bin Laden and every last Lancaster kid.

Except Henry.

"Goals," he says.

"Best senior year ever," I yell.

Henry spins me around and sets me back on my feet. Then he kicks through the ice at the edge of the lake and wades in with the Jet Ski. I wade in, too, and climb on behind him. He revs the motor to life, and it's louder than a full military assault.

If the Marine Police weren't onto us before, they definitely are now.

But it doesn't matter. Henry launches us off into the dark, and I clutch onto him for dear life. Then we're flying across the lake, and I scream because (a) why the hell not, and (b) who gives a shit, and (c) we're Henry and Cleves, and everybody else can suck it.

We own this lake and this stolen Jet Ski and this ghost town night.

We'll figure the rest out later.

Culver Neighborhood Watch
Does a Really Great Job

The Marine Police never catch us.

We come back after half an hour, because it's so cold that we'd probably die if we stayed out any longer. I lose my balance while I'm disembarking and fall face-first into the water.

"She's beauty and she's grace," I sing. Or sort of atonally yell through chattering teeth, if we're being honest.

Henry leans off the Jet Ski to pull me up, but then of course he falls in, too.

I let go of his hand and pull a glob of mud out of my hair. "She'll fall flat on her face."

He tries to get up. He falls over again. We're winners through and through.

Eventually we get the Jet Ski back on the trailer and into the garage—and by "we," I mean "Henry," while I do what

I would optimistically call "quality control," but mostly consists of shouting unhelpfully whenever the wheels start taking out the shrubbery. Then Henry shuts the garage door, but instead of going back out to the car, he heads inside.

"Want anything?" He's already in the kitchen. I'm right behind him, dripping lake water all over the perfect hardwood floors. The cops will have a clear roadmap of events when Norfolk Howard reports a burglary.

"A sauna," I say as he digs around in a cabinet and unearths a lone bag of chips.

Henry rips the bag open but leaves it on the counter. He snags a beach towel from a closet, tackles me with it, and sends us crashing into the breakfast nook, where of course we knock three chairs over. "God, you're freezing," he says.

"Yeah, well, I fell in a lake."

He pulls a leaf out of my hair. "This was the best idea."

"I'm not going to argue. I'm just saying my entire body is caked in frozen mud."

He leads me out of the kitchen and points up the stairs. "There's a shower straight up and to the right. The room across the hall has plenty of clothes."

I pry my shoes off, but I still leave footprints all the way up to the most concerning bathroom I've ever encountered. Two of the walls are solid mirrors, and the other two are floor-to-ceiling windows, and I can't figure out how to close the blinds, so I shower in the dark, obviously.

Wrapped up in a fluffy and fashionable Howard-Boleyn towel, I head for the room Henry was talking about and flip

343

the lights on. The second I see everything, I do a stage-worthy uncontrollable shiver.

It's Anna's room.

Creepy factor: off the charts.

There's a fancy sound system, so I turn it on, since I'm kind of freaking out and I want the company. It's classical piano, but not Hannibal Lecter-ish and not Edward Cullen-ish, either. Dramatic and flashy. The walls are super-white with big paintings in black frames, and they're all aggressive abstract things with lots of texture. Past a giant bookshelf is another black-framed masterpiece, but this one isn't art. It's photos.

Which of course I need to investigate, for journalistic reasons.

There's Anna and George and Parker on the pier. Anna and George dressed up outside a church. Anna and a bunch of girls in front of the Arc de Triomphe. Anna and Katie on a boat. Anna playing piano. Anna and Henry, and she's laughing so hard she's blurred.

She looks so real, it legit feels like prom never happened and any second she's going to come in like, *what are you doing in my*—

Then there's a hand on my shoulder, and I go through the ceiling. And scream. And almost lose my towel. So by the time I turn around, I have one hand clutching the towel shut and the other in a velociraptor claw configuration.

Henry's standing there, dying of laughter.

"Not funny," I say, waving my claw in his face.

He goes over to Anna's closet and throws an unimaginably pretentious dressing gown thing at me.

"Dude, you know sexy bathrobes are absolutely not my aesthetic." I smooth my towel down. "Isn't there a T-shirt somewhere?"

"Maybe in Mary's room." He disappears, and I decide hey, what the hell, and put the dressing gown on. It's very asylum-escapee-aboard-the-*Titanic*.

Henry comes back in and cracks up again. "You should wear that to school tomorrow."

"Only if you wear that," I say, because he's in kelly green prepster shorts with whales all over them and a shirt that at first glance looks like your typical screen-print Che Guevara face, except it's Martin Luther instead of Che, and it says *I've got 95 problems.*

"Beggars can't be choosers," he says, handing me a bikini top and shorts so short they'd get you expelled if you even *thought* about wearing them to Lancaster High.

"No way," I tell him, and go tramping around like the Ghost of Girlfriends Past until I find George's room.

I scrape together a moderately workable outfit of the bikini, the obscene shorts, a shirt that says *EXTRA SALTY,* and the dressing gown, because it's really growing on me. When I get back, Henry's sitting on the floor paging through one of Anna's books.

"Okay, don't you find it slightly creepy to be sitting in Dead Anna's room wearing Dead George's clothes listening to Dead Beethoven?"

"Rachmaninov," he says. "And you don't have room to talk."

I wave the dressing gown sash in his face. "I'm just here for the boat theft."

"You live in Anna's old house."

"Is it also built on a sacred burial ground?"

"I'm serious. You didn't know?"

I stare at him. "Excuse me, what? The Boleyns used to live in my house?"

He nods.

"And it never occurred to anybody to mention it?"

"It's not like you really knew them."

"Okay, but you'd think somebody could've found the time to be like, oh, hey, you live in the haunted Boleyn house."

Henry sets the book down. "It's not like the whole school knows your address."

"You do! And what about—I don't know. Katie? Parker?"

"You know I didn't want to talk about her. And I don't think Katie even knew that was their house. She was never in town until she moved in with Norfolk, and the Boleyns were gone by then. And Rochford—who knows." He shrugs.

The Parker thing is bothering me. I've been trying to be Switzerland, but I'm starting to feel like neutrality might be a little risky. Especially since Parker and Henry both think I'm on their side.

I'm the worst double agent in history.

"Okay, but what if Parker's not really playing me?" I say.

"Hey, Cleves." He glances up over my head. "It says 'gullible' on the ceiling."

"Very clever, asshole. I'm sorry the Dead George getup has failed to make you witty."

"And I'm sorry the Dead Anna bathrobe has failed to make you charming."

I dig back into the closet and find a totally ridiculous old-Hollywood hat, a gauzy scarf, and a pair of leopard-print ankle-breakers. I emerge in full costume, waving another double-middle-finger salute. "I'm charming as hell."

"Sit down before you hurt somebody." He grabs my hand, and I dive for the floor and lose the hat and one shoe. And also land practically on top of him.

"Watch it. I'm figuring you out," I say. "You've got a pattern. Get me into a room that isn't mine when I'm cold and emotionally vulnerable. Make sure there's something classical playing, and I'm dressed like the total ingenue I am, and nobody knows we're alone—"

He leans closer and brushes Anna's scarf out of my face. "Is it working?"

My heartbeat's at a full gallop. It *is* working. It's totally working.

But apparently I still have some tiny shred of decency left, because I sit up and say, "I can't hook up with you while I'm wearing your dead ex-girlfriend's seduction bathrobe."

He smirks. "You don't have to be wearing it." And then he does a fake-sexy eyebrow wiggle, but damn him, his fake-sexy is still legit-sexy, and I'm pretty sure he knows it. It doesn't matter if he's wearing a shirt with a five-hundred-year-old joke on it and shorts that scream "irredeemable douchebag." It doesn't matter that he smells like Norfolk Howard's Old Spice and Lake Mad Max. It's that stupid I-own-this-place confidence of his. He's so sure of what he wants that you end up wanting the same thing.

"No no no no no," I say, before the overwhelming majority

of me that doesn't give a damn whose nightgown I'm wearing can destroy the last few brain cells that are still hanging on.

"I know," he sighs, and then he leans back against the wall. We sit there listening to Rachmaninov for a minute, and then Henry says, "Why did we break up, anyway?"

"Hilarious."

"For real."

I honestly don't even want to talk about it, because I'm not the one who did the breaking up. But if he has to ask, he has to listen to whatever bullshit I feel like concocting. "Um, because we never should've been going out in the first place? Because we were only going out because it made sense, like, intellectually, and you're so codependent—"

"Thanks."

"Come on. You suck at being single. And you were over me the minute I freaked out about your Camaro attack."

"*You* weren't into *me*."

"I never said that!" I untangle Anna's scarf, ball it up, and toss it at the closet, but it unwinds like a comet and hits the floor five feet short.

"Not to my face."

"Dude. You're the one who told everybody we never sealed the deal because you felt like you were kissing your sister. Which is interesting, seeing what happened last Thursday—"

"I never said that." Now he looks pissed.

"That's my line. And I wasn't finished. You acted all weird after that night in your car, and—"

"I thought you didn't want— I thought you didn't like me like that."

"Get real," I say, like I'm twelve, but I'm way too annoyed to come up with a better zinger. "I've had a thing for you since our first week of Overachiever Camp, okay? I just thought I was about to get cannibalized. Slasher vibes aren't considered an aphrodisiac where I'm from."

He gets up and throws Anna's crap back into the closet. "You wanted me to go out with Katie."

"I said I was fine with it because I thought you liked her."

"It was your idea!"

I pull off the stupid dressing gown. "It was *never* my idea."

"Then why the hell did you tell Rochford everything?"

"Like what?"

"How we didn't go all the way," he says. "How it wasn't working, and I should dump you for Katie—"

"I literally never said that. I mean, the first thing, but that was it. Parker said *you* didn't think it was working."

Our eyes lock. Rachmaninov slams out a few particularly dramatic chords.

"Rochford," Henry says quietly.

I don't want him to be right about her, but all of a sudden it's crystal clear that she broke us up. And maybe that move could fit in with her Henry-is-a-murderer theory, except for the part where she immediately suggested Katie as a replacement girlfriend—which, if she was expecting future murders, was a pretty cold move.

So apparently she doesn't believe any of her bullshit after all. Apparently she's just fucking with me. And Henry. Again.

This looks so shady, I should probably make a *Dead Queens* post about how Cat should watch her back.

349

"It always comes back to Parker Rochford," Henry says. "Every damn time."

I can't even think of a response, so I just get up and hang Anna's dressing gown in the closet. When I sit back down, I slide in close so I'm leaning against Henry, but the potential makeout moment is over. This is just about being near the only person I can actually trust in this whole shitshow.

"So what should I do?" I finally ask.

He squints at one of the paintings. It looks like those ink-blots you can use to figure out your secrets: If you see a knife, you're probably a killer. If you see a kitten, you probably aren't a killer. If you see boobs, you're probably an eighth-grade boy.

"Act like we never talked," he says after a minute. "Like you aren't onto her. Sooner or later she'll give herself away, and we'll figure it out from there."

The painting just looks like a lot of expensive nothing. "Okay," I say.

We stand up, and Henry pulls me into a hug. It's totally platonic but ridiculously intense at the same time. Like we're about to go to war.

Finally we pull back, but Henry leaves his hands on my arms and looks right into my eyes again.

And he says, "Don't trust anybody."

Operation Desdemona

Nobody Expects the Fort Wayne Inquisition

What Henry may not have realized is what a shockingly untalented actress I am.

I get to Hampton Court Friday morning and promptly make a moron of myself by laughing way too hard at a joke Brandon tells. When Erin looks at me like, *what,* I laugh even harder, and then I high-five Parker for no reason and excuse myself to the library, where I proceed to make a very aggressive vaguepost about the lost art of not being a pathological liar.

I don't even attempt lunch. I just hit the library again.

Rationally this would be a perfect opportunity to maybe (a) actually read *Othello,* because I do want to pass twelfth grade; or (b) research colleges, because if I do manage to graduate, it would be good to have somewhere to go; or (c) pre-

pare for Potential Future Day Job #000, Person Who Makes
No Meaningful Contribution to Society.

Instead I spend the whole time trawling through *Lancaster
Tribune* archives.

Here's the thing: I'm pretty sure Anna did set up the Tower
fireworks, and she might've even been trying to get Henry
back for Jane and all the shit-talking. But I still don't think
she was trying to kill anybody, and if I can just find some
damn receipts to post on *Dead Queens*, maybe people will stop
being such dicks about her. And also stop accusing everybody
and their mother of murder. And also stop inviting Cat Parr
everywhere.

Except there's nothing. I mean, there's something, obviously. But it's about as uninformative as nothing.

May 20: *Two dead in Howard Heights fire.*

It barely even qualifies as perfunctory. It's two paragraphs.
Explosion, prom night, details remain unclear.

Enlightening.

There are articles about it every day for a month, but
there's never anything that means anything. The last article
says, *A representative from the Sheriff's Office confirmed that the
May 19 fire at the Lancaster Country Club has been ruled accidental. Howard Estates CEO Elizabeth Howard-Boleyn declined
comment.*

That's literally it. Other than the mind-boggling number
of editor-deleted comments on every single page that even
sort of references the fire.

Censorship is the real villain in this town, in case you were
wondering.

So I text Eustace: prom. why did people start saying anna was trying to kill people?

He texts back practically before my message goes through.

Eustace: Necklace. Duh

Me: right, but why MURDER-kill? not accident-kill?

Eustace: Cleveland, Cleveland, Cleveland

Me: useless, useless, useless

Eustace: Ms. Parr won't think I'm useless when she gets my story about a gold Camaro driving into Howard Heights at midnight last night

Me: breaking: fuck you

Eustace: Calm down. You're old news. Word on the street is he's into Erin now

Me: that's the least believable thing you've ever said

Eustace: Didn't say it was true. He's acting the same as always with Cat

Eustace: At least in public

Then he sends me the devil emoji twenty separate times,

and the resulting buzzfest compels the librarian to come over and chew me out because "this isn't social hour!" When I tell her it's my lunch block, she starts rambling about how I should write a letter instead of texting, which is definitely the solution I need right now.

So, you know, *ainsi sera*, or whatever.

But I successfully avoid Parker. Which means that the closer we get to the shopping trip, the more I'm trying to weasel out of it. Friday night I text her that I might have to do a family thing. Saturday morning I take it up a notch and tell her I have a headache, which isn't even a lie, because thinking about hanging out with her and Cat all day *is* giving me a headache.

She doesn't text back.

Anyway, I'm crossing my fingers that she's icing me out for being lame, but then at literally the exact second my phone flips over to ten o'clock, the door flies open, and there's Parker in full shopping attire.

"Cleveland, get up, we're going!" she says and starts throwing things at me.

I'm still in bed, so the only weapons I have are my pillow and my computer. "I'm sick!" I yell.

A shoe flies past my head and hits the wall, and a layer of lake mud cracks off and rains down onto the sheets. "You could at least try to make your voice sound hoarse," Parker says, flinging a pair of jeans onto the bed and crouching down to dig for a shirt.

"Migraine."

"You don't get migraines."

"I do when people break into my room at the crack of dawn and start assaulting me with my own belongings." Especially people who deliberately get guys to dump me and then lie about it. "Who let you in?"

"Amelie." She pauses on the shirt I nabbed from George's room. It's inside out, but I'm totally sure she's going to detect his cologne or something and bust me. Then she drops it and grabs a sweater instead. "Get dressed. I don't want to keep Cat waiting."

"I can't go to Fort Wayne. My ankle monitor will detonate."

She throws the sweater at me. "You can't hate Cat *that* much."

"Yeah, and you can't like her that much."

"You're coming." She glances at the closet.

Anna's Hollywood hat is on the doorknob. Where I hung it, like an absolute genius, after wearing it home, also like an absolute genius.

Parker's across the room before I can blink. "What the hell? This is Anna's."

"Um." All I can think is, holy shit, I would make the world's worst criminal. Or spy, which is what I'm supposed to be right now, and I'm starting to wonder about the lasting effects of Henry's bike-slide head injury, seeing as he actually approved me for this role. "No, it's not."

"She got it in Paris. God, the last time I saw her in it was spring break at Lake—"

"It was in the attic," I say before she can telepathically determine that Lake TJ Maxx is exactly where I got it.

"Was there anything else up there?"

I'm not even sure we have an attic. "Um, not much. I don't remember."

"Which is it?"

"What?"

"Not much, or you don't remember?"

I need to make friends with dumber people. "Um. Amelie's the one who went up there. She thought the hat would complement those rocket pajamas you love so much."

She narrows her eyes. "You're acting so weird."

I grab the clothes she threw at me and hop out of bed. "Gotta get ready."

Parker stands outside the bathroom while I brush my teeth and try to manufacture a better lie-face. "When did she go up there?" she says through the door.

"Um. Thursday."

"Why?"

"Um. You know. Looking for lightbulbs. It's a science fair thing. Electricity."

"Are you high or something?"

My Parker-curated floor outfit looks better than half of what I've worn to school in the past two weeks. "On life. And liberty. And also the pursuit of happiness."

"I bet. Hey, can I go up there and look around?"

I throw some water on my face. "Don't want to make us late to pick up my favorite editor-in-chief."

"I meant tonight. When we get back."

"Um."

"Perfect," she says. "Aren't you ready yet?"

"Very sympathetic, coming from the girl who does her hair to go to a hair appointment."

By the time I finish my minimalistic beauty routine and surreptitiously scope out the ceiling—there does, in fact, seem to be a trapdoor between my room and Amelie's—it's pretty clear that (a) there's no way out of this expedition, (b) there's also no way out of attic exploring, and (c) Parker knows I'm up to something. Shocker.

I let Cat have shotgun, and she and Parker gab nonstop while I play the classic role of Annoyed Teenage Offspring On Electronic Device In Back Seat. I'm on *Dead Queens*, combing through the notes on my anti-slut-shaming manifesto. We're past two thousand at this point, which is kind of unbelievable until I look back to yesterday and realize an Actual Legit blog reblogged me. You know, one of those ones attached to an Actual Legit website, with Actual Legit writers who do Actual Legit stories.

And now it's fully unbelievable.

Once we're in Fort Wayne and out of the car, I'm contemplating wandering off and seeing if Parker and Cat even notice, but right when I'm about to split Parker pulls us over to a bakery and says, "I've been dying to try this place." She leads the way in.

And there's Lina Aragón, sitting there reading.

So that's weird.

Cat goes, "Lina!" and runs over and *hugs* her.

So that's also weird.

Then Lina says to Parker, "I thought you were going to tell them."

So that's also weird.

And then Parker goes, "I was, but—" and shrugs.

So I say, "Okay, am I the only one who has no idea what's happening?"

Parker looks at Lina and Cat and me and says, "Sit down, you guys." So we do, and then she says, "I'm sure you're wondering why I brought you all here."

"Holy shit, is this the part where we find out we have superpowers?" I ask, because really, it's like she *wanted* me to say it.

But she's got her Tyrannosaurus Rochford face on. "It's about Henry."

Which is exactly when I figure out that whatever Henry predicted Parker was going to do, she's doing it. Right now.

Cat catches on right when I do. "If this is about the thing from last week—"

"It's about you," Parker says.

Cat glances at Lina, and Lina nods. "You're sure?" Cat asks, and Lina nods again.

Parker starts up in this very polished voice. "You're not safe, Cat."

"I've got it under control," says Cat, because of course she does. She already has three college acceptances. She probably also has her retirement home picked out.

Parker scoffs. "No offense, but Anna thought she had it under control, too, and I love you, but you're not her."

"Fortunately," says Lina, right as Cat goes, "Exactly."

And then everybody looks at each other like, *Whose move is it?*

"Okay, so this identity politics tangent is fascinating and everything, but can someone please fill me in on what's going on?" I ask, because I still feel like I'm missing several very important parts of this equation.

"I *told* you," Parker huffs.

"I don't mean about the…you know." I improvise some murder-y sign language. It's supposed to look like stabbing, but it comes off more like emphatic sports fanning. "I mean, I thought we were shopping."

And at least Cat says, "I thought this was a shopping trip, too."

Lina scoots her chair back. "Why don't we each say what we're doing here?"

She'll be a damn good ambassador someday.

"Any chance you guys want to relocate?" I ask as a woman pushes a stroller right past us.

"It's all good. Howard Estates owns this place," says Parker, like we're in some Crips and Bloods turf war and gang-claim logic counteracts her perennial paranoia. "And I'll start. I'm here to save Cat's life."

She's said it fifty million times by now, but it sounds freshly ridiculous every single time.

"I got everybody together so we can come up with a plan to protect you," Parker says to Cat. "I didn't tell you because I didn't want you to bail."

"Kidnapping," I say. "Again."

Cat looks over at Lina. "Do you trust Cleveland?"

I lean in. "Hello. Right here."

Lina nods. Which is a tad guilt-inducing, given my current spying-and-lying gig. On the other hand, I'm not the one who started the spying-and-lying trend in the first place.

"And Parker asked you to come here to convince me about—" Cat does my murder-mime thing. It's the best thing that's happened all day.

Lina nods again. "I'm on my way home for the break. Parker's giving me a ride the rest of the way."

"So you want us to—what? Join your gang?" I ask Parker. Which, yes, I'm kidding. But I'm also only barely kidding, because that's the point we've reached on this wild ride of accusation-lobbing.

"Protect Cat. Duh. You're his best friend, and Lina was with him for like twenty-five years. If we work together, we can get inside his head."

"You guys seriously think Henry's a killer?" I say. "Come on."

Parker stares at me like I'm the outlandish one. "Yes."

"I never said that," Lina tells me. "I said someone set up the fireworks, and it wasn't Anna."

"Close enough," says Parker.

"What about you, Cleveland?" Cat asks.

"I'm here for the shopping."

She goes full Ms. Parr. "Seriously."

"Let's just say I'm somewhat skeptical about Henry's ability to *murder* somebody."

"Come on!" Parker practically yells, and the tragic grad student at the next table jumps. "I told you everything!"

"Yeah, and I'm reserving judgment."

Cat raises her eyebrows. "That's new."

"Character development," I shoot back. "And also, I want to know what we're doing."

"We're stopping Henry," says Parker. "We're going to figure out a safe way for Cat to break up with him."

She's sounding suspiciously reasonable.

"And then we're going to trick him into confessing and get him thrown in jail for the rest of his effing life."

False alarm.

"Maybe we should focus on the first thing," I say. "Especially since you're the only one who thinks Henry murdered anybody."

"That's not exactly accurate," Cat says, and we all stare at her.

I shake my head. "Two days ago you were ready to strap Rochford into a straitjacket."

"Two days ago," she says deliberately, like a politician referencing some unspeakable act of war instead of, you know, a high schooler referencing some unspeakably crazy conversation, "I didn't trust you."

"Me?" Parker and I ask at the same time.

Cat nods toward me.

"This is what I get for selflessly redacting Parker's death threat?"

"You're friends with Henry," she says, and for a second, I'm sure Eustace told her exactly what kind of friends we are. "But I talked to Lina yesterday, and she said you weren't the type to rat me out." She folds her hands together. "I've been suspicious of Henry since last spring."

"What?" Parker sounds totally shocked, like what Cat's saying isn't incredibly tame next to her own story.

"George never kept his mouth shut," says Cat. "I don't think Anna was cheating. I think Henry decided she was too much to handle, and then it turned into character assassination."

"So you don't think she staged the explosion?" I ask. I can't even keep up with who thinks who said what and who did what. The minute they release me from my latest kidnapping, I'm going straight to the craft store to buy a hundred yards of string and a thousand thumbtacks, because every obsessive genius in cinema history can't be wrong when it comes to connecting implausible theories in a visually compelling way.

Cat shakes her head. "Anna just wanted to prove she wasn't cheating. It doesn't fit her motives. But it fits Henry's. Maybe it was the bike accident, or the guilt when Lina left. Maybe he just got tired of Anna. Hypothetically, he scares her into giving up, and he frames her, so he comes off looking like the victim. His image stays intact."

The grad student heaves a massive sigh at the book he's reading. Sad Grad really gets me.

"It worked," says Cat. "Maybe too well, but maybe just like he wanted. And then Katie happened."

"You think he killed Katie, too?" Parker's practically breaking out the champagne.

"I'm saying I went from suspicious to—" Cat does a there-you-have-it motion. "I wanted to get a closer look."

I blink. "So you tricked him into going out with you?"

"He's predictable," Cat says with a shrug. "His rebounds

are always the opposite of the girl he's done with. Lina was popular and she followed the rules. Anna liked being controversial. Jane was agreeable. Cleveland was different. Katie was a little shallow—"

"Excuse me," Parker and I cut in at the same time.

"I'm not saying I agree. I'm saying that's the profile she fit."

"Wow. So much for your editorial disdain for unsubstantiated gossip," I mutter.

"I liked Katie," Cat says, totally level. "But when he started looking for a rebound, I knew he'd want somebody more academic, more responsible, probably not as young. Someone like me."

She's not just the editor-in-chief. She's an actual criminal profiler straight off some FBI show. In a second she's going to whip out a photo album and start pointing out secret messages in the way Henry combs his hair.

"So when I asked if you tricked him into dating you, you could've just said yes," I say.

"I thought I could get a better look from the inside."

"What's your endgame?" Lina asks. She looks kind of shell-shocked by the Agent Parr revelation, too.

Cat hesitates. "I'm not sure."

"Beautiful," I say. "You recruit a fake boyfriend on the off chance he'll spontaneously incriminate himself for murder, but you have zero idea how to pull it off and zero idea what you're going to do if you *do* pull it off?"

"And what if he KILLS YOU?" Parker semi-shouts. I'm starting to see how she and Katie and Tom got caught.

Cat's still so unruffled I'm starting to suspect she's from the same emotion-free alien planet as Jane Seymour. "He's not a cold-blooded killer. He's emotional. Cheating sets him off because it's an insult *and* a betrayal. As long as I don't cheat, I'm safe."

"Anna didn't cheat," Parker snaps.

"You're literally the one who told Henry she did," I say.

"Oh my God. When are you going to wake up and realize he's lying to you?" She's still edging fairly close to yelling. "The point is, Cat's not safe. We need a plan. But before we do anything else, we're going back to Cleveland's house and checking out the attic."

She stands up and sweeps out of the bakery, and she's the one with the car, so it's not like the rest of us can do anything except follow her out.

But I stop at the door to text Henry first, because the way things are going, Parker's going to hijack Air Force One to skywrite a list of fully unbelievable accusations before today is over. And then possibly blitzkrieg Henry's house.

I mean, he warned me about her, but this is excessive.

So I type: SOS. parker wants revenge and you're the target.

Public Service Announcement:
Your Attic Is Probably Cursed and You
Definitely Should Not Go Up There

In what may be a personal first for Parker, we make it to and
from Fort Wayne without acquiring any clothes, shoes, or
manicures. There's not even a debate. We just go straight to
my house and straight to the attic trapdoor.

"Come on, Parker, Amelie said there's nothing up there."

She drags a chair out of the library. "We're looking anyway."

"What if you just talked to him?"

"Good luck with that," Lina says. She's playing spotter, and
Parker's climbing onto the chair in her very knifelike stilettos.

"It makes sense to get all the information we can first,"
says Cat, steadying the chair as Parker gets her hands on the
ring in the door.

"I'm just saying, it's kind of sounding like we're about to turn into a pitchfork mob, and wouldn't it make sense if—"

"First of all, what the hell is a pitchfork mob, and second of all, no," says Parker. She pulls the ring, and the door opens with the most ungodly screeching noise known to man.

Parker hops off the chair—yes, hops, in her knife-shoes. She pushes the chair off to the side and Cat unfolds the ladder. They're both up in the attic so fast I don't even have time to argue back, and Lina follows them up. I'm on my way after her when my phone buzzes.

Henry: What do you mean, revenge?

Me: for george and anna

Henry: Hard to get revenge for both at once since his death was her fault

"Cleves, get up here!" Parker yells from somewhere in my ceiling.

Me: i'll keep you posted

Then I climb up into the attic and it's the exact opposite of whatever I was expecting, which wasn't much—like, plywood and cobwebs. The rafters are stained really dark, and the rest of the ceiling is off-white and all weird angles, so it feels like those half-timber buildings they had back in ancient England. There's a couch and a coffee table and a seriously overloaded bookshelf. Off in another corner is a sort of art-fully messy collection of blankets and pillows, all of which look far too frou-frou to be decorating an attic floor.

"So your sister's a liar," says Parker.

I somehow manage not to say, *Well, it takes one to know one,* mostly because I'm too busy staring at the fully furnished se-cret room I never knew I had in the house I never knew was Anna's. Who leaves a room-sized time capsule when they move? That's some ghost-story shit right there.

"Is this how it looked when the Boleyns lived here?" Lina asks. She's at the bookshelf, running one thumb over the ti-tles. Just in case one of them is *How to Murder Your Boyfriend* or *What to Do If You Think Your Boyfriend Might Murder You,* I guess.

Parker nods. "Pretty much. God, this was the best place to hang out."

"Okay." Cat's moving on to the investigative portion of today's itinerary. "I'll look through the books with Lina. Is there anything we should be watching for?"

"A signed confession from Henry," I say. "Or Anna. Or Jane. Any signed confessions you can find, really."

Parker follows Cat over to the bookshelf. "I don't know. You're the one who's good at this spy stuff, right?"

Cat doesn't dispute that, which is great, because if there was one thing I needed in my life, it was for my nemesis to turn out to be a scrappy girl detective who still doesn't trust me. Also, I'm starting to think I should've chosen a different nemesis, because aside from her censorship fetish, Cat's turn-ing out to be objectively awesome.

"So I guess I'll handle the managerial aspects," I say after a minute.

"Look over everything else," Cat directs without glancing up from the book she's examining, which I'm pretty sure is a dictionary. "See if anything's out of place."

"Holy crap. You're right. Somebody moved the couch an inch to the left."

"Cleves," says Parker. "Just look. And then come help us with the books."

So I wander around checking the walls for encoded messages and looking under the couch for weapons. Ten minutes yields exactly one discovery—a note in pen on the underside of the coffee table, in baby-Parker bubble letters: *Parker Boleyn.*

Which would be great material for making fun of her, because Modern Parker would have a total field day if any of her girls started scribbling that kind of thing on their geometry notebooks, let alone on other people's furniture, but given the circumstances it's actually super depressing, so I keep my mouth shut.

See? Cat isn't the only appropriate one.

Anyway, once I've scanned every square inch, I flop down in the pillow nest. My phone buzzes, and it's Henry: Are you still with Parker?

By the time I type yeah, my taskmasters have figured out I'm slacking. "Are you done?" Lina asks. She looks like she's ready to win a fight. Possibly an entire battle. I'm not fully comfortable with this, since I'm still not sure if she's done being mad at me for being too Team Anna at the Siege of Notre Dame. Which you'd think wouldn't matter anymore, given what we're doing, but if there's one thing I've learned this week, it's that we're all double-crossing traitors.

Or something.

So I just go with, "I'm investigating thread counts."

"Can you start on the right end of the top shelf?" Cat asks.

"As soon as I finish my thread count investigation."

Parker finally tears her eyes away from the books and looks at me with the sort of dramatic wistfulness typically reserved for fifty-year-old photo albums. "You know, the very first time I slept with George was right there where you're sitting."

"Ew. Good to know." I start to get up, but of course the ten thousand blankets slide around and I halfway fall and something stabs me in the hand. I yelp and everybody looks over to see me bleeding like one of those saints who gets sainted when they develop unexplained Jesus-wounds. "God, Parker, what the hell were you guys into?"

Lina pulls back the blankets and Cat digs around. "Found it," she says, holding up a little notebook with a pen hooked into the spiral at just the right angle to inflict stab wounds.

Posthumous stabbing. I count this as a solid vote in the Anna-did-it column.

"Hey, how did that get up here?" Parker's over with the rest of us now, and sure enough, the cover has her initials on it.

"Maybe you were scheduling your sex appointments."

She smacks me with a pillow. "No, I mean—that notebook's in my room. Or at least it was last weekend."

All three of them look at me, like maybe I broke into Parker's room to steal last year's cheerleading notes and hide them in Mr. and Mrs. George Boleyn's conjugal blanket-fort. "What? I don't know, either."

My phone buzzes and I glance down and see another text from Henry: Is Cat with you?

And then Parker shrieks the most intense oh-my-God I've heard from her since End of the Road. She's staring at the first page. So I look, too, and…it's a notebook.

"What?" I ask.

"Oh my God. Oh my effing GOD." Parker points at the *This belongs to* line, and okay, it's definitely not her handwriting, even though it's her name.

"Anna wrote that," says Lina.

"So…she was gearing up to murder Parker and assume her identity? Plot twist."

Cat glances at me. "Whatever she was putting in here, she didn't want anyone looking at it. So she made it look like it wasn't even hers."

"And if anything happened, whoever found it would give it back to Parker," Lina adds.

Parker's got an incredibly pale-faced thing going on, and when she flips the page her hand shakes, but then she gets it under control because, you know, years of training.

The first page says *May 11* in the same pointy, tiny handwriting. Parker reads the first line out loud. "'I don't know what's going on, but I know I'm screwed. Yesterday he said, 'I could bring you down just as fast as I raised you up.' Obviously that's bullshit, because I'm the one who got myself here, but—'"

Parker looks up at us and laughs, just a little giggle, but

a split second later she's full-on cracking the hell up. "God, that's so Anna."

"Keep reading!" says Cat.

So Parker gets herself back together. "'—but I don't even know what I did. He knows I didn't cheat. But everyone believes him because he's Henry, and Jane's so fake sweet no one believes she'd scratch my name out on the prom nominations if she could.'"

Parker pauses again but nobody nags her. "'I'm sure Lina's laughing about this from whatever fresh tropical hell she's in, because here I am with some girl tricking Henry into getting rid of me, and of course that's what everyone thinks I did to her. We're going to get rid of Jane just like we got rid of Maggie—'"

"Who's Maggie?" I ask.

"Maggie Shelton. She graduated last year," says Lina. "Henry paid too much attention to her back in April."

Parker nods. "Anna had me tell Maggie that if she didn't stay away from Henry, she'd be dealing with some very private pictures going public."

"And I'm supposed to believe Anna's the innocent victim here?"

"Just because she wasn't innocent doesn't mean she wasn't a victim," Cat points out like she's some sage on a mountaintop.

"Exactly," says Parker, and then she keeps reading. "'—just like we got rid of Maggie, but this time Henry's going down, too.'"

I slide in closer so I can read over Parker's shoulder. "This sounds a lot like a confession."

"It's not. Listen to this: 'I have to figure out what he's try-ing to do without him knowing I'm doing it, so when Henry does whatever he's going to do to make everybody hate me even more, I'll have proof.' See?"

"That doesn't mean she didn't decide to get revenge. That's what she's *talking* about."

"We've got to read the whole thing," says Cat.

So we do. It starts out pretty uneventfully: Henry says some-thing dickish, Henry yells at Mark, George says something shitty about Henry. Then on May 14, Anna starts *following* Henry, because that's definitely not something a vigilante would do.

She follows him to Jane's house the next day—and there's a picture she printed out and taped in the notebook so she could delete it from her phone in case of, I don't know, the NSA forwarding it to Henry.

"This is exactly what the defense needs for an airtight alibi," I say. "Don't worry, Anna couldn't have done it, and here's a picture of Jane Seymour's front door."

"She was covering her bases." This is Cat, not Parker, sur-prisingly enough, since Parker's been covering the role of Chief White Knight with great gusto.

I check in with Lina, because apparently she's my only pos-sible ally in terms of looking at *Confessions of a Teenage Prom Queen* with any shred of objectivity. "Okay, I'm willing to bet everything in this attic that you never followed Henry around taking pictures of Anna's house."

"There are quite a few things Anna did that I didn't," Lina says.

"Wow. Four for you, Lina Aragón."

Anyway, after a few more Seymour house creepshots—
made substantially more interesting by the fact that there's a
life-size stone wolf in the front yard, and in one of the pictures it almost looks real—we get a play-by-play of Henry
walking into this charm bracelet store two doors down from
Le Overpriced Croissant.

"Dude, this is next-level," I say when Parker turns the page,
because here we have a picture of the store copy of Henry's
receipt. He bought a necklace with a heart charm, apparently,
but that's beside the point since Anna openly admits to getting the receipt for "her records" after telling the poor innocent store lady that she's Henry's fiancée.

"That was for Jane." Parker flips another page and points
to the next morning's notes: Henry tried to give Jane the
necklace, but she wouldn't take it, *because she's playing hard to
get*, Anna writes. *Wonder where she learned THAT trick.* "He
got her to take it at prom," Parker adds. "That was when the
fight happened."

The necklace-ripping: another sign of Anna's unimpeach-
able stability.

We keep reading, and by Friday—T-minus one and a half
days until the march up the scaffold—all we have is a remarkably complete Henry itinerary.

"See?" says Parker. "She wasn't plotting."

I give her my best *are you serious* look, and of course it can't
hold a candle to her well-honed eyeball daggers, but it's the
best I've got. "Yeah, because otherwise she would've been
like, 'Oh, and after I caught this prime footage of Henry going

through the McDonald's drive-thru, I rigged up the Tower to explode'? Come on."

She throws the eye-daggers. "Whose side are you on, any-way?"

"I'm not on a side. I'm a neutral third party on the side of truth and justice."

"That's interesting, because it seems like you're on the side of 'I still have a major thing for Henry.'"

"Like you guys aren't biased!"

"I'm not," says Cat.

"You literally signed up to be his girlfriend just to bring him down!"

"Not to bring him down. To find out the truth."

She's the undisputed champion of pedantic semantics. "Right. And the truth is Henry isn't a murderer just because Anna didn't take a selfie at a fireworks stand."

Then I reach for the notebook and flip a page, and there's a fireworks stand.

But Henry's the one walking in.

"GIVE ME THAT RIGHT NOW!" Parker screams straight into my ear, even though the book is right in front of her. She grabs it and proceeds to wave the picture violently in our faces. "I told you! It's proof! She pulled it off!"

You know that feeling when you trip, but you catch your-self, and even though you don't actually fall, you get that shot of adrenaline and your whole body goes cold, like it still thinks you're about to plaster your face to the pavement? Yeah. That's how I feel right now. And the picture might not mean what Parker thinks it means, but I can't even clear that up because she won't stop shaking it around and shrieking about how great Anna is. So after ten seconds of that I start yelling, too: "Parker! Let me see it! Come on!"

Finally Lina gets a hand on the notebook and Cat gets a hand on Parker's arm and Parker lets go.

"Chill," I say. "He's just buying the roman candles."

"Bull-effing-shit," says Parker.

On the opposite page there's a picture of Henry coming out of the store carrying a ton of bags. "She followed him almost to Ohio," Cat reports. "That big store right on the border, you know? You can see it from 35. Next to the giant cross."

"Symbolism. Fantastic," I say, but the falling-on-my-face feeling is taking over my entire body.

"Obviously." Parker's totally shrill. "He couldn't go any-where close."

"And a bigger store means they're less likely to remember anybody," Lina says.

"She said he was inside from three fifty-five to four twenty," Cat reads.

"Blaze it," I mumble, because my mouth is on autopilot. Because all my mental energy is going toward freaking the fuck out.

Henry didn't do it. He couldn't have. Anna set him up.

"Look." Lina's pointing at a caption. "She used company cars so he wouldn't notice her following him."

Cat's nodding. "And she thought the fireworks were for a party she didn't know about, for Jane and everybody, and the Tower was just a cover to get her out of the way."

I'm still freaking the fuck out.

Cat turns the page, and Parker shrieks again. It's two pictures: a long receipt with a million things on it, and then a picture of some permission slip or whatever you sign when you buy that many explosives at once, in case you end up killing your girlfriend.

"That's not Henry's signature," I say. "It's not even his name. It says Rex something."

"It's his fake," says Lina, and then Cat helpfully reminds us you have to be eighteen to buy fireworks and besides, this way there's zero trace of Henry buying anything.

They won't stop talking. And they're *excited*. Like it's the best news they've ever heard.

I get up to go back down the ladder and get the hell out of the attic, but with the way I'm feeling I don't think I'll be able to navigate it without taking it headfirst and breaking my spine, which I'm sure Parker would blame on Henry. So I just get as far away from everybody as I can, which is the couch, and then I sit there death-gripping my phone, because hey, at least it's real, and right now I need something real to hold on to until I can talk to Henry and find out what really happened.

Anna set him up. It was her. It had to be.

It wasn't Henry.

Correspondent Is
Extremely Done with Boys

"**C**leveland. Hey. Are you okay?"

The couch is no longer a Cleves-only zone. Parker's next to me and Lina's sitting on the coffee table holding the notebook and Cat's crouching in front of me like I might spontaneously pass out.

"Is that an actual question? We just found out Henry might have blown up the Tower."

"Might have?" Parker says like I'm the one casually accusing my best friend of murder, terrorism, and generally being evil.

I blink at her. "So no, I'm not okay, and it's kind of disturbing that you guys are."

"Well, we weren't surprised," says Lina.

I give them a long look. "You guys are making me feel like an ass," I finally say. "I mean, Parker, you practically died in that fire. And Lina, you guys were together forever. But I'm the one flipping out. Please slap me."

They wait like they're not sure if I'm kidding, so I attempt a laugh, and then they laugh, too—a little too enthusiastically, but whatever.

My phone buzzes, and everybody looks at it, and of course it's Henry again: Hello??? Is Cat with you?

"What the hell are you doing texting a murderer?" Parker tries to grab my phone, but her talons aren't the best on hard surfaces.

"He's not a murderer. And you sit with him at lunch."

"Because otherwise he's going to murder me, too!"

"He's not a murderer!"

She grabs for the phone again. "He bought the fireworks. He framed Anna with her necklace. He threatened me. It's airtight."

My phone's going off again. This time he's calling me.

"Don't answer it," Cat says. "Text him back. Tell him you don't know where I am."

I stare at Henry's face on the screen. "He knows you're shopping with us."

"He's going to get suspicious. Say I had to skip it. I'll get Erin to cover for me."

"Um, isn't it more suspicious if we're actually lying?"

But she's already setting up her alibi, so I go ahead and text him. If I thought lying felt like shit before, I wasn't even vaguely prepared for this.

"I need to talk to him," I say.

"NO." It's three-part harmony.

"Can't we give him a chance to explain himself?"

"He's had plenty of chances," says Lina.

"I just—" What's bothering me the most is everything we talked about at Lake Maximus. You'd think he'd trust me enough to tell me the truth if it was an accident. Or even just—I don't know. Not talk about it. It's freaking me out the way he blamed Anna and Parker instead.

But it's not like I can mention it, because (a) they'd figure out I was an unsuccessful double agent for thirty-six hours, although now I appear to have progressed to the rank of unsuccessful triple agent; and (b) I'd have to include our lake escapade; and (c) I'd have to admit I was open to believing Parker was a criminal mastermind—which in retrospect was stupid, given how she couldn't even hack *Dead Queens* without outing herself.

So I go with this excellent non sequitur: "Why did you trick Henry and me into breaking up?"

"I didn't trick you," says Parker. "You agreed with everything I said."

"Dude. You totally played us off each other."

"Do we really need to do this right now?" Cat asks.

"YES," Parker and I tell her.

"Maybe you guys can work this out while Cat and I start figuring out a plan," says Lina, and the two of them head back down the ladder.

Parker glares at me. "I was saving your damn life, okay?"

"That excuse only works if you didn't throw Katie at him in my place."

Her eyes flash actual fire. "Take that back. Right now."

"I'm not blaming you. I'm just saying, it doesn't make sense to get me away from him if you were just going to give him some fresh cannon fodder. You told me he liked her!"

"He did, okay?" Parker grabs the notebook and stares at a picture of Henry loading fireworks into the Camaro. "But how was I supposed to know he *liked* her, liked her? I thought he liked her like—you know, the way he liked Anna's sister. Or Liz or Maggie. Just like, you know, hey, she's hot. I thought he'd hook up with her, not ask her out."

"So you're a pimp. Awesome."

"You know what I'm saying. I never thought anything was going to happen. She was falling all over herself about Tom, okay?"

It's pretty close to believable. In the context of how unbelievable my life has gotten, at least. "Why didn't you just tell me? Instead of sneaking around breaking us up?"

"Yeah, because you totally would've believed me."

Fair. "Well, why were you helping Katie and Tom—"

"I was trying to keep her from getting caught. They were already together, and she didn't get it, so what the hell was I supposed to do? She wasn't even being careful, and she was dating a murderer."

"You've got to stop calling him that. You're making it sound like he was *trying* to kill them."

"Yeah, and you've got to stop acting like it was just a prank. They *died*, okay?" She flips past the fireworks to Anna's last entry—it's prom day and she's freaking out because she can't find her phone or her necklace. It ends with *I'm so over this. Henry probably stole my necklace to give to Jane with that cheap trash he bought. I dare him to try, because you know it will look like shit with the future double chin she has going. I'm clearly the superior choice, be-*

cause I have a little neck. Ha. I'm losing it, right? Here's to a flawless prom. And maybe once it's over everybody can finally stop hating me.

The opposite page is blank.

"That's so Anna," says Parker. "It's like she's not even gone. And it effing kills me every time somebody talks shit about her. But I can't say anything because—"

She tips her head back and does a completely symmetrical tear-flick thing at the corners of her eyes. "God, I'm so sick of ruining my makeup over that asshole." She tear-flicks again. "You don't even know how glad I am that you made it out alive, okay?"

And then she hugs me so hard I legit see stars.

I said it the last time I got blindsided with a new twist in the world's most twisted prom night: I don't know what's true and what's not.

I still don't know.

Maybe Anna freaked out and jumped to conclusions, which in her defense is a defining feature of youth culture in Lancaster.

Maybe Henry's scared to tell the truth because whatever was supposed to happen at the Tower went so wrong, nobody would believe there was ever a non-disastrous way for it to go.

Or maybe Henry's a liar.

I've heard every possible version of the story. Now I have to figure out what I actually believe.

And I'm going to have a metric fuckton of questions for Henry the next time the Amazons let me talk to him. Like what he was doing at that store and what really happened on prom night and why the hell he tried to set Parker up.

I mean, I'm not saying he was a murderer.

But I *am* saying he owes us some answers.

At Last, an Answer to "Will I Ever Use This in Real Life?"

After we finish our Hallmark moment, which does actually get me feeling ten million times closer to my actual self, we call Lina and Cat back up.

"Okay," says Lina, and we all wait for her to direct us, of course. Possibly the only positive development of this ill-fated attic adventure is that Queen Lina and Tyrannosaurus Rochford are done hating each other, meaning I'm no longer being iced out by association. "We figured it out."

"That was fast," I say, but it's barely a surprise since they're both so stupidly smart. Leave them alone for another hour and they'd probably achieve world peace, which would be a major bummer for Parker, since this would lead to the end of pageant interview questions and, ultimately, pageanting itself.

Cat shrugs. "Henry made it easy. And Shakespeare helped."

THE DEAD QUEENS CLUB

She slaps my beat-up copy of *Othello* down next to Anna's spy book.

I sneak a glance at Parker, but she's nodding. Apparently I'm the only one who doesn't have the Complete Works memorized. "Everyone dies?"

Lina lifts her chin, and the way she does it would come off looking Mussolini-ish if it was Cat and straight-up ridiculous if it was me, but she makes it look imperial. "We're calling it Operation Desdemona," she says. I kind of expect some massive digital display to pop up next to her. "What does Henry hate more than anything else?"

"Being single," I guess.

"Being cheated on," says Parker.

Lina nods at her. "Right."

"It's an insult to his masculinity," Cat says, like we're in my mom's Angry Feminist Writing seminar. "And it's humiliating. That's why he couldn't just dump Anna and Katie. He had to get them back for making him look bad."

Parker's getting the dagger look going again. "Anna didn't even—"

"People thought she did. The damage was done."

I'm not exactly sure where this line of philosophizing is supposed to be getting us. "Wait," I say. "We want answers. Can't we just...you know, ask?"

They look at me with a rich variety of disappointed expressions.

"Yes," Cat says after I've been sufficiently shamed. "If we want to hear a new version of the same cover-up story. But if we want the truth, we have to turn the pressure up."

I settle back into the couch, because clearly we're in for a long ride. "So you're going to cheat on Henry, and then if you die in a tragic debate-club podium malfunction, you'll be like, 'I told you so'?"

Lina answers instead of Cat. "She's not going to cheat." She taps *Othello*, which I'm beginning to wish I'd read. "We make it look like she's talking to somebody else. Then we make him think they're going to meet, and I guarantee he'll try to confront her. The rest of us will show up before he has a chance to do anything."

"Okay, but what happened to Katie happened in, like, a second," says Parker.

"We'll always have someone close enough to stop him. We won't leave anything to chance," Lina tells her.

I mean, they're brilliant and everything, but there's at least one serious flaw in this plan. "Are you just going to hire a stripper to play the guy?" I ask. "Because Henry's definitely going to see through it if Cat starts making a locker shrine to a stock image."

"TJ," Cat says.

"Who?"

"Thomas Seymour. Jane's brother."

Apparently the entire Seymour family suffers from forgettability. "Sorry, Mata Hari. Henry knows TJ's in Belarus."

"Belgium," says Cat. "But he's coming home next week for Christmas."

"Except his family doesn't live here anymore."

"Henry's going to think he's going back to campus first. And visiting Cat," Lina says.

"Just...telepathically, or something? Or am I supposed to post that on *Dead Queens*?"

"Cat's going to leave her computer unlocked," Lina says.

Parker looks highly skeptical. "You can't trust TJ. He'll totally cave if Henry talks to him. And anyway, he's creepy. I don't know why you like him."

"Maybe I've stopped giving a damn what anybody else thinks about who I like," Cat shoots back, and it's feisty enough that Parker and I both do a double take.

"Wow, Ms. Parr." I grab a book off the table and fake-fan myself with it. "And here I thought your style was the eternal high road by all censorship necessary."

"My style," she says, "is navigating Lancaster High School with the best grades I can get, the fewest enemies I can make, and the best future I can set up for myself. That doesn't mean I don't have a personality. You just haven't gotten to see it yet, because we're not friends."

I'm staring, and Parker's in hysterics. *"Cat,"* she gasps out. "You need to be like this all the time. It's an actual tragedy the way everybody just thinks you're, like, appropriate."

Cat makes a totally disgusted face. "They're not the ones trying to manage five APs and date a murderer. Speaking of which, Cleveland, I'd really appreciate a retraction on that essay Eustace wrote about—'upwardly mobile serial monogamy'? Was that the headline you gave it?"

"My writers write whatever they want."

"Your writers write whatever gets attention," says Cat. "Which is exactly what the *Ledger* looked like last year when

Eustace and his anti–Anna bandwagon gave the cheating stories enough credibility that two people ended up dead."

Parker takes a two-second laughter intermission to go, *"Damn."*

"People listen to you, Cleveland," Cat tells me. "You can do anything you want with that. But sometimes standards are a good thing."

I'm temporarily stunned into silence, because Cat 2.0 does kind of maybe have a point. Other than like ten things that need a strong rebuttal. "Right, but—"

"We're not telling TJ," says Lina.

We do a synchronized meerkat head-turn toward her.

"Um," I say. "What?"

"The plan," says Ambassador Aragón. "We're making a fake account that looks exactly like TJ's, but he'll never know. If Henry tries to get to him, he'll just keep saying he doesn't know what Henry's talking about."

I'm still off-balance from finding out Cat is actually the fight-me type, and I'm picturing her at Williams or Swarthmore or wherever, walking into her dorm and seeing that some unsuspecting legacy has claimed the top bunk. And then Cat will take off her earrings and her blazer and proceed to put that girl in her place, possibly with actual fisticuffs.

I kind of don't hate her anymore. I actually kind of love her.

I definitely need to hire a new nemesis.

"Hey. Hello." The new-and-improved Cat is snapping her fingers in my face. "Are you listening?"

"Henry stalks you. We stalk him. We ask him why he blew

up the Tower and he says he was just trying to scare Anna. We tell him not to do it again. We all live happily ever after."

"The part where she said you're not allowed to talk to him about this. Any of this."

"Um, freedom of speech," I say, just to stay on-brand, but then I tell her that yeah, I won't. Because whatever's going on with Henry, I've gone from defensive to annoyed. There's no way in hell he wasn't trying to manipulate me two nights ago when he drove me all the way out to the lake to convince me Parker was evil. You don't do shit like that if you're not hiding something.

And you also don't do shit like that if you care about somebody the way I thought he cared about me. Which, okay, feel free to laugh, because I'll be the first to admit my chronic inability to be alone with Henry without trying to jump his bones is interfering with my rational thinking skills. Fine. But he sure as hell has been acting like he cared, and now it's looking more and more like it was all part of the game to make sure somebody's on his side.

For the record, I still think it was an accident. The death part, that is.

But the way he's been covering it up isn't an accident.

The more I think about it, the more I realize how pissed off I am with his royal majesty. And how goddamn grateful I am to be surrounded by a pack of girls this badass.

"Operation Desdemona," I say, and I swear I'm going to read *Othello* soon, for real, for Desdemona's sake. "I'm there. You don't even *know* how there I am."

Does Lancaster High School Even Have a Journalism Teacher? Parent~Teacher Association Raises Concerns

We all get code names, of course. That's my first assignment. I assign it to myself right there in the attic. Parker and Cat are making the fake TJ account and blowing up Cat and Fake TJ's chat log. Lina's poring over the spy book and writing out the ops plan. I'm supposed to be helping her, but after a few minutes the lack of code names becomes too glaring to overlook.

Parker is MGB, short for Mrs. George Boleyn. Lina is The Queen, of course. Cat's The Ref, short for Reformation, since I can't get over her secret sass. Henry gets a name, too, for thoroughness, and I go with his football number, but Roman numerals to be both classy and confusing in case our correspondence falls into hostile hands: VIII.

And I'm The Ex-Files. For obvious reasons.

Anyway, thank God I bothered coming up with code names, because I'm carrying most of the weight in the first phase of Operation Desdemona, and without an alter ego, I'm not sure I'd be able to pull it off. Fortunately, the Henry-Erin rumor has gained some traction by Monday, and that's a decent distraction.

This may have something to do with a certain Eustace Chapman masterpiece I posted on *Dead Queens*. With Ms. Parr's full blessing, because now that she's (a) editor-in-chief, (b) early-admission-accepted at like four schools, and (c) successfully dating an alleged murderer, her newest mission in life is (d) making sure everybody's primed to believe she's down to cheat, which means she needs a motive.

Or something.

Anyway, Phase One starts with Cat texting Henry after a long day of marveling at the wild-eyed look Parker's sporting, thanks to her insatiable thirst for vengeance. Cat forwards us the texts in real time:

The Ref: Can we talk? Rumor about you and Erin is freaking me out

VIII: You know it's bullshit

The Ref: Do I?

VIII: Come on, Brandon's my best friend

The Ref: And Erin's mine. Your point?

VIII: I'm not cheating

The Ref: Meet me in the office after class? We need to talk about this

VIII: I'm not cheating

The Ref: See you at 2:00

Henry doesn't text back, but Cat swears he'll be there. So I march boldly onward to the live-action part of Phase One, fortified by a bottle of Mountain Dew plus half of Christina's Red Bull, which I was hoping would make me feel like a snowboarder who does flips while throwing up gang signs, but it just makes me feel like throwing up, full stop.

My job is to just happen to be in the journalism office when he shows up. In reality, I've been pacing—a challenge, given the shortage of floor space—for ten minutes and staring so hard at my phone that an asteroid could take me out and I wouldn't even notice.

The door comes flying open just as I'm about to do another about-face. I dodge quickly enough that I don't get a door to the eye, but the dodging results in a collision with the York chair, and all the shit I piled back on it after our murder talk takes a header into the linoleum.

"Hey," says Henry, like the deceitful deceiver he is. "Where's Cat?"

It's on. "Um," I say. But then Lina's ops plan filters back in through the subclinical panic attack I'm having. "Cat had to move her car."

If he thinks I'm lying, he doesn't show it, although we've already proven I suck as a Henry polygraph. "Cool. I'll wait."

That's exactly what he's supposed to say, but then he's supposed to sit down at the computer and bump something so it wakes up. Then boom, there's Cat's incriminating chat with Fake TJ. Instead, he leans back against the door. So not only is he not discovering any cheating, but he's also impeding my only asteroid escape route.

"So are you here for a makeout session?" I ask after a pause that's probably five seconds but feels like five centuries.

"The opposite," he says. "Cat's about to lecture me about that stupid rumor. You know it's bullshit."

I wander over to the desk and start examining Cat's latest Starbucks cup, like maybe that will lure him in. "I think I should plead the Fifth on that one."

"Come on! You know I'm not hooking up with Erin."

"Based on your undying fidelity?"

"Shut up, man." But he's laughing, and he grabs a scarf off a chair and throws it at me.

"I'm not the one asking the girl I'm trying to cheat with if she thinks I'm a cheater." I swat the scarf out of the air, which triggers a second Dust Bowl, and I'm so busy coughing it takes me a second to notice I hit it straight onto the keyboard, and now the screen's on.

"Give me a break. It's Erin."

"So? She's hot. And smart."

"And a bossy know-it-all. I don't get how Brandon deals with her."

I scoot closer to the desk. I just have to see if everything looks like it's supposed to, with the chat log in one corner of the screen and the article Cat's writing on the other side. "Maybe because Brandon's not threatened by independent women."

"Have you met any of my exes?"

"Yeah, and the one you've never hated is the one four out of five dentists agree is totally bound to—you know, obey and serve and sit around being agreeable." I glance at the computer again.

"In case you haven't noticed, Jane's not the only one I don't hate," he says, but before I can respond to this modern-day sonnet, he adds, "You're really twitchy."

"Mountain Dew. Spiked with Red Bull."

He fake-gags. "Well, nobody ever said you weren't all about the good times."

"Don't make me tell Cat you're still trying to tap this." Something blinks in one of Cat's browser tabs, and obviously I have to look again.

"She won't buy it. She's too hung up on the Erin thing. God, what do you keep looking at? Were you guys watching porn or something?"

"Nailed it." I slide in front of the screen, and of course Henry tries to see around me.

He moves in a little closer and I keep playing reverse chicken. He's laughing. "Seriously, what is it?"

I can't figure out where the I'm-a-liar real nerves stop and the Ex-Files-faking-it fake nerves start. "Nothing. Cat was working on something and she said to make sure nobody saw it."

Henry's two inches away from my face. "Come on, aren't you curious?" he asks. He puts one hand down on the desk on either side of me, so I'm seventy-five percent surrounded by Henry and twenty-five percent backing into the computer.

"I don't know. I mean—"

He kisses me. And I kiss him back, which I swear to God is just a panic reaction. Mostly.

Then he pulls back and whispers, "You know if I cheated it wouldn't be with Erin."

"Wow." I swipe the back of my hand across my mouth. "Way to Lothario that moment to death."

"Way to play watchdog for a girl you hate."

"Way to try to seduce me into spying on your girlfriend."

"We're pranking," he says. "Goals."

Then he actually has the nerve to go in for the kiss again.

But I do the classic fake-left-go-right, so he lands on the side of my face. Honestly, I'm in the mood to slap him at this point, because he's definitely, without-a-doubt hitting on me to get me to do what he wants.

And because this definitely, without-a-doubt is making me have some very unpleasant second thoughts about that night at Lake Marxism when he pulled the exact same move right after he told me Parker was a big bad liar.

I rein it in somehow—full credit to my accountability buddies—and do my most over-the-top pseudo-sultry whisper: "Never should've dumped me."

He rolls his eyes and moves one arm so I can escape. "Let's see what she's hiding."

"Yeah, because checking in on your girlfriend's every move is a normal part of a healthy relationship. Especially while you're waiting for her to show up so you can tell her you're not cheating. And then when you get thirty seconds of free time, you're like, hey, cool, time to make out with that girl I dumped three months ago."

He looks at me. "You need to lay off the Mountain Dew and Red Bull."

"And you need to lay off the stalker act."

"You're acting so weird. I know you want me to dump Cat, but I'm—"

"Really?" I'm too pissed off to worry about where I'm going with this. "Did it ever cross your mind that maybe the world doesn't revolve directly around you?" Which is a lie in this case, since Operation Desdemona does, in fact, revolve directly around him. But come on.

"Calm down. Cat's already going to bitch at me—and by the way, I do care about her, so—"

"Yeah. You care so much you're spying on her."

"Fine. If it bothers you so damn much, I'm not even going to read—" But then he glances at the screen with an angry hand-wave to prove his point, and I guess the months of hardcore paranoia have sharpened his powers of observation, because a split second later he's back to the two-handed desk grip pose, except this time I'm not blocking the computer.

He stops cold. Seriously, he's not even blinking. Or breathing. He's just staring straight-on at the chat window.

Then all of a sudden he unfreezes, spins around, and takes the one long stride between the desk and me. I back up just for the sake of Newton's laws or whatever, but I stumble right into a tower of yearbooks and they all come crashing down and then I dead-end into the wall.

"You know," he spits out.

"Dude. You're freaking me out." I'm actually hoping Mr. Lee will barge in, because forget Operation Desdemona, right now I'm just focused on Operation Not Having Henry Rip My Head Off.

"You know about Cat!"

I back myself a little harder into the wall. "We're not even friends, and you need to chill."

"Where is she?" He's actually snapping right in front of my face. If I had an emergency call button, I'd be slamming the shit out of it.

"She went to her car! Jesus, Henry, what's going on?"

He gets even more in my face, practically makeout proximity, but after a second of nuclear staring he shoves off the wall and jerks Cat's screen around. "Look."

I take a couple of tentative steps out of the yearbook rubble and start edging toward the door. "She's talking to somebody. Whatever."

"It's TJ Seymour."

"Is that supposed to mean something to me?"

"The guy she had a thing for."

I move another inch toward the door. "So? You said he was in Bulgaria."

"Belgium. And it doesn't matter. Cheating is cheating."

"She's not cheating just because—"

"She's hiding it! She told you not to let anybody look." Henry slaps the screen. "He's coming home for Christmas, and she's meeting him."

"That doesn't mean anything."

"And Katie was just reading the Bible out there in the woods with Tom? Get real."

"Just because she—" I start, but then whatever my mouth was planning on saying sort of fizzles out, because my ears are playing a nonstop loop of Henry saying *She's CHEAT-ING on me*, and it doesn't even matter whether he's talking about Anna or Katie or Cat. It's all the same.

It's all rage.

He grabs his phone, and I figure he's about to send Cat the mother of all hellfire texts, but instead he makes a call and I seize the opportunity to move another baby step toward the door.

"Yeah, fine, don't answer," he snarls out after a minute. "Don't call me back, either. But you know what else you better not be doing, TJ? Meeting my girlfriend tomorrow night. You don't fuck with me. You should know that."

He hangs up and jams the phone back into his pocket.

"You swear to God you didn't know," he says.

I actually cross my fingers behind my back. "You know I would've told you."

He studies me so hard I swear he can see into my brain. "I can trust you," he says, like he's testing the idea out.

I nod. I'm still crossing my fingers.

"I can trust you." This time he sounds like he almost believes it. "Nobody else, you know that? I can't even trust Brandon anymore. Not after this shit with Erin."

I'm not sure how a rumor about Henry having a thing for Brandon's girlfriend makes Brandon untrustworthy, but whatever. Clearly I don't have a natural aptitude for power-hungry scheming, unlike everybody else in this damn school.

"We're in this together," he whispers, and his voice—the way it's strung so tight, it's on a whole different frequency—makes my heart drop straight into my stomach. It doesn't matter what the girls think, or what an asshole he was being a minute ago. Right now, he's just Henry, and I'm just me.

No matter what he's lying about, he's not lying about feeling alone. I'm the only person he trusts, and he can't trust me, either.

"We're in this together," I say, and then I take his hand and holy shit, I didn't know it was possible to hate yourself as much as I do right now. He's going to find out about me, because he always finds out when he's being lied to. And when he does, it's going to ruin us.

"You can't tell Cat," says Henry.

I nod.

He goes back to the door, and he's still holding my hand, so I follow him until we're both right next to the blinds Parker shut last week. "She can't know I'm onto her," he says. "I have to make sure it's the truth."

I nod again.

"Tomorrow night," he tells me.

"What about it?"

"That's when they're meeting. She never said where, but

I'm going to follow her, and I'm going to find them, and—
Well. You know."

I'm pretty sure my heart actually stops beating. "I *don't* know," I choke out.

"I'll handle it," he says. That's all.

He squeezes my hand so tight it hurts.

And then he walks out and slams the door behind him.

Nothing to See in Howard Heights; Definitely No Plotting at All

"Holy shit. You guys. Holy shit."

I should probably start trying harder in the quotations department, but whatever. You try being the world's worst actress in a situation that's rapidly becoming life-or-death and then having to wait two hours before you can even talk about it, because cheerleading practice is that damn important, and also the *Ledger* deadline can't wait.

That's right: I had to sit through two hours of newspaper with Cat ten feet away and not even talk about it. Because Parker's immediate response to my NEED TO MEET NOW!!! text was Attic 4:30 don't talk here.

Then of course she insisted on smuggling Cat and Lina into Howard Heights under a bunch of cheer paraphernalia in case anybody's monitoring the traffic. And then driving into her garage. And then I had to drive my mom's car to Parker's house, which is one block away, and drive into the garage to get them, and then drive back into my garage.

Choreography: It's not just for cheerleading routines anymore.

Anyway, by the time we're in the attic, I'm about to lose it. So all things considered, my greeting is remarkably articulate.

"What happened?" Lina asks. She's been in hiding since Saturday, which she's playing off as Quality Time With Isabel and Fernando, even though it's actually mission-driven sneakiness, since according to all three of my co-conspirators, it's better if there's no chance Henry knows Lina's home.

I give them the rundown, minus the part where Henry kissed me and I nearly went turncoat and then also nearly slapped him. When I finish, they all wait like they're not sure I'm done, and then Cat literally goes, "That's it?"

"What do you mean, that's it? He lost it!"

"What's that thing your newspaper friends are always saying?" Parker asks. "Breaking?"

"I'm serious. He had a whole new personality."

"Not really," Cat says. "Remember how he went off at End of the Road?"

"That was an extenuating circumstance!"

"So is this."

"Yeah, but—"

"But what?"

I can't even defend myself, because the more I try, the more everything feels wrong. The stupid spirit bottle prank. The way he never told me about Liz and Mary and Maggie, even though we talked about everything.

The way he kept me close after we broke up.

Who knows if any of it was even real?

I know this is the general train of thought that leads people to march on Washington raving about lizard people, but really. It's not like I'm the only one getting jumpy.

"Anyway," Cat says, "that's what we wanted to happen."

"He wants to follow you to meet TJ!"

"Perfect."

Her idea of *perfect* leaves a lot to be desired. "I thought we wanted it to happen at school or something. Now we have to fake a date and we don't have a TJ."

Lina reaches for Anna's notebook. "But knowing when he's going to confront her is the biggest advantage we could have."

"He'll know something's up," says Parker.

I double-point at her. "Right. Thank you. And we need witnesses."

"We *are* the witnesses," says Cat.

"And isolation helps," Lina tells us. "If he thinks he's alone, he won't play it safe."

I'm not buying it. "Where can we set it up so they're alone? It's not like Cat's going to go cow tipping."

"The river," says Cat.

Parker flinches. "Do you *want* to die?"

Cat shrugs. "It's prime hookup territory."

"Not since Katie died!" Parker looks like she wants to throw them out of the attic. "Nobody goes out there anymore!"

"Even better."

"No." Parker's totally in Cat's face. "He killed Katie out

there, okay? You really think three of us hiding in the woods can stop him from doing it again?"

"We don't know for sure that he killed Katie," says Lina. "And yes, we can stop him, *if* he tries anything. He's not going to hurt Cat right in front of us."

"You don't have to come if you can't handle it," Cat says.

And who knows if she's aiming for reverse psychology, or if The Ref just doesn't give a shit, but either way, Parker throws an expert pair of eye-daggers straight at her and grabs the book from Lina. "Are you kidding me? I can handle it. Let's plan this damn thing and bring Henry down exactly like he deserves."

Stalking: The Trend That's Sweeping the Nation

So this is the part where everybody leaves Lancaster High School after cheerleading and basketball and debate, and four girls with nothing in common except one major vendetta transform into a girl gang on a secret mission for revenge and justice.

Kind of.

Cat kisses Henry goodbye, since supposedly they're all good again. Then she leaves to work on a story, and everybody buys it because come on, it's Cat. So she heads to her car, and I follow Henry to the Camaro, because Ex-Files's current assignment is to keep tabs on VIII until everybody's in place.

"So what's next?" I ask. "Hotwiring a tractor at Grandma Howard's farm?"

Cat's sitting in her car, texting, and Henry's watching her

so intently you can see the laser trackers beaming out of his eyes. "Not tonight," he says.

"Dude. Take a picture. It'll last longer."

He tears his gaze away for one frame. "She's texting TJ."

"I'm glad you're psychic now. I bet Penn really goes for that kind of thing."

"That article is bullshit," he says. "She's meeting him and she came up with the worst cover ever. I'd expect more from Cat Parr."

"A girl really can't win with you, can she?" Sitting here talking about his perpetual girlfriend drama pulls me right back to the night before homecoming. Two months ago, I thought the Katie plot was funny. Now I feel like an accomplice.

"She can win if she doesn't cheat."

"Double standard much?"

Cat finally starts her car. Henry lets somebody get in line behind her, and then he pulls out of his parking spot. "I don't want to hear it," he says.

"In that case, let's go break into Norfolk's house and drink all his liquor."

"We're following Cat."

"Right now?"

"Why not?" He turns onto the road.

"Um, because nobody meets up with their secret lover in broad daylight?"

"You never know."

"Okay, then what about because Cat *does* have a story and she's totally business before pleasure?" I slide my phone out, pull up the Operation Desdemona group text as nonchalantly as possible, and type @The Ref: you're being followed, go straight home.

"Right," says Henry.

"Okay, then what about because I have to be home soon? I can't spend all night on a stakeout."

Henry snorts. "You don't have a curfew."

"I do since we disappeared to Lake Max Azria and I got home at midnight in a stranger's booty shorts." In reality, Mom may or may not have bought my halfway-true story, but I was intact and sober so she didn't even lecture, other than an obligatory college comment.

"You jumped out your window to help me with home-coming."

"Yeah, and we all know how well that worked out."

He shoots me a dark look. "Don't go there."

"I just—" I cut myself off when Cat goes straight at the intersection where she'd have to turn to get home. And then, a block later, she turns the other way. Toward Lina's house, which was the plan, but that was before we knew Henry was going to start following her the second she left school.

Of course Cat doesn't text and drive. Damn her respon-sibility.

"I need to call my mom," I say, which is stunningly unbe-lievable, but we're three blocks from Lina's and I'm desperate.

"And then you'll start acting like a normal person?"

I call Cat. "Because helping you stalk your girlfriends is the definition of normal?"

Finally, after another interminable block, Cat answers, but

before she can even ask what's up I say, "Hey, Mom, I'm going to be late, because I'm with Henry and we're stalking Cat Parr."

"Shut up!" Henry looks fifty percent amused and fifty percent pissed, so while Cat's asking whatever she's asking I talk over her again.

"No, yeah, we're just hanging out. I'll text you, okay?" I hang up and pray to Saint Desdemona that Cat's geniusness won't desert her in her hour of need.

"This isn't her street," says Henry. "Where's she going?"

"Probably her meth dealer's house." Cat's on Lina's block now—big imposing houses on both sides of the street. Parker pointed Lina's house out the night we biked to the park, and I said something like, *of course she grew up in a castle*, because the Aragón-Castilla house is a limestone fortress.

"Maybe she's meeting TJ at the park."

"For a hot slide-biking date?" Cat's going to be in front of Lina's house in three—two—

She keeps driving. It takes all my remaining willpower not to do some type of seat-belt-compatible victory dance.

"TJ Seymour," Henry's saying. He passes Lina's house without even glancing at it. "I should've seen it coming. He was all over Cat at Brandon's end-of-summer party, remember?"

"I knew like four people then. Are we really just going to follow her? Can't we at least recycle something?" I can hear the caffeine overdose in my voice and I should probably shut the hell up at some point, but I can't. Not with that *She's CHEATING on me* loop still playing in my head. "This is a pretty unimpressive scheme. I'm disappointed."

Cat takes a left at the next corner—we're in the old downtown now, just up the hill from the courthouse. "You won't be," says Henry.

The way he's pulling me into whatever he's doing is freaking me out. And it's freaking me out that he's always done it, but up until Parker waved Anna's spy book in my face, I liked it. We were best friends and confidants and partners in pranking, and it was the best.

Now it feels way too possessive. "Can't you just pretend you guys were never going out? Like with me?"

"You didn't cheat on me."

"I'm just saying, it's not like you and Cat were ever madly in love or anything, right?"

"Apparently not."

Cat slows down and takes a right into the library parking lot. "Prostitution ring in the reference section. Told you."

Henry coasts into the lot next door. It's St. George's, the big old Catholic church, made of the same limestone blocks as Lina's house. "You don't know she's not meeting TJ," Henry says, eyes glued to the mirror.

Cat heads over to the book return, drops something in, and goes back to her car. "She's leaving him a love letter. If we wait, TJ's going to leap out of the bushes."

"Right." Henry's not laughing.

"Seriously, what if she *is* cheating? Is it really that big of a deal?"

He breaks his restraining-order-worthy stare. "Are you kidding me?"

"You can't tell me you've never cheated on anybody."

"That's not the point." When Cat turns back onto the street, he lets a car in between them, and then he takes the turn so fast the tires actually squeal.

"Because you're a guy and she's a girl? Come on. That's so fucking sexist, Henry."

"Because nobody cheats on me! I could be with any girl in this damn school, you know that? I could replace her in two minutes. Nobody fucking cheats on me!"

This is officially the least fun I've ever had with Henry, including the thirty seconds his dad was yelling at us while I was shirtless. "Narcissistic personality disorder isn't a cute look on you."

"It's not about narcissism. It's about respect. You don't go out with somebody and then make them look like—you don't do that shit. I just want everything to work out for once. It shouldn't be this impossible to find a girlfriend who gives a shit about the future, too."

"You mean like Lina?"

He slams on the brakes. We're literally in the middle of the street, and every driver in Indiana hits their horn. "Don't talk about Lina. You know better than that."

Normal people don't get this angry over their high school girlfriends. Hell, normal people don't get this angry over their *marriages*. "Dude. You're freaking me out."

"Grow up, Cleveland," he says, then sends us screeching back into motion and onto Cat's street. He street-parks two driveways down—if you can call stomping your brakes so hard the car actually jumps from the impact "parking"—and punches the steering wheel. His eyes are still fastened on Cat, who's unlocking her front door.

"If growing up means having anger management issues and being a dick, I think I'll just stay seventeen, thanks."

It's like he doesn't even hear me.

So I open the door, and he snaps out of the sniper zone, locking one hand on my arm before my foot can even hit Cat's neighbor's yard. "Get back in the car."

"Let go of me."

"Get back in the car." It's the voice from the bonfire, right before he started punching people. That night I was pretty sure he'd limit it to Francis and Tom. Today, I'm starting to think he'd punch a baby if it looked at him wrong. And yes, it's damn scary.

"Henry. Let go of me. Please."

He grips my arm tighter for a second, and then he lets go. I don't shut the car door, but I don't get out, either. I'm in way over my head and also, I'm really worried about Henry. Like, worried he's going to lose it and drive straight into Cat's house, and worried he's in the middle of a breakdown, and worried about whether this side of him is new, because either way, it's looking really bad. Like either the girls are right about him, or he's just had the worst luck ever, and now we're pushing him over the edge on purpose.

These options are equally not-fantastic.

Not to mention that the end result is me sitting here stalking Cat when I'm supposed to be distracting Henry long enough that Cat and Lina can pull off some more car choreography maneuvers and get back to Parker's for the final round of prep.

"Get back in the car," Henry says again, but he doesn't sound like he's method-acting as an authoritarian dictator anymore. He just sounds exhausted.

I get my phone out. "I'm texting Christina to pick me up," I tell him, and shoot Sneak out back to Operation Desdemona.

"Cleves. Get back in the car. Please."

"Not until you swear you're done with whatever the hell that was."

"I'm sorry," he says. "I didn't mean it."

"You didn't mean to practically get us killed, or you didn't mean to flip out on me, or you didn't mean to be a chauvinistic ass?"

"I didn't mean it. Any of it."

I still don't shut the door.

"There's a lot going on, okay?"

"Yeah, and maybe you should see a shrink instead of taking it out on your girlfriends."

"I'm not crazy. Don't even say that."

"I didn't." I shut the door. My phone buzzes, but I don't even think about checking it.

He stares at Cat's house some more. "Everything's falling apart."

"Meaning?"

"Everything. My leg's getting worse again. I won't even be starting if it doesn't get better. You know how that looks to Penn?"

"Like you're injured? It's not like you're trying to play varsity."

"It looks weak. I'm some jackass with a cheating girlfriend and a jacked-up leg and my dad let the factory close, but that sure as hell doesn't stop him from telling me everything I'm doing wrong. Everything my brother would've done better."

"You'll be out of here in like six months. You just—"

"My mom died eight years ago next week," he says.

That shuts me right up.

Henry laughs that empty laugh again. "See? Nobody wants to talk about that. Not even my dad. He changed into a different person, and everything fell apart. And so I figured, you know, I can fix this. Be a fucking winner. Earn our name back."

"You're going to," I tell him. "Come on. You're doing everything right—"

"The more I try to fix it, the worse it gets."

"Because you hurt your leg and you might not be starting five for a couple of weeks?"

"Because I keep making the wrong decision. I thought Lina was perfect, but she never gave a shit about Lancaster. I thought Anna was perfect—" He cuts himself off.

Okay, so clearly there's no good way to handle your mom dying and your dad giving up when you're still a kid. But Henry has to stop trying to save himself and his family and the entire town—like that even makes sense—by burning through girlfriends and going postal when they don't magically save his dynasty.

"I feel like maybe you've done enough trials of the girlfriend hypothesis," I say.

413

"I just—I keep thinking, if I get a fresh start, you know—"

I lean forward so I'm almost in the way of his porch-staring. "Henry. Come on. I know you think the perfect girlfriend is the missing piece, but seriously, it's not that big of a deal. Look at everything else you've done."

"Yeah, but it's really fucked-up that I can't find one damn relationship that works, right?"

"I'm just saying maybe you should be single for a few months. For everybody's sake." If he'd crack a damn smile, I'd feel nine hundred percent better about everything.

He finally looks at me. "I can't do that until I fix this."

My phone buzzes again, and I almost jump out of my skin. "Do I even want to know what you mean by that?"

"Settle this thing with Cat and TJ. Stop Parker. *Fix* this."

Even the most creative of interpretations can't turn that into a good thing. "Just promise me you're not going to do anything stupid, okay?"

Now he smiles. Except I can't tell if it's real or not.

If we mean anything, or if he's just manipulating me.

I open the car door once more, and this time I jump out for real. "I can walk home," I say, and Henry smiles again, and I almost want to get back in and tell him everything and ask him what the truth is and believe whatever he says.

But I don't. I walk away.

And when I get to the end of the street and take one last look over my shoulder, he's still staring at Cat's door, like I was never even next to him.

Students Go Above and Beyond on English Assignment

I'm turning into quite the fan of catharsis walking. A few more dramatic events, and the track team is going to scout me for some event that doesn't have a speed requirement. But there's something really great about pounding the pavement with nobody in your face telling you who to believe and what to do. Like you can make your own decisions for once.

And this is the decision I make: I can't trust Henry anymore.

Better late than never, right?

So I'm charging back up toward Howard Heights, skipping every song that comes up until I get to another angry one and thinking about how great it's going to be when a bunch of girls show Henry what the hell is up, especially since three-fourths of us are on his list of conquests.

Fuck prom. This is personal.

I'm almost back at the school when somebody blasts me

away with their horn. I don't even turn—I just flash them a middle finger. Then the honking wonder starts yelling loud enough that I can hear them through my headphones.

Which is just the opportunity I need to vent some rage.

So I spin toward the cars waiting for the light to change and I start shouting about how no girl in the history of the world has ever heard some prick catcalling her and been like, "Okay, I'll jump in with this asshole and ride off into the sunset," but I only get a couple of words out, because it's not some guy. It's Cat with her head out Lina's window.

"Get in!" she yells.

I jump into the back seat and pull off my headphones as the light turns green. "Did he see you leave?"

"He's still in front of my driveway," Cat says. "Lina was two streets over. I went out the back."

I lean into the front seat. "FYI, Henry's basically foaming at the mouth. And occasionally acting like he's about to cry. Or totally snap."

Cat just nods, but Lina says, "Good."

"So much for that whole bit about how you still love him."

Lina looks at me with a solid steel glint in her eye. "It's not about that anymore," she says. "This is justice. For all of us."

One round of human smuggling later, and we're in Parker's room: Operation Desdemona Phase Two HQ. We're all in black except Cat, who's supposed to look normal, so she's in a sparkly ensemble that seems like overkill for a woodland hookup.

"You're leaving your house at eight," says Lina, standing with her hands on her hips under a giant prom portrait of Parker and George. Which is a pretty morbid thing to have watching you all day every day if you ask me, but Parker hasn't.

Cat nods. Parker's doing her makeup, although I'm not quite clear on why she needs a TV-ready face for this.

"The rest of us are out ten minutes later. Far enough back for them to get into position, but close enough that we'll be there before anything happens." Lina looks at me. "Anything from Henry?"

"Nothing."

"Good," says Parker. She steps back to give Cat a once-over. "You're perfect. TJ's going to love it."

"Thanks." Cat checks the mini microphone clipped to her bra strap. She's planning to catch Henry's multi-murder confession. I'm guessing she's just going to catch a lot of yelling.

Parker uncaps the lipstick she was using on Cat and does a good ten laps around her mouth with it. When she does the pucker-pop thing at the end, her lips are bloodred.

"Really, MGB? Is this prom?"

"I hope not," she says, grabbing the eyeliner next. "I want to dress for this, okay?"

Her particular version of "let's wear black" is skintight and deadly. Which is totally her style, kind of like Lina's military aesthetic and my kick-your-ass-on-the-way-to-a-show look. "The Catwoman attire isn't enough?" I ask.

She executes perfect wings on her first try. "Listen, Ex-Files, you're supposed to dress for the job you want. And I want to be the one who gets revenge for Katie and George and Anna."

Lina steps past Cat—who's looking a bit like a hostage, given her normal outfit and our hodgepodge of vendetta girl gear—

and picks up the lipstick and takes her turn. When she finishes, all three of them stare me down until I say, "Okay! Fine!"

So Parker does my eyeliner while Lina does her own, and okay, yeah, this is actually a solid idea. And I'm pretty sure Katie and Anna would approve.

Then Parker has to take a bunch of group selfies, which is great because I'm starting to get nervous, and now we can pretend we're just getting ready for Halloween six weeks late. Parker fixes everybody's hair while Lina goes over everything in the notebook and Cat reads us the tell-all she wrote for *Dead Queens.*

"I'm submitting it right now," she says. "Queue it for midnight, Cleveland."

"I don't know. I'm not sure it's...*appropriate.*"

She's not entertained. Even her eyeliner isn't entertained.

"I mean, it's not personal. It's just a question of editorial standards."

"CLEVES." Parker swats at my phone. "Queue it, or I'll post it right now."

So I do, of course, although I'm really looking forward to four hours from now, when we've all discovered the errors of our ways and I can unqueue it. "I'm glad we have a backup plan in case we die," I say. "Great thinking."

"It's not in case we *die.*" Cat's still looking ultra not-okay with not being editor-in-chief of my life. "It's in case anything goes wrong. The truth will be out."

"Hold on. Let me queue my will, too. Just in case."

Cat eagle-eyes me. "Is my post scheduled?"

"Dude. Relax. Yes."

She's still eagle-eyeing so hard that all she needs is an American flag behind her and we could make a small fortune selling T-shirts of her at truck stops all across Indiana.

"Right here. Look." I stick my phone in her face. "I don't hate you anymore, okay?"

"I appreciate the qualifier."

"I appreciate your continued disdain for my life choices."

"Likewise," says Cat. But there's a rogue smirk under her man-killer makeup, and I can't *not* laugh at this point, and once I'm laughing, it sets her off, too. And then we're really and truly cracking the hell up right here in front of Parker's *In Memoriam* wall hanging.

"You *guys*," Parker says. "It's time to go."

So we get ourselves together and Lina leads the way downstairs, and somehow just the way she holds her shoulders makes me feel pretty much like an imaginary attack soundtrack is playing.

At least until we get downstairs and Parker's mom goes, "Hold it right there."

All four of us stop in our tracks and look over into the living room, and there's Mrs. Rochford and five other Howard Heights power-moms. They've all got wineglasses in their hands and Bibles on their laps.

This is it: foiled by Miss Indiana Emeritus.

"Is this that English project you were talking about?" Parker's mom gives us a smile that proves without a doubt that Parker isn't adopted. "You girls look fantastic."

Parker pageant-smiles right back. "We're filming at Cat's house. See you later!"

"Good luck!" the moms chorus.

Well, except that one of them also says, "We'll pray for you!" Which may, in fact, be what we need. Bible club wine-moms: don't underestimate them.

We pile into Parker's car and head out. Once we're a minute or two past the gates, Lina and Cat dig themselves out of their cargo camouflage and I say, "I can't believe we're really doing this."

"I can't believe Jane isn't here," says Parker.

"Who?" I ask, for tradition's sake.

"God, and it's not like she doesn't know."

"We've got Fake TJ to represent the Seymour faction." I peer into the dark. "What do you guys think is going to happen tonight?"

"We're going to kick ass," says Parker.

"We're going to get answers," says Cat.

"We're going to get redemption," says Lina.

Parker turns onto the street where we're dropping Cat off and pulls up to the curb. They all look at me, and as I look back at three possibly deranged girls with their hidden microphones and their weaponized eyeliner, I know I picked the right side in *Lancaster Prank Wars: Ultimate Escalation Edition.*

I slide my aviators down, even though it's dark, because Ex-Files absolutely wears sunglasses at night. "And we're going to show Henry who he's really dealing with," I say.

Seriously Just Stay Out of the Damn Woods, Says Local Teen

Thanks to the incomparable plotting skills of Queen Lina and The Ref, the plan kicks off exactly the way it's supposed to. Cat disappears, and two minutes later, she texts us from her driveway: In the car. VIII still two houses down. In another minute, she passes the end of the street we're lurking on.

Two cars later, there goes Henry's Camaro.

My phone buzzes again. I look, and it's a *Dead Queens* notification. My first thought is basically just one long expletive, because I was really hoping it was going to be Henry saying, you know, *Cat's leaving, so let's break into her room and hack into her computer and add typos to all her papers*, or something else that would slide us back to the good old days when our crimes were limited to gambling, trespassing, and a willingness to drink shitty beer.

Call me unadventurous, but I prefer my bad boys to stick with non-capital offenses.

Anyway, the resulting emotional tornado is really not okay, so I read the stupid *Dead Queens* ask just for the distraction, except instead of some gossip crap, it's from the Actual Legit Blog that didn't hate my ASKING FOR IT post.

"What the serendipitous fuck," I say.

Parker goes straight onto high alert. "What happened? Is it Henry?"

Which is unhelpful, but whatever. "This site seriously just asked if I'm interested in being one of their high school guest writers."

"Okay, but that isn't helping us save Cat's life. We're in the middle of something right now."

"Oh. Then I guess I'll just tell them, 'Yeah, thanks for offering me literally the coolest gig in the universe, but I'm pursuing a potential future day job with the Northern Indiana chapter of the mafia, and—'"

"You're supposed to be our comms op! Right, Lina?"

"Right," says Ambassador-Turned-General Aragón. "Focus. But congratulations."

I put my phone down. "God, don't you want to follow him right now? Jump out at the next light and be like, 'Hey, asshole, here's a stalking citation, and good luck getting another girlfriend this time'?"

"And also a murder citation," says Parker. "Three murder citations. God, I'm so ready to get him back." She glances back at Lina. "How come you never did anything to him? Like, last winter. You know the whole school was on your side."

"Interesting, coming from somebody who wasn't," Lina says.

"Anna was practically my sister!"

Lina shakes her head. "You were my friend, and then overnight, you weren't."

"I'm sorry, okay? I didn't know Henry was going to make your life hell or that you were going to leave without saying goodbye."

Lina doesn't look pissed at Parker, not that a sliver of somebody's porch light is the best for sussing out micro-expressions. She's just watching the cars go past.

"Everybody thinks I'm this backstabbing bitch," says Parker. "But it's bullshit, just like everything everybody said about Anna. She was so smart and ambitious, and all anybody remembers is that she stole somebody's boyfriend."

"What people said about Katie wasn't fair, either," I tell them. "She's dead, and all they want to talk about is who she slept with instead of how she was the sweetest person ever, and the least selfish, and the most fun."

We're silent for a minute. Then Lina says, "That's why I never went up against Henry."

"What?"

"I didn't want that to be what everybody remembered about me. The girl who started a war because her boyfriend was being awful." She shrugs.

"Well, if you ever change your mind, just text Eustace," I say. "He'll rally the troops in three seconds."

Parker snorts. "Who needs to rally the troops? This is better revenge than anything they could do. It's playing him exactly the way he needs to get played."

"It's not about revenge. It's about what's right," says Lina.

"Maybe for you."

My phone buzzes. It's Cat: On the road.

That's our cue.

Parker pulls onto Broadway, and we head downtown and out to the bridge. When we turn onto the maintenance road, the déjà vu gets way beyond tolerable, particularly because Parker is driving slower than her running pace.

"Can you go any slower? Like, is it physically possible?"

"Do you see these branches? Do you see this *gravel*?" Parker asks. "This car isn't going to be another Henry casualty."

"Seriously, they're both going to die of old age by the time we get there."

"Would you rather walk? We can't speed through the woods or Henry will hear us." This was an argument in yesterday's strategy session, actually—how far Parker should drive. Lina thought coming in on foot before anything started was the best way to do it, because she's intrepid as fuck, but Cat thought a backup getaway car made sense. I voted against a mile of hiking. Parker was on the fence, but she ended up siding with those of us who aren't warrior princesses.

So we crunch along at five miles per hour and stare at every branch we haven't seen since homecoming.

"God, I can't stand this road," says Parker.

The path in front of us is lit up, and so are the branches just to the side, but a few feet out it's pitch-black. I shiver. "I wonder if anybody will ever party out here again."

"Of course they will," Lina says. "Maybe not next year,

but they'll be back the year after. They'll forget she was real. She'll just be another story."

Parker gets to where we're stopping, just out of sight from the turnaround, and does a three-hundred-seven-point turn to give us the getaway angle we need.

This is it.

We look at each other with several variations on a *holy shit* expression theme, and then we're out of the car and into the woods. Single file, hugging the edge, because Cat was supposed to lead Henry out to the bank right by the drainpipe for maximum setting-based guilt, but if that didn't happen, we're a little less likely to walk ourselves into having to explain why we're taking a stroll through the haunted death forest in all black and excessive makeup.

Then we round the last bend, and there's an extra car in the lot.

Lina does the pedestrian equivalent of slamming on the brakes. She stops in her tracks and throws her arms out so Parker and I can't sprint for the mystery car.

"Dude," I hiss. "This doesn't feel right. We need to get out of here."

"No," says Lina, totally non-negotiable. "We stay."

"We're in the creepiest woods ever, and whenever the hook-hand killer jumps out and starts scraping through the car roof, he's going to get all the way through before Parker can get us out, because she's incapable of hitting the double digits on—"

Parker elbows me. "Can we not make murder jokes when we're tracking a murderer?"

"He's not a *murderer*. He wasn't—"

"Cleveland," they both say.

"He's not going to roof-hook us to death!"

"This is so not the time for this conversation!" Parker's doing her Maximum Impact Whisper-Scream.

"Exactly. So let's get the hell out of here."

"We're not leaving Cat alone," says Lina. "I'm sure there's an explanation."

"Maybe it's TJ. Life imitates art."

"He's in *Belgium*," Parker whisper-yells.

"Maybe it's Cat's actual secret boyfriend."

Parker grabs Lina's arm. "What if Henry figured it out? What if Cat's really on his side and we're walking into a trap?" She pulls out her phone.

Lina covers Parker's screen, which is a blinding here-we-are beacon. "We can trust Cat."

"We can't trust anybody!"

"Do what you want, but I'm not leaving," says Lina.

"But we—"

And then there's a gunshot. An actual fucking gunshot coming from the river, and then a scream.

Lina's running before I even get a grip on what's going on. Parker's right behind her. My brain is absolutely telling me to run the opposite direction, or dive into the bushes and pray to God I camouflage, but I can't let Lina and Parker go by themselves. So I dash after them and hope to hell that the mystery car is a park ranger or a cop or something.

They're across the lot and down the trail and I'm crashing after them when Lina slams on the brakes again. Parker smashes into her and I barely avoid the pileup. We're right at the edge of the woods, looking at the most unbelievable scene I can come up with.

Halfway across the river, there's some kind of fence locked around the drainpipe so you can't get over to the other side, and Cat's backed up against it, clinging on to the chain link. Henry's right in front of her yelling, "Drop it! Drop it!"

And at our end of the drainpipe, a few feet off the bank, there's Jane Seymour with both arms out in front of her, holding a gun.

What. The. Hell.

"Get away from her!" Jane screams.

"Not until you drop the gun!" Henry shouts.

"Get AWAY from her!"

"Oh my God," Parker whisper-shrieks. "We have to do something!"

"Give it a second," says Lina. "We have to figure out what's going on first." Which yes, good plan, because (a) where the hell did Jane Seymour come from, other than Illinois; (b) where the hell did Jane Seymour get a *gun*; and (c) where the hell did Jane Seymour learn how to *use* said gun, since she seems very damn confident about this entire thing and as far as I'm aware, there's not a Girl Scout badge for shooting ex-boyfriends?

Also (d) when the hell did Jane Seymour turn into an actual Wild West outlaw?

"Jane, put the gun down." Henry has his voice back under control now. He holds one hand up and takes a couple of steps away from Cat.

"I'm not putting it down until she's safe!"

Cat's still holding on to the fence. It looks weirdly shiny, like it shouldn't be welded onto such a rusty piece-of-crap drainpipe. I guess this was Lancaster's response to Katie dying, which fuck them, because now Cat's stranded. "Jane, put it down," calls Cat. "We can talk this out."

Henry spins back toward her and practically slams her into the fence. The metal clangs, and Cat shrieks and loses her balance for half a second, but she gets her other hand back on the fence and stays on. Henry's gripping on to the fence now, too, pinning Cat to it. "You're going to let me do the talking," he barks.

"Let her go!" Jane screams.

"Put the gun down and tell your brother to show his damn face."

"TJ's not here and Cat's not cheating and I'm not dropping the gun until she's safe!"

"She's fine, Jane. You—"

"She's not fine! Don't lie to me! At least say it to her face like you said it to me."

"I don't know what you're talking about."

"Shut up!" Jane shrieks. She's the loudest person I've ever heard, and also possibly the bravest, and the fact that I'm thinking this about *Jane Seymour* is so surreal, it can almost distract me from how somebody could get shot to death if she sneezes at the wrong second. "Yes, you do! You said to remember what happened to the girl before me!"

"The girl before you was a cheating bitch."

"You killed her! That's what you meant!"

Henry actually laughs. I've never been as scared of anything in my life as I am of him right now. "She did it to herself. You know that."

"She never even cheated!"

Henry tenses up, and the fence rattles. "She did. You know that, too."

"You just wanted it to be true so you could get rid of her!"

"You don't believe any of that. Who told you that?"

Before Lina can stop her, Parker goes flying out to the bank. "I did."

The shock only shows on Henry's face for a second. "Rochford. I should've known."

"Should've known what?" Jane's still screaming everything she says. I'm really damn glad I'm nowhere near the line of fire, but I'd feel a lot better if she weren't pointing the gun at Henry and Cat.

"I should've known Rochford would be the one to get to you. She's crazy, Jane. She cracked when George died."

"No," says Jane.

"It was her fault I found out about Anna, so it was her fault Anna blew up the Tower. She has to believe it was my fault, so she doesn't have to admit she's the one who killed George."

"Don't say that!" Parker shrieks.

"They found Anna's necklace under the fireworks. And Anna texted you and Cleves right before it happened. That quote—you know that meant she was getting her revenge." Henry sounds so calm and collected, it's hard not to believe him. It's like the first conversation we ever had, when he told me he was going to be famous.

Like it's a fact. Like you can't possibly believe anything else.

"No," Jane says again, but she doesn't sound quite as sure this time.

"Stop it!" Parker's screaming at Jane instead of Henry now. "Don't listen to him!"

"You're upset, Parker," Henry calls. "You're not thinking clearly. You haven't since George died."

"Don't talk about George! Don't you ever say his name again!"

"I miss him, too," Henry says.

"You killed him! Just like you killed Anna. Just like you killed Katie—"

"Katie fell. You almost did, too, didn't you?"

"Shut up!" Jane shouts, and she lowers her chin like she's going to shoot again. Henry puts his hands up and Parker shrieks and Cat yells at her to stop. I really want to take the gun out of the equation, but the only way I can do that involves a suicide leap at Jane in which we'd both end up in the river.

"Shoot him! Do it!" Parker yells.

"No!" Henry and Cat shout.

"Just shut up! Just let me think!" Jane's frozen in place with the gun locked on Henry, who's backing into Cat like she's some kind of reverse human shield.

And then there's a new voice, steady and low: "You don't have to drop the gun."

It's Lina, standing next to Parker on the bank. I didn't even notice her stepping out of the trees in the total insanity of the last thirty seconds, but there she is.

Henry looks like he's seeing a ghost. He doesn't bounce back this time like he did when Parker ran out of the woods. "How—what—"

"Let go of her, Henry," Lina tells him.

He does. It's automatic.

"Jane, you're in charge here, because you have the gun," Lina says. Which feels like a lie, because holy shit, The Queen is living up to her name right now. "But I think we can all get out of this without getting hurt."

"I have to make sure Cat's safe." Jane keeps twitching, like she wants to turn around and look at Lina, but she's afraid to look away from Henry.

"We'll make sure that happens, okay?"

Jane finally does glance over her shoulder for half a second, but then her head snaps right back to Henry. He's still two inches in front of Cat. "Okay," says Jane.

"Do you trust me?" Lina asks.

"You can't—" Henry starts, but Jane shouts, "Don't!"

She waits for a second, like she's testing him, and then she answers Lina: "Yes."

"Okay. Good. I trust you, too, okay?"

Jane nods.

"I think you should come back off the drainpipe. It's not safe out there."

"I'm not putting the gun down."

"That's fine. It's your call. Just come back so you won't get hurt."

Jane hesitates. Then she nods again and starts backing toward the bank with the gun still up. She's only a few feet out, but it takes forever.

When Jane's finally on solid ground, Parker heaves such a huge sigh of relief you'd think the whole problem was solved.

Call me a cynic, but I'm really not convinced.

"Okay," says Jane. "Now he lets Cat go." She glares at Henry. "Now you let her go!"

"You think I'm going to fall for that?" Henry calls. "If I let her go, you're going to shoot. I'm not about to trust you as long as you're listening to Parker's shit. She's got issues, Jane, you know that."

"Stop telling me what to think!" Jane shrieks.

"Jane, you don't have to do anything you don't want to do, but you want Cat to be safe, right?" Lina asks.

Jane nods again. Her arms are starting to shake.

Lina takes a step forward, almost in front of Jane, but not quite. "Do you trust me?" she says again, but this time she's talking to Henry.

He looks away.

"Henry." The way Lina says it stabs me right in the heart. It's like even though she's facing him down thinking he killed people, even though he was so cruel that she left Lancaster without saying goodbye, even though he tries to act like she never existed—even with all that stacked against him, it's like somehow all she wanted was to see him again. Like somewhere under everything, she really does still love him.

Henry keeps looking away.

"Henry, if I'm holding the gun, will you let Cat go?"

He stares at the water. Right where Katie fell. Then he looks Lina in the eye and he nods.

"Jane, will you let me take the gun?"

"I can't put it down. You don't know what he's going to do."

Lina steps back so she's next to Jane. "I won't put it down until she's safe."

Jane steals another glance at her. "Do you know how to handle a gun?"

"I'm Isabel Castilla's daughter."

Jane almost laughs. Parker does laugh, a little hysterically. Then Jane hands Lina the gun and collapses onto the bank.

"Let Cat go," says Lina. She looks totally comfortable with the gun in her hands. "Hold on to the fence and shift to your right. Let her walk back to us. She doesn't deserve to get hurt."

Henry shakes his head and mutters something, but he does exactly what Lina told him to do. For a second he and Cat are face to face, gripping on to opposite edges of the fence, and Cat's sizing him up like she doesn't quite trust him not to do a kamikaze dive off the bridge with her.

"You can do it, Cat, come on!" Parker shouts.

Cat lets go of the fence.

Thank God we brought a cheerleader.

After a thousand years of suspense-walking, Cat gets to the bank and Parker grabs her. Lina's still got the gun trained on Henry. He takes a couple of steps forward and Parker shrieks, but Lina stays steady.

"So what happens now?" Henry asks.

Lina doesn't answer. Henry takes two more steps forward.

"Shoot him!" Parker yells. "You can't let him get away with this!"

Henry keeps walking.

"Do it!" Parker's voice gets higher.

"You heard her," says Henry. "Do it." He's ten feet from the bank now, maybe fifteen from Lina. "I hurt you. I made your life hell."

But Lina doesn't want revenge.

I know she won't shoot. And Henry knows it, too.

Which means in ten seconds he'll be safe, and two seconds after that somebody's going to dive for the gun, and—

Then I'm dashing out of the woods and straight onto the drainpipe.

"Stop," I gasp, skidding to a halt in front of Henry. I'm too scared to look down, so I just look straight at him and for the first time ever, he looks like he doesn't know what's going on.

"Cleves," he says. He grabs my shoulders, and Parker screams, and Lina says his name, low and even, like *don't you dare try anything*.

"Cleves," he says again, and then he laughs, because that's apparently all anybody can do tonight. "Tell me you know what they're doing."

"Vengeance and justice." I'm staring him right in the face, and it feels like my voice is going to crack, but it doesn't.

"You don't believe them."

"Yes, she does!" Parker shouts.

Henry looks over at Parker and Cat and Jane, and then at Lina, who's straight behind me. I'm positive she's still got the gun pointed right at Henry. Which technically means right at me.

"She's not on your side," Henry tells them.

"She is!" Parker's almost shrieking again.

Henry's grip tightens, but he laughs like he doesn't believe her. "She's been on my side the whole time. She told me you were plotting something. She knows you're a liar, Rochford."

"Stop it!" This time it's Jane.

"Tell them I didn't do it," says Henry. His eyes are back on me now, ice-blue and intense even in the dark. He's being a controlling asshole, and I came here to get him back for it.

But there's something under the scary-confident shit. The Tragic Backstory and the way he slammed his fist against his bad leg the night of End of the Road. The way he asked me if we'd be okay that night we did the spirit bottle prank.

He really does trust me.

And I really want to trust him.

"Tell them, Cleves," he says. His voice is all bravado, but I can see in his eyes that he's faking it.

"I—" I cut myself off.

"Don't listen to him!" Parker screams.

I flinch, but Henry doesn't even blink. "Tell them."

"Tell me," I finally say, but this time my voice does crack. I clear my throat and say it again: "Tell *me*."

"What do you mean?"

"Tell me you didn't mean it," I say, and then my legs just sort of give out. I sit down way too fast and Henry almost-falls right along with me.

"Of course I didn't mean it, because I didn't *do* it." His eyes

435

are different now. He's back to his king-of-the-world self. The one I used to trust.

"I know it wasn't Anna," I tell him.

"Bullshit. Rochford's lying."

Suddenly I feel like I'm going to cry. Or puke. Or pass out and fall into the river. "Anna took your picture at the fireworks place."

"I was buying the shit for her party! You know she's exactly the kind of person who'd set me up like that!"

I breathe in and try not to look down. Henry's hands are still on my arms, holding on to me so tight that if one of us fell, we both would. "Stop telling me what to think."

"You don't—"

"Henry."

He stops talking.

"I know the party was your idea."

"She set me up." He's using the When-I'm-Famous voice. I don't trust it at all anymore.

"She didn't do it. I *know* she didn't." I take a deep breath. "I know you set up the fireworks. But just—just tell me you didn't mean for it to happen like it did, okay? Just tell me that. Please. It was a prank. You didn't mean it."

"I didn't mean it because I didn't do it."

"I'll believe you. I swear." Every time he lies, I move one step closer to knowing for sure, for real, that Parker and Cat and Lina are right. He isn't lying because everything went wrong.

He's lying because it went exactly the way he planned it.

"I didn't *do* it, Cleves!"

"Yes, you did." And now I'm crying, like an idiot, and he's still not letting go of me, and it's like I'm not even in my own head anymore. Like I'm watching from fifty feet up, Henry and me on the bridge and Lina behind us with the gun and Cat and Parker and Jane watching. Because as freaked out as I was about him setting up the fireworks to teach Anna a lesson, this is so many times worse I can't even process it.

"It was Anna," says Henry.

"Tell me you—please, Henry, I swear to God, I'll believe you," I choke out.

"Anna did it. You know she did it. They found her necklace. She texted you and Jane."

"She didn't!" Parker bursts out. "She lost her phone. You read it in her notebook, Cleves, remember?"

He said it before, and I didn't even think about it because Jane was about to shoot somebody. How Anna texted us right before everything exploded, and it only made sense if she knew.

Except it really only made sense if Henry knew, because he was the one who took her phone, just like he was the one who took her necklace.

"You did it on purpose," I whisper.

His face is completely closed off.

"You killed her. Say it."

His hands are locked so tight on my arms they feel like tourniquets.

"Say it!"

Nothing.

My head's blurring everything together—tonight and prom

and homecoming, and it's like Katie's right here in front of me. Katie begging and Henry yelling and that scream—

"You pushed her!" I'm shrieking now, and he won't let go. I can see Katie's face, gentle and earnest and caught in the middle of a bunch of guys who treated her like shit when she was way too good for them. When she was just trying to make things right and do what Henry wanted, make him happy, this whole no-other-will-but-his thing, even though she could've been so much more if she had the chance—

I hear her scream again, and it's so real I scream, too, and finally I wrench away from Henry and get up. Then there's another scream, but it's not Katie, and something crashes and the gun goes off again, so loud it kills all the rest of the sound.

Someone's grabbing me, and then I'm off the bridge and onto the ground, eating dirt. The gunshot's still ringing in my ears. Lina and Parker are on the ground, too, and Lina's yelling, and the gun is in Parker's hands now and Lina's hands are up. Cat has me by the arm and Jane's blocking the drainpipe and Henry's stranded where I was before Parker jumped Lina. He's crouched down and saying *Don't. Don't. Please.*

I can hear again.

"Are you okay?" Cat's saying, and I wonder if maybe I got shot and just didn't realize it, like those people who walk into the ER with a knife sticking out of their backs, which is exactly how I feel right now.

"Don't move!" Parker shouts at Henry.

"Put the gun down," says Lina. "You don't know what you're doing."

"I know exactly what I'm doing!" Parker edges to the left so she's got an angle on Henry instead of Jane.

"Get your finger off the trigger," Lina tells her, a little more strained.

"Admit it," Parker says to Henry.

He starts to straighten up. He's shaking. "You can't—"

"Admit it!" Parker twists sideways and pulls the trigger and everything goes white again.

"Parker. Please." Henry's crying now.

"Admit it, or the next one isn't going to be a warning shot." She's terrifying. The makeup and the outfit and the gun she clearly has no fucking idea how to use.

"I didn't—"

"This is your last chance!" Parker aims, and her hands grip tight on to the gun. She's wearing pink nail polish, which is the dumbest thing I could notice right now, but it's better than dealing with the fact that my best friend is a murderer.

His head drops. There's dirt on his face and he looks scared as hell, but I don't feel sorry for him anymore. Not one bit.

"Kill me," he tells Parker.

He's not bluffing this time.

"Don't," Lina gasps.

Henry looks at her. And then Parker. And then he pushes up onto one knee, like he's proposing. "It doesn't matter what I say. No one's going to believe you. You're as dead as I am."

"Tell us what you did." Parker's voice is trembling.

"You already know."

"Say it."

He stares straight at her. Straight down the barrel of the

gun. "The Tower. End of the Road. I meant it." He doesn't flinch. "And they deserved it."

That's it. That's all.

Henry lifts his chin. "Do it. Kill me," he says again.

Parker aims. Her hands shake.

And then Henry laughs. "You're never going to do it. You're going to let me go again, and nobody's going to believe you, because you're a liar just like Katie and Anna and George—"

She pulls the trigger.

Once upon a Time Things Did Not Suck

The first summer we were at Overachiever Camp, Anna and Jane and Katie didn't even exist yet. Henry was so in love with Lina it was actually kind of disgusting and okay, fine, I lied before. I didn't *sort of* have a thing for him. I completely and stupidly and embarrassingly had the most distracting crush on him in the history of sad summer camp crushes.

I'm serious. It was tragic. Especially because I'd never been a crushy girl until that fateful dorm lounge selfie meet-cute. And because he was so obvious. Like, of all the boys at a camp full of staggering IQs and philosophical wonders and assorted brilliant weirdos, I had to fall for the one blatantly hot human magnet jock boy. The literal quarterback who also happened to be a songwriter and the kind of guy who would sneak out on the roof to run a poker club. Smart, but in an easy kind of way. Unbelievably popular. Unsurprisingly taken by a girlfriend so impressive she seemed like she should be fictional, or at least canonized. Funny, and he thought I was funny, too.

And then there was that confidence. The way he could make you believe anything. The way he said he was going to be famous. The way he said Lina was perfect. The way he said I was the best thing at Overachiever Camp.

It was, like, two weeks after we met—one of our first successful poker nights, and by "successful" I mean none of the math freaks counted cards and also, I really cleaned up in the mixed currency of money and contraband—when Henry decided we needed to sneak out. The roof was inarguably ours now, so it was time to conquer new frontiers.

We were going to sneak out the basement door, which we'd jammed open for curfew-bending purposes the day we met. The problem was that the basement stairs were heavily guarded by the night sentry, whose formal title probably wasn't "night sentry," and the elevator didn't open into the basement from the inside unless you had a staff key. Basically—and this is after everybody else went back in and it was just Henry and me—we decided one of us had to create a distraction to get the sentry away from sentrying so the other one could get into the basement and call the elevator down to let the first one out. And then we'd be free.

Originally I was supposed to be the distraction, since Henry was definitely more athletic, which seemed like a stair-access speed advantage, but then we considered my atrocious acting skills and decided Henry needed to be the liar. I snuck down behind one of the couches in the first-floor lounge with my eye on the sentry. She was sitting at the staff desk, reading a refreshingly unintellectual book and humming along with the office radio.

So I'm in stealth mode, and Henry comes up to the desk and goes, "Sorry to bother you this late, but I happened to look out my window and there's a guy in the lot messing with car doors."

"Okay," said the sentry without looking up.

"Thanks." Henry turned back toward the door, and then he called over his shoulder super casually, "Oh, and you should probably have the security people look up who owns the white Honda at the end of the second row, because he got the trunk open on that one."

The sentry froze. The lounge door swung shut behind Henry. And then the sentry actually leaped over the desk to get out of the office faster. It was such an impressive display, I forgot for a second that I was supposed to be running for the basement. By the time I got down, Henry had already texted me to call the elevator.

"Holy shit. She was out of there in two seconds," I said when the doors slid open.

Henry grinned. "She's working on her thesis, and she smuggled a manuscript out of the rare books collection for the night. It's in the trunk of her car."

"How the hell did you know that?"

He just laughed.

"And how'd you get to be such a good liar?"

He pushed open the basement door and led the way out. "It's not lying if you believe it when you're saying it," he told me.

"That's deep. It's like the power of positive thinking, but for criminals."

We were on the sidewalk by then. Just walking along, Henry seemed so in charge of everything that even if we'd run into the night sentry, she probably wouldn't have bothered asking why we were wandering the streets three hours past curfew.

"Listen, Cleves," he said as we crossed the street to the pizza place, "you never know when you're going to need to get away with something. The more you remember, the better your chances of winning."

"Remind me never to get on your bad side, Dr. Evil."

He held the door for me. "I'd never play you. You're in the inner circle already."

"Damn. I've never been so elite before."

"Get used to it," he told me. "As long as you're with me, you'll be a VIP everywhere. I'll make sure it happens."

"Because how else would you escape the dorms after midnight, is that it?"

He wrapped one arm around my shoulders and pulled me into a booth. "Because you're the best, and you're on my team now."

Just like that.

And maybe it was because it was one o'clock in the morning or maybe my overwhelming crush left me particularly vulnerable to flattery. Maybe it was just Henry, because that's the way he always was. You couldn't say no, but why would you want to?

Anyway, whatever it was, I felt ten times more awesome than I should've. He'd picked me, and that meant something. Stupid or special or tricked, I was on his team, just like he said.

And I wasn't sure what the game was, but I was positive we were winning.

I didn't know how much we had to lose.

Correspondent Honestly Doesn't Have the words for This

The first thing I hear is Lina's voice.

We have to go. Come on, Parker, I'll help you. Let's go. He's not worth it.

Lina's tucking the gun into her waistband. Parker's on the ground next to her.

No. No. I promised George—I promised—

Parker's getting up, and then she's collapsing against Lina and sobbing so hard it makes my heart hurt.

I promised.

He knows. You won, Parker.

Then another voice joins in and somebody's in front of me, blocking them out.

We did it.

There's still dirt in my mouth.

Are you okay? Come on. Let's get out of here.

Henry's lying on the ground right where it meets the drainpipe.

"You—" I gasp out, to Parker, because Henry was right: She's as dead as him now.

And then Henry's arm moves. He's not dead. He's just curled up, lying in the dirt, with that empty smile totally gone. Crying.

All the air rushes out of my lungs. A giant breath I didn't even know I was holding. I'm still sitting on the ground, but I sink back into it and everything plays back so hard it's like the gun going off one more time.

There's something hollow in my chest that wasn't there before.

Henry's not dead, but he's gone. All these months I thought I knew him so well, and it's like I never even knew him at all. And the truth is worse than any bullshit story I ever threw at Eustace and Hans and Christina.

I can't believe it's true. I mean, I know it is. But I can't believe it. I *refuse* to believe it.

"Let's go," Cat says.

A few yards over, Jane's with Parker, and Parker's still crying, but her chin's up now. Cat's a couple of feet away from me, watching Henry. He still won't look up.

"Cleveland," Cat says. "Let's go."

"I can't."

Then Lina's next to me, sitting down in the dirt. She takes both my hands, like it's a sleepover séance, and I wish it was. Get the séance gods to bring the real Henry back.

I look at Lina and I say it again: "I can't."

"You can," she tells me. "You will."

I'm not even sure what she means, but I'm positive she's right. And she has to know. More than I'll ever know, probably, but she's not going to leave me alone to dig my way out.

"We both will," I say. It's not even half as strong as I want it to sound, because let's be real, I'm not even halfway to wrapping my brain around everything I just found out. But it's what I want to tell her, because holy shit, she deserves it.

She squeezes my hands tighter for a second and then she says, "Imagine us in full armor."

And then she lets go and gets up to wait with Cat.

I stare at Henry for a second drawn out so long, it's like that life-flashing-before-your-eyes thing. Like in that second, I see the night we met and the night he chose me and the night we stole the Jet Ski. Everything.

But then I look away.

He chose me, but I'm not choosing him back.

I stand up.

"Next time," Lina tells Henry, "I'm not going to knock her down. I'm going to let her take the shot."

"You know I'm not afraid to pull the trigger," says Parker. She's not crying anymore.

Cat pulls her phone out and taps the screen. Henry's voice comes out, tinny and muffled, but completely recognizable: *They deserved it.* "You're done," she says. "Your name. Your legacy. Everything that matters to you is in our hands now."

He doesn't look at her. I guess once everybody knows everything about you is a lie, it's not worth lying anymore.

Lina's the first one to walk away. Jane's right behind her,

and then Parker. Cat gives Henry another long look and tells him, "We're clearing their names. You try to stop us, and we'll ruin your life."

Then she joins the rest of them, and it's just me left. And finally, Henry looks up.

He didn't mean for any of this to happen, probably. He didn't know what to do when everything with his family got fucked up. He wanted to turn everything around, and he didn't know how to stop.

But that doesn't even start to justify the shit he did.

"Cleves—"

"Don't." My voice doesn't waver. "We won't have to ruin your life. You did that to yourself. And if you want to fix it, that's up to you. I'm not your partner in crime, and I'm not just one of your—one of the six."

"I'm—"

"It's not about you. It's about me."

And then I leave him. For good.

The King Is Dead

We walk back to the parking lot together. A girl I thought I hated, and a girl Henry almost convinced me to hate, and a girl Henry wanted me to forget about, and a girl I almost did forget about.

And me.

"I can't believe you tried to shoot him," Cat says.

"I can't believe Lina stopped me," Parker answers.

"I can't believe Jane stole her dad's gun and drove here from Chicago," says Lina.

Jane makes a prim little scoffing noise, and it's such a classic Jane sound that I freak out all over again about her savior streak. "I couldn't let him hurt Cat. When TJ texted me about that message from Henry—I mean, I couldn't. Not after Katie."

We keep walking. We're past Cat's car and Jane's, crunching down the creepiest road in the world, but it isn't creepy anymore. "I can't believe Henry did it," I say.

They don't laugh in my face, even though I wouldn't blame them if they did. Which is awesome, because no matter how many ways they tried to tell me, I really didn't believe it until tonight. He was my best friend. It's not like I actually thought he was capable of *killing* somebody.

But right now, it so isn't about that.

"We've got to do a tribute so good, nobody will even remember the rumors," I say.

Next to me, Cat links her elbow into mine. "I'll cover print media. You cover digital."

"And I'll do PR," says Parker.

I laugh, and it's not the hysterical laugh we've all been passing around tonight, or the horrible cold laugh Henry used when he stopped trying to make us think he was somebody he wasn't. "You mean you'll make your JV minions retweet me."

"Whatever. They'll do anything I tell them to do. They already put your *Dead Queens* URL on the away stands."

"That was you guys?"

"Obviously," she says. One hundred percent Tyrannosaurus Rochford.

"For real, though," says Jane. "We're going to make sure they're remembered."

"The right way," Lina adds.

We're almost to Parker's car now. I have no idea where we're going, but it honestly doesn't even matter, because wherever it is, we're unstoppable. I mean, just look at us.

Goals.

"Ten years from now," I say. "We have to promise. We'll all be here for homecoming. It's what Katie wanted."

"Deal," Parker agrees. And then she's linking arms with Lina and Jane, and Jane and I make the last link, and there we are. An unbreakable chain of girls Henry seriously underestimated.

"Ten years," Lina says, "of doing all the things we never could've done if we never stood up to him."

"Ten years of knowing we stopped him at six," says Cat.

"And knowing what we're made of," Jane adds.

We stop in front of Parker's car, but we don't unlink, and I swear I just want to stay a girl gang with all of them. And that means Katie and Anna, too.

You better fucking believe I'm there, now and forever, for every single one of these girls.

"What's that quote?" I ask. "That thing Anna used to say?"

I'm half expecting them not to have a clue what I'm talking about. But Lina raises her chin and Cat squeezes my hand and Jane sets her jaw.

Parker closes her eyes for a second. Her makeup is smudged, but she still looks perfect.

"Ainsi sera," she says.

That's the way it's going to be.

Teenage Girls Achieve Immortality

It turns out I didn't have to figure out the truth after all. I just had to say it. Out loud.

We pull up to the away stands in Parker's car. She's letting me drive for once, which has me more than slightly concerned for her welfare, but we'll sort that out in the morning.

Tonight, we've got better things to do.

Cat covers print media and I cover digital. We're both typing so hard, I actually wish Eustace would show up and start a pool on which one of us is going to crack a screen first.

Parker does PR. So do Jane and Lina.

For the record, if anybody ever tells you that End of the Road is Lancaster's biggest party, they're wrong. Because right now, on a very unwelcomely cold night in December when everybody responsible is doing something boring like working on their college applications, I'm basking in the blinding glow of Parker's brights and the possibly toxic fallout from Walmart's finest neon-pink spray paint.

"Oh my God, we're done, right?" says Parker.

Lina takes a step back with her paint roller dripping onto the grass. "Not yet."

And Jane says, in exactly the type of proper little voice I now associate with gun-slinging outlaws, "Suck it up, Rochford."

Parker sprays her hair neon-pink.

Next to me, Cat looks up from her screen. "My story's ready," she says. "Are you posting yours tonight, or waiting until morning?"

"I mean, you're the editor-in-chief," I tell her.

"Savage."

"Thank you." I scroll down my draft. We both started with the post we queued in Parker's room, except now it's been updated, since we've had some actual breaking news come in. And also because let's be real, *The Dead Queens Club* and *The Lion Ledger* have slightly different editorial standards.

But we've got the truth. We've got Anna's evidence. We've even got a recording of Henry admitting he did it.

It's not going to be enough, though. When Cat mentioned that—at which point we were all crammed into Parker's car on the way to Walmart, because what else can you do in Lancaster after you almost murder a murderer—I very nearly took my hands off the steering wheel to dive into the back seat and clock her in the face.

Once we'd all survived that moment, made infinitely more dramatic by Parker's car-related shrieking, we came to the conclusion that yeah, Cat was probably right.

Even if we press charges, he won't go to jail. Not for long enough to mean anything, anyway.

But that doesn't mean we lost. It just means we're getting creative.

"I think you should publish it tonight," says Cat. "We can't sit on a story like this."

"Agreed." I flip back to the draft I'm writing. "Want to proof it first?"

She takes my phone. "If by 'proof' you mean 'censor,' then yes."

Here's the other thing Cat was right about: Once the truth is out, it won't matter if Henry is in jail or not. All the over-achiever shit he's always been so obsessed with—his name, his reputation, his when-I'm-famous world-domination plan— it's over the second I hit *Post*.

By the time the sun comes up, everybody will know what he did.

"Well," Cat says, "it's not *Ledger* material, but I think it will work."

"Breaking: Cat Parr approves a Cleveland story. Journalism dies."

She smacks me with my phone. "Breaking: Cleveland chooses an appropriate topic. Journalism lives."

"Guys," I yell, and Parker and Lina and Jane look over at us. "Come here."

"Oh my God, *thank* you," says Parker, and she flings her spray-paint can down with exactly the amount of drama I've come to expect from Miss Indiana's Outstanding Almost-Killer.

"Okay," I say. "I'm posting the story. Last chance to knock me out and steal the byline."

"Do it," says Lina.

So I do. And then we all sit there staring at the little *Posted!*

icon and, in my case, feeling badass enough that I can almost forget I lost my best friend tonight.

Sometimes words are the best weapon of all.

Finally Jane goes, "Hell yeah!" so emphatically that her hair rains paint specks all over my screen.

Ugh, Jane Seymour.

Then we all high-five and shriek, and Parker does some impossible cheerleading gymnastics, and I reach into the car and turn on the radio and blast the silence away with the same stupid pop song Katie's phone was singing that night at End of the Road. I may have a somewhat laissez-faire approach to religion, but I solemnly swear that it's her actual angel self speaking to all of us through the lowly vessel of northern Indiana's best Top 40 radio station.

And I also swear the headlights get brighter, and Parker's and Jane's and Lina's very mediocre artwork is, at this exact moment, a thing of beauty that leaves every Renaissance masterpiece in the dust. Half the away stands wall is blacked out, at least as high up as Parker-on-people's-shoulders can reach. The portraits of Anna and Katie are pretty shitty, but we'll bribe Hans into fixing them, and anyway, anybody who looks is going to know exactly who they are.

Besides, the headline totally gives it away.

LONG LIVE THE QUEENS

★ ★ ★ ★ ★

Acknowledgments

So. This is for real. My elementary-school self is *losing it.* Thank you, so very very much—

To Logan Garrison Savits, for finding me in the slush pile and deciding I was worth a shot. Logan, I will always owe you!

To Sarah Burnes and Julia Eagleton, for bringing me the rest of the way to where we are now—and hopefully far beyond. And to Mary Pender, for coming on board with Cleves and her friends and taking them in an entirely new direction.

To Lauren Smulski, for making the editing process more fun than should be legal, and for matching my enthusiasm for all things Tudor. And to everyone at Inkyard Press, for making this story an actual thing.

To my parents, for always encouraging me to pursue what I want, even when that includes a degree in saxophone performance and a year in the Caribbean. To my brother, for fort-building and the *Canterbury Tales.* And to my extended family, especially my late grandfather Art Haist.

To my own girl gang! You are too numerous to name (yes, I'm that lucky), but it would be unforgivable if I didn't shout a few of you out: Cadence Woodland, London BFF and Cat Chat confidant; Liana Mack, New York BFF and Rio soul sister; Jessica Kelley, partner in gossip and YA murder; Emily Lundin, "passionate!"-ly; Katie Williams, secret-keeper; and Suzanne Burns, writer of outstanding four-word book reviews.

To the wonderful writing community at the Muse, and to Ellen Bryson and Lydia Netzer in particular. Your scathing feedback is my favorite.

To the teachers who not only tolerated my excessive personality but supported my writing obsession: Rob Fraser, Karen Grass, Becky Crossett, and Melissa Larsen.

To everyone who has cheerfully endured my rants about Katheryn Howard. I stand by every last word, but I do recognize that first dates, backstage lineups, and club bathrooms are not necessarily contexts in which people want to hear how devoted I am to changing the narrative on the queen of my heart.

To Eustace Chapuys, for your 500-year-old gossip.

To the historical women I love so dearly: Katharine of Aragon, Anne Boleyn, Jane Seymour, Anne of Cleves, Katheryn Howard, Kateryn Parr, and Jane Parker/Boleyn/Rochford. You *all* deserved so, so much better.

And finally, because I must (and also because I'm a loyal Episcopalian), to the man without whom this book would very literally not have been possible: King Henry VIII. In your own words, *Company is good and ill, but every man hath his free will.*